Carys Morgan is torn between two worlds.
One bright. The other shadow.
One familiar. The other filled with magic.

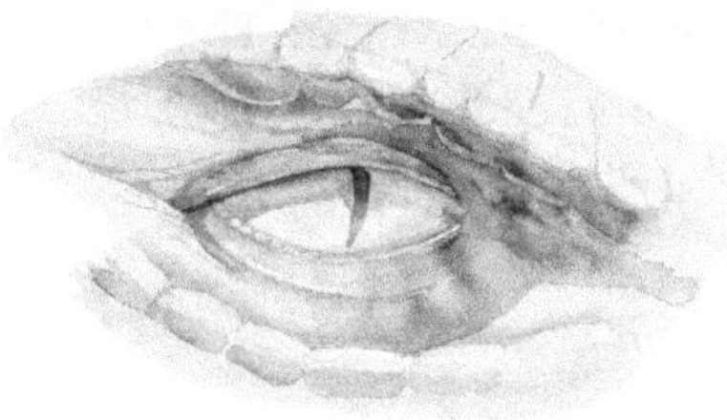

In one life, Carys is an assistant mythology professor in Northern California. In the Shadowlands, she's a dragon rider with close ties to royals, fae, and powerful magic wielders. It's not just differing worlds that Carys must navigate but the love of two very different men who wear the same beloved face.

When the Anglian king dies, Carys returns to the Shadowlands where a brittle peace accord threatens to crumble. As war looms and old gods begin to wake, Carys will have to choose between the two men vying for her heart and the two worlds that promise very different destinies.

Dragons, fae, and a fantasy world that is at once familiar and entirely unique—*USA Today* Bestselling Author Elizabeth Hunter is a master at her craft, unspooling complex worlds and characters into an addictive page-turner you won't be able to put down!

PRAISE FOR ELIZABETH HUNTER

"What an exciting installment in The Shadowlands series! The entire time I was reading this book I was either smiling or sitting on the edge of my seat."

— THIS LITERARY LIFE

"Adventure at it's best....plus dragons! Prepare for your sleep schedule to be interrupted until you finished this delicious read. I for one - Could. Not. Get. Enough. ...I got swept up in the color and layers of this world and all of its characters. I was so happy we got to go deeper into what makes this land tick."

— TXBRITGAL, GOODREADS REVIEW

"A second journey into the Shadowlands is totally mesmerizing. I am fascinated by the characters, magic and locations. A masterful crafting of a complex story encompassing myths, mystical creatures and gods of old."

— LINETTE, GOODREADS REVIEWER

THE SHADOW PATH

SHADOWLANDS BOOK II

ELIZABETH HUNTER

THE SHADOW PATH

SHADOWLANDS

BOOK TWO

ELIZABETH HUNTER

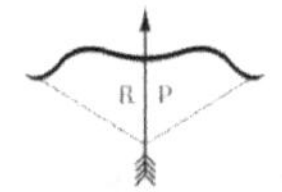

For every reader willing to walk through the forest
And into the unknown

PROLOGUE

The queen sat bolt upright in bed as a voice echoed across the sea and into her mind.

"Who did this? Who brought iron into this place?"
"Not iron. Steel."
"No!"

"Ah!" The queen clutched a hand over her heart as it raced in terror. "My love!"

A moment later, a silhouette appeared in her doorway. The light fae prince strode toward the queen, kneeling at her bedside in the golden hall beneath the earth.

"I feel her." He gripped his wife's hand. "She is in Alba. I will send—"

"Too late." She clutched his hand with a gasp. "It's too late!"

"You murderous hag!"
"And?"
"You're dead."

A slice of pain cut across the queen's chest and she bent forward, screaming in pain. The prince gathered her into his arms, holding her as she suffered her daughter's dying wounds.

A burning pain across her knees, then a gutting slice across her belly.

The queen clutched her abdomen, her hands pressed over the womb that had stretched with miraculous life, filled with a child that could only come from the will of the gods.

She panted as she felt her daughter's last breath.

Felt the blade cut across her neck.

Then she felt nothing at all.

The queen's hollow chest filled with rage, and she screamed in agony and anger.

Child of my blood.

Child of my blood.

Anu, they have killed the child of my blood.

"She's gone!" The queen wailed over and over, rocking back and forth in her husband's arms. "She is gone! I have nothing," she cried out. "Our daughter is gone."

The prince picked her up and cradled her in his arms.

She laid her head against his chest, and in her heart, she felt the burning fire of rage bloom.

He would die.

All of them would die.

The world would feel her wrath.

"It is time," the prince whispered. "My love, it is time."

ACT I

CHAPTER ONE

"So once we answer that question" —Carys looked out over the small lecture hall— "we are forced to ask ourselves another one. What do these stories, these intensely human stories that are often violent, often grim, but can also be redemptive, mean to us as modern humans?"

She faced a mosaic of faces when she looked at her students. Many were watching her, others were typing furiously on their laptops, far too many were looking at their phones, and at least two sophomore boys were slumped over with their eyes closed.

"When we examine mythological archetypes from around the world like..." She waited for hands.

A freshman girl in the front row raised hers, and Carys nodded.

"Catastrophic floods?"

"Yes. Another one." She pointed to a boy in the back who had his hand up.

"Trickster gods," he said.

"Excellent." She was relieved that even though the semester was wrapping up and they were taking their final the following morning, her students were still engaged. "Another one?"

"Uh, reaper myths?"

Carys pointed at the student. "Psychopomps and afterlife guides. Great one."

A boy in the front row cleared his throat. "Is this stuff gonna be on the final?"

Carys nodded. "If we're talking about it today, it's a good guess that you're going to see it tomorrow."

One of the sleeping sophomores roused himself and rubbed his eyes. "Uh, twins. Divine twins. Feral twins."

Carys forced a smile to her face. "Can't forget that one." She glanced at the clock and heard the side door to the hall creak open. The next crop of students was probably arriving for their nine-thirty classes. "Okay, so that's the question we're asking, right? What do these stories that cross cultures and time mean to us today in the modern world? Why bother studying any of this stuff?"

"Because it fulfills an English requirement?"

Carys smiled as scattered laughter ran across the room. "Thank you for the most obvious answer, Paul. Any other reason?"

A familiar voice with a deep Scottish brogue spoke from the side of the room. "Because in learning what our ancestors believed, we might learn more about who we are and who we want to be."

Carys turned and met Duncan Murray's brilliant green eyes. He was leaning against the wall of her classroom, clad in worn jeans, a green-and-blue-plaid flannel, and a dark green Barbour jacket.

Her heart leaped in her chest. "Great answer." She forced herself to turn back to her students. "Don't forget you can use your printed-out notes on the final, so make sure you bring them to the testing center tomorrow."

As soon as she started to wrap up, all her students started packing their books.

"Also, you were a delight and I want to thank you for braving the eight a.m. time slot." Carys rushed through her closing remarks. "Good luck on your finals, rest up, eat something green for all the gods' and goddesses' sakes" —more laughter as all of them started heading out of the hall— "and have a great summer! English majors, I hope I see you again in the fall."

"Thanks, Professor Morgan!"

"Have a great summer too."

A soft-spoken girl passed by the lectern. "I'm going to try to register for your Classical Mythology in World Literature class in the fall. Does it fill up fast?"

Carys started getting her own notes together to clear out for Dr. Ramirez, who was probably already in the building. "It rarely fills up because it's a three-hundred-level class." Her eyes kept darting to Duncan, whom more than one student was eyeing with interest as they passed. "So I doubt you'll have an issue, but if you do, just email me, okay?"

"Awesome." Her smile was relieved. "Thanks."

"Good luck on the final." Carys had little doubt the girl would ace it. She was one of her top students.

"I heard this was your first class back after your sabbatical," the girl said. "I just wanted to say it was one of my favorites."

Carys's heart nearly burst. "Thank you. That means a lot. I can't lie—I was nervous coming back." She saw Duncan walking over from the corner of her eye. "But I had a great time with you guys. You made this class really fun."

"Thanks." The girl's cheeks were a little red when she looked at Duncan; then she nodded at Carys one more time before she headed toward the door.

Which left Carys alone with Duncan, laird of Murrayshall, who was once again looking like an advertisement for the Scottish Tourism Board.

"Hey." She leaned on the lectern and tried to act cooler than she felt. "This is a surprise. I didn't know you were coming to Baywood."

Duncan had visited once, just after the Christmas holidays and right before she started work again, but when they'd talked the week before, he'd made no mention of flying to California. "I mean... a nice surprise, but what's up?"

She had a sneaking suspicion this wasn't just a social call.

"What can I say, Professor?" Duncan hung his massive hands in his pockets. "I couldn't keep away from the glorious Northern California weather."

"The sun is shining today." She pointed toward the door. "I saw it."

"Professor Morgan." The corner of Duncan's mouth inched up as his low voice curled around her professional title, his tongue rolling the *r* in Morgan. "It's giving me ideas, Carys."

Now it was her face heating. "Come on." She saw students start to trickle in for Dr. Ramirez's class. "You caught me at the end of work, so walk with me and tell me what you're doing here."

Duncan followed Carys out of the lecture hall and into the bustling humanities building at Baywood State University. The college town on the Northern California coast wasn't quite as foggy that late-May morning as it usually was, and the last of the ocean mist was burning off as Carys and Duncan walked down the stairs and across the north quad.

"So how are you?" She glanced over her shoulder, wishing she'd worn something slightly more appealing than her oversized tweed blazer, jeans, and a Cranberries band shirt that morning. "Been over to the other side lately?"

By "other side," she meant the Shadowlands, the alternate realm where magic and myth weren't just something Carys taught out of books. A realm where magical twins called Shadowkin existed at the will of powerful and scheming fae.

"I have been, yes." Duncan glanced at her from the side. "Is your dragon around?"

"If you mean is he on campus, no. After four weeks of very bored class attendance, Cadell finally realized that no dark fae strike forces were likely to kidnap me in the middle of Baywood, so he usually hangs out on the other side of the fae gate behind my house while I'm in class." She frowned. "Why?"

Duncan paused under the shade of a spreading ash tree. "Do you remember the Anglian king, Edgar?"

"I never met him, but I remember the name." Carys had only traveled to the Scottish Shadowlands, called Alba, but all the realms of Briton had their own king or queen.

"Well, Edgar is dead."

Carys felt the news like a punch to the stomach. "Poison?" Her own Shadowkin, Seren, had been poisoned by the human mage who'd been her closest friend. "Was he assassinated? Was it fae or some kind of—"

"Fell off his horse while he was boar hunting," Duncan said. "Split his head open. Died instantly."

"Oh, that's..." A relief? "That's terrible."

"Aye, it is, because that means his bampot of a son, Harold, is going to be the king." Duncan rolled his eyes. "I knew Harold when he was a kid. Complete arse."

"You knew him when he was a kid. He might have matured since then."

Duncan shrugged. "Maybe. Either way, there's a new king in Anglia, and I received a message from your uncle's man in Cardiff last weekend." He held out an elaborately decorated envelope with her uncle's seal on the front.

Her Uncle Dafydd was her own father's Shadowkin and the sitting king of Cymru.

"I was instructed to hand deliver it to you," Duncan continued, "which is why I am here." He smiled a little bit. "Not that it's a hardship. We never got to Yosemite on my last trip."

"I can't help that there was a snowstorm." Carys couldn't stop her smile. "What does Dafydd want?" She reached for the envelope with trembling fingers.

"I didn't read it of course, but since a private plane to London is waiting for you and Cadell, I have a feeling that your uncle wants you and your dragon at the coronation."

Carys's heart started to race. "Why me?"

Duncan's eyebrows went up. "Because you're nêrys ddraig, Carys. You're a Cymric dragon lord now, and since Seren is dead, you're also the closest thing that Dafydd has to an heir."

"I just think it's ridiculous to even consider me for the job." Carys walked through her kitchen door and immediately hung her work bag on the hook by the door. "Come on in." She pointed to his shoes. "Boots off."

Duncan huffed, but he bent over and took off his shoes as Carys walked to the stove and started a kettle.

"You're his daughter's Brightkin." Duncan rose to his full height, ducking under the arch that separated the living room from the kitchen. "You're nêrys ddraig—"

"Barely!" Carys spun, leaning against the counter while the water heated for tea. "I've only been training six months, and most of what I'm doing is just archery. The Chahta dragon riders do not fight like the Cymric ones—which Cadell reminds me of pretty much every training session I have."

Duncan frowned. "I thought your uncle coordinated your training with his allies. He couldn't send over a Cymric trainer?"

There were two dragon nations in North America, and the friendliest to Cymru was the Chahta nation, who lived in the Mississippi Valley.

When Carys and Cadell had finally found the fae gate behind her house—well, when her best friend Laura had revealed it to them—it caused more than a bit of stir.

"Just because the Chahta are a friendly dragon nation, that doesn't mean they want Cymric soldiers on this side of the ocean." She heard the kettle start to boil and reached for two of her mother's earthenware mugs that hung underneath the wooden cabinets. "It was complicated enough getting permission from Laura's people to allow Cadell to live here and use their gate."

The past six months of her life had been a riot of revelations and a crash course in a brand-new world.

And she'd also had to go back to work teaching three classes at the college. Unlike Duncan, she was not independently wealthy.

Carys tore open two tea bags and plopped them in the mugs, then took a deep breath and poured boiling water into each mug, enjoying the rising steam scented with black tea, bergamot, and orange.

She turned and saw Duncan looking at the photographs pinned to a corkboard on the wall. "How is Laura? And what's Kiersten up to? Has she seduced the dragon yet?"

"She's tried her hardest, but I think..." Carys couldn't stop her smile. "I think if that dragon has any affections under his scaled armor, they may be directed at someone else."

Duncan's eyebrows rose. "That sounds like a story that needs whiskey."

"You're not wrong." But it wasn't time for that kind of gossip when a royal coronation was looming over her head. "Laura is good. Busy with work—she's working on that new solar project for the tribe she was talking about over the holidays."

"The one for the elders' village?"

"Yep."

Laura—who was Brightkin like Carys—was one of the designated pauwau inwe of her people. The Yurok, unlike the majority of the population of Baywood, knew about the Shadowlands, and in every generation there were Brightkin chosen to cross the gates to serve as representatives between the two worlds.

It was how Laura had immediately recognized Cadell as a dragon.

"I just don't think I'm equipped to be Dafydd's heir. Not even close. It's not that I don't want to have a relationship with him, but Seren trained her entire life to be queen. And whatever a queen needs to be, it's not... me."

She turned and saw Duncan leaning against the arched doorway, watching her as she set the mugs on a carved wooden tray. His admiring gaze made her cheeks warm up. "Tea is ready."

She set it on the island her father had built between the kitchen and the living room. Duncan pulled out a stool on the other side and sat down gingerly.

"Am I going to break this?"

Carys smiled. "Cadell sits on it, so I can't imagine it won't take your weight."

She squeezed a bit of lemon into her tea and sipped the fragrant, warm concoction, waiting for it to soothe the lump that had landed in her stomach the moment Duncan had mentioned returning to Briton. "I just don't know if I can do this."

He cocked his head. "Do what?"

"Be... whatever they want me to be."

"You don't know what they want from you." He shrugged. "Right now all they want is your presence. Your summer break is starting at work, right? The timing couldn't be better. You have three months free."

Carys set down her mug. "You have to understand. You haven't crossed over the gate here. I know my bloodline is in Briton, but the Shadowlands here? They feel... safer. More like home."

Laura's Shadowkin—a warm and maternal village healer named Kere—was the one who had led Carys and Cadell across the fae gate near Mad Creek. Crossing over to the Pauwau Aki—the common name for the Shadowlands in North America—felt far more familiar even though the magic there was like nothing she'd studied in books.

"It's hard to explain," Carys said.

Duncan nodded silently, sipping his tea. After a few minutes, he straightened up, set his mug down, and looked Carys dead in the eye. "So don't explain it. Show me." His eyes were glittering with antic-ipation.

"You want to cross over to the Shadowlands here?"

He shrugged. "I've only ever been to Briton," he said. "Maybe it's time to broaden my horizons."

Laura walked with them through the forest, a glossy blue-black raven perched on her shoulder. "It'll be faster if I send a raven through. Chuck can usually find Kere faster than I can."

Laura and Carys were as familiar with these paths as they would be walking the friendly streets of Baywood, while Duncan's footsteps sounded like a bear lumbering through a hardware store.

"You named your raven Chuck?" he asked.

"Not really." Laura glanced at the bird. "I think he named himself Chuck."

The bird let out a throaty caw.

Laura Thompson was a beautiful Yurok woman with an oval face, high cheekbones, and deep brown eyes. She was shorter than Carys, and her curvy figure had been the envy of both Carys and Kiersten when they were kids, though Laura had never had much time for fashion or anything that took time away from school.

Her long black hair fell in a single braid down her back, and while she might be guiding them into a magical shadow world, she wore the typical Northern California uniform of sturdy hiking boots, jeans, and a flannel shirt under a waterproof jacket.

"Kere will meet us at the gate," Laura said. "And I've told Chuck to bring someone to take you across, Duncan."

As an adult, Laura had become a civil engineer and worked on projects for the state, the forest service, and the Yurok tribe. But she was also a person who could cross between the worlds.

The gate knew Laura and Carys, but because Duncan was new, he would need a guide native to the Shadowlands. And because nothing was born in the Shadowlands except by magic, Carys knew their guide wouldn't be human.

"I deeply appreciate it." Duncan's lairdly accent was in full force. "And thank you for allowing me to cross over."

Laura glanced back at him. "You're Lachlan's kin, aren't you?"

Carys's two best friends still considered Lachlan a friend even though her former boyfriend—ex seemed a little too harsh—had returned to the Shadowlands of Scotland the year before and they hadn't seen him since.

"How is Lachlan?" Laura asked.

"He's doing well." Duncan spoke from behind Carys. "Busy. His brother Rory has returned to court, so that's been... interesting."

Carys had never met Rory, and even though Lachlan sent her letters nearly every day, he hadn't mentioned Rory.

Okay, what is that about?

Carys tucked that bit of information away as they crossed over a small stream flush with spring runoff. As they walked farther into the forest, the ground grew softer and the air around them was thick with small insects taking advantage of the last warmth of the day.

It was close to nightfall, and the drooping sun cast long shadows through the massive trees. Dust floated through high beams of light, and the sound of their footsteps was swallowed by the dense underbrush.

As they approached the gate, Carys saw the wisps—the luminous bright souls floating through the forest—dipping down like dragonflies to skate across the lush ferns, flying up into the trees and circling them as they grew closer.

"You're right," Duncan murmured. "It feels different."

Laura glanced over her shoulder. "Kheta Inwe are not like your fae, at least not from what Carys has told me."

Kheta Inwe—the Old People—were the magical creatures that controlled the gates in North America. They were fae, but Carys had never felt malevolence from them like she had from the fae in Briton.

"Same rules apply here as there though," Carys said. "They're a little bit nicer, but they're still tricksters. They still love playing games with humans."

"So don't give them your name," Laura said. "Don't make them any promises. Don't eat their food. And *definitely* don't take anything from their forest."

"Think I've learned that lesson well enough for two lives."

Duncan's head was swinging from one side to the other as they walked.

The waning sunlight was golden through the trees, the forest floor was springy with fresh green shoots, and all the patches of snow had finally melted. Carys breathed in the damp scent of bark and moss, closing her eyes as a wisp dove down and hovered right next to her ear.

She closed her eyes for a moment, trying to ignore the melancholy sigh.

"Are they the same here?" Duncan asked softly.

Carys nodded.

The Shadowlands was a mirror world. Every person in the Brightlands had a twin in the Shadows, but not every twin was allowed to live and grow.

A lucky number were given to humans on the other side of the gates to raise as their own children. But some were taken by magical creatures, and the rest only existed as these bright lights, wandering between the worlds until their Brightkin died.

It was a sad existence for the wisps, but even though some of their light seemed to flicker, others glowed and raced, as if they were eager to lead Brightkin into the other world.

"Almost there." Laura shrugged, and Chuck lifted from her shoulder, angling his wings to dive toward a fallen log before he rose into the air and disappeared between the trees.

Laura walked to the side of the massive log and turned. "The village is right on the other side of the gate," she said. "If Kere is awake, it won't take long."

Nightfall in the Brightlands meant dawn in the Shadows.

Carys braced her foot against a rock and hooked her thumbs in her pockets. "Did you see Cadell today?"

"No." Laura stared into the green veil of the forest, her eyes fixed on the place where Chuck had flown. "I was working."

"He was asking about you the other day."

Laura rolled her eyes. "He asks about everything," she said. "That dragon is the most curious creature I've ever met in my life. I can barely give him an answer before he's asking another question. He's like a child."

Carys narrowed her eyes. "Is he though?"

"Cadell?" Duncan asked. "You're talking about Cadell of Eryri? The dragon Cadell?"

Laura shrugged. "I guess."

"Duncan has known Cadell for years." Carys turned to Duncan. "He's a little more... talkative with Laura than he is with other people."

Duncan's eyebrows went up again. "Is this the whiskey conversation?"

"It is."

A loud caw sounded from the forest.

"That's Chuck." Laura pushed away from the log. "And the two of you don't need to be gossiping about me when your whole" —she waved her hand toward them— "situation is complicated enough."

"Pfft." Carys frowned. "I don't... We're not—"

"Together," Duncan said. "Yet. But you're right." He walked past Carys, shooting her a smile before he followed Laura toward the clump of bushes where Chuck was waiting. "And it's only complicated because Carys needs time."

Carys shot the back of Laura's head a dirty look before she followed both of them down the slope, across a creek, and toward a stand of blooming dogwood where a woman was waiting. She turned to face them, and Carys was struck again by how startling it was to see her old friend's exact face in another person.

"Well." Duncan halted. "Is that what it's like when people see Lachlan and me together?"

"Yes." Carys nodded. "Exactly."

Kere was Laura's twin, and the only difference between them was that Kere wore three delicately tattooed lines down her chin.

"Carys." She held out her arms, walked to Carys, and pressed her forehead to Carys's. "Good to see you." Then she turned to Duncan and waved him down to her level before she pressed her forehead to his. "It's good to meet you. Any friend of Carys's is welcome here."

"Thank you."

"Sister." Kere walked to her Brightkin and repeated the greeting. Then she turned to face them. "Okay, follow me and stay close."

Kere walked around the clump of trees, and the three of them followed her.

Only to freeze when they saw a massive black bear rising on two legs as they walked into a small clearing.

"This is Abukcheek." Kere patted the bear's side. "He'll lead us across."

Carys turned to Duncan, who was frozen and staring at the bear. "Okay, I did tell you it's a little bit different here."

"That's a... very large bear."

"He's a shifter."

"Right. A shifter bear," Duncan muttered. "So much better."

Carys took his hand and shook him a little. Duncan blinked and started walking.

They followed Laura, who followed Kere, who followed their black-coated ursine guide. The trees grew denser and the forest darker. The wisps flew around them, swirling and dancing in the heavy darkness.

Carys kept Duncan's hand in hers, just as he'd done for her when she crossed the gate in Scotland. "I promise it's not far."

"It's so dark."

Carys looked up at the living sentries that guarded the portal between the human world and the magical. "The trees are older here."

The redwoods seemed to grow taller and thicker as they walked, crowding out everything around them. No sunlight. No stars.

The world pressed in to the point where Carys didn't know how the bear guiding them could even make it through the narrow alley of gnarled reddish bark.

The scent of green life was thick in her throat until the air seemed to loosen, the wisps sighed and flew away, and a pearl-grey light peeked through the cathedral of massive trees.

The bear in front of them started to gallop toward the light, but Kere and Laura walked hand in hand, strolling into the gentle light that opened up and bathed a forest meadow where flowers bloomed, a gentle stream trickled, and birds were beginning to sing.

Kere turned to Duncan and Carys and smiled. "Welcome to Pauwau Aki, Duncan Murray."

Carys could feel her dragon approaching, and the low, rumbling voice in her mind was like gentle, distant thunder.

As they walked into the meadow, she lifted her face to the cloudy sky to see her dragon soaring overhead, wheeling and turning in the grey morning light, his emerald-green wings outstretched and red fire glowing in his belly.

Nêrys, there you are.

CHAPTER TWO

"I was about to cross the gate to look for you." Cadell sat on a log around a friendly fire in a clearing. "You should have been here an hour ago."

He was clad in leather armor, his muscled arms bare, as if he didn't feel the morning fog at all. He stretched out his massive legs and leaned toward the fire.

Dragons really loved fire.

"Duncan showed up at the college," Carys said. "We had a cup of tea before we walked over. I'm sorry if you were worried; we kind of lost track of time."

Men and women were bustling around the village, getting ready for a busy spring day as children ran around the camp, calling to their friends and gathering their belongings from long, low cedar-plank houses that were halfway dug into the ground. The roofs were covered in redwood shingles, and from each house, a grey stream of smoke rose from a clay chimney.

It looked like a typical morning as children grabbed knapsacks for school, parents readied them for the day, and others headed off toward the forest to hunt or fish.

Though the faces were as familiar as the ones in Baywood, everyone in the village spoke a dialect of the local Yurok language that Carys was still trying to learn. But though she didn't speak the common language, the Shadowkin in Kere's village had always made her feel at home.

Cadell turned to Duncan. "Perhaps you think that I've become derelict in my role as Carys's protector—"

"No one was thinking that, Cadell." Carys tried to stop him.

"I have learned that there are no malignant forces in Baywood—other than the typical human dangers," Cadell continued, "but also that I can feel Carys from this side of this gate. The old growth forest exists in both worlds, so the gates are more porous than they are in Briton."

Duncan frowned. "That's interesting."

"Should she be in danger, I have timed my arrival at the college where she works to under fifteen minutes." He took a deep breath. "Now that I tell you that, fifteen minutes is too long. Nêrys, I should continue guarding you at work."

"You really shouldn't," Carys said. "You scare the students."

"Then they're too easily frightened."

Duncan cocked his head. "That's interesting about the gates. And that bear who guided us—"

"Right?" Carys leaned forward. "Magical shifters from here retain form on the other side of the gates, at least as long as they remain in the old growth forest, which... I have a lot of theories."

Duncan nodded. "I'm sure you do."

Cadell sat up. "Did the cross human return to Baywood in order to court you properly?" He turned to Duncan. "What gifts did you bring her? Jewels? Cows?"

Duncan's face turned red. "I didn't exactly— Not that I wouldn't like to, but—"

"That's not why Duncan came to visit, Cadell." Carys tried to turn the conversation away from her very confusing love life.

At her words, the dragon seemed to expand in size. "Then what is wrong in Briton?"

"Edgar is dead." Duncan lifted a hand. "Hunting accident. No foul play is even being considered."

Cadell grunted. "Humans are so fragile."

Just as he said it, Laura walked over and handed him a massive platter with a giant roasted salmon. "Fragile?"

Cadell didn't flinch, but his attention shifted immediately to the pretty woman who gave him food. "Your bodies are not as durable as dragons, bears, or wolves. If your bones weren't solid, I would classify you with birds."

Laura crossed her arms over her chest. "Keep irritating me and I'll show you how solid my fist is."

The dragon frowned. "I would never insult my host. You misunderstand me."

Laura sighed. "Whatever, Cadell." She plopped down on a log next to Duncan and across from the dragon. "So why did you fly all the way here about the king dying? He has an heir, right?"

"He does." Duncan continued, "And he's already in control of the country. Harold has trained his whole life to be king, so the transition is going smoothly. But there will be a coronation, and Carys's uncle would like her there."

Cadell's chest puffed out. "As is appropriate for a nêrys ddraig in the royal line." He nodded and broke off a large piece of salmon. "We'll make preparations to leave immediately."

"No worries," Duncan said. "Dafydd's man in Cardiff already sent a plane. It's waiting in San Francisco."

Cadell swallowed a large bite of fish before he spoke. "We can fly to Briton from here. The Chahta would not permit Cymric soldiers to live near them, but they did allow Mared to deliver a coracle for Carys to train. We can travel that way."

"And be there next week," Duncan said. "The coronation is in four days."

The dragon's mouth was a grim line. "I hate flying in the metal tubes."

Carys raised her hand. "Excuse me. Uh, thanks for making all these plans without even asking me what I'd like to do, but no, thanks."

Cadell's head swung toward her. "You're going."

"I don't actually have to though?" Carys wanted to go back to Briton—of course she did—but the idea of landing in another sticky political mess when she was still getting used to dragons and magic and having power she couldn't predict sounded like a *horrible* idea. "I have lessons with my Chahta trainer this week. I was planning on spending all summer practicing my archery, and Cadell was going to start on swords and stuff."

"Swords are cool," Laura muttered.

"Exactly." She looked at Cadell. "We've talked about this. We have plans."

The dragon was unmoved. "Plans change when there is a coronation and the king of Cymru requests your presence."

Carys didn't have a great response to that, so she looked at Laura. "What do you think? I'm not his heir. I'm barely a dragon rider."

Laura kicked out her feet and crossed them at the ankles. "Listen, I hate people planning my life as much as anyone, but you do have a role. I think you need to go." She shrugged. "It'll probably be a week of parties and boring dinners, a long-ass ceremony or two, and then you come home. You can spend some time with your uncle. You know that's probably all he really wants. The coronation just gives him a good excuse to call you home."

Carys wanted to scream. "You do realize that just by saying that, you're practically guaranteeing that something shitty is going to happen to me, right?"

And her current concept of home felt very, very tenuous.

Yes, she was born in Wales.

Yes, her extended family was there.

But she had grown up in Northern California. Her parents were estranged from their families, and everything Carys knew was in California.

Except for Duncan.

And Lachlan.

And her uncle and aunt, who were both in the Shadowlands.

So *home* was uncertain at best.

Laura lifted a steaming mug of what smelled like mint tea. "I don't think you can get out of it, so you should consider it a paid vacation. You're flying to England on a private jet, dude."

Cadell turned to Duncan. "*Dude* is a common term of address in California, and it can be applied to all genders. It expresses a general sense of camaraderie, but it can also be used in insults. It is sometimes hard to distinguish which is which."

Duncan nodded. "I appreciate the information, Cadell."

"Fine." Carys smiled at Laura. "Then you can come with me as an honorary representative of Turtle Island."

Laura snorted. "I wasn't invited."

"I think that is an excellent idea," Cadell said.

Laura gaped at him. "What? Why?"

The dragon was silent.

"You'd be able to keep Carys company." Duncan spoke up. "I know for a fact that Dafydd would love to meet more of her friends. He's about as welcoming a host as you can imagine, so it's not a bad idea."

"I'm not a leader here." Laura looked around. "Kere is a healer. Most of the humans here have some kind of magic even if it's just a little bit, but I don't have any mysterious powers like Carys does."

"Don't lie," Carys said. "You can read runes."

"That's not magic."

"It is power though." Cadell looked at Duncan. "As a pauwau inwe, Laura Thompson has been trained in magic, and while she is not fae-touched like humans born into the shadows, she can access some elemental magic."

"I'm just a go-between for our people both here and there," Laura said. "It's not the same."

"If it helps, I don't have any magic at all," Duncan said.

"A go-between is exactly what Carys needs," Cadell said. "Someone from her life here to accompany her and give her council on her role in Briton."

Carys hated to see Laura uncomfortable, but she had to confess she loved the idea of having someone from home come with her.

"Please?" Carys tried to make her eyes as doe-like as possible when she turned to her best friend. "Please, please, please?"

Laura humphed. Then she huffed. Then she sighed. "Okay, but if things get weird, I'm ditching all of you and going on a pub tour or something."

Carys couldn't say Cadell's face was beaming, but he looked less terrifying than usual. It was strange and somewhat disturbing.

She turned to Laura and made her hands into a heart. "I love you so much, and I owe you so much chocolate."

"Yes you do, and also you're the one who has to tell Kiersten that we're taking a vacation without her," Laura said. "I have paid time off and she just got back from Iceland, so you know she's stuck here all summer."

Carys turned to Cadell. "We'll let Cadell tell her."

Cadell's expressed turned from mildly happy to grim.

"So who is your Chahta trainer Cadell was talking about? Iniwe?"

Carys looked up at Duncan and smiled. "Jealous?"

"Maybe." He glanced at her. "I already have to share too much of your attention with other people. I don't want more."

She snorted. "So antisocial."

"I've a mind to be plenty social with you."

They walked along the edge of the forest, the massive trees stretching up into the fog that rolled in from the ocean.

By the afternoon, the fog would burn off and the pearl-grey sky would emerge, but there would be no sun. There was no moon or stars. The Shadowlands—no matter what part of the earth they were in—resided in a dreamy half-world where sun and moon didn't exist.

The only light that came from the sky was caused by the terrifying and mysterious thunderbirds that occasionally raced across the horizon, their shrieks so loud they made the trees sway, and the flap of their wings created light shows within the clouds.

The forest and the earth around her were alive in a way that Carys could see with new eyes, and she wondered if her mother had seen them the same way.

Tegan Morgan had talked to the trees. She'd sung to the deer and the birds. Carys had always thought her mother was a fanciful artist, but Cadell was convinced that Tegan wasn't from the Brightlands at all. Carys's dragon was convinced that the brilliant paintings Tegan had produced in her short life could only have come from seeing the Shadowlands of Briton.

"So." Duncan spoke again. "Iniwe?"

"Yeah." Carys grinned. "She's amazing actually. She's from... I guess it's around Mississippi in the Brightlands. Archer. Javelin thrower. All-around badass."

"Ah." His face brightened. "So you've been learning how to be a nêrys ddraig from an American."

She smiled. "No such thing as America here, Laird Duncan."

He nodded. "Right."

"But the dragons from Chahta..." Carys's smile grew. "They're stunning. I mean, they're kind of like Cadell, but their bodies are a lot longer and they have all different colors. It's been amazing to learn from her and Minko—that's her dragon—all the different flying and battle styles, because obviously they don't have coracles." She turned to him. "Oh! And feathers. Chahta dragons have these beautiful feathers around their faces, and Iniwe says that the dragons in Aztlán have even more feathers, and of course that would make sense because the mythology and cult of the feathered serpent is so prominent in Mesoamerican history, so—"

"Carys, you're rambling." Duncan stopped and leaned against a massive redwood. "What's wrong?"

She glanced at her feet. She looked at the dark earth and the verdant-green moss that covered the rocks. She breathed in misty air that smelled of salt and cedar.

"I don't know where I belong anymore." She blinked away the tears that wanted to rise. "I don't know where my family is from. At least, not my mother. If you'd asked me two years ago where my home was, I would say—without a moment of hesitation—that it was Baywood."

Duncan turned and looked at the village in the distance. "They don't treat you like a stranger."

"I know." She nodded. "They're wonderful. As soon as Laura realized what Cadell was and what I was, she immediately went to Kere and told her about us. Offered both of us passage. Told us that the forest was our home too." She smiled a little bit. "The children all adore Cadell. He's so good with them, and he takes them flying almost every day if their parents allow it."

Duncan muttered, "He's a very confusing dragon."

"He misses his children." Carys swallowed the lump in her throat. "And I'm the reason he's missing them. Because I can't face the fact that this place isn't really my home anymore. That it can't be."

Duncan walked to her and lifted her chin, his callused finger rough on her skin, but it felt so good. So... real. "You'll make your home where you want it to be, Carys Morgan. You have to be the one to choose your path. No one else."

She looked into his brilliant green eyes. "And if I wanted to move to Scotland?"

"Fuck yes," he blurted. "Brilliant idea. I'll help you pack."

Carys smiled. "I had a feeling you'd say that."

"You say the word and I'll move heaven and earth to make it

happen." He tapped her chin. "Don't forget I'm filthy rich. Feel free to take advantage of me."

"Is that so?" She had a feeling he wasn't just talking about money.

Duncan stepped closer, and she could feel the heat of his body through her wool sweater. "I haven't forgotten how your lips taste. Haven't forgotten how you feel in my arms. Have you forgotten, Carys?" He leaned down, his lips inches from her ear. "Would you like a reminder?"

She closed her eyes, and his scent grew stronger. He smelled like cut grass on the edge of a forest. She remembered his kiss too. She remembered how it felt to have her body pressed to the firm planes of his chest, wrapped in his embrace.

Everything about Duncan lit her up. If Lachlan had been like the sun, Duncan was fire.

He was grumpy as hell at times; he was also kind, thoughtful, and honest.

"It would be so easy to fall into this." Carys opened her eyes and stared at the cable-knit sweater that covered his chest. "To fall into *you*. I'm not even going to pretend it wouldn't be."

"You think I wouldn't catch you?"

"I know you would." She looked up and her heart ached. "But you know why it's not simple."

Duncan had feelings for her. So did Lachlan. And Carys had feelings for both of them. It wasn't just about picking one brother over the other; it was about two different lives.

"Until I know what kind of life I want—who I even am—I can't give you my whole heart." She put a hand on his chest. "Because that's what you deserve. My whole heart or nothing."

Duncan put his hand over hers, pressing her fingers close until she could feel his heartbeat underneath her palm. "You deserve that too, Carys Morgan. You deserve a man's whole heart. And don't you forget that ever."

CHAPTER THREE

Less than twenty-four hours later, Carys was in a black car, riding though the rainy streets of London with Duncan sitting in the front and Cadell and Laura with her in the back. She wasn't sure how much their driver knew about anything because he was sent by Duncan's mother, so she kept her voice low when she talked to Cadell.

"So" —she glanced at Laura— "what is London called?"

Cadell stared at her. "London."

"No, in the other place."

"London," Cadell said. "London is London no matter what side of the shadow you fall on."

"Really?"

Laura folded her hands and looked out the window. "It's a very old city, and both Old English and Welsh people called it London. Or some variation close to that. Some people think it was founded by the Romans, but it's older than that."

Cadell's eyes glowed. "You've done research into Briton."

"I research every place I go," Laura said. "I like to know things."

Cadell nodded. "A truly admirable trait."

Of all the humans that Cadell could get attached to, Carys could not think of a single one more unreceptive to male attention than Laura. It wasn't that her friend didn't like men, but she'd been burned.

And not by a dragon.

"Almost there." Duncan rubbed his eyes. "Glad we didn't arrive at rush hour."

The streets were nearly deserted at three in the morning, but it had still taken over half an hour to drive from London City Airport to Duncan's family home in Belgravia.

Carys had never been to London before, so she'd been disappointed that they were arriving in the middle of the night. However, once she saw the traffic at three a.m., she was more than happy to delay a city tour.

They crossed the River Thames, the wide black tributary that snaked through the old city, for the second time that night, and then they were driving on surface streets as rain spattered on the roof and dripped down windows to create a kaleidoscope from the colorful lights of the city at night.

Carys didn't know what time it was, and she wasn't even sure what day it was, so when they pulled up to a glowing white row of houses across from a neat park, the only thoughts in her head were: Feet up. Sleep. Food.

"Holy rich people's houses, Batman," Laura whispered. "I knew Duncan came from money, but holy shit."

Cadell said, "The laird comes from great wealth on his father's side, but his mother comes from even more. This is her home. She doesn't enjoy Scotland."

"Right." Laura's eyes were as wide as saucers when the door opened and the uniformed driver held his hand out for her to take.

They all hurried toward the door, which was opened before they could even reach the bell.

"Duncan." A woman in a grey uniform held out her arms. "Come out of the rain. Quickly."

All four of them entered the house, and before Carys knew what was happening, her coat was whisked away, her luggage had disappeared, and someone was ushering all of them into a cozy parlor where a fire was burning and a meal was set out to eat.

"Mr. Cadell." The woman gestured toward a table near the fire. "The laird was quite specific about your diet." She motioned to a platter containing a standing rib roast and nothing else. "I hope this meets your expectations."

"Excellent." Cadell sat at the table and immediately began devouring the roast before Carys and Laura could even sit down.

"Don't wait for the ladies, dragon." Duncan held Laura's chair for her and waited for both of them to sit down. "God knows we don't want you to start feeding on Mother's spaniels."

Carys sat down, but her head was swinging side to side.

She'd seen Duncan's estate in Scotland, but though this house was smaller, the wealth on display was far more obvious.

There were no suits of armor, weapons on the walls, or plaid cushions. But there were graceful landscape paintings, china on the table, and oil portraits of various stoic ancestors staring down from shadowy corners.

"This is your mother's house?" Laura asked. "So big money, right?"

Duncan nodded as he reached to uncover a silver tray. "Very big money. Her mother's family has owned this house since the 1840s or something. My uncles also live in the neighborhood. All filthy rich."

"But you live in Scotland?"

"I prefer it." There was a dish with medallions of some poultry on the tray along with roasted potatoes and carrots. "I don't like the formality here, but I can appreciate her cook." He served Carys, then Laura. "Dig in; then we should get some sleep."

Carys took a bite of the roasted bird, which was probably pheasant or goose or something very English. She didn't care what it was—it was delicious, and she'd had no idea how ravenous she was until she took a bite.

"How long are we staying here?" Laura asked quietly. "And where do we find a gate?"

"I know a gate, and we should probably cross tomorrow." He looked at Carys. "Your uncle is expecting you. You'll be staying at his estate in London on the other side."

Cadell lifted his head from his systematic destruction of the beef roast to say, "There's a gate nearby. I can feel it."

"Correct," Duncan said. "In fact, there's one within walking distance. Most of the gates in London are attached to rivers, and the old Cye Bourne is only a few blocks away."

Cadell lifted his head. "The Cye Bourne? You don't mean to take them under the Night Bridge, do you?"

"Knightsbridge?" Laura narrowed her eyes. "If this is Belgravia, that's the neighborhood right next to us. South of Hyde Park?"

"Knightsbridge is the modern name," Duncan said. "But in the Shadowlands, it's not knight with a *k*. It's called the Night Bridge because a market happens every night, and being right next to a fae gate, it's a very... interesting market."

"A market right next to a fae gate?" Laura asked. "Let me guess, not exactly legal, right?"

"Not in the slightest." Cadell's face was grim. "It's a *troll* market, and at night humans are traded there like property. They also trade in wild fae and other magical creatures. Potion dealers. Black mages, and every sort of contraband from the Brightlands. Duncan, you cannot take them there. Do you want me to burn down a troll market and instigate war with Anglia?"

Carys raised a hand. "I'm going to say that's a very bad idea right before a big fancy royal event, so maybe we find another place."

"It's the closest fae gate to the house," Duncan said. "Believe it or not, it's the easiest passage. Trust me, nothing is going to happen. One, we'll be crossing over at dawn when the legal market sets up, and two, we have a guide."

Cadell was still unhappy. "What kind of guide can get us safely through a troll market?"

Duncan glanced at Carys. "A familiar one."

CARYS SLEPT like a log in a massive four-poster bed layered with the most luxurious bedding that had ever touched her body.

This. This was what separated the rich from the poor, she decided. This was why wealthy women in San Francisco always looked so well rested.

Okay, it was probably also Botox, but the sheets had to be part of the equation.

She sat up when she heard a tap on the door. "Yes?"

"I have a tea tray, Professor Morgan."

Carys rubbed her eyes and jumped out of bed. She'd been hoping for coffee, but tea would do. At this point she wasn't picky. She threw on a thick cotton robe and slid into a pair of lush slippers someone had set next to the bed, then walked over and opened the heavy wooden door.

A woman in a grey uniform was on the other side. "If you'd like me to wheel the tray in, I can set it up by the table."

"I have a table?" Carys looked over her shoulder. "Oh, I have a table."

There was a round table with four chairs sitting underneath a tall window that looked out over the garden. Carys could see ferns rising up beneath the dark wooden windowsill, and—shock of shocks—it was raining again.

"Thank you." She opened the door wide, and the woman wheeled the tray in, the wheels almost silent on the thick Aubusson carpet.

There wasn't only tea but also a tiered platter of fruit and pastries, and Carys's mouth was already watering when she noticed the croissants.

The maid spread a white tablecloth, then went about setting the teapot and the plates on the table. "Full breakfast will be served in the morning room at ten, but the laird requested an early tea service for his guests since you all arrived so late last night." She turned and smiled at Carys. "I imagine the jet lag is quite disorienting. If there's anything else you need, please ask. My name is Rose."

"I'm… honestly not sure what time it is."

Rose looked at a neat watch with a black band on her wrist. "It's eight thirty-two, miss."

"Thank you." She walked over and lifted the lid of the teapot to smell the familiar and happy scent of Lady Grey drifting up.

Duncan. He always knew what she would want. "This looks great, but will there be coffee at breakfast?"

"Of course." Rose nodded. "I understand that Miss Thompson is in the adjoining room. Would you like me to wake her or allow her to sleep?"

"Uh…" Laura could be a bit of a bear when she woke up. Carys raised a hand to stop the maid. "Why don't you let me do that? Might be safer."

The maid nodded brusquely and walked toward the door. "If you have any other needs, please just ring the bell." She pointed at a brass button over the light switch near the door.

"That's actually a bell?"

Rose nodded. "Yes, miss. Please ring us if you need anything else." A second later, the door was closed and Carys was alone again.

She walked to the door to the adjoining room and lightly tapped. "Laura?"

Carys heard shuffling, and then the door swung open.

"Why am I awake when the bed is literal heaven?" She wrinkled her face and sniffed. "Is that tea?" She sighed. "Carys, I need coffee. You know I need coffee."

Carys gently led Laura toward the table. "I know, and there is going to be coffee with breakfast—I already checked. This is just a little bit of tea and some snacks so we don't wake up hungry."

Laura blinked at the stacks of fruit and pastries. "This is a snack?"

"Trust me, you're going to want to eat as much as you can on this side because food isn't quite the same on the other side."

"Oh, I know that." Laura sat in the chair, and Carys sat across from her. "There's a reason I rarely eat salmon back home. Because any meal in the Shadowlands? Salmon. Roasted salmon. Smoked salmon. Salmon with greens. Raw salmon for festivals. Salmon soup. Salmon stew."

"I love salmon, but that's a lot."

"You have no idea." Laura bit into a croissant, and her eyes rolled back. "Oh my God."

"That good?"

"The butter." Laura devoured the pastry in three more bites. "You want me to eat, I'll eat."

"Good." She glanced at the door. "I wonder who the mysterious guide is going to be?"

"Do we really need one?" Laura frowned. "Cadell is a *dragon*. We've all crossed over to the Shadowlands at other gates. Another guide seems unnecessary."

"I don't know, but fae gates here are not as friendly as they are back home. Duncan's probably right on this one." Someone knocked on the door, and Carys rose to answer it. "He's probably being overly cautious, but having some kind of magical escort that knows this gate isn't a bad idea, especially if we're walking into a troll market."

"Okay, but who?" Laura frowned. "How many fae does Duncan know who are just randomly hanging out in the Brightlands?"

Carys opened the door and looked up into the intoxicating blue eyes of the last person she'd been expecting.

The corner of Dru's mouth curved up and he bent low, taking Carys's hand in his own before he placed a courtly kiss on her knuckles. He looked up and smiled. "Carys Morgan, daughter of two worlds, it's so good to see you again."

CHAPTER FOUR

"You called the bartender?" Carys followed Duncan, who was following Dru, with Laura at her side and Cadell at her back. "If he's here, who's watching the Four Crowns?"

Dru glanced over his shoulder with a smirk. "You don't even realize what a question that is."

Dru—no last name given—was a dark-haired fae of mysterious origin who made his life in the Brightlands for a reason Carys didn't know. He was the owner and keeper of the Four Crowns pub in Scone, which as far as Carys could tell, had no magical connections except for Dru.

"Four Crowns pub," Carys said. "Four crowns of Briton. Trust me, I got the connection months ago."

"Ha!" Laura smiled. "That's clever though."

Night had fallen in the Brightlands and they were as rested as they were going to get, so they were headed to the mythical Shadowlands of London via a troll gate accessed via a Chinese restaurant on Knightsbridge's main road.

It was only a fifteen-minute walk from Duncan's family home, but the wind was brutal and Carys was already chilled to her skin by the time they turned left and the pedestrian traffic picked up.

"Not far now." Duncan glanced over his shoulder. "How you doing, dragon?"

"I'm ready."

"*Ready?*" Duncan's eyebrows went up. "No. Pick a different answer, because I don't like that one. Calm. Calm would be an excellent answer."

"I'm not calm," the dragon muttered. "I'm ready."

He rolled his shoulders under a large wool coat that Carys had forced on him after he tried to leave the house in nothing but his sleeveless leather armor.

Her dragon was ready to return to the Shadowlands. Carys could tell by the set of his jaw. He'd been in human form far longer than he liked.

Of course, he'd have to remain in human form until they passed through the gate and arrived at her uncle's house unless he wanted to create an international magical incident.

"Attention to the humans." Dru fell back as Laura and Carys gathered on either side. "A short lesson about where we're going."

Carys pulled her coat closer around her body as a gust of wind cut through the street, which was bordered by town houses. She glanced to the right and saw a man in a black overcoat leaning against an archway and smoking a pipe.

Belgrave Mews.

"The London you're going to encounter on the other side of this gate is nearly as diverse as the one in the Brightlands," Dru continued. "Whatever you think you know from movies or popular books, you would be better to forget it."

"Tell us about the trolls," Carys said.

"They are mostly harmless as long as you remember what they're there for," Dru said. "They want to trade, they want to eat, and they want to *not* be noticed."

"If they didn't want to be noticed, seems like a bad idea to start a giant black market right in the middle of London," Laura said.

Dru stopped walking and stared at her. "Why are you here, human?"

Laura lifted her chin. "Because Carys is my best friend, and I have a really good bullshit detector no matter what magical species I encounter."

Dru nodded. "Very well." He started walking again. "Don't look into a troll's eyes. Glance, don't stare, no matter how strange they look. Unless you're buying what they're selling, do not linger."

Glance, don't stare. Glance, don't stare. Carys repeated it like a mantra because this was going to be really hard.

Trolls were a fascinating mix of contradictions. Old Norse in origin, it shouldn't surprise her that there were trolls in Anglia, considering the Norse influence through both blood, conquest, and trade.

In some legends, they were small and fae-like. In other tales, they looked almost exactly like humans. And in others, they were tall and monstrous.

Basically, Carys was trying to prepare herself for anything.

The traffic as they turned onto Knightsbridge was bustling as the main road filled up with cabs, buses, and cars inching along, passing elegant hotels, and tooting their horns when the automobile in front of them didn't go as fast as they liked.

They continued through a busy intersection and walked through a construction tunnel before the road suddenly grew much more quiet and the lights seemed to dim.

Duncan muttered, "They feel him coming, for sure."

"What did you expect?" Cadell said. "If you wanted to slip in unnoticed, you shouldn't have invited *him*."

Carys glanced at the back of Dru's head and noticed that he seemed to grow taller before her eyes.

Light fae were usually taller than the average human, but the dark-haired bartender did such a good job blending into the human world that she hadn't noticed before.

Dru's chestnut hair fell in waves around his face, covering his pointed and gold-pierced ears, and his manner, unless you were talking directly to him, was mild.

Laura leaned toward Carys. "Who is this guy?"

"As far as I know, he's a fae guy who owns a pub in Scone." But Carys was starting to feel like there was more to the story than what she knew.

"Here." Dru stopped at the glass door of a Chinese restaurant. Unlike the bustling pub next door, the restaurant was dark, and the red lanterns hanging in the windows were not lit.

Despite the darkness, Dru pushed the door and it swung open. He walked through, leaving Duncan to hold the door for the rest of the party.

A moment after they walked through the door, a stout Asian woman in a yellow dress appeared from a hallway at the back of the shadowed restaurant. "We're closed!" She gasped a little bit when he saw Dru. "You."

"It's me." Dru hung his hands in his pockets and stared at the woman. "I'll be taking them downstairs."

The woman appeared to grow in stature before Carys's eyes. No longer a forgettable middle-aged restaurant proprietress in a yellow dress, she was nearly as tall as Duncan, and when she shook her head, Carys could see gold rings lining her pointed ears. "He won't like it."

"He won't know I've crossed over unless someone *tells* him." Dru's gaze drilled into the fae woman. "Is that going to be you, Lian?"

Lian cocked her head and looked at the dragon, the three humans, and the fae standing in her dark restaurant. "I didn't see you, but he will." One dark eyebrow lifted like a bird in flight, and then she disappeared back into the dark hallway from where she'd emerged.

Dru watched her leave, then turned to Carys and smiled. "My people. So dramatic." He walked to a hallway that Carys hadn't noticed before, pushing aside a red beaded curtain before he disappeared into the shadows. "Come, Carys Morgan. Day is dawning in the Shadows, and the market is waiting for you."

THE MAZE of passages beneath the restaurant was eerily quiet. Nearly as soon as they descended from street level, Carys could see the weeping blue lights of the wisps begin to glow overhead.

"The fae built this gate long before the city was established." Dru spoke quietly as they walked. "It was only marshlands then. But the tides of the ocean shifted, and the old god who was this river retreated into the Shadowlands. Over time, the humans changed the course of the river, but the gate stayed."

Carys saw nothing in the blackness, but she listened for the sound of Dru's voice and followed him, her right hand grasped in Duncan's and her left clutching Laura's.

She couldn't say exactly when the shift came, but she felt the claustrophobic press of brick and mud give way and the air around her expanding. The wisps danced and sighed in her ears. There were dark whispers in the distance, and when the first glow of light finally touched the horizon, she didn't see trees but the shadowed silhouettes of figures walking to and fro.

The ground beneath her feet turned from brick to mud to cobblestones, and she could hear water flowing in the distance.

"I've never seen a gate like this," Laura whispered behind her. "What is this place?"

They emerged into an alleyway where the fog was so thick Carys could barely see Dru's head as he led them into what looked like a cross between the Alemany Farmers' Market in San Francisco and a flea market.

It was early morning, and the air smelled of fish, mud, and damp wool. Along the banks of a slow-moving river, she saw figures of every shape and size setting up shops.

There was a barrel-chested creature with a forked black beard, piercing eyes, and a plaid kilt setting out leather goods. Belts, bags, and what looked like an ordinary backpack with a pair of mouse ears silhouetted on the front pocket.

Across from the leather shop, a tall, willowy female figure with bright white hair that resembled cotton candy was setting out glass bottles filled with potions of every color. Beside her, a shorter version of herself was setting out comic book playing cards from the Bright-lands in a single row.

Laura's eyes went wide. "Is that allowed here?"

"Shhh," Dru whispered. "Don't stare."

"Not technically," Carys whispered. "But you see more crossover here than in Baywood."

Carys had never seen a hint of the Brightlands in the Shadow-lands of California save for some clothing styles and Shadowlands takes on things like lunch boxes and modern fashion. But artifacts from one world crossing over? Not a single one.

She put her hand on the stash of treasure in her coat's inside pocket and hoped no one could read her mind.

What are you hiding, Nêrys?

Oh right. Dragon. She glanced over her shoulder and saw that Cadell was wearing the hint of a smile.

No shifting yet, she thought at him.

I know.

Mental communication had become second nature to her in the months she'd been training with Cadell.

Do you still have my bow?

I do.

Cadell had been the one to suggest Carys take her compound bow with her. It had no steel or iron and was made exclusively of carbon fiber and aluminum, both materials that the fae allowed in the Shadowlands, though aluminum wasn't common.

Cadell had packed her bow in the large bag he carried on his back, and as the market grew more and more crowded, Carys drifted closer to the safety of her dragon.

"Pike," a thick man barked from the riverbank. "Fresh pike and perch today."

She glanced at the fishmonger's swarthy face, a silver beard covering the lower half and a pair of pointed ears peeking from a red cap.

"Pike," he called again. "Fresh fish from the river."

As more and more creatures arrived at the market and more stalls were set up, Carys could see why the mythology about trolls was so varied.

There seemed to be no rhyme or reason to any of them.

The trolls setting up in the market were tall and short, stout and slender. There were creatures that reminded her of trees and ones that seemed completely made of moving rock. The only common feature appeared to be a certain roundness to the face and nose, larger-than-average pointed ears, and a wild aspect that Carys couldn't quite put her finger on.

"Wood and stone," Laura whispered. "They're elementals."

Carys nodded. "Maybe that's it."

Unicorns had elemental magic too, but they were otherworldly in their beauty while the trolls that ran this market looked like they could melt into a forest or mountainside in the blink of an eye.

There was a stall selling comic book T-shirts and another selling vegetables. There were fishmongers with scales on the backs of their hands, and a thin fae woman sat under a tent surrounded by a stack of books, some of which appeared to be reading themselves.

Once again, Carys was overtaken by the ordinary strangeness of everything in front of her eyes.

"Looks like most of the more… interesting stalls have closed up for the day." Duncan fell into step beside her. "You happy, Cadell?"

"I'll be happy when we get to King Dafydd's estate." His eyes scanned the street in front of them, sweeping back and forth as a red fire glowed at his throat. "Surely you feel it, human. Even though you're mundane."

"Mundane," Laura said. "My all-time favorite word. Cadell, you do know how to make a girl feel special."

"I was talking about the blacksmith. There is nothing mundane about you." Cadell's eyes never stopped scanning, and he stepped in front of a short rocky-skinned vendor who walked toward Carys, holding a bright paper flower. "No," the dragon growled.

"Rude." The small troll backed away and disappeared behind a table draped in brightly dyed wool.

"There's no need to be hostile," Carys said. "He was just offering me a flower."

"Nothing in this market is offered freely," Dru said. "The dragon is right. He probably smelled your coffee and was going to try to pickpocket you."

Duncan looked at Carys. "You didn't."

"Listen, I have heard your warnings about introducing geographic anachronisms," Carys said. "But whatever crazy things are about to happen to me, I am not facing them without coffee again." She put her hand on the contraband in her inside pocket, the prize she'd been hiding from Cadell. "I have enough instant to last me and Laura for a week. Don't test me."

"I knew you were my best friend for a reason." Laura grasped Carys's hand again.

"Do you see the bridge?" Dru pointed to a steeply arched stone bridge that crossed the river. "That's our way across the Cye Bourne."

They climbed stone stairs and walked up and over the bridge, stopping at the peak of the arch to survey what they had just passed over.

Duncan smiled at her. "London looks a little different here, doesn't it?"

Carys smiled and nodded. "Yeah. A little bit."

Instead of skyscrapers and townhomes, the London of the Shadowlands was a flat city of wooden buildings and thatched roofs. Two- and three-story buildings hugged the banks of a massive, wide river that twisted and flowed slowly toward the sea.

"The Cye Bourne is only one of the rivers that flows into Great Tamis." Dru leaned on the edge of the bridge and looked into the distance. "There it is, Carys Morgan. The oldest god of Anglia."

Flowing steadily through the middle of the city, the Tamis River slugged along, bordered by thick reeds and rock walls that shored up embankments on either side.

There were wide pathways and markets like the one they'd just passed through, and in the distance, poking its head from the low wooden buildings, stood a great stone tower that overlooked the heart of London.

Carys looked down at the slow-moving Cye Bourne as fishermen in wide, flat boats threw out nets and poled slowly downstream. Small fae creatures with bright wings fluttered from one side of the river to the other, and otters played in the thick green verge.

"We should keep walking," Cadell said. "We're starting to attract attention."

Dru pulled a black cloak up and over his head. "Come then. Just on the other side of the bridge, there's a fork in the road."

As they crossed over the bridge and saw the wide green embankment, a few market stalls selling morning snacks to passersby, Carys saw that Dru hadn't been joking.

She nearly laughed out loud.

Past the bridge there was an intersection of two paths, one that led into a dense forest and another that led farther along the river on the other side of the Cye.

And at the juncture, there was a large stall selling brass cutlery.

Forks. There were forks in the road. Someone had a sense of humor.

"Oh, for fuck's sake." Duncan growled. "He didn't."

"Who didn't?"

The tall Scotsman stalked past Dru and marched over to the

cutlery stand, leaning over the counter-height table and looking at someone on the other side. "Who the fuck let you two out of Alba?"

From behind the counter, Duncan's mirror image stood up, and Carys's heart started to race when she saw her former boyfriend for the first time in over six months. "Lachlan?"

The russet-haired prince shot her a beaming smile and happiness lit his eyes. "Carys!"

"Well," a growly voice came from behind a curtain before it swung to the side and a grey-haired, stony-faced creature emerged. "This should make things more interesting."

Duncan, Cadell, and Carys spoke at once. "Angus."

CHAPTER FIVE

Carys walked along the wide, stone-lined path that cut through a large wood on the other side of the Cye Bourne with Duncan on one side and Lachlan on the other.

"This is Hyde Forest," Duncan said. "Once we pass through it, your uncle's estate is on the other side."

"Are we still in the city?" Carys didn't know London well, but she was pretty sure that in the Brightlands, Hyde Park was right in the middle of town, and they looked like they were heading away from the city, not into it.

"In the Shadowlands," Lachlan said, "London has spread farther toward the mouth of the river. Most of the traffic goes by boat, so that's where the majority of people have settled. This area here" — Lachlan gestured to the dense woods around them— "Hyde Forest and Kingswood, is primarily occupied by the lords of Anglia and the wolves."

Wolves. Carys tried not to shiver, because she'd only seen the legendary shifting wolves from a distance. From what she'd heard though, they were magical creatures that were fierce, warlike, and owed their allegiance to the Anglian throne.

Cadell and Laura were walking behind them with Dru in the lead. A heavy cloak covered most of Dru's face, hiding the deep blue sigils that marked his cheeks and forehead. As he walked through the drifting fog, small sprites and zipping wisps danced around him, alighting on his shoulders and swirling around his head.

Sometimes he appeared to whisper to the tiny fae creatures, and Carys would swear she heard more than one sparkling laugh before a sprite or a wisp flew away into the trees.

A laugh bubbled from Laura, and Carys looked over her shoulder. "What's so funny?"

"Oh, little halfling," Laura said in a very bad English accent, "have you had your second breakfast yet?"

She looked at Duncan on one side and Lachlan on the other. "Ha ha."

Dru glanced over his shoulder with a smile. "You do resemble the good people of your homeland a bit, Carys Morgan."

"I look like an ellyll?" Carys couldn't stop her smile. "My hair isn't curly enough."

"Nevertheless," Dru murmured, "you should take honor at the compliment."

The fae people of Cymru, the ellyllon, were shorter than the fae in the rest of Briton, and myths and legends said they were some of the oldest magical creatures on the island. They had curly hair, darker skin, and mostly walked barefoot.

Carys had only met one, a fae woman named Naida who resided in Alba for mysterious reasons. Unlike the rest of the fae Carys had met, Naida was less conniving and more helpful.

But walking between two much taller Scotsmen and led by a mysterious fae escort, Carys realized they probably did look more than a little bit like a very lopsided fellowship.

"You're one to talk." She glanced over her shoulder at Laura. "Is Cadell two feet taller than you? Three?"

Cadell said, "I'm one foot and seven inches taller than Laura in the imperial measuring system."

Laura raised an eyebrow. "I'm not contesting my halfling status. Not as long as it gets me a second breakfast."

Cadell immediately took the pack from his back and handed Carys, then Laura, an apple. "Eat. Both of you."

Carys grabbed the apple and bit into it, only to see Lachlan staring at her with smiling eyes. "What?" She grinned. She couldn't help herself. When Lachlan looked at her like that, it felt like sunshine on her face. "Do you think I look like a hobbit too?"

"Your hair isn't curly enough." He glanced down at her shoes. "Your toes are a little bit hairy though, so maybe—"

"Hey." She smacked his arm, but she couldn't be mad at him.

Lachlan laughed. "You know, I jumped at the chance to come to Harold's coronation," he said. "Even though he's not my favorite person."

"Oh yeah?" Carys felt her cheeks warm. "Couldn't wait to dig into those famous Anglian royal banquets, right?"

"The food is far better in Anglia than in Alba," Cadell said. "They have greater access to spices from the continent."

Yet another misconception Carys was going to have to get over.

"I can't argue with the dragon," Lachlan said. "But it wasn't the food I was looking forward to." His green eyes were fixed on her face. "It's good to see you again."

Carys glanced at Duncan, highly conscious that the man hadn't said a thing to her since Lachlan showed up. "What's Angus doing here?"

Duncan kept his voice low. "He won't be staying." He glanced down at her. "But he had something of importance to deliver while I'm here."

Something of importance had to be Duncan's dragon-steel sword that he and Angus had forged in Sgain. According to Duncan, there were rumors about the sword now, but they were just rumors.

"Is that wise?" Carys asked. "To bring something like that to a royal coronation?"

A steel sword in the Shadowlands was akin to a weapon of mass destruction according to the fae.

"Just a precaution." Duncan stared straight ahead.

Lachlan glanced at his Brightkin. "Perhaps you're being overly cautious."

"Perhaps I like to be prepared," Duncan growled. "Some of us don't have their father's army to watch their back."

Before they could start snapping at each other, Carys jumped in. "We should go for a walk later," she said. "I've had time to catch up with Duncan, but it would be good to catch up with you too."

"Wonderful idea." Lachlan's smile was a triumph while Duncan's face only looked more stormy.

Great.

She wasn't trying to cause a problem, but Carys wondered why Lachlan hadn't mentioned his brother returning to court. It sounded like Rory's arrival had caused some upheaval, and she wondered why he hadn't written to her about it.

Lachlan's voice lightened. "How did the end of the semester go? First classes after your sabbatical. Were you stressed?"

"Not at all." She caught herself. She could always be honest with Lachlan. "Okay, that's not true. I was at first, but when I got into class and started interacting with the students—"

"It all came back." He nodded. "I told you it would."

"You were right." She smiled. Lachlan had always been encouraging. It was one of his best qualities as a person. "How are your parents?"

"Thrilled. They officially have all their children back in Alba. My sister Nora has returned from Ireland and recently married one of the Northern chiefs. She's spending some time in Sgain though and working to renovate and update the library."

"Your mother must be pleased."

"She is, and my father is less of a tyrant with his favorite child close." Lachlan smiled. "Neither Rory nor I can hold a candle to Nora in his eyes. He is—as you would say in the Brightlands—a complete 'girl dad.'"

"I'd heard Rory was back too." She glanced to her right. "Duncan mentioned it."

"Hmm."

"That's it?" Her eyebrows went up. "Just a 'hmm'?"

"Rory is back from Cymru with ambition on his mind." Lachlan's sunshine expression clouded. "We'll talk more about that later." He glanced at Duncan. "Duncan, how is your mother?"

"She's doing well," Duncan said quietly. "Thank you for asking."

Dru looked over his shoulder. "We're crossing into King Dafydd's estate." He pointed ahead where the massive English oak trees, birch, and alder thinned out. The fog was lifting, and the stone-lined path disappeared, leaving them walking on a hard-packed dirt road rutted with carriage tracks.

Moments after their group left the cover of trees, Carys saw them. Flying through the drifting fog and slipping in and out of the clouds, half a dozen dragons filled the sky.

Dragons. An entire horde of dragons.

Her heart raced, and she turned to Cadell. "Go. I know you want to."

Dru added, "It's safe here. I'll make sure she gets to Dafydd's castle."

"As will I," Duncan said.

"And I," Lachlan added. "I'm staying nearby."

The fire in Cadell's eyes matched the glowing fire in his throat. "My children are near. I can feel them."

"Then go!" Carys impulsively reached up and gave him a hug. "Go. I'm safe on Dafydd's estate. You know I am. Give them my love."

"Thank you, Nêrys." Cadell stepped away from her, handing his pack to Duncan before he ran toward the open field, his human body shimmering away as his arms reached to the sky, swiftly growing into massive wings that lifted his iridescent green body from the prison of the ground and into the sky that was his home.

Laura let out a small breath as her eyes followed Cadell's path into the clouds. "That never gets old."

"Nope." Carys felt his joy in her heart, and she nearly called him to come and grab her in his giant claws to carry her into the air with him. *One of these days I want to meet your children, Cadell.*

One day you will.

"Come." Dru motioned them toward a pair of massive bronze gates set into a high stone wall. "Your uncle will be expecting you." The corner of his mouth turned up. "And we must get our halflings a proper second breakfast."

"Carys!" Dafydd's voice boomed through the hallway Dru led them to. "You are most welcome." He left his chair and walked toward them. It appeared a small banquet really was laid out. "Most welcome, my dear."

"Dafydd." Carys was immediately enveloped in a hearty embrace that reminded her so much of her father it brought an unexpected rush of tears to her eyes. "It's so good to see you." She held on far longer than she intended but noticed that Dafydd did the same.

"Well." When he finally pulled away, he dashed a bright sheen of tears from his eyes. "You're looking well."

"As are you." She blinked back her own tears and stepped back and held out her hand for Laura. "I brought a friend from California. I hope that's okay."

Dafydd's face registered surprise, but it gave way immediately to pleasure. "Of course. You must treat my home as your own." He held out a hand. "A pleasure to meet you, my dear."

"I appreciate your hospitality." Laura shook his hand. "I'm a friend, but I'm also a pauwau inwe of the Yurok people. I'm born

Brightkin, but I'm an ambassador between our people on both sides of the gates."

"Yes, I have heard of this," Dafydd said. "An excellent system. I believe it fosters better relationships between the fae and the humans in your country."

"We think so."

"Welcome to our islands and to my home," Dafydd said. "You are most welcome. I will inform Harold's people that an ambassador from across the sea will be joining our party. I can assure you they will welcome such an esteemed guest."

"You're very kind."

Carys looked at the empty seat on the other side of Dafydd's chair. "Where's Eamer?"

"Back in Cymru," Dafydd said. "Looking after things while I am here." He lowered his voice. "After what happened in Alba, there has been some... hesitation about Eíran participation in the coronation."

What had happened in Alba was nothing less than a revelation of treachery from two Eíran noblewomen. Regan, the daughter of the Eíran queen and a powerful sorceress, had assassinated Carys's Shadowkin—Dafydd's daughter Seren, the heir to the Cymric throne. She'd also kidnapped Carys and nearly killed her before she destroyed Duncan's home.

Only Carys knew that Aisling, Seren's best friend and a granddaughter of Queen Orla of Éire, was truly responsible for Seren's death.

"Duncan." Dafydd greeted the tall blacksmith. "So good to see you. And Lachlan of course." Dafydd shook hands with both of them. "Glad your father could spare you for the event."

"He wanted Rory to catch up with the chiefs," Lachlan said. "I was able to get away."

"Only because you're the most likable, my boy." Dafydd clapped Lachlan on the shoulder and led all of them to the table filled with food.

Seren's death and Carys's kidnapping were sordid crimes

surrounded by more rumor than fact. Carys wasn't surprised that the Anglian court was suspicious of the Eíran throne, particularly when Queen Orla was so closely aligned with powerful fae.

"Is Queen Orla coming to the coronation?" Carys asked.

"Oh yes. She and Prince Cian are due to arrive via fae gate for the welcome banquet." Dafydd pulled out a chair for Carys and clapped his hands for the servants. "More food for our guests, Angharad. And call for Anwyn and Dylan to join us."

"Very well, my lord." A woman in a neat suit nodded brusquely and immediately began barking orders at the staff in Cymric.

Carys had been brushing up on her Welsh, but the dialect of her mother's language was different in the Shadowlands than what she could learn in the Brightlands. Still, a little of it made sense.

"Anwyn and Dylan?" Carys reached for a bowl of roasted turnips only to have the spoon snatched from her hand as Duncan started to serve her.

"Let me," he murmured.

"Thanks."

"And sausages?" Lachlan took two from a platter and set them on her plate. "Remember, it's colder here."

"I'm fine." She held up her hands. "That's plenty. Both of you." She looked at Laura with wide eyes, but her best friend was trying to stifle laughter.

"You've done this to yourself," Laura whispered.

"Shut up." Carys now had two large Scotsmen hovering over her, trying to feed her, and she was about ready to boot both of them out the large double doors when those doors parted and a pair of soldiers walked into the hall.

"Carys." Dafydd stood again, followed by everyone at the table. "Your cousins, my dear."

She turned and saw two fierce warriors glaring at her, a man and a woman, both clad in leather armor that looked similar to dragon-wear and sporting long, curved swords at their waists.

"These are my younger brother's children," Dafydd said. "Anwyn the eldest, and Dylan, her younger brother."

Both were dark-haired and bore more than a passing resemblance to Carys. They had the same dark brown hair and vivid blue eyes. Both were of medium height, and Anwyn carried a long scar that dragged from her left cheekbone nearly to her chin.

It did nothing to detract from her striking looks; both of Carys's cousins looked like complete badasses.

"Hello." Carys didn't know what to do with her hands. She didn't think a handshake would be welcome when both of them had one hand on the pommel of their swords and the other was fisted as they stood at attention.

"Lady Carys." Anwyn spoke in English. "Welcome to our uncle's home. And welcome to the company of nêr ddraig. Cadell is a wise and worthy dragon." She gave Carys an assessing look. "We trust he has chosen well."

Trust wasn't exactly screaming from their expressions, but Carys decided they were both playing polite for now.

For now.

"Both Anwyn and Dylan are dragon lords," Dafydd said. "The pride of the Cymric royal family."

Anwyn and Dylan both bowed deeply before they stood up straight.

"You honor us, Uncle," Dylan said. "We are servants of the throne."

"We look forward to flying with Carys," Anwyn said. "Rumors say that you are nearly as accomplished an archer as Seren was."

"That would be an exaggeration," Carys said. "I'm still training."

Anwyn's mouth twitched in what might have been a smirk. "Of course you are." She turned to Dafydd. "Uncle, we are training with your guards. If there is nothing else you need from us, we should return to them."

"Have you eaten?" Dafydd asked.

"We ate at first light," Dylan said. "As is expected of our company." He glanced at Carys, then back at Dafydd. "Unless you have need of us—"

"Go." Dafydd waved them away. "We'll have to arrange for some family time when you are not so busy."

Family time was about the last thing that Carys imagined these two wanted. "It was nice meeting you," she called out to Anwyn's and Dylan's retreating figures. "See you later."

Everyone sat again, and Carys immediately noticed that her food had gone cold.

"They adored Seren," Dafydd said. "I'm sure the three of you will enjoy getting to know each other as soon as they have time."

"Oh, they hate me." Carys sat in a large embroidered chair in the chambers that Dafydd had prepared for her. "They hate me *so* much."

Laura was sitting in another chair near the fire, holding her hands out to warm them. "They might have loved your Shadowkin, but they were also mentally preparing their own coronations after Seren died," Laura said. "Now you show up—bonded with your Shadowkin's dragon and wearing Seren's face. They're not going to be your biggest fans."

Carys dragged her chair next to Laura's and kept her voice low. "I don't want to be queen of Cymru," she whispered. "But I feel like that's Dafydd's idea, and it's not a good one."

"You're not Seren."

"Exactly!" Carys kept her voice to a hissed whisper. "I'm a mythology professor from California. I don't even speak Welsh. There is no way I would make a good queen."

"So you need to make that clear to your uncle," Laura said. "Just like you need to pick a Scotsman. Because two is kind of too much."

"Easier said than done." Carys sat back with a groan. "Do you want to pick for me?"

"As of right now, I'd pick Lachlan," Laura said. "Because I know him, and I don't know Duncan nearly as well. But from the look on your face right now—"

"What look?" Carys sat up and schooled her expression. "I have no looks."

"—and the fact that you didn't leap into Lachlan's arms the moment you saw him at the market," Laura continued, "I'm guessing the affections are getting a little blurry these days."

Carys squeezed her eyes shut. "How do you pick between two good men?"

"Well, Lachlan lied to you and Duncan didn't." Laura shrugged. "Don't get me wrong; I get it. If you wanted to get picky, you could even say that I've been lying to you my entire life by not telling you about the Shadowlands."

"You didn't lie to me. Don't be ridiculous."

"But I didn't tell you the whole truth," Laura said. "Because we're not supposed to. And that has probably been drilled into Lachlan's head from the moment anyone found out he'd gone through a gate. So I have some sympathy for him."

"You can relate to him." Carys nodded. "That makes sense."

"I also watched Lachlan drag you back to life when I was really scared for you." Laura's voice got soft. "So I can't be unbiased. I love Lachlan, and I love how happy you were when you were together. That doesn't mean that Duncan isn't also a wonderful man, and I recognize the fact that Lachlan was married to your Shadowkin makes things impossibly messy."

"Yeah, it really does." Carys sighed. "Did you really not know that Lachlan was Shadowkin when he showed up in Baywood?"

Carys's best friend had said she didn't know, but sometimes it was hard for Carys to imagine she couldn't sense anything different about the Alban prince.

"I knew he was different, but he was from an entirely different country," Laura said. "Had he shown up with Duncan, of course I would have known. But on his own?" She shrugged. "He didn't have magic in the Brightlands." She scooted forward. "Wait, so does he have magic here? What do they call it here when humans—"

"Fae-touched." Carys stretched out her legs, growing sleepy with a full stomach and a roaring fire. "He's got a bit of musical magic here."

"And Duncan?"

"Nothing." She shook her head. "He's a normal Brightkin. Unlike me."

"You know what Cadell and I think."

Laura and Cadell were both of the opinion that Carys's mother Tegan wasn't born in the Brightlands at all. Which meant that somehow her mother had made it from the Shadowlands of Cymru to the Brightlands of California and bore a child, which should have been impossible.

But Carys was clearly more than mundane, so that was the best theory they had.

"I'm going to fall asleep," Carys murmured. "Is that okay?"

"I'm about to join you." Laura yawned. "We have full stomachs and our bodies think it's three in the morning. Or maybe in the afternoon. We've got jet lag and shadow lag."

"Is that a thing?"

"It is now." Laura stood and took Carys's hand. "Come on. Let's nap in your bed because I don't know where mine is yet, and that thing looks like it could bunk a small army."

"We'll just sleep for a couple of hours." Carys was already falling over.

"Sure. That sounds like a plan."

Nêrys?

"Cadell is calling me."

"He's back already?"

Carys had the same thought. *Are you already back?*

I told you my children were close by. His voice was warm and happy. *I will see them again, but I wanted to return to you.*

I'm going to sleep for a while. Wake me up in a couple of hours?

Understood. You and Laura should both rest. Tomorrow is going to be a busy day.

I met my cousins. She sent her thoughts to her dragon. *They hate me.*

Cadell's rumbly voice came back to her mind. *They are thinking of their own position in the Cymric court.*

"Surprise, surprise," she muttered.

"What surprise?" Laura crawled under a heavy, fur-lined blanket.

"Nothing." Carys patted her arm. "Let's get some sleep."

She closed her eyes and opened them moments later to Cadell's voice in her mind.

Nêrys.

She sat up and noticed that it was completely dark outside. "Okay, so that was more than a minute." She reached across the bed and shook Laura's leg. "Hey. It's night already."

The cross human is looking for you.

"Duncan?" Carys rubbed her eyes. "What does—"

A rapping at the door interrupted what she was going to say and had Laura sitting bolt upright in bed.

"But scales aren't sexy," Laura blurted.

Carys looked at her and raised an eyebrow. "You're going to tell me about that dream later." She crawled out of bed and walked to the door, cracking it open and not at all surprised to see Duncan on the other side. "Hey. What's up?"

His eyes were dancing. "You want to see something brilliant?"

"Brilliant as in cool? Or brilliant as in something that will require brainpower?"

"Brilliant as in cool," Duncan said. "Doood."

"Please don't say *dude*. It sounds very wrong." She looked over her shoulder at Laura. "Okay, let us change our clothes and we'll be out in a minute."

Duncan couldn't stop his grin. "Cool."

God, he was so adorable when he didn't care about being goofy.

Carys closed the door and leaned against it, her heart beating in rapid rhythm when she remembered Duncan's smile.

"That smile is making me lean to the grumpy one," Laura said.

"You're no help." Carys walked toward the wardrobe where she knew she'd probably find a bunch of Seren's old clothes. "No help at all."

"I know," Laura said. "I am the worst."

CHAPTER SIX

Dressed in woolen clothing to keep away the evening chill, Carys, Duncan, Laura, and Cadell went riding through Hyde Forest on horses borrowed from Dafydd's stables.

"So" —Carys nudged her mount toward Laura's— "what do you think so far?"

"Of this place?" Laura looked around as the fog drifted between the trees, wafting in long feathers that curled and wrapped around them before moving on. "The fog is familiar but not much else."

"The magic feels different than back at home, right?"

Laura glanced at her, a heavy wool cloak masking much of her face. "I've spent a lot of my life going between the two worlds. I have to say, this place? It feels... unsettled."

"What does that mean?"

"I mean the magic here" —Laura dropped her voice— "there's something *restless* about it. It feels off to me, but maybe that's just because it's not what I'm used to. But it makes me uneasy. I feel like everything is on edge."

"Do you think it's the coronation? Because the human government is changing?"

"Maybe." Laura shrugged. "Like I said, I don't know this place well enough to say, but if I were feeling this back in the Pauwau Aki that I know, I would think there was conflict brewing." She glanced over her shoulder at Cadell. "Not among humans but among the magical creatures. It's not the people who are restless; it's the magic."

Carys fell silent and nodded.

"Like I said, I don't know this place well, so I could be wrong." Laura glanced back at the dragon behind them. "I hope I'm wrong."

Laura let her horse fall back to ride beside Cadell, and Carys continued forward.

"Are we headed back to the troll market?" Carys asked. "I thought that wasn't a good idea at night."

"We're not." Duncan rode a little ahead as the horses walked through Hyde Forest. "We're going to a spot a little downriver from the Night Bridge. I want you to see the Tamis at night."

"Ah," Cadell spoke from behind them. "I know what the blacksmith is thinking. A pleasant outing then."

"What is it?" Laura asked. "Don't keep us in suspense."

Cadell said, "But suspense will heighten your pleasure."

Carys barely managed to muffle her snort.

Laura cleared her throat. "Want to try that again?"

"Prolonged suspense will heighten the pleasure of what you are about to experience."

"Right." Laura was hard to embarrass, but Carys heard it in her voice. "So you're saying you enjoy anticipation."

Cadell said, "I believe *you* will enjoy anticipation. It's a common trait in humans."

Laura kept her voice deliberately mild. "Not in dragons?"

Duncan fell back to walk his horse beside Carys and lowered his voice. "Are they always like this?"

"Yes."

Duncan glanced over his shoulder. "Poor dragon." He kept his voice low. "Does he have any idea how transparent he's being?"

Carys shook her head. "I don't think so."

"I suppose I know how he feels. It's hard having something you want right in front of you and feeling like you're not allowed to touch."

"Not *allowed*?"

He raised an eyebrow. "Someone told me that she needed time."

Carys felt the zing of attraction between them. It would be as easy as breathing to take what Duncan was offering.

She could move to Scotland.

He could move to California.

Carys knew it would be good. Maybe it would be better than anything she'd ever had. Better than the fumbling boys in college. Better than Lachlan even.

After all, destiny was on their side.

"Carys Morgan." Duncan made his brogue thick. "Slide yer leg over and ride in front of me." He spread his legs and scooted back. "I've got just the spot for ye, lass."

Her cheeks flushed. "That's a lot of weight for your horse."

"Ye're nothin' but a feather. It's been too long since I've had my arms around you."

"You're shameless." Her cheeks were on fire.

"Not yet, but if ye're looking for shameless, I have some ideas."

"Duncan!" She had to laugh or she would explode. "Maybe you need to take Cadell's advice."

"What's that?"

Carys nudged her mount forward. "Enjoy the anticipation."

Cadell's voice rose behind them. "Dragons are practical and appreciate planning ahead so we can act in accordance with desired expectations."

Laura said, "So you're saying that if I want something from you, I should state my desired expectations clearly?"

Cadell's voice dropped to a low rumble. "Do you want something from me?"

"Not right now." Laura kicked her mount a little and sped up to pass Carys. "Duncan, you're slow. Let's speed this parade up; I'm freezing."

Duncan smirked and nudged his horse to ride faster. "Follow me."

It was a good thing Carys had been practicing her horseback riding in California, because once Duncan sped up his mount, he didn't stop until the horses let out a high whinny of joy and the trees sped past them in a blur.

They kept to the clear cobblestone path, but Carys could see lights in the forest around them as they rode, and the bright golden glow of eyes peeked from the shadows.

Wolves.

"Watch the horizon," Cadell shouted, "when we turn this corner."

Duncan led them to the left when the path forked, and in the distance, Carys saw a blue-green glow emanating from the darkness. Drifting through the forest, hundreds of singing voices carried on the wind.

Duncan began to slow their pace.

Carys caught her breath, her eyes fixed on the growing glow in the night sky. "What is it?"

Cadell smiled. "The river fae."

The blue-and-green glow grew brighter and brighter, and as Carys watched, lights flew into the sky overhead. A pure, golden voice sang from the far side of the river, and from the darkness voices sang back in a language Carys had never heard.

"Who are they?" she whispered.

"Well, there's the high fae court of Temris—that's in Ireland," Duncan clarified. "Éire. But all over Briton, all over the land, there are wild fae. Powerful creatures attached to rivers or forests or... anything really. They're not part of the political life like Prince Cian is, but they're still very powerful."

"What is that?" Carys kept her voice low. "What are they singing?"

Duncan slowed his horse to a walk, keeping to the edge of the tree line. He shook his head. "I don't know. They sing every night, but I've never heard them like this. Some boys in the stables were talking about it after dinner, and they said we should ride out and see." He smiled, his eyes fixed on the light show before them. "I'm so glad I listened."

Cadell drew up beside them with Laura on his right side. "They're singing a kingsong. It's a welcome chorus." The dragon shook his head. "I have not heard this song in many years."

Carys saw others in along the edge of the river, other riders and people on foot, all peering through the trees as the dark and slow-moving span of river that stretched before them came alive in the darkness.

There were adults and children of every color and type of clothing. Children walked down to the banks and set shining candles along the shore. Adults lit lanterns that floated up and over the river, reflecting light below.

"It's so beautiful," Laura whispered. She blinked shining tears from her eyes.

Shadowlands London might be different than Brightlands London, but what Carys saw on the dim bank of the river was a tapestry of human and magical creatures.

Stout trolls conferred with human neighbors, pointing at the bright lights dancing among the reeds. A long-haired fae woman helped the human children light the candles, whispering something that made them laugh.

Carys had never seen a scene like it. The fae lights over the river appeared like a luminous display that might happen for a holiday or a celebration, and the echo of their singing drifted across the water and filled the night sky with an ethereal beauty.

"Is it for the Anglian king?" Carys asked. "Is this to celebrate the coronation?"

"The fae do not recognize human rulers," Cadell whispered.

"Neither the high fae or the wild. This is for something else. Something far more powerful."

Below the water, golden ribbons undulated in time with the music, and some vast and terrifying creature rose from the deep, breaching the surface of the water before it slid into darkness again, taking its golden glow with it.

"Is that a sea monster?" Carys whispered.

"It's the Great Serpent." Cadell's voice was reverent. "He lives in the depths and is the guardian of the Tamis River and all her creatures. The kingsong has called him to the surface." The dragon whispered something under his breath that sounded like an incantation or a prayer.

Carys wanted to go closer. She wanted to wade into the long grass along the riverbank, hang on to the willow branches, and dip her fingers into the gold-brushed water. A tug in her chest told her that nothing dangerous lurked there.

Of course, it was entirely possible that's exactly what the river wanted her to think.

The song continued, as did the light show. Dancing blue and green lights appeared overhead, swirling in patterns that weaved like intricate knots in the black sky.

There were no stars because the fog was too thick to see the sky, leaving the fae lights to illuminate the darkness in magical whorls and golden threads.

Laura was staring at the edge of the water. "Carys, look."

She tore her eyes away from the dancing lights to see dark silhouettes perched on stones upstream and away from the crowds. They were sitting along the edge of the muddy riverbank. The pert heads of otters mingling with otherworldly creatures left her blinking in disbelief.

"Cadell," Laura whispered, "are those mermaids? Selkies?"

The dragon glanced at the edge of the water where Laura was pointing. "Don't point." He grabbed her hand. "The mermin have traveled upriver." He frowned. "Very unusual. They rarely leave the deep water. They're very shy."

One of the mermin must have caught their scent or their sound, because the creature with long, weedy hair and pale grey skin turned, bright blue eyes glowing in the darkness. They hunched their bare shoulders, whispered to the otter, and both creatures dove into the black depths of the river and disappeared.

"I want to go closer." Carys nudged her horse to the right, making for a dark, shadowed copse of trees a little closer to the river. "If we go over here, we can see more and we'll be away from the candles."

She nudged her horse—a sweet-faced dappled grey mare—closer to the darkened bunch of trees, aiming for a fold of blackness that would hide her from the view of the river fae. "No one will see us over here."

"Nêrys, wait for me," Cadell whispered. "Laura, where did you go?"

"Carys, don't go that way." Duncan kept his voice low. "Wait for..."

Before she could turn back for Duncan, the fog closed behind her, blanketing Carys in gentle silence.

"Oh, fantastic." There was something going on, and Carys didn't feel like facing it on horseback when she wasn't an expert rider. "Hello?"

The darkness and the fog were immense. There was something supernatural happening, but nothing was telling her instincts to run.

She slid off her horse, keeping one hand on the reins as she led the creature under the low-hanging branch of a hawthorn tree. "Hello?"

Just as she passed under the tree, a black crow landed on her shoulder, letting out a rude "Caw!" before it flew away.

Carys felt her before she heard her.

"Hello, Carys Morgan."

She spun around to see the Crow Mother sitting on a tree stump, stirring a pot that hung over a cooking fire.

"You." Carys looked over her shoulder, listening for Cadell, for the river fae. For anything other than the drifting silence of the fog that enveloped her. "Why am I not surprised?"

"I've been waiting for you." The woman looked up at Carys, her black eyes shining from a face surrounded by dark, curly hair. "We have unfinished business, you and I."

CARYS'S HORSE nudged her shoulder, but she stood frozen in front of the powerful fae woman who had lured her into some fold of shadow that not even Cadell had detected.

Usually fae ground had some wards or warnings that her dragon could detect. This hollow in the Shadowlands had given him no notice at all.

"Who are you?" Carys asked. "Are you really fae? Or are you something else?"

The Crow Mother tsked. "It's not the time for questions, Carys Morgan. You made me a promise."

"I know." Carys spoke carefully. "Have you decided to collect on that promise tonight?"

Carys had traded a single passage to the Brightlands to this powerful fae in return for Seren's lost journal. It was the journal that had revealed her killer, so it had been worth it. But then Carys had left for the Brightlands without fulfilling her debt.

So seeing the Crow Mother wasn't exactly a surprise. Carys had fully expected to run into her again, but a little warning would have been nice.

The mare at her side whinnied, and the Crow Mother, who sometimes called herself Branwen, looked at the creature. "I see you, Epona's kin. This child is not one of your daughters, and she and I have struck a bargain of our own free will. This is not your concern."

The grey mare neighed, stamping her foot a little bit.

"Nevertheless," Branwen said, "she will uphold the old laws or I will take payment in the way that I see fit. If your mistress objects to this, she can fulfill the debt herself." Branwen's eyes lit up. "Oh wait. No, she can't. She's as stuck here as I am." She turned her gaze back to Carys. "You have a debt to repay."

Carys was tired of the double-talk. "So what do you want to do? We're not that far from the Night Bridge. I'll take you right now if you want."

Was she dreaming, or did her horse's neigh sound a little bit like a laugh?

"So eager to be rid of your obligation?" Branwen asked.

"You seem eager to collect," Carys said, "so come on." She waved in a hurry-up gesture. "It's morning in the Brightlands. I can't guarantee you'll see the sun because it's England—it was pouring rain when we left—but if you want to go, I'll take you."

Branwen smiled, her eyes lit with amusement. "You've grown in confidence. I enjoy this, Brightkin."

"Okay, cool." She took her horse's reins again and started to turn her around under the hawthorn branches that encircled them. "Follow me and I'll take you right there."

"What's the rush?"

Carys turned when she heard an unexpected male voice. She frowned at the last person she'd expected to see. "Dru?"

The tall fae had a brown wool cloak wrapped around his shoulders and pulled up over his head. The blue sigils that marked his forehead and cheekbones sparkled in the light from the cooking fire that Branwen tended, and his eyes seemed to glow in the darkness, reminding Carys of the fairy lights dancing over the river.

The Crow Mother rose when she saw the fae enter her clearing. A sly smile took over her face. "Is it Diarmuid himself before me? The wandering Oberon returned at last? What, has the stubborn Mab finally returned your affections, dear boy?"

Dru pulled his cloak closer around his body, but he didn't take his eyes from the Crow Mother, nor did his face register the slightest hint of worry. "You're speaking nonsense, Badb. Why do you trouble my friend tonight? We all know your plans are still in the nest.”

“Are you the reason the river folk are singing a kingsong and the serpent has risen from the deep?” Branwen chuckled. “Oh, won’t Cian be pleased?”

They were speaking in riddles that Carys couldn’t decipher, so she leaned into her horse’s side and watched carefully, filing every word away to write down later.

“You let me worry about Cian and don’t bother yourself with mortal matters, old one.” Dru glanced at Carys. “Let the girl leave us and we may speak freely.”

“Speak as you will, for she knows nothing.”

“She’s a creature of two worlds, and she’s her own part to play. Speak at your peril, for the Night Queen hears our dreams.”

“Rhiannon is gone from the Shadows and shelters in her own world.”

“And yet her daughters live, as do yours.” Dru leaned closer and seemed to grow taller before her eyes. “Depart from this place and cease your meddling, old one. Your time has passed.”

“My time is reborn as I am.” The Crow Mother leaned forward, her face in shadows from the cooking fire. “As I always will be.”

In the flickering lights, Carys saw Branwen’s face shift from a mature woman with dark hair to a young maiden. In a blink, she was a weathered crone. Then before her face changed again, the cooking fire went out and the hollow of the tree was cloaked in darkness.

What was she?

Mother, maiden, crone. A triple fae? Carys needed her books. She needed a library!

She gasped when a warm hand grasped her arm. “Who—”

“It’s me.” Dru let her arm go, opened his palm, and a soft blue light illuminated the black. “Relax.”

Carys let out a breath. “What are you doing here?”

Dru ignored the question. “Such odd companions you’ve collected, Carys Morgan.”

"Does that include you?"

"Naturally." The corner of Dru's mouth turned up, and he pulled his cloak farther over his face.

"How did you find us?"

"The ward she placed around this tree was weak—I sensed your presence as soon as I entered the forest."

Carys stared at the empty ground where the Crow Mother had been sitting. "Where did she go?"

"Oh..." Dru sighed. "Where all of them go when they're finished causing trouble." He threw his cloak over his shoulder and patted the side of her horse. "This mare is a fine animal. You should stay close to her while you're here. She carries her mother's spirit."

"Her mother?"

Dru took the mare's reins from Carys. "Most horses in Briton carry a bit of the goddess Epona in them. She's one of the oldest gods on the islands." He smiled brightly at the horse as he led her under the hawthorn branches. "Some creatures are closer to the goddess than others." He patted her neck. "You lovely darling." Dru glanced at Carys over his shoulder. "Her name is Leuca. It means bright one."

"Leuca." Carys put her hand on the mare's side. "You're lovely, Leuca." Her hand remained on the horse's neck as they walked back into the forest. "I don't know how, but she was very reassuring when the Crow Mother trapped me in here."

"You weren't actually trapped." Dru leaned down. "That's important to remember, Carys Morgan. You're never trapped with them unless you *believe* you are."

She heard loud whispers in the forest, and Cadell was yelling in her mind as soon as she emerged from the fog.

Nêrys!

"I'm here." She waved into the darkness as Dru tossed the glowing fire into the sky. The fog caught it, turning the night into something more like dawn.

"Carys?" Clopping hoofbeats sounded in the night a moment before Duncan and Laura appeared from between the trees. Duncan slid off his mount and walked over. "Good God, you disappeared into thin air. What the hell happened?"

"Where did you go?" Laura's eyes were the size of saucers. "I swear, I was right behind you, and then just... Poof. Gone."

Carys shook her head. "I'm honestly not sure what happened."

Where did you go? Her dragon was shouting in her mind.

"Calm down," she hissed, looking at the sky. "You can land now. I was never in any danger, Cadell."

"It was just a little mischief from the Crow Mother." Dru handed Leuca's reins back to Carys. "She couldn't have kept them for long. It was a temporary ward, and Auld Tamis's magic is strong this close to the water."

Carys looked toward the river, but the glowing blue lights were gone. "Oh shoot. I missed it."

Dru smiled. "It was a lovely show though, wasn't it?"

Cadell walked through the forest, glaring at Dru and at Carys. "You need to discharge your debt to that fae woman and be done with this bargain."

"I tried, but according to Dru, she's not ready yet." Carys shrugged. "Whatever that means."

"Dragon, don't be too eager for your mistress to settle her debt." Dru pulled his cloak closer around his body. "And all of you should ride back to Dafydd's. I can feel the wolves stirring in the forest."

Carys looked at Dru, watching how the tall fae seemed to shrink into himself, his power growing less and less obvious by the moment, and she remembered Cadell's words: *The fae do not recognize human rulers. This is for something else. Something far more powerful.*

"Any idea what that singing was about?" Carys asked Dru. "It sure was beautiful."

Dru smiled and melted into the shadows of the forest. "Good night, Carys Morgan. And don't forget to give Leuca an apple when you get back to your uncle's stables. They're her favorite."

Duncan frowned as Carys mounted her horse. "Who's Leuca?"

CHAPTER SEVEN

The next morning—way too early—a knock sounded on Carys's door. She rolled out of bed, threw a cloak over her shoulders, and walked to the door. "If you're coming to light the fire..." She pulled the door open, her jaw dropping when she saw Lachlan in the hallway. "Lachlan."

The corner of his mouth turned up. "You said something about lighting a fire?" He glanced down at her bare feet. "What are you doing? This isn't California, Carys." He shuffled her into the chamber, shutting the door behind them as he picked her up like she weighed nothing and plopped her on the bed.

"What..." Carys put a hand flat on his chest. "Uh, Lachlan, in case you didn't realize—"

"I'm not assuming anything." He kissed her cheek. "Yet." He bent and searched around the edge of the bed. "Stockings, Carys. You're going to catch cold wandering around a castle with bare feet."

She swung her legs over the edge of the high bed. "Are you being serious right now? When did you turn into my granny? Not that I knew my granny, but you know what I mean."

At that, Lachlan straightened, nudged her knees apart, and slid between them, bracing himself on the edge of the bed as he leaned into her. "What was that?"

Carys's breath caught. "Uh... nothing."

Before he returned to the Shadowlands, Lachlan had been practically living with her. They were together for months, and he knew every inch of her body, every one of her buttons, every trick that turned her on.

He didn't even need to touch her to light a fire.

"Hi." She swallowed the lump in her throat. "You're here early."

"I wanted to take you riding this morning." He didn't move, his arms remained braced on either side of her hips, his lips inches from her own, their breath mingling in the cool morning air.

"Riding sounds fun."

"Yes." His eyes dropped to her lips. "I thought it would be nice to catch up on news." He licked his lips, and she could see how red they were.

It was his tell. Lachlan's lips always flushed when he was turned on.

"Lachlan?"

"Carys."

"Riding sounds fun, but you're going to have to let me get dressed."

"I could do that, or I could help you get dressed. Or undressed." His eyes met hers. "I don't have a fixed plan."

Having sex with Lachlan would be a mistake. She'd allowed herself a sentimental night with him months ago, and it had left her feeling conflicted and confused.

Was she tempted?

Yes.

Did she know it wasn't a good idea to sleep with her ex-boyfriend who had been married to her Shadowkin and possibly still had feelings for his dead wife?

Also yes.

She put a hand on Lachlan's chest and felt the warm, steady beat of his heart under her palm.

He placed his hand over hers and held it there.

"Is that for her or for me?" Carys asked.

"For you." His voice was soft. "It's always been for you, Carys. You're as different from Seren as Duncan is from me."

Carys closed her eyes and drew her hand back. "Yeah." The mention of Duncan's name was enough to kill the mood. "You know Duncan and I—"

"I know your heart is conflicted," Lachlan whispered. "I understand, Carys. I truly do."

She closed her eyes and leaned back. "You and I are from different worlds. I can't forget that."

"It didn't matter before."

"Because before I didn't know."

Lachlan sighed and stood up straight. "Ah, mo chridhe. If I loved you less, it would be easier to step aside."

Okay, when he said things like that, Carys wanted to pull her former lover into bed and forget all the wise and mature boundaries she'd set for herself. "Riding. Riding is good. Let's go do that. Did I tell you about my horse?"

Lachlan took a step back, a smile flirting around his lips. He knew exactly what he was doing to her. "I'll find the kitchen and pack a breakfast for us. You need to eat. Get dressed and meet me at the stables. You can introduce me to your horse there."

"Perfect." She started to slide out of bed, but Lachlan caught her around the knees and she gasped.

"Don't forget stockings." He lifted her leg and kissed her bare ankle. "It may be summer here, but remember to dress warm."

WHEN CARYS ARRIVED at the stables, she was surprised and not surprised to see Dru in some kind of intense conversation with Lachlan. The tall fae was speaking in low tones to the Alban prince, and he was dressed in heavy woolen clothes that were covered with straw.

Was Dru sleeping in the stables? Carys didn't know what to make of the odd man, and she hadn't spent enough time with other fae to know what was and wasn't normal.

As she'd learned in her previous foray into the Shadowlands, what the books she'd studied said was true and what was *actually* true were two different things.

Carys hung back, watching from a distance, but the two men didn't notice her. The fog had cleared, and in the pearlescent morning light, Lachlan looked like a young, golden god. His reddish-brown hair fell to his collar in waves, his shoulders were thrown back, and the clothes he wore made him look every inch the prince that he was.

Dru, on the other hand, looked like the mythical Green Man wandering out of the forest, his hair wild and threaded with feathers and bright blue beads that matched the markings on his face.

But as he spoke with Lachlan, his chin was tipped up and the way he looked down his nose didn't match the grubby clothes he wore. Dressed in rough clothing or not, there was something distinctly regal about Dru, and Carys was starting to wonder why the fae had crossed back into the Shadowlands.

"Is it Diarmuid himself before me? The wandering Oberon returned at last? What, has the stubborn Mab finally returned your affections, dear boy?"

Was Diarmuid Dru's true name?

Carys found herself examining what she remembered from the Crow Mother's cryptic words in the forest the night before. Oberon was easy to decipher; he was the king of the fairies in folk stories and Mab was his queen, but they had broken apart. In some stories, Oberon had even imprisoned Mab.

As far as Carys knew, the high fae of Briton had no king or queen in this realm as humans did. The closest the fae had to a ruler was Prince Cian, the consort of the Eíran Queen Orla.

"Are you the reason the river folk are singing a kingsong and the serpent has risen from the deep? Oh, won't Cian be pleased?"

Kingsong? Oberon? Carys had a sneaking feeling that fae politics were going to get a lot more complicated with Dru's return.

She walked forward, and as soon as Dru spotted her, he stopped talking and snapped something in Gaelic at Lachlan.

Lachlan turned, saw Carys, and his face lit up like the sun. "And there she is. We were just speaking about your appointment with the Crow Mother last night."

Dru said, "*Appointment* is an interesting word." He turned and whistled. Moments later, Leuca trotted out of the stables, already saddled and bridled, as if she was waiting for Carys to arrive.

"Leuca!" She stepped forward and caught the mare's reins in her hand. "Good morning." She grabbed an apple from her pocket and held it out. "I was hoping to see you this morning."

"You speak as if she understands," Lachlan said.

"She does." Dru whispered into the horse's ear and drew his cloak around his body. "Your uncle was kind enough to let me stay on his estate as I have no home in Briton anymore."

"In the stables?" Carys accepted Lachlan's hand as she mounted her horse. "The house is massive. I'm sure there's a room available."

"No, thank you." Dru smiled and looked at the forest. "I prefer the stables." He patted Leuca's neck. "It's a pleasure to be near wild things and warm hearts."

"I'll speak to you later," Lachlan said. "Carys, shall we?" He patted his saddlebags. "I've packed a meal for us."

"Excellent." Her stomach was rumbling. "Dru, we'll see you later?"

"I'm here." His voice was grim. "For good luck or bad, we'll see in the end."

Carys and Lachlan walked their horses out of the yard and onto the road. She was silent, breathing in the morning air and drinking in the pearly morning light.

"Why didn't you tell me about seeing the Crow Mother last night?"

Carys looked to the right. "Because we were flirting in my room when you came to wake me up, and mysterious fae sorceresses were the last thing on my mind."

Lachlan smiled. "Fair enough."

The lane outside Dafydd's estate was a broad boulevard that bordered multiple grand estates, all of them bound by stone walls that enclosed vast green lawns dotted with grazing sheep.

Carys could see the crush of the city in the distance, but while they'd be smack into Brightlands London riding just north of Hyde Park, in the Shadowlands, the rolling land north of the woods was strewn with massive stone houses, grazing land, and scattered stands of forest.

Lachlan handed her an orange. "A bit of home from the continent for you. An ambassador from Gaulle came for a visit this morning. And please tell me if you see the Crow Mother again. She's trouble."

"I'm *going* to see her again. I have to." Carys took the orange and immediately began to peel it. "This is a treat. Don't tell me there's coffee too."

Lachlan smiled. "None but what you've brought with you."

"Does everyone know about that?" she whispered. "If you guys try to steal my stash, I'm going to get mean. Be warned."

They passed from the wider road into the park, and immediately the trees around her felt wild. There was an eerie silence under their branches, and she realized there was little to no birdsong even though it was morning.

"You know, in the redwood forest, sometimes visitors complain that there aren't many birds." Carys looked around at the ancient tangled oaks, twisting elms, and delicate birches. "But they don't realize all the birds live so high up that you just don't hear them."

"I did notice that, but I'd never put it together with the height of the trees."

"But here..." Carys looked at the hardwood forest. "There should be birds, right?"

"There are birds," Lachlan said. "But these woods have very old magic and they're hunting grounds, so the birds might avoid it even during the day. I doubt many of them nest here."

"Hunting grounds?"

Lachlan nodded toward the land behind them and to the left. "This park and the Kingswood are wolf territory. We're not in any danger during the day, but make no mistake. If you stray off the pathways at night, they will find you."

She heard footsteps to the right, and it might have been a trick of the light, but she saw something moving in the underbrush.

"Lachlan?"

"I hear it. They're around, but they shouldn't bother us. We're foreigners, but we're guests of the king." He moved closer even as his horse became restless under him. "Calm, Attalus."

Carys put her hand on Leuca's neck, leaving her palm on the warm animal's body. She felt a hum of serenity even as the flicker in the forest came again, this time accompanied by a crashing sound in the distance.

"Should we go back?"

Lachlan's mouth was a grim line. "It's daylight in the park, and we're guests of King Harold," he bit out. "There should be no danger."

Nêrys?

"Cadell is close." The dragon had remained at Dafydd's estate, not particularly adept at flying through the bunched trees of the park in beast form.

I'm with Lachlan, and there are wolves in the forest.

Cadell's voice came back to her mind in a calm, even cadence. *The forest is their home.*

True. "Is this making you nervous?" She was watching Lachlan, whose eyes were sweeping from left to right. "Should we go back?"

"No." His jaw was set in a firm line. "They have no cause to bother us."

Cause or no cause, the crashing sounds were coming closer. The wolves were not masking their approach, and while Lachlan, Carys, and their horses waited near the path, a column of massive, grey- and brown-coated wolves filtered through the brush and out of the forest and began circling the riders, yipping in excitement, then positioning themselves in formation around them.

A perfect circle of preternaturally large wolves surrounding Carys and Lachlan and staring at them as they sat crouched and ready.

Carys wasn't afraid, but she was feeling... cautious.

There were no snarls or growls, but their utter silence felt more daunting.

She'd run into wolves in the Brightlands, but these creatures were nothing like timber wolves. They weren't wild in the least. Many of them wore gold or silver bands around their shoulders. Not a collar, but something that almost looked like a wolfish pauldron.

"Good morning to the pack." Lachlan spoke calmly to the largest wolf, who waited in front of them. "We are guests of Dafydd and Harold, taking a morning ride through the king's land. Who do we walk with this morning?"

A moment later, Carys saw her first wolf transformation.

A massive white beast with grey shoulders stepped forward and walked toward them, its body shimmering like a mirage a moment before a tall man with a shock of grey and black hair emerged, his body covered in leather armor fitted to his frame like a second skin.

"I am Godrik of the Eskari." The wolf's voice was low and menacing. "And you are foreigners trespassing on the territory of Harold, king of Anglia." His grey eyes narrowed on Carys. "Brightkin are not welcome in this place."

"Your aggression is unwarranted, Godrik." Lachlan kept his voice even but firm. "Has Anglian hospitality fallen so low that the king's guests are unwelcome in his woods?"

Godrik stared at Carys as if Lachlan wasn't even there. "State your business, Brightkin."

Carys racked her brain, trying to remember what the forest rangers said about wolf encounters.

She was pretty sure you shouldn't turn your back to them. Maintain eye contact, but don't stare too intently because that could be interpreted as a challenge to their territory.

"I am the Brightkin of Seren of Cymru," Carys said. "The niece of Dafydd of Cymru."

"You are Brightkin, not of the Shadows."

"I am also a nêrys ddraig, bonded to Cadell of Eryri."

That made the wolf blink. "And yet you ride on a horse like any other human?"

Cadell, she called to her dragon in her mind, *might be the time to make an entrance.*

Don't move.

"I've called to my dragon." Carys sat back on her horse and waited. "He's not very far away." In fact, seconds after she'd called to him, she could feel Cadell approaching.

Lachlan urged his mount forward. "I know your father," he said. "The wolves of Eskari are clan brothers with the wolves of Yorvik, who border Alban lands. We have no quarrel with you."

Godrik kept his eyes on Carys, settling back on his right leg with his hands braced on his hips as two wolves came to flank his right and left side. "The Alban chief's son is a guest of Harold and may pass without warrant through any of the kingswoods." He nodded at Carys. "She is a foreigner and has no such passage."

A thundering roar sounded from the air, and seconds later, Carys felt Cadell circling overhead. The dragon let out another ferocious roar, and Godrik looked up. His eyes went wide, and he looked at Carys again.

"So you're the one." He frowned slightly, and then a mask fell over his face and the soldier was all that remained.

Cadell circled the woods, lowering in ever-smaller circles until the dragon landed in a crowded clearing a short distance from the pathway, letting out a gust of hissing steam that blew like heated fog through the trees.

"I didn't know he could do that," Carys muttered.

Tell them nothing. Seconds after he landed, a storm-faced Cadell was stomping through the woods, aiming straight for Godrik, who braced himself as a dozen wolves moved into position behind him.

"You doubt my lady's word?" Cadell snarled at Godrik. "Do the Anglian king's *dogs* question my lady's right to walk in a territory where she was invited?" He stood between Carys—who was still sitting on Leuca—and the wolf pack, an angry tower of consternation in green leather armor. "She *honors* you with her very presence."

"Cadell of Eryri." Godrik inclined his head, holding out his hand as the wolves around him began to pace and snarl. "We have no quarrel with you."

Cadell pointed at Carys. "If you have quarrel with my nêrys, you have quarrel with me."

Lachlan swung off his horse and stepped between the two massive men. "Hold, friends. Let us talk in calmer voices." He looked around at the wolves gathering close. "We are allies, after all."

Carys leaned forward. "Cadell, should I—"

"Stay where you are." The dragon looked at Carys's horse, and Carys would swear that they were speaking with their minds because Leuca took a careful sidestep toward the path.

"Carys." Lachlan's voice was a soothing brush of charm that cut through the tension in the clearing. "You're fine. We're all friends here."

"Do you distrust our ability to reason?" Godrik couldn't hide his sneer as he took another step toward the dragon. "Or do you distrust your own, dragon?"

It was only then that Carys realized just how tall Godrik was. Until Lachlan stepped between them, she hadn't noticed, but the wolf was nearly as tall as her dragon but of stockier build.

"I'd like to just point out that the reason you were unhappy with me walking through the forest was because you thought I was Brightkin and a foreigner, and since Cadell has arrived and confirmed that I'm nêrys ddraig, the entire reason for all... *this* has now been answered, so..." She waved her arms. "Can we all be happy now?"

Cadell glared at Godrik.

Godrik glared at Cadell.

Lachlan, as imposing as he normally was, looked like the little brother trying to break up a fight.

"What's this?" A bright voice came from a short distance away. "Godrik, is that you?"

Carys turned and saw a round-faced, cheerful woman with curly blond hair walking up the path. She wore something that looked like a uniform and carried a bow and arrow strapped to her back. "And Lachlan." She grinned.

Godrik took a step back and bowed to the woman. "Lady Wynn-flad. I didn't realize you were in the wood this morning."

"Winnie." Lachlan let out a breath. "Good to see you. I was riding with Carys through the park this morning and we had... a bit of an interruption."

"Good to see you too. The castle is absolutely buzzing with preparations for the welcome banquet tonight, so I'm trying to escape." The soldier walked with a light step and a keen eye. She glanced at Cadell, then at Carys on her horse, immediately taking the measure of the situation. "You must be Dafydd's niece."

"I am." Carys decided to offer the woman her name. She didn't look even a little bit fae. "I'm Carys." She didn't need her last name.

"And I am Dafydd's niece. I'm also from the Brightlands." She gestured toward Cadell. "And this is Cadell, my dragon."

Godrik took another step back, and the wolves that had been in formation around him sat on their haunches.

"Lady Wynnflad." Cadell turned to the newcomer and inclined his head. "It is an honor to meet a captain of the Kingsguard. I have heard much about your prowess in battle." He turned to Carys. "Lady Wynnflad is the king's cousin and one of the captains of King Harold's guard. She is also an expert archer."

"Call me Winnie, please." Winnie stepped forward and extended her hand up to Carys. "It's a great pleasure to meet you, Carys of the Brightlands. I knew Seren by reputation only, but it was a good reputation."

"It's a pleasure to meet you too." Especially since the arrival of the king's cousin seemed to have dissipated the tension that had filled the woods only moments before.

"Welcome to London." Winnie's eyes lit up. "My cousin Harold is eager to meet the woman from California who can speak to dragons."

CHAPTER EIGHT

It was the end of their first full day in the Shadowlands, and the welcome banquet for King Harold's coronation guests was at nightfall.

"I guess when you've got guests traveling from all over the world, you don't waste time." Carys looked over Laura's head into the mirror.

Her friend—knowing that she was attending a formal event—had packed the traditional regalia of the Yurok people, an intricately beaded tunic she donned over warm wool leggings and a long leather shirt she'd brought in anticipation of the cool Anglian weather. Her feet were encased in leather boots and laced up to her knees, and she had a braided headpiece made of willow and hazel fibers.

"It's good." Laura leaned forward on the dressing table, applying makeup that would mimic the traditional chin tattoos that were commonly worn in Pauwau Aki. "We dance. We eat. This Harold guy is coronated." She narrowed her eyes. "Is coronated a word? As soon as I said it, it sounded like a medical procedure."

"I have no idea." Carys was dressed in one of Seren's gowns, a draped garment in bright red with emerald-green trim that weighed nearly as much as she did. She affixed the golden dragon brooch on her shoulder and the green leather vest over her bodice. "This thing looks like dragon skin."

"No, it doesn't." Laura glanced at Carys's clothes. "Dragon skin is almost see-through. It has that iridescent, pearly quality in the light."

"Seems like you've been looking at Cadell's skin quite a bit." Carys tucked a piece of her hair back into her braid. "Like what you see?"

"Stop." Laura rolled her eyes. "That dragon is impossible."

"Impossibly attracted to you." Carys nudged her shoulder. "Just admit that you're interested."

"He's like... five hundred years old or something."

"And? His horde breeding days are over as far as I know. That means he can make any match he wants to at this point in his life."

Laura stared into the mirror. "That sounds so sad. Like he's an old bull put out into pasture."

"That's not what it's like at all. Dragon families don't work like human ones. He had responsibilities to his horde before, and now he's more of a free agent."

"Can we change the subject to *your* love life?" Laura finished her makeup and stood. "How was your breakfast with Lachlan? After the wolf incident, of course."

"Kind of killed the mood if you know what I mean." Carys grabbed a purse sitting on the table and slipped her feet into her dancing shoes. "Are you ready?"

"That was a quick change of subject," Laura said. "Which means you need to tell me more."

"In the coracle." Carys nodded toward the door. "We're gonna be late."

THEY FLEW to Harold's castle by dragon coracle, a round wooden carriage clutched in the claws of Dafydd's dragon Mared as Cadell flew ahead of them over the city of London where fires lit the darkness and revels gathered the citizens of the city to squares and parks for coronation week celebrations.

Duncan was sitting to her left and Laura to her right. Dafydd, Anwyn, and Dylan had flown to the castle first, and this was Mared's second journey.

The surly blacksmith hadn't said a word to her since they got into the coracle. In fact, he hadn't said a word to her all day.

Moody much?

Carys peeked through the narrow rectangular window cut into the coracle and saw dragons in the distance, far-off shadows with massive wings, soaring over the river, flying in from the east.

Cadell, who are they?

The dragon answered in Carys's mind. *They are balauri from the east, Nêrys. Emissaries from the dragon kingdom of Valachia. Harold has cultivated them as allies. Wary allies, but the Anglians are making an effort.*

Are they friendly with Cymru?

No. But they're equally unfriendly to everyone, so we don't consider them a threat. They keep to the continent.

Carys watched the massive red beasts with skin the color of blood as they flew closer. "Laura, come look."

Laura scooted closer and peered through the window. "Does that thing have two heads?"

"I think so."

Mared wheeled away from the group of balauri and started to descend. Carys braced herself as the ground grew closer.

"Okay—the bottom is curved, so imagine a boat landing on the ground." She held Laura's hand. "We're going to rock forward for a hard beat; then the door will pop open and that braces the thing. I'd advise just keeping your seat until we stop rocking."

"Arms and legs inside the coracle at all times?"

Duncan snorted.

Carys lifted an eyebrow. "You look very nice tonight, Laird Duncan. Are you going to dance with me?"

He turned his brilliant green eyes on her, and Carys was not prepared for the way his intense gaze made her melt. "I'll claim your *first* dance if you'll have me, Professor Morgan."

If you'll have me. When his voice was low and rumbly like that, Carys wanted to crawl into his lap and sniff his neck.

Nêrys, Mared is about to land. I'll be on the ground to escort you.

Cadell's voice in her head was enough to snap her out of her blacksmith-laced stupor. "Uh, yes. Absolutely." She glanced at Duncan. "The first dance is yours. Also, Cadell says we're about to land."

"Good." Duncan stretched his legs out, and there was a glint in his eye. "I'll make sure to claim you after the banquet."

"So feral," Laura whispered. "Curious what you just committed to there."

"I was just having the same thought," Carys muttered as the coracle touched down with a thunk. The wooden vessel rocked once, twice, and then the door released, swinging down to the grassy meadow where Carys could already see Cadell waiting in green leather armor.

The dragon's eyes were fixed on Laura, but he tore them away and looked at Carys. "Nêrys." He held out his arm. "I will be your escort."

Carys turned to Laura. "Can you walk with Duncan? Cadell and I should—"

"Go!" Laura urged her out of the coracle. "You've got a role to play. I'm just here for the dancing and the food." She looked up at Duncan. "Hey, sexy Scottish dude, you got an arm for me?"

Duncan bowed his head and held out his elbow. "My lady of the Baywood, would you allow me to escort you to the castle?"

"Oh, see..." Laura smiled. "That works for you. Like, so well. You should do that more."

"D'ya think?" Duncan winked at her as Carys walked toward Cadell. "I'll keep that in mind."

Carys and her dragon escort walked down a pathway lit with torches toward a garden party she could see in the distance.

The Anglian night had joined in the new king's hospitality; the air was balmy and the breeze off the river as gentle as a mother's kiss. The castle gardens were alive with spring flowers. Trees in full blossom, bulbs bursting from the ground, and fairy lights dancing in the shadows beyond the trees.

As soon as they approached the gardens, a liveried usher snapped to attention and took the card that Cadell handed him.

"Carys, Nêrys Ddraig and Lady of Cymru, and Lord Dragon Cadell!"

Carys appreciated that in a gathering with more than one fae guest, full names were not being thrown into the air and they were using titles instead.

"Laird Duncan of Murrayshall and Laura, Pauwau Inwe of the Yurok people of California."

Carys and Cadell were already walking into the party, which might have been in the gardens but was no less formal than in a castle hall.

She could see the head table in the distance, surrounded by men and women dressed in uniforms similar to what Winnie the archer had been wearing earlier in the day.

Harold was easy to spot as they walked down the center aisle to be presented. He was a tall, plain-faced man whose most prominent feature seemed to be the flowing brown locks that fell to his shoulders and the gold-rimmed spectacles on his nose. His beard was thick, braided in two forks and decorated with bright gold beads. His nose was prominent, and his eyes were dark in the flickering blue-and-white fae-light.

To his right, King Dafydd sat on a slightly lower seat, wearing a simple gold circlet on his forehead. A humble king with a dragon standing at attention behind him. He was speaking to Harold in a low voice and gave Carys a nod. Anwyn, Carys's cousin, was seated on Dafydd's right.

Just past Anwyn, Lachlan watched Carys with a smile in his eyes. He was wearing a gold circlet similar to Dafydd's but decorated with a single green stone. Beside him, a woman with flowing blond hair and a single gold sigil on her forehead drank from a crystal goblet. A unicorn in Anglia? Interesting.

"The Lady Carys, Nêrys Ddraig of Cymru," another usher announced. "And Lord Dragon Cadell of the Horde of Eryri."

"Lady Carys," Harold said to them. "And Lord Dragon Cadell. The thrones of Briton greet you, and the royal house of Anglia welcomes you to London."

Carys offered him a low nod as Cadell had instructed her earlier. "I am grateful, King Harold. Congratulations on your coronation, and we appreciate your hospitality."

That was all she said and all she was expected to say. She didn't bow because she wasn't Harold's subject and to do so would have been a slap at Dafydd, who was—technically speaking—her king.

The usher showed them to a table on the left side of the garden, where they were shortly joined by Laura and Duncan.

"Okay, this is so fascinating," Laura whispered. "But who the hell is that boss queen to Harold's left?"

Carys glanced up and looked at the left side of the table where another line of dignitaries was sitting.

"That *boss queen*" —Cadell kept his voice low— "is Orla, high queen of Éire. And next to her is Prince Cian, her consort and the closest thing to a fae ruler in Briton."

"*That's* Queen Orla?" Carys didn't know why she was expecting someone older except that she'd met Orla's granddaughter, who'd been the same age as Carys. "Holy wow."

Orla was the single most beautiful woman Carys had ever seen in her entire life. She wore her raven hair in intricately woven braids, and bright jewels decorated the elaborate, lacelike silver crown on her head.

Regan's mother. Carys could see echoes of the sorceress in the queen's face, and just for a moment, Orla turned brilliant blue eyes toward Carys, as if she could hear her thoughts.

Their eyes met for only a second before Orla's shuttered and looked away.

Perhaps she was seeing Seren's face. The face of the woman her daughter and granddaughter had killed.

Did she feel guilt for stealing Dafydd's child?

Did she feel anything at all?

A second later, the queen's eyes moved back to the head table, and she inclined her head toward King Harold as he spoke to her.

She was the picture of grace and royalty. Her gown looked like it was woven from moonlight and silk, and while her hair showed silver threads at the temples, her skin was unlined and glowed like a pearl.

"She's human?" Laura asked. "Entirely human? I'd assumed she was fae."

"She's not mundane," Cadell said. "She's a trained magic user, but she is human."

"Then I need her skin routine," Laura muttered.

"Her beauty regimen would be being wedded to a fae prince." Duncan nodded toward the regal, golden-haired fae man at Orla's side. "Magical unions have been known to keep humans young for a long time."

Prince Cian was tall, broad-shouldered, and as stunning as Orla in an overtly masculine way. His jaw was shaved smooth, and his golden hair fell like a waterfall over his shoulders. His crown was wrought of finely woven gold, and though he didn't bear the title of king, his demeanor was as royal as any figure at the head table.

His eyes surveyed the welcome banquet, and he looked down his nose at the gathered company, clearly a bit bored by the ceremony.

Laura looked at Cadell. "So does *any* magical union keep a human young?"

"Yes," the dragon said quickly. "At least, that is what I have heard."

Duncan shot Carys a look, and Carys couldn't stop her smile.

Transparent. Cadell was so transparent.

"So that's Orla." Carys examined the fae prince beside the Éiren queen. "And Cian is a light fae?"

"Yes," Cadell said. "But trust me, the lightness in him only extends to his hair and his eyes."

Cian was Orla's equal in beauty and grace. The two regents seemed to move as one, dark and light, human and magic. They were mirrors of each other, their expressions dual masks of benevolent power as they surveyed the banquet.

In the royal garden, fae, humans, and magical creatures of all kinds mingled and sprites danced overhead, their high, bright voices creating a background of joyful music to accompany the feast.

Soon after Carys and her friends were seated, human servers in bright red uniforms spread through the garden, serving roasted game, root vegetables, and fresh fruit in massive platters that filled the center of each table.

Dafydd rose to his feet and lifted a goblet filled with red wine. "To our host," he shouted. "To King Harold and his house."

"Hear, hear!" Lachlan called. He spoke to the crowd, but his eyes landed on Carys.

"Eat." Duncan placed what appeared to be an entire goose leg on the plate in front of her. "You'll need your energy for dancing."

THE ORCHESTRA CUED UP, and a pair of pipers stood at the entrance of the garden as the tables were moved back to the edges of the lawn. Quick-moving servants had already laid out a wooden dance floor as the musicians assembled just before the king's table.

In the bustle of the party, Carys watched as the king's careful orchestration of seating broke down into magical and nonmagical creatures.

The willowy fae guests gathered together on the far side of the room, whispering and watching the humans, who continued to drink and raise their voices ever higher.

"It's easy to spot the wolves now," Carys told Cadell. "There are so many of them."

"They serve the Anglian throne, and their clans are rewarded with the best hunting grounds across the country." Cadell spoke softly. "It allows Harold to control a large territory, but make no mistake, many common people resent it."

"If they're as territorial as they were this morning in the park, I can see why." Carys spotted the massive wolf lord called Godrik at the back of the room. "No love lost between dragons and wolves, it looks like."

"North Wolves are touchy. They aren't native to Briton."

"Neither are unicorns." Carys saw a group of the peace-loving creatures mingling with the fae and some of the human guests.

"Unicorns are beloved wherever they go," Cadell said. "How could they not be?"

Only about half of the unicorn guests were still in human form while the rest had already transformed into ethereally beautiful horses with twisting horns. They wandered along the edges of the garden and through the trees while the sprites that lit up the garden followed them with joyful abandon.

Cadell kept his voice low. "Did Lachlan claim your first dance?"

"No."

"No?" The dragon's voice went up. "Surprising."

"Duncan claimed it." Carys frowned. "Does it matter?"

"It's not a commitment." Cadell cleared his throat. "But... it is a precedent."

"See, why don't you tell me these things?" The back of her hand hit his armored stomach. "I need to know stuff like this, Cadell."

"I assumed you knew." He shrugged. "I suppose I should not have."

"Who claimed Laura's first dance?"

"Me." The corner of his mouth twitched up. "I confirmed my place yesterday evening."

Of course he did. "Okay, well, it's not a marriage proposal or anything."

"No." Cadell turned his face to the pipers, who were starting to play. "But it is a precedent."

"Again, I don't know what that means." She clamped her mouth shut as the dancing started.

"These are the stag dancers," Cadell said. "They start any formal Anglian dance."

It was ceremonial dancing, and nothing like what Carys had experienced in Scotland. A company of brightly clad men in red-and-blue outfits walked into the garden, carrying massive racks of deer antlers over their shoulders. As the pipes sounded and drums beat, they wove together like a braid, singing a deep chorus in a language Carys immediately knew.

"Old English," she whispered. "I recognize it."

"How?" Cadell curled his lip. "It's from the continent."

"From the continent like... a thousand years ago."

He lifted his chin. "Still, it's not nearly as beautiful as Cymric."

"And you're not biased at all, of course." Carys smiled. "Trust me, if you'd been forced to read *Beowulf* as many times as I have, you'd recognize it too."

The stag dancers finished their chorus and dance, were greeted with applause, and then the violins in the orchestra immediately broke into a bright dancing song that had couples lining up in a more familiar set.

"Okay, I can follow along with this one," Carys said. "This is kind of like the dancing in Alba."

"Good, because Duncan is heading toward you." Cadell raised his eyebrows. "As is Lachlan."

Indeed, the two brothers were walking straight toward her with Duncan having a slight head start because of his position on the ground instead of the head table.

"Carys." He hadn't exactly run, but the laird hadn't strolled either. "If you'd join me?" He held out his hand, and Carys took it just as Lachlan arrived.

"Don't give me that look." She glanced over her shoulder as Duncan pulled her away. "He asked; you didn't."

Lachlan's mouth was a thin line. "I assumed—"

"Well, you shouldn't have," Duncan snapped. "You should never assume anything, especially not with Carys." He put his warm hand over the fingers that rested in the crook of his elbow. "Lady Carys?"

"I'll dance with you later," she said to Lachlan before Duncan led her away.

Once they reached the dance floor, she turned to Duncan, facing him and bowing before she took his hand again to let him lead her through the dance. "Was that really necessary?"

"Absolutely yes." His lifted his chin, and though his hair was shorn close to his head, he was just as regal as Lachlan in that moment. "I take nothing for granted with you, Carys. And I want no confusion." He pulled her close, and she could feel the heat pouring off his chest. "I aim to win your heart. In my opinion, our destinies are tied together and always have been."

Duncan angled her to the side, and they walked through the column of dancers together, the music making her feet move almost as if by magic.

Carys's heart was beating fast, and it wasn't only from the dancing.

Duncan guided her across the dance floor in circles, weaving in and out of the other dancers, spinning her under the light of the pixies whirling overhead.

Duncan twirled her around, then pulled her close. "I'll be your man if you'll have me, Carys Morgan. I'll live where you live. Follow whatever path you want to take. The shadows. The light." His arm was firm around her waist, and her breasts were pressed to his chest as he tilted her chin up so she was looking into his eyes.

Her breath caught at the warm emotion in his eyes. Gone was the churlish blacksmith. Banished was the antagonist Scot who couldn't wait to be rid of her.

"Duncan." She whispered his name.

"I love to hear my name on your lips." They were still in the middle of the dance floor. "I don't think I liked my name before I heard you say it. It was a curse to me. The legacy of a hard man who loved nothing but himself."

Carys felt tears gather in her eyes. "You never talk about your family."

"Ask me anything and I'll tell you." The music changed, and couples shuffled around the dance floor. "I'll tell you whatever you want to know."

Carys felt weightless in his arms. She wanted to feel his lips on hers. She wanted to fold herself into his arms and sleep against his chest.

"If you trusted me to hold you while you slept, it would be the greatest honor of my life," Duncan whispered.

Carys blinked. "Oh my God, did I say that out loud?"

His eyes crinkled with laughter. "Aye, ye did."

Her face was on fire. "Okay, the song ended. We better move."

Duncan took her hand, weaving their fingers together. "I know you're going to dance with Lachlan." He bent and whispered in her ear. "But you're going to think of me when you're in his arms."

CHAPTER NINE

Carys did dance with Lachlan, and she did think about Duncan most of the time. From the sour look on Lachlan's face, he knew it too. She also danced with Godrik, though there was little conversation, and she danced with her uncle twice.

Laura appeared to be the belle of the ball, and Cadell was forced to be patient as every lord and a few ladies of Anglia took the opportunity to dance with the interesting foreigner from across the ocean who was visiting the Anglian court.

Carys loved to see her friend being celebrated. Back home, Laura was the responsible eldest sister, backbone of her family and tribe and mainstay at every community function. Here, she was a carefree diplomat of sorts and a fascinating visitor from another continent.

"Your friend is rather pretty, isn't she?"

Carys smiled. "She's more than pretty, don't you..." Her smile fell when she turned to the right and saw the familiar face of the Crow Mother, who was sitting at her table. "What are you doing here?"

She looked around, but no one seemed to notice the dark-haired woman dressed in black save for a lone fae woman on the other side of the room who stared at the Crow Mother with ice-blue eyes.

"What are you doing here?" she asked again. Meanwhile in her mind, she was shouting for her dragon. *Cadell, where are you?*

Nothing.

It was as if a fog had wrapped around her mind.

"No use calling for the beast," the Crow Mother said. "My magic is far older than his." She looked at the head table. "There's so much magic and feasting in this garden, it's the perfect time to act." She narrowed her eyes on Orla. "The queen will bring me her offering, and then everything will fall into place."

"What offering?" She had to be speaking about Orla. There was only one queen on the dais since Harold wasn't married.

"I take offerings of all kinds," the Crow Mother said. "Magic. Blood. Babies."

Carys barely managed to stop the shiver. "What do you want from me?"

"What you've promised, Carys Morgan, daughter of two worlds. Passage to the Brightlands so I can..." She smiled. "...see the sun. Among other things."

There was no way Carys could go back on her promise now; she'd struck a bargain. "I'll meet you in the morning at the Night Bridge then."

"No need." Branwen stood. "We'll go now."

"I can't." She looked around. "I'm a guest here and—" It was as if a hand reached up and covered her mouth.

Carys panicked.

"No need to be afraid, dear one. You're going to give me what was promised, and then you'll return safely to the Shadowlands." Branwen stood, reached her hand down, and took Carys's in her own.

Carys had no choice but to follow her, mute and manageable. She shouted for Cadell in her mind, but the Crow Mother's power was too great. Fog crept around them, just as it had in the park and on Branwen's mountain fortress in Alba.

Without any recourse and compelled by magic, Carys lifted her skirt and followed Branwen into the trees.

"Harold thinks his wards are powerful." Branwen spoke to Carys as if they were friends. "But the wolf mages have earthly magic. More brutish than elegant." She glanced over her shoulder when Carys didn't speak. "Oh, forgive me." She waved a hand, and Carys felt her lips loosen.

"How are we going?" She was already plotting her escape. "You have to know we're miles from the Night Bridge. And that's the only gate that knows me in this area, so how—"

"Have a care, Carys." The Crow Mother interrupted. "You think I haven't thought of these things?" Branwen led them through the forest bordering the castle gardens, and moments after they entered the trees, Carys saw a dark carriage emerge from the shadows. "If it were only me, I would simply fly with my crows." She turned and patted Carys on the cheek. "But you need more... terrestrial accommodations."

As they approached the carriage, a black door swung open and the shadows loomed in front of her. Nothing appeared to be pulling the carriage, but even so, the box jolted ahead as if invisible beasts were ready to move.

Carys didn't feel fear. Not exactly. The Crow Mother needed her to open the gate, which meant that—at least for now—she was safe. Then after they passed through the gate and into the Brightlands, the old fae would lose her magic.

Which would leave Carys in Brightlands London with no way back to the Shadowlands and Laura and Duncan unless the gate decided that she was familiar enough to welcome. In theory, she should be able to find her way back.

In theory.

"Up you go." The Crow Mother boosted Carys into the carriage, and the door slammed behind her.

"Wait, aren't you going to—"

"Ar aghaidh linn!"

There was a creaking sound, and the coach jolted forward, Carys locked in the black box with a single window to watch the dark woods roll past.

If Carys did find her way back to Shadowlands London, she'd land in the troll market in the middle of the night, when all the security in the city was focused on Harold's palace.

One problem at a time, Carys.

Cadell would realize she was gone. Soon the dragon was going to realize she was gone, and once the Crow Mother's fog lifted, Cadell would find her.

Her dragon could always find her.

THE GLASS WAS DARKENED, but Carys knew immediately when they arrived at the night market. There were torches lit along the river, and blue lights floated over the water in the distance. Raucous laughter pierced the fae fog, and eerie music competed with the sounds of merriment for space in the night sky.

It seemed that all of London was celebrating, whether it was in a fancy palace garden or under an old stone bridge.

The laughs fell to whispers as they passed through the market, and when Carys peeked through the smoked glass, she saw wide eyes of all shapes and sizes watching them.

Trolls of every shape and element stared as they passed. Rocky-skinned vendors; pale, watery-faced artisans; and ethereal passersby.

Also in the shadows, she could see humans and smaller magical creatures trudging in the background. Some were standing behind tables, and others carried crates on their shoulders.

All of them looked as if they were wearing some kind of charm, because their faces were obscured. From one moment to the next,

Carys could see an eye clearly, then a mouth. But never the entire face at once.

What magic was happening to these enchanted humans?

The coach stopped at the mouth of an alley, and the door creaked open.

Carys waited for Branwen to appear before her.

"Well?" the fae woman asked. "Are you getting out, or do I need to compel you?"

"*Can* you compel me?" Carys was wondering just why she'd been so quick to follow the old fae into the forest, but she had a vague recollection of something in her belly pulling her into the woods.

"Hmm." The Crow Mother eyed her. "Not as easily as I should." She waved. "Come now. Fulfill your half of the bargain, and our deal will be complete."

"That's it?" Carys wanted assurances. "I walk you through the gate into the Brightlands and my debt to you is complete?"

She smiled. "When you say it like that, it makes me think you owe me more."

"Nope." Carys put mental shutters on either side of her face and pointed it toward the familiar alley where Dru had guided them only two nights before. She wasn't seeing the humans in thrall to the trolls. She wasn't seeing the chains or the ropes or the magic that bound them.

Not that night.

Not until it was finished.

"Let me see." Carys slowed her steps as she walked across the damp cobblestones. "I need to feel for it."

She was dragging her feet—she knew exactly where the gate was. She could see the blue will-o'-the-wisps flying up and down the narrow passageway, darting this way and that as they flew toward the gate.

Carys ran her fingers along the dirty stone wall, anchoring herself to the solid reality of the buildings as the darkness pressed in.

Other than the fae gate behind her house in California, she'd never walked through a gate on her own before, much less guided a magical creature through the passageway.

Grit and moss gathered under her fingertips as she walked, and Carys absorbed everything her senses could detect.

The sound of her boots slapping on damp stone.

The press of dark shadows on either side of the narrow alley.

The smell of the river and roasting meat from the market.

What kind of meat? She didn't want to guess.

Her fingers dragged over a gritty line of brick; then cold fingers grabbed her wrist.

Carys jumped back, yanking her arm away from whatever creature had grabbed it, but she wasn't able to get away from the shadows, and instead, she dragged a tall, thin figure covered in wool rags.

The Crow Mother uttered a breathy curse and snarled, "What are *you* doing here?"

The creature lifted its head, pushed back the dark cowl around his wild hair, and Dru stepped into a beam of light coming from a second-story window.

"What trouble are you about this night, mother?" The corner of the fae's mouth turned up. "And what trouble have you dragged my friend into?"

"None but what she bargained for, Diarmuid."

Carys was a little bit shocked that Dru considered her a friend, but in the company of the Crow Mother, she'd take it. Cadell still couldn't hear her, and she didn't have any kind of weapon secreted in her ball gown.

That was a lesson learned.

"Hey, Dru." She let out a slow breath. "Kind of surprised to see you here."

Was he following her? Following the Crow Mother?

Or did Dru have his own schemes that had nothing to do with either of them?

Dru hooked his thumbs in the band of leather around his waist, lifting his chin and pushing his shoulders back. He was the canny bartender again, not the Green Man, the woodland prince, *or* the beggar in rags.

"This woman made that bargain not knowing your true nature," he said.

"But she made it nonetheless."

Carys whispered, "I did make a bargain, Dru."

Dru nodded. "And so you'll pay the old one." His eyes narrowed. "I do wonder what you're about."

Branwen cackled. "You'll find out in time, and it's no trouble for you or your kind." She leaned closer to Dru. "In fact, it might just be to your benefit."

A muscle in Dru's cheek jumped, and a glimmer of light ran along the sigil at his right temple. "I'll go along then. I see that Carys's dragon is absent from her company this night. I'll be happy to be her guide."

"I tried calling him," Carys said. "But I couldn't seem to connect."

"Not necessary," the Crow Mother said.

Dru's voice crackled with power. "Try to stop me, old woman."

Carys put a hand on his arm. "I would appreciate having company on the way back."

"Very well." She cocked her head. "The elf prince is correct. I cannot stop him from following us."

"Let's get on with it." Dru glanced over his shoulder. "There's a dragon in the air."

THE BLACK SHADOWS of the fae gate were just as dense as Carys remembered, and Branwen clutched her hand as they walked, hissing in surprise a few times but never releasing her.

It could have been minutes. It might have been an hour.

Carys followed the narrow corridor and the blue lights of the wisps where they led her, ducking around corners and stepping over obstacles that seemed to reach up from the ground below.

She felt a tugging in her belly, a pull of knowing in her gut as the pressure in the air eased and the whispering in the shadows eased away. When Carys saw a low light gleaming from the end of the passageway under the shop on Knightsbridge Road, she blinked in surprise.

Not only had she led the Crow Mother to the Brightlands, but the sun was shining in London.

Branwen was whispering under her breath, and her fingers dug into Carys's wrist. "We're there. We're nearly there now."

The rabid excitement in her voice made Carys want to wrest her arm away and run back to the Shadowlands, but she couldn't get away from the old fae if she tried.

This is your promise.

Do this and you'll be free.

The wisps pressed around her, high and hissing voices that sighed and tickled her ears. They were speaking in hushed tones so fast that the mass of their voices crowded into Carys's mind, and she felt the beginnings of a headache starting to grow in her temples.

Under her feet, she felt the change from smooth earth to wooden floor, and moments later, her toe hit the first low step.

"Ouch!" she whispered. "I don't know why I'm whispering." Carys turned and started up the stairs but turned when she didn't hear anyone behind her. "Are you there?"

"Am I welcome then?" The Crow Mother looked up, and her eyes were luminous. "Am I welcome in the light?"

"Come on." Carys gave her a hurry-up gesture and kept climbing. "This is what you traded for, remember?"

"Not far now." Dru kept his voice mild. "Up you go, old mother, into the land that's forgotten who you are."

The Crow Mother sang, "But they'll remember me again."

Carys glanced over her shoulder to see the woman's dark eyes had faded to the color of a winter sky, and her cheeks were pink. She looked... surprisingly human. Her magic was draining, and she was becoming mundane.

They climbed a half flight of stairs, and Carys pushed open the leather-padded red door that swung into...

A bustling restaurant with a crush of early-morning diners. Silver carts sped by, laden with stacked trays of dim sum as servers shouted orders across the room.

Branwen blinked, and then a huge smile spread across her face. "Children of light."

Someone rushed toward them, speaking in rapid Chinese, and Dru answered them in kind as the Crow Mother dragged Carys toward the door.

They burst through the glass-fronted door and onto a bustling street crowded with cars, pedestrians, scooters, and bikes.

"What is this wonder?" The Crow Mother spun in place, turning her face up to the morning sun as she spread her arms and whispered something under her breath. "This decay and this dirt?"

Decay and dirt? Well, that was one way to look at the human world.

"Okay." Carys watched her carefully, but in the morning sunshine, the Crow Mother looked like a completely ordinary human woman even if she was preternaturally pale and more than a little morbid. "Well, here you are. The sun is beautiful, right?"

It *was* gorgeous, and so bright Carys wanted to strip off her wool tunic and bathe in the light. She took a deep breath of air that... Well, it wasn't fresh. But it also didn't smell of magic or trolls or river monsters, so there was that.

Dru walked onto the sidewalk behind them, dodging a green scooter that sped by. "There you are, old mother. Is the sun as you remember it, or are you waiting for the moon?"

The Crow Mother's head swung back and forth so quickly, Carys worried it was going to twist off completely.

Dru snapped, "Badb."

The Crow Mother turned her pale grey eyes toward Dru, and the corner of her mouth turned up in the hint of a smile. "I'll be going now, Mo Diarmuid. I trust you won't tell anyone what's happened here."

"That's a ridiculous request that I have no intention of keeping," Dru said. "And neither does Carys. We're not your confidantes." He nodded at the street. "Go. Cause your little mischiefs, whatever they might be." Dru took Carys's hand and drew her away from Branwen. "We'll be off."

As Dru pulled Carys back from the sidewalk and into the restaurant, she kept her eyes on the black-haired woman until she melted into the passing foot traffic along Knightsbridge Road.

She looked up at Dru. "What's the rush?"

"There's trouble on the other side of the gate," Dru said, his voice grim. "The dragon is not pleased."

CHAPTER TEN

Walking back into the darkness, Carys could hear the wisps screeching in high, panicked voices.

"What the hell happened?"

Was Laura okay? What about Duncan?

"The moment you took the Crow Mother through the gate and her magic waned, the dragon could sense you." Dru cocked his head. "From the sound of it, he is expressing his displeasure at your absence."

They rushed through the twists and turns of the Night Bridge passage to emerge in the narrow, dark alley where a pile of broken crates smoldered into ash.

"Cadell?" Carys reached out in her mind. *Cadell!*

Nêrys? Cadell's mental call was more of a bellow. *Where are you?*

"Come on!" Dru shouted. "Between your dragon and Dafydd's, they're about to start a war."

I am fine! Calm down!

There was a roaring sound in her head but nothing intelligible.

The moment they stepped onto the main road that led toward

the river and under the bridge, Carys saw what Dru was talking about.

The troll market was in chaos.

Market stalls were overturned, and in the distance, Carys saw two dragons perched on the stone archway of the bridge, roaring into the foggy night as smoke billowed around them and tents and ramshackle buildings burned.

Cadell, calm down. I am fine. The Crow Mother ambushed me at the banquet, but Dru went with me to fulfill my bargain and now I'm back.

Where are you?

I am with Dru.

Stay with the fae until I can find you.

She didn't know how he'd find her in the confusion and chaos of the burning troll market.

Furtive creatures lurking in the shadows had emerged, and what had previously passed for some kind of order had burned to the bone.

"Come on!" Dru grabbed Carys's wrist in his right hand and dragged her through the chaos. He had a silver saber in his left hand, and as they walked, he brandished it at more than one hulking monster that emerged.

Anything that could fly was already gone, and the air was still and dark save for the flicker of dragon fire. The lane was covered with smoldering canvas tents, aluminum pop-ups from the Brightlands, and a collection of old patio umbrellas.

"Where are we going?"

"I'll take you to the dragon." Dru looked up at the tall buildings on either side of the market. "He won't be able to fly through here."

Some trolls were swiftly packing their wares, trying to avoid notice and get away, while others seemed to have taken the dragon's violence as permission to wreak their own kind of havoc. There were thieves scurrying about, shoving whatever they could find into sacks or stuffing things down their shirts.

Humans and magical creatures bound in chains had wrapped

those bonds around the necks of their captors or were actively fighting against those who had captured them.

Carys saw a dark-haired woman stab a rocky-skinned troll in the belly. The troll bellowed and fell back, gripping its stomach where the rough blade was buried. The body twitched and spasmed, and the woman bent down, yanking at the chain that bound her ankle to the troll's.

The old bronze wouldn't give way. Angry tears streamed down her dirty cheeks, and she screamed in frustration.

"Dru!" Carys pulled on his arm, pointing to the crying woman.

The tall fae paused, scowling as he looked between the woman and Carys.

"We have to help her." What would happen to her if her troll captor survived?

And what if he didn't?

Dru dragged Carys to the flaming market stall, then rolled the limp body of the troll over before he brought his silver sword down across the troll's ankle.

There was a sick thunk, a red spurt of blood, and the knobby foot detached while the body remained still.

"Come on." Dru pulled Carys away from the woman, who slipped her chain from the bloodied stump, hiked up her skirts, and ran.

"Can she be punished?"

"Not by human authorities." Dru dodged a low-flying group of pixies that swooped down the center of the lane. "Slavery like that is illegal."

Carys looked around the market and noted all the humans and magical creatures in chains. "Doesn't seem too secret though."

"There are more illicit activities happening tonight because of the coronation." Dru used the pommel of his sword to bash in the face of a gnarled creature who limped toward them with murder in his eyes. "The Kingsguard is occupied closer to the palace. Stay close to me."

Nêrys, where are you?

Dru is taking me to the bridge. Stay where you are; I can see you from here.

Dru's grip on her wrist never wavered, not even when a scream came from behind them.

Carys spun around just in time.

A scale-cheeked troll barreled toward them with a raised axe. "Ya weaselly, murderin' fae bastard!"

"Dru!"

Carys yanked her arm away and Dru released her, bringing his hand up, his palm glowing with flashing blue light as the troll attacked.

Dru's silver blade clashed against the axe, and a glinting magic pulse slammed against the troll, punching him back, but not before the edge of his axe sliced across Dru's jaw.

"No!" Carys was still in a ball gown and had no weapons on her, but she reached for the shorter silver blade she saw at Dru's waist, yanking it from its scabbard as Dru fell.

"Carys!" Someone in the distance bellowed her name.

It sounded like Duncan or Lachlan, she couldn't tell which.

She jumped on the troll, who had fallen to the ground with the force of Dru's magic, and didn't hesitate to plunge the dagger into his shoulder. The blade found purchase, and blood sprayed across her cheek. The troll bellowed and threw his burly arms around her, trying to crush her on his chest, but two hands gripped her ankles and dragged her from its grip.

She scrambled to her feet and ripped off a piece of her gown, running on adrenaline as she pressed the dirty cloth to Dru's bleeding jaw and shoulder.

"I'm fine!" He grabbed at the rumpled lace.

"You're hurt!"

"Leave me and run to Cadell!" Silver blood soaked his jaw and neck. "Carys, you have no weapons. Run!"

The chaos was growing, and she heard trumpets in the distance.

The Kingsguard?

Carys scrambled up the cobblestone-covered slope that led to the bridge, keeping her eyes on Cadell, massive and bellowing fire from his ruby-red throat.

Nêrys.

The moment he saw her, he spread his wings and lifted into the sky.

"I'm here!" She held out her arms, and Cadell swooped down and grabbed her in his massive claws.

Nêrys. His voice was like a sigh once she was back in his grasp. *Belen's protection was on you.*

Cadell took to the sky, Dafydd's dragon Mared at his left wing, when Carys shouted into his mind.

You have to grab Dru! He was injured protecting me.

Cadell flew high, turning in circles over the river, likely communicating with Mared.

The fae has earned a favor for protecting you, he finally said. *I can see him near the bridge.*

Cadell turned in the sky and arrowed back toward the troll market, roaring with a mighty bellow before he dipped down, hovering over the wreckage of the market as he enclosed Dru in the talons of his right foot, lifted away from the smoking stalls, and flew into the air.

CARYS RESTED in Cadell's claws, looking to the right to see Dru similarly gripped.

Dragon claws were not the most comfortable perch for riding through the air, but Dru's eyes were closed, and she saw his face peaceful in the red glow of Cadell's body. He leaned back, his long legs dangling from the cage of dragon claws.

Carys reached up, running a hand along Cadell's iridescent skin.

Beneath her hand, the fire glowed from his belly, warming her and setting her mind at ease.

In Cadell's claws, she was safe.

The cross human and the prince were at the market. Her dragon spoke in her mind. *The Kingsguard had just arrived moments before you found me.*

A flood of dread in her belly. *Are they safe? Do we need to go back?*

They were in the company of the Kingsguard, mounted with weapons and archers at their back. I would not worry about your suitors, Nêrys.

Carys tried not to worry, but it was impossible. She was also worried about Dru, who was still as the dead as he rode in Cadell's claws. *Dru is injured.*

I smell his blood. He will need healing.

Can you heal him?

Cadell let out a great huff of air. *My magic will not be effective on him. He's an old creature; he needs healing from his own kind.*

Carys was wondering where she might find a fae healer when she felt Cadell start to descend.

She turned to look at Dru, whose eyes were open and watching her. "You need a fae healer," she shouted. "Where do you want to go?"

He shook his head, but Carys could see the wound on his jaw was still weeping.

"Was that troll axe poisoned?"

"Probably." He closed his eyes. "They like poison."

"Don't be noble." She pointed at Cadell's claws. "You're bleeding on my dragon."

"Don't worry about me." He put a hand on Cadell's foot. "I appreciate the quick escape, but I'll be quite well with some sleep."

There was no moon and no stars in the Shadowlands, and the fog was thick and endless until they broke through the clouds and Carys saw the light of a bonfire in Dafydd's courtyard.

Your uncle is waiting.

"Do you think they noticed that I disappeared from the banquet?"

"Yes." Dru's eyes were still closed. "Ballroom politics. You'll have to answer for your absence."

"And the destruction of the troll market?"

Dru seemed to shrug. "Harold should thank you for that."

Cadell circled slowly, Mared right behind him. Moments later, Carys and Dru were gently placed in the middle of the castle yard, and Cadell transformed soon after, followed by Mared, who immediately walked to Dafydd's side.

"In Modron's name, I am relieved that you are safe." Dafydd walked to Carys and embraced her. "I was about to send Anwyn and Dylan to search for you."

Her Shadowlands cousins stood back, their shoulders back and arms at attention, still dressed in their banquet finery.

Carys, on the other hand, had a ripped dress covered in troll and fae blood, scorched at the edges and with mud at the hem six inches deep.

Anwyn and Dylan looked super excited as they looked down their noses at her.

Hoping the trolls might finish me off? Carys didn't think her cousins would've been all that disappointed if she'd met an untimely end.

"Right." She stood up straight. "So the Crow Mother kind of trapped me at the banquet. I had to go with her to pay back a favor." She tried to smooth her dress over her legs. "But things got a little... fiery."

Anwyn glanced at Dru. "You consort with fae?"

Everything about the woman irked Carys. "Oh, I don't consort with them," she said. "But I do help them chop off troll legs when the occasion calls for it." She walked over to Dru and knelt at his side.

The fae man, for his part, was still on the ground, staring into the fire as silver bled from his jaw. He seemed not to notice that he was in the presence of the Cymric king and a cadre of nêr ddraig or surrounded by dragons.

"Dru?"

He was whispering into the flames in some strange tongue, and Carys didn't know if he needed help or simply—as he claimed before—to be left alone to heal.

"Dru." She put her hand on his shoulder. "What do you need?"

He rolled over, placed his lips to the earth, and whispered, "Dewch ataf fi."

Come to me?

Carys recognized the Cymric phrase. Who was Dru calling?

Carys heard horses in the distance, and it sounded like a company of soldiers was riding toward them. From the forest, wolves bayed, and the flames in the bonfire leaped to the sky.

Lachlan and a group of Alban soldiers dressed in blue-and-white uniforms rode into Dafydd's courtyard and circled the fire, and Duncan rode with them. The blacksmith wore a black coat, his formal kilt, and a stormy scowl.

"Carys!" Duncan bellowed across the yard. "Where the hell have you been?"

"We were worried." Lachlan was about to dismount, but then he looked at the ground. "What is that?"

Carys was kneeling next to Dru when she felt it. There was a hum in the ground beneath her, and though Duncan dismounted and ran to her, she couldn't take her eyes from the earth.

"Carys!" Duncan threw his arms around her and pulled her away from Dru. "Earth magic. He's calling for earth magic. Stay back."

The land seemed to breathe up and out, and silver threads that looked like roots emerged from the soil, glowing and rising, rising, rising under Carys's hands.

Every human in the courtyard stopped and stared as the ground beneath them sighed like a tired mother.

"Carys?" Lachlan called her name. "Are you—"

"It's not me." She looked at the wounded fae. "I think it's Dru."

The soldiers stayed on their horses, who skittered back from the fire.

Dafydd, Anwyn, and Dylan froze.

Carys stayed in Duncan's arms, both of them kneeling next to Dru, who stared in the direction of the dark woods in the distance.

There was a light coming toward them, as small as a wisp that seemed to grow.

And grow.

The wolves in the woods went silent as a figure walked out of the darkness and toward the fire.

Duncan growled, "Dru, what have you called?"

"Easy, my friend." The fae's eyes were glowing and content.

She was small, as petite as Dru was tall. Her skin was the color of polished oak, her eyes a brilliant blue. Her dark, curly locks were threaded with braids, and her delicate pointed ears were pierced with a line of intricately woven gold hoops.

Anwyn gasped. "Ellyllon."

The small fae stared at Dru with a flood of tangled emotion filling her eyes. "You return to this place but call to me only now, when you have need of my healing?"

Dru closed his eyes. "Naida—"

"I do not need your excuses, Diarmuid."

He lifted his hand, palm up, silver fae blood staining his graceful fingers. "I am your servant."

"You are no one's servant," Naida whispered, "least of all mine."

Dru closed his eyes. "My love—"

"Stop talking." She walked over, sparing only a glance at Carys and Duncan before she knelt next to Dru. "Carys Morgan, do I owe you a favor for saving him?"

She shook her head. "I was only doing what I could. He saved me from the violence at the market tonight."

"Did he now?" Naida's eyebrows went up as she took off a cloak made of silver-grey fabric and embroidered with flowers, then threw it over Dru. "A selfless act? Don't make me question your identity."

Despite her harsh words, Naida's hands were gentle, and Dru

stared at her like she was the sun, the moon, and the stars wrapped in one.

A smile curved the corners of his mouth. "You are more beautiful than ever."

"And you've lost blood." She glanced around the fire. "We'll be back when he's healed."

"Back?"

The silver threads that covered the ground glowed and pulsed with magic, and Duncan grabbed Carys and scrambled away from Dru as the ground beneath them heaved again, like a giant beast taking a breath.

Naida's cloak seemed to grow, covering both her and Dru under its silver span, the threads of the cloak reaching down to twine with the glowing threads reaching up from the heaving earth.

The ellyllon put her hands into the dirt, whispered something, and the ground opened up and swallowed them both, leaving a massive fairy mound in the middle of Dafydd's courtyard.

CHAPTER ELEVEN

The world around Carys swam in shades of grey and red. The red of the fire at the market. The black and grey of the fog-dampened cobblestones. The heated red of troll blood spraying across her face. The silver of magical roots growing out of the ground.

"Carys." A soft whisper in her ear, and strong arms held her.

It was Duncan. She recognized the smell of metal and fire with an earthy undertone. He smelled of the forge and fresh soap.

Her back rested against his broad chest, and his arms wrapped around her. Their legs were tangled together, and Carys had the vague memory of changing into a nightgown by the fire and pulling him into bed beside her. She hadn't wanted to be alone.

"Carys."

"Shhh." She kept her eyes closed. The bed was warm, and the covers over them were heavy. Resting in Duncan's arms felt like being encased in a weighted blanket with the added benefit of smelling his soap.

"What kind of soap do you use?" she murmured.

"My soap?" There was a laugh in his voice.

"Aye." She mimicked his accent. "Your soap."

He pulled her closer and sighed. "Hmm. Mary makes it from goat milk, I think. She uses whatever kitchen herbs are in season. This batch was made in the summer. I think it has rosemary."

"Can I get some?"

"Yes." His teeth nipped her ear. "But you have to come to Murrayshall House."

"That's fair." She turned a little and looked over her shoulder. "Did you sleep with me all night?"

His green eyes shone. "Aye, I did. I tried to leave, and you seemed put out. Pulled me right into bed and then fell asleep in minutes."

"Well..." She snuggled back into his chest. "You're very comfortable."

"I'm glad you slept well." He inched back. "You needed it."

Carys wiggled closer.

Duncan scooted away.

She glanced over her shoulder. "What are you doing?"

Duncan raised an eyebrow. "Ah, lass, it's morning and you're not the only one who woke up."

"Not the only..." Oh. As she cuddled closer, she felt what he was talking about. "Ah. I understand."

"You don't seem to be moving away." Duncan didn't move either.

"Neither are you." Carys pressed her lips together and tried to contain her smile. As she'd expected, Duncan was as well-endowed as Lachlan, but his body had a mass and weight to it that made everything about him new and intriguing. His arms were different. His chest was more muscled.

She scooted back and wiggled a little.

"Hmm." Duncan's morning voice was a delightfully smooth rumble that made her ears purr. "Carys Morgan, you'll be the death of me."

She pulled his arms around her shoulders. "I have no idea what you're talking about."

Duncan chuckled low in his throat. "Be a menace then."

Her mind flashed back to the night before. "You were yelling at me."

"You scared me witless. You disappeared from the banquet, and not even Cadell knew where you were. What the hell happened?"

"Let's just say that I'm no longer in debt to the Crow Mother. She decided last night was the time I needed to pay up."

"Hmm." Duncan let out a low, unhappy grumble. "The power of that fae woman worries me."

"Doesn't matter anymore." Carys closed her eyes and let out a sigh. "It's done. Debt fulfilled. Bargain finished."

"I have a feeling we haven't heard the last from her, but as for your bargain with her, you're correct." He kissed her shoulder. "You're well and done with her. Thank the heavens."

Carys closed her eyes and leaned her neck to the side as Duncan's mouth moved from her shoulder to her neck, the warm velvet of his lips contrasting with the rough stubble of his beard.

Her skin prickled in awareness.

She was tempted. She was so tempted.

Duncan was right there, and she wanted him. Her body was screaming at her to turn and take whatever she wanted. He was ready, and she was too.

But bodies weren't the problem. Her attraction to Duncan hadn't ever been in doubt.

"So you went to the Brightlands." His lips trailed soft kisses along her skin. "Did ya think about staying once you were there?"

"It was sunny in London."

He laughed. "So that's a yes?"

"No." She blinked. "Actually I didn't. Dru was with me, and all I could think about was getting back to Laura." *And you.*

"You're a good friend," he whispered. "I had my eye on her. Once everyone realized you were missing, I made sure she had a carriage back to Dafydd's with his guards before Lachlan and I went to look for you."

Her heart swelled. "You're a good man."

"She's a guest here. And your best friend. You can trust me to take care of her. I know what it's like to be a stranger."

"And that's why you're the laird of Murrayshall."

His laugh was low. "Because I can call a carriage?"

She turned and met his eyes. "Because you think about the details, Duncan. No matter where we are."

He took a strand of her hair between his fingers. "Just helping a friend."

She whispered, "Thank you."

His lips were right there. She wasn't ready for everything Duncan wanted, but she couldn't forget the memory of their kiss.

His eyes fell to her lips, and he mouthed her name. *Carys.*

She closed her eyes and inhaled the scent of rosemary and metal. His breath touched her lips and—

"Lady Carys!" A pounding came at the door. "The Kingsguard is in the hall!"

"The Cymric dragons caused a riot on the Night Bridge." Wynnflad, newly promoted Chief Captain of the Kingsguard, stood at attention in Dafydd's hall. "King Harold is not pleased. It's the eve of his coronation, and there are foreign emissaries from the continent here."

Carys had been called to Dafydd's hall with Cadell, only to be greeted by a company of the Kingsguard standing at attention in front of her uncle's table. She had thrown on a pair of linen leggings and a tunic while Duncan waited in her sitting room, but she felt distinctly underdressed with everyone in uniform.

Dafydd shrugged his massive shoulders. "One of my nêr ddraig was attacked by a troll illegally trading in human slaves in the night market. Her bonded dragon responded in the appropriate way. If a troll or two was injured, that is not our concern. They were criminals. Harold should be *thanking* my niece."

The captain sighed. "There were two dragons sitting on the

Night Bridge, spewing fire across the west side of the Cye Bourne. There were reports of fae involvement." Winnie was clearly exasperated. "They were out of control. We haven't seen a sign of the Great Serpent since last night."

Dafydd looked at Cadell. "Were you out of control?"

"Of course not, my king." He glanced at Winnie. "And at no time would we harm the Great Serpent. He is the guardian of the river and her creatures; all dragons of Briton revere his power. As soon as I located my lady," he continued, "I retrieved her and left the market."

"After lighting half of it on fire," Winnie countered.

"We were defending ourselves from troll aggression." Mared stood at Dafydd's shoulder. "We could sense Lady Carys's presence, but none of the market vendors were forthcoming and more than one implied that we should do anatomically impossible things."

"They were insulting you, so you started a riot?" Winnie said. "Dafydd, you must see—"

"As a complete coincidence, the Cymric throne is delighted to announce a redevelopment project on the east side of the Cye Bourne and the Night Bridge neighborhood," the king said, interrupting her. "In honor of King Harold's coronation. Consider it a gift from Cymru to Anglia. We'll even build a guard station there to oversee the market." Dafydd nodded toward Winnie. "Though of course we shall expect the Kingsguard to offer their soldiers to staff the outpost."

Winnie opened her mouth, then closed it. "I will convey your... *gift* to King Harold," she finally said, then turned to the guards behind her and nodded at them. "You may go. I have a matter to discuss with the Cymric king and do not have need of you," she told her lieutenant. "Wait for me in the courtyard."

"Yes, Captain." The lieutenant nodded at Dafydd before swiftly departing the hall.

After they were gone and Winnie was alone with Dafydd, Carys, and the two dragons, she pulled out a chair and sat down. "Seriously, Your Highness?"

"Winnie, it's not my fault that Carys needed to use the fae gate near the market. That neighborhood is lawless, and Edgar should have dealt with it years ago."

Mared crossed her arms. "We did you a favor, driving off the worst of that lot."

"My cousin has been king for less than *two weeks,*" Winnie said. "You think he's had time to deal with the troll markets and all the other things his father overlooked?"

Dafydd turned to Carys. "Winnie is an old friend and a trusted advisor of the new king. She spent time in our court as a child."

"Why do you think I'm such a good archer?" Winnie smiled at Carys.

"I can speak freely then?" Carys asked.

"Of course." Winnie nodded. "What do you have to say?"

"I was taken from the banquet to the troll market by the Crow Mother." She wasn't sure Winnie knew who that was. "She's a fae sorceress, and I owed her a debt."

"I know her by reputation." Winnie frowned. "She's a powerful creature. How did you come to owe her—" Winnie held up a hand. "You know what? I don't want to know."

"Wise," Cadell muttered.

"The Crow Mother mentioned something to me at the banquet that the king should know about." Carys was relieved that she could speak to someone about what Branwen had told her at the banquet. "Before she took me, she looked at Queen Orla and said: 'The queen will bring me her offering, and then everything will fall into place.' I don't know what she was talking about, but I have a feeling that Orla is not a friend."

"An offering." Winnie glanced at Dafydd. "Do you have any idea what she was referring to?"

"None." Dafydd's brow furrowed. "What could Orla offer the Crow Mother that she hasn't given already? After decades of union with Cian, Orla's more fae than human."

And also the mother of a fae child, but Carys didn't know if Dafydd had shared the knowledge of Regan's origins with anyone outside of those who'd witnessed Regan's death, which was only Carys, Dafydd, Duncan, and Lachlan.

Dafydd turned to Carys. "We *have* been in contact with Harold about the maps that Seren drew before she was killed. About the land bridge that Regan appeared to be building between Éire and Briton."

Winnie nodded. "I even went with Anwyn when she surveyed the islands. So far, no new land masses have appeared."

"That means nothing," Cadell said. "Cian is the power behind Orla's throne, and fae plan in centuries, not years. Seren's murder could have been the first step in their plans."

"Harold knows what really happened to your Shadowkin," Winnie said. "We also know that publicly, Queen Orla has claimed that Seren's killer was working on her own. Even though it was her own daughter."

"It's possible that Regan's death meant the death of whatever Orla was planning," Dafydd said. "That has been our hope."

"But an offering to the Crow Mother?" Winnie pursed her lips. "I agree with the dragon. It sounds like they're still plotting."

"If Orla and Cian had no idea what Regan was up to with Seren, I'll eat a haggis in one sitting," Carys said. "She knew. And Regan also had allies in the Anglian court; she said as much to me when she thought I was going to die."

Winnie scowled. "I'm not saying you're wrong, but the problem is, Harold was not on good terms with his father. King Edgar was enamored with Orla. Always. And he was closer to the high fae than Harold would like. As Orla has aged—even though she doesn't look it—Cian has taken more and more power."

"So Harold agrees with us?" Carys glanced at Cadell. "He thinks Queen Orla is plotting something with the fae?"

Dafydd nodded. "That's one of the reasons I wanted you here for the coronation. Winnie has been our liaison with Harold. She and Lachlan have been speaking with me about the plans they fear Orla is making. It's the other reason Eamer didn't come with me. Her mother is powerful, and she doesn't want to be used as a pawn. We both felt she was safer in Cymru."

"So we all suspect Orla and Cian are planning something, but no one has any idea what it is?" Carys looked at Cadell. "You guys have spies, right?"

Winnie smirked. "We're not supposed to spy on our allies."

"Bullshit," Carys said. "All countries spy on their neighbors."

Winnie said, "They may not be... *spies*, but magical creatures gossip worse than humans do."

"What do you mean?" Carys asked.

"The wolves have heard rumors. Fae gates that have been dormant for years are waking."

According to Carys's sources, wolves loved war. She glanced at Cadell. *Can the wolves be trusted?*

Some of them.

Dafydd added, "We've heard the same from the dragons. Fae gates are shifting. The trees are growing faster, and old magic is waking."

"Are there wolves in Éire?" Carys spoke aloud. "Do they have—I don't know—connected clans? Can they find out more that way?"

Winnie shook her head. "The fae hunted and drove the wolves from Éire long ago, so we have to acknowledge there is bad blood between the fae and the wolves, but I don't think Godrik would lie to me about this. His people have seen strange things around fae gates here in Anglia."

Dafydd said, "And Lachlan says the Alban unicorns have also raised concerns."

Cadell stepped forward. "Concerns like what?"

"Activity in barrows they thought were abandoned centuries ago," Dafydd said. "Magical activity near gates that have been all but dead."

"Godrik's people have reported unseasonable vegetation that smells like magic in Essex," Winnie added. "We'd like to investigate more, but I have to be very careful who to trust even among the

Kingsguard. Much of the leadership is still loyal to Edgar's memory, and Harold is a new king. My cousin trusts me and Godrik right now. Not many others."

"Cadell and I can help." Carys looked at Dafydd. "Right?"

"Absolutely." Dafydd nodded. "Robb and Elinor are in agreement with Eamer and me that Orla and her ambitions are not in keeping with the Queens' Pact. Her union with Cian has pushed her toward fae interests instead of human. We think she's looking to exert more than her share of power in Briton."

"*Balance* is what is needed in Briton," Mared said. "Not ambition."

"Meet with us here," Carys said to Winnie. "Between Cadell and me, Duncan and Lachlan, we can help you and Harold." Carys sat up. "Laura can help too. She can read runes, and she's smart as hell."

Winnie looked at Carys. "You're proposing an alliance?"

Dafydd beamed at Carys. "I told you, Winnie."

"Oh no." Carys held up her hand. "This is not me making a play for the Cymric throne. That's a whole other problem, Uncle Dafydd."

Unfortunately, Dafydd was still beaming.

"I'm just saying that until Harold is situated," Carys said, "until he has confidence in his guards, he has backup from Cymru and Alba, right?" She looked at Cadell. "We can work quietly. I'm sure Lachlan and Duncan will help us figure out what's going on."

Cadell raised an eyebrow. "Lachlan and Duncan will do anything you ask them to. Backward and hopping on one foot if necessary."

"I don't need the sarcasm," Carys muttered. "That's not necessary."

Winnie couldn't hide her smile. "Godrik and me, Cadell, Carys, your American friend, and the two Alban boys. That makes seven of us. Seven isn't a bad number."

"It is not," Dafydd said. "Let us meet after Harold's coronation tomorrow, Captain. For now I'll send a company of my people to the Night Bridge to reinforce Harold's troops and start on our..." Dafydd glanced at the dragons. "...new development project. We'll get all this cleaned up by tomorrow; I guarantee it."

CARYS WAS WALKING out of Dafydd's morning room when she heard footsteps to her right. She turned and saw Anwyn walking toward her from a long narrow corridor with daylight at the end. The armor-clad woman saw Carys, stopped, then leaned back on her right foot and lifted her chin.

Carys had a feeling that Anwyn practiced that expression in the mirror, because the angle of her head displayed the long red scar that looked like a claw mark down the side of her face.

The effect was a little terrifying.

"I understand you had a misunderstanding at the troll market last night. The Kingsguard requested a report."

"Uh..." Carys had no idea what she was supposed to tell Anwyn about their agreement to help King Harold figure out what was going on with the fae in Anglia.

Better to leave that for Dafydd to share. "It was a misunderstanding, but the Anglian guards had to kind of make a statement, I guess." She lifted a finger. "Don't let your dragons burn down markets in London again. Blah blah blah."

Anwyn's eyes narrowed. "My brother says you came back to the house covered in blood."

"Not mine," she said quickly. "But there was a troll I had to... stab. To get away."

Anwyn's expression never changed.

And Carys didn't know how to stop talking. "I think *that* troll was pissed off because there was another troll who was holding a human woman captive and she was trying to get away, but her leg was chained to his, so Dru and I—well, Dru had the sword—we kind of chopped off... the troll's leg. The first one, not the second one. The second one I stabbed, and then there was blood spray." She spread her hand over her face. "Kind of everywhere. But I wasn't hurt. Just the troll. Trolls. Two of them."

Still very little change in expression. Carys was starting to wonder if one of the things they taught at the dragon academy was how to not display any human emotion.

"You speak very freely," Anwyn finally said. "I would advise you not to share that story with just anyone."

"But you're not just anyone, right? You're kind of my cousin."

"I suppose we are related. In a way."

"Right." Not warm and friendly, but Anwyn was definitely looking at her with slightly less distaste than she had before.

"I appreciate your boldness," Anwyn said. "And your sense of justice. Human and fae slavery is hideous, and I know Harold's people are trying to stamp it out."

"It seems like it." She pointed over her shoulder. "It sounds like King Dafydd is going to help."

Anwyn nodded. "Queen Eamer speaks highly of you."

"Queen Eamer is very kind." Carys's voice softened. "And wise. I was hoping I would see her this week, but I understand why it was important for her to stay back in..."

"Caernarfon." Anwyn motioned toward the corridor behind her. "Are you engaged?"

"Engaged?" God, was everyone curious about her love life? That was unexpected coming from such an obvious soldier. Anwyn's expression didn't exactly scream "girl chat."

"Do you have some place you need to be?" Anwyn asked. "I was looking for you because the younger soldiers are practicing archery this morning, and my uncle said you are gaining proficiency."

"Oh!" Carys smiled. "I'd love to do some practice shooting if that's what you're asking."

"I am." Anwyn didn't exactly seem thrilled about the idea, but she also wasn't glaring at Carys anymore. "Demelza also says that you have a compound bow, and I'd love to examine it."

"Demelza?"

"My bonded dragon."

"Ah. I do. And I'd be happy to show you." Carys pointed toward the staircase. "I'll get it and meet you outside?"

There was finally a spark of interest in Anwyn's eyes. "Excellent."

ANWYN PULLED BACK the string of the compound bow after she'd nocked the arrow. Carys instructed her on how to use the release.

"Okay, you're holding it exactly right. Do you see the loop?"

"I do."

"Once you've aimed, you're going to squeeze that release like I showed you. Keep that left arm angled out just a little so the string doesn't hit you on release."

Dylan said something in Cymric.

"It's the same with a long bow." Anwyn released the arrow with obvious expertise, hitting the target dead center as the soldiers around her murmured in approval. "Very good. Very smooth. Tremendous range. But slow. It takes too much time to set up a shot."

"It is much slower than the short bow that Yurok people use," Carys said. "I've been training on that one and my range isn't as good, but it's definitely faster."

"The power is remarkable." Anwyn examined the weapon. "An excellent machine."

"I feel like it's something you could reproduce here, but I don't know about the fiberglass parts," Carys said.

"It would be difficult with the materials we have available." Anwyn shook her head. "Individual weapons? Perhaps. But nothing we could scale."

"Understandable."

Anwyn handed the compound bow back to Carys. "And what do you use for shooting from a coracle?"

"This one. The compound bow." Carys lined up and took another shot, trying to ignore the curious eyes of the Cymric troops on her.

She didn't hit the target dead center the way that Anwyn had, but she didn't miss the target entirely. There were a few murmurs of approval, and then the majority of the men and women looking on returned to their own shooting.

"I use a short recurve when I'm focusing on speed, and like Cadell said, finding supplies for this one in the Shadowlands is not easy, so it's important to learn both. I'm getting better with the recurve, but for accuracy and range, I've been training with this one. All the Chahta dragon riders use compound bows."

"You're not bad" —Anwyn's mouth angled up at the corner— "for someone who's only been training for six months."

"Appreciate it. I'd like to spend more time on this and less on dancing, but there's a party tomorrow and I'm required to attend."

"You're a curiosity. Walk with me." Anwyn set down her own bow and started strolling behind the practicing archers. "You were a scholar before this?"

"Uh..." Carys smiled. "Yes. And I still am. I have to work. I teach at a university in the Brightlands."

"What do you teach?"

"Mythology and world literature."

Anwyn froze. "You teach poetry?"

"I mean, that's part of it but—"

"Not tactics? Political science? Not even military history?"

Carys blinked. "There's politics *and* history in literature and mythology, but no, most of what I teach is more in the humanities area. Poetry, if you like. Philosophy. Things like that."

Anwyn blinked and muttered something in Cymric.

"Listen." Carys lowered her voice. "I know that our uncle envisions some kind of... role for me here, but I want you to know that I don't see things that way. I don't— I'm not Seren. And I don't want to be."

Anwyn stepped back and did the looking-down-the-nose thing

again, showing off her scar. "And yet the scholar with only six months of archery training has bonded with a legendary dragon, is a passable archer, and stabs trolls in the marketplace while trying to free human captives."

"I don't get what you're trying to—"

"You're brave and bold," Anwyn said. "And Eamer says you're smart. You could learn quickly. My brother thinks you're trying to maneuver me out of the way to take the throne. Is he right?"

"No. He's not right."

"Should he be right?"

Carys frowned. "What are you saying?"

Anwyn shrugged. "I love my country. And soldiers don't always make the best leaders. Look at King Harold. He prefers books to the blade, but that doesn't matter because he's smart enough to promote Wynnflad to be his Chief Captain. Winnie is the soldier so Harold doesn't have to be."

"I don't want to be queen of Cymru."

"No?" Anwyn started to walk away, keeping her eyes on the backs of the practicing troops. "Well, maybe that means you should be."

ACT II

CHAPTER TWELVE

The morning of King Harold of Anglia's coronation was overcast and cool, but the window out of Carys's room overlooked Dafydd's garden where flowers of bright red and yellow burst from the ground, giving the appearance of sunshine even where none existed.

A light knock came at her door.

"Come in."

A maid entered the room and immediately moved to tend the fire in Carys's hearth. "Good morning, Lady Carys."

"Good morning." Carys couldn't remember the woman's name. In Dafydd's London house, there were far more servants than in the castle in Sgain. She'd been in London a few days, and she was still seeing new faces every morning she woke up.

"Carys?" A sleepy voice came from town the hall.

"In here."

"Okay, this is so weird. I've never spent this much time out of sunlight before." Laura wandered into her room after the maid, yawning and scratching her head. "Growing up in Baywood, I thought I could exist without it, but this is on another level."

"I know." Carys turned away from the windows and leaned on the small table as the maid finished with the fire and rolled a cart with steaming trays into the room.

"Will you take your breakfast in Lady Carys's room, Miss Laura?" the maid asked.

"That would be great. Thanks." Laura plopped down in the chair across from Carys and watched the maid bring the cart over. "You know, I'm going to go back to Baywood eventually and I'll have to make my own breakfast every morning, and it will be tragic."

Carys smiled. "If you want Cadell to deliver a charred deer carcass to your front step daily, that can probably be arranged."

"Tempting as that is" —Laura rolled her eyes— "I will pass."

Carys sat down and lifted the teapot the maid set on the table. "Just water?"

The maid nodded. "Freshly boiled, my lady."

"You're wonderful."

The maid's cheeks dimpled with pleasure.

They waited for the young woman to leave the room before Carys hurried to her knapsack and dug for the tiny tubes of instant coffee she'd smuggled into the Shadowlands.

"Come on, come on," Laura urged her. "Don't hold out on me. They brought fresh cream."

"You know what the Shadowlands has taught me? Honey in coffee is surprisingly delicious." Carys brought two instant coffees to the table and handed one to Laura. "Your daily fix, my lady."

"You're not a dragon rider—you're a goddess." Laura tore the packet open with her teeth and poured it into the delicate glass teacup on the table before she added water. "Oh, sweet, sweet coffee."

Carys was just as eager to get her caffeine fix. She poured the steaming water over the dried coffee before she handed the teapot to Laura and stirred.

The distinctive aroma of roasted arabica filled the room.

Nêrys. Cadell spoke in her mind. *You have brewed coffee.*

It's not good for dragons, Cadell.

Coffee is not good for dogs. It has no detrimental effect on dragons, and you know it.

"Cadell wants to poach our coffee," Carys said. *Next time you should bring your own.*

The dragon had discovered a love for very strong coffee after moving to Baywood. It was a love that Carys could appreciate, but that didn't mean she was sharing.

There was another knock on the door.

Laura narrowed her eyes and sipped her coffee. "Be careful."

"I will be." Carys left her steaming ambrosia on the table and walked to the door. She opened it a sliver and saw Duncan on the other side. "Hey."

He was dressed in loose woolen pants that hung on his narrow hips and wore a tunic open at the neck.

"You have coffee in there," Duncan muttered in a throaty growl. "I can smell it."

"You should have brought your own," she whispered.

He put his hand flat on the door and pushed his way into the room. "A packet or I'm telling the dragon."

"Duncan—"

He caged Carys against the wall and kicked the door shut with one determined foot. "You smell delicious." He leaned in and put his face near Carys's neck. "One cup of what you're drinking will buy my silence and whatever else you might want from a lonely and very eager-to-please blacksmith."

Laura coughed loudly.

Duncan turned to her with narrowed eyes. "You have company."

"Yes, just letting you know that *I am in here*, and also the dragon already knows about the coffee." Laura sipped from her cup, smacking her lips before she blew some of the steam in Duncan's direction. "And if you wanted to get rich in this place, a thriving business in black market coffee would do the trick."

"If I wanted a fortune in millet, I'd agree with you." Duncan grabbed Carys around the waist, wrapped a burly arm around her, and whispered, "Please. My lady. My queen. Goddess of Baywood, bless me with your coffee."

Carys shivered at the scrape of his beard against her neck. "I have limited quantities, Duncan."

"Tell me what you desire." His breath was on her neck. "I will be your willing servant if only you'll—"

"Give the man a coffee or get a room," Laura barked. "I do not need a front-row seat for your messed-up love life, Carys."

Carys wanted to feel Duncan's lips in other places that weren't her neck, but recognizing that neither of them needed an audience, she gently pushed his shoulder back and nodded toward the table. "Sit down and say nothing to anyone about what you're about to drink."

He grabbed her hand and kissed the inside of her wrist with fervent adoration. "Lady, I am your servant."

Laura muttered, "Damn it, why does shit like that work?"

"Every time." Carys felt her heart racing, and she hadn't even had her caffeine yet. "I'll get you a packet, but next time plan ahead."

Duncan's eyes were fixed on her until Carys turned toward the wardrobe.

"I think Dru drilled it into my head that nothing from our world could pass through the gates so often I never even considered bringing coffee." Duncan slumped in the chair next to Laura and yawned. "I imagine he meant steel and technology, but I took it to mean everything."

"Coffee comes from Africa," Laura said. "They don't have it here?"

"According to Cadell" —Carys walked back to the table with a packet of coffee and an earthenware mug from the cabinet— "it's more common in the Middle East and Eastern Europe, but it still hasn't caught on in Western Europe."

"And definitely not in Briton." Duncan reached for the mug and the packet. "But facing a day of Anglian ceremonies is going to be so much better with caffeine." He grabbed Carys's hand and kissed her knuckles again. "Thank you."

Carys managed to ignore the fluttery feeling in her belly when she felt Duncan's lips on her skin. "Apparently Eamer picked out our clothes and had them sent over to make sure we were all presentable," she said. "She flew everything to Dafydd by dragon last night."

"Doesn't surprise me," Duncan said. "Lachlan's mother sent clothes for me since I'm officially in the Alban court's party."

"I've never been to a coronation before," Laura said. "But I did attend the installation of the Wykanush high chief a couple of years ago. It was..." She sighed. "...a very long week."

"Thank God this one only lasts a day." Duncan sipped his black coffee and closed his eyes in bliss. "But Anglian ceremonies tend to have a lot of stag dancing, a lot of beer, and the wolves like to get crazy. So stay close, both of you."

CARYS, Duncan, and Laura were dressed and ready by late afternoon. They flew by coracle and landed in a large meadow that sloped down from the hill where a massive bonfire was already burning. There were stag dancers circling the fire, and a great stone throne had been erected at the apex of the mound that was the highest point in London.

"That's Lud's Hill." Duncan raised his voice as they walked off the coracle, trying to compete with the pounding drummers that weaved through the milling crowds. "It's the center of ancient Anglia. The first of Harold's ancestors is buried beneath it. According to Shadowlands history—"

"Lud," Carys said. "King Lud, right? He was a pre-Roman British king." She frowned. "That's wild that they have the same history here."

"There's some debate," Duncan said. "No one is sure if Lud was real or a myth, but for tradition's sake, *that's* Lud's throne, so that's where Harold will sit to officially take power."

It appeared to be built for a giant. According to what Dafydd had told her, it was made of sarsen stone and etched with Anglian history and the names of the kings and queens who had ruled the south of Briton for over a thousand years.

Carys wished she could see the etchings better, but the closest they were going to get in this gathering was about halfway up the hill where she could see Cymric banners waving in the torchlight. A royal box for the nêr ddraig was elevated from the crowd and guarded by Cymric soldiers with bright green uniforms.

Nêrys, you have arrived.

"I just heard Cadell." She spun around, looking for the dragon. "He's here."

We just landed. She spoke to the dragon in her mind as they crossed from the meadow into the maelstrom. *Duncan is with us, and we're headed to Dafydd's box.*

Be careful. There are many fae here, many wolves, and a large gathering of trolls. There might be fighting with a crowd this size.

"Cadell is worried about fights," Carys said. "Duncan?"

"Uh..." He shook his head. "With this many people—no matter what world you're in—it's a possibility."

"This is crazy." Laura stood on her tiptoes to scan the mass of people that was flooding the riverbank. There were boats packed with folk who had gathered on the river, and fae lights danced in blue and purple overhead. "I've never seen this many magical creatures and people anywhere in the Shadowlands before."

"London is massive in both worlds," Duncan said. "I'm sure American cities are the same."

"Yeah, that's probably why I avoid them," Laura said.

"Carys, keep your arm in mine." Duncan held it out and locked her forearm against his side. "This crowd is something else." He held out his left arm. "Laura, you too."

"Gladly." Laura locked her arm with Duncan's and kept her eyes on the ground as they trudged up the earthen hill that was already churned and muddy from so many feet.

For this ceremony, Cadell would not be there to escort them unless something went very wrong. He and all the Cymric dragons save Mared waited like towering sentinels in the meadow west of the hill, guarding the ceremony with their presence.

On the eastern side, Carys saw a line of blood-red balauri positioned in much the same way. To the south, lines of red-coated guards dominated the field, the wide bridge, and the riverbank where it appeared that every Londoner in the Shadowlands had gathered to watch Harold climb from a barge on the Tamis River to Lud's Hill, where he would sit on the same throne his father and grandmother had when they'd claimed the seat of power on their own coronation nights.

To the north and beyond Lud's Hill, more soldiers had gathered, dressed in blue and silver, and in their midst, she saw moving figures that glowed with ethereal light as a large company of unicorns joined the Alban troops to guard the northern border of the ceremonial hill.

"Wow."

Carys didn't miss the ceremonial touches. Alban troops guarding the north, Cymric dragons guarding the west, Anglian troops in the south, and red balauri guarding the east and the skies nearest to Continental Europe.

But if the Queens' Pact ruled all of Briton, what had the Éiren nation provided as part of the ceremony? Their absence was noticeable.

"Orla and Cian are here?" Carys looked at the other royal boxes, but they were in the distance and it was hard to see who was in them.

"I'm sure they are," Duncan said. "Somewhere."

"Okay, this is crazy." Laura's voice rose over the pounding drums that grew louder as they approached the hill. "But also amazing."

As they approached Lud's Hill, Carys looked at the wooden platforms erected for royal guests, visiting dignitaries, and Anglian nobles. She was searching for the Éiren contingent, but she saw no sign of Orla and Cian.

She tugged Duncan's arm.

"Aye, lass? If you have a question, I'm as lost as you are. I know this hill is where Saint Paul's Cathedral is located in the Brightlands, but I have no idea—"

"Where is the Éiren box?" She scanned the crowd. "And their defenses. I see Alban unicorns mixed with Lachlan's soldiers, and Cymric dragons buttressing Dafydd's troops, but surely the Éirens and the fae are here too. As the fourth kingdom in the Queens' Pact, wouldn't they... I don't know, contribute?"

"Cian and Orla are there." Duncan pointed at a large group of brightly dressed fae on the eastern side of the hill. "Mixing among the fae. But they won't have brought any soldiers."

"Why not?" As they climbed into the Cymric box, she scanned the teeming throngs of London that spread along the river. There had to have been a half a million people or more.

"I believe the Éiren army is small," Duncan said. "And their general is the crown princess Finola. She'll be back in Éire if her mother is here, I'd guess. But as I said, they don't have a large army. They mainly depend on fae mages for their defense."

Carys wondered whether Harold would even welcome Éiren troops on Anglian soil, knowing what had happened with Orla's own daughter.

Laura shouted, "This is not like the high chief's ceremony at all."

Duncan shook his head. "I've never seen the like."

There was nothing dignified or ceremonial about the coronation so far. The entire spectacle felt more like a sporting event than a solemn ceremony.

"But the Éiren throne *are* allies," Carys said. "At least publicly, right?"

Duncan raised both eyebrows. "You know, you never explained

why the Kingsguard was at Dafydd's house yesterday. Anything you want to share?"

"Yes." She'd have to if their alliance to support Winnie became a reality. "But not tonight."

Duncan growled. "Carys, I can't help if I don't know—"

"Lachlan!" Laura shouted over the hubbub. "Carys, there's Lachlan!"

She saw him in the distance, standing in the Alban royal box with various nobles and dressed in blue finery with silver and blue flags flying overhead.

Her former boyfriend was surrounded by guards and courtiers, leaning down to speak to a silver-haired woman in a red cape with fur trim while another courtier—a being that Carys guessed might be a unicorn—waited to speak to him.

He nodded gravely before he turned to the waiting unicorn and shook his hand, clasping it between his own as he listened to whatever the older man was communicating.

Lachlan looked serious and consequential.

He looked... like a king.

And Carys suddenly realized that all this ceremony and pomp— all the tradition and heraldry—was all something that Lachlan would face some day. King Robb was in good health, but King Edgar had been too.

This was Harold's present and Lachlan's future.

Something in her heart cracked.

And eased at the same time.

Nêrys, you feel sorrow.

She tried to calm her heart. She didn't want Cadell worried about her. *I'm just seeing clearly, I think. Maybe for the first time.* She clutched Duncan's arm a little tighter. *Lachlan will be king someday.*

If he wishes it, Cadell said in her mind. *Yes, he will.*

Where does that leave me?

Wherever you want, my lady. If your uncle has his wish—

"Oh no, we're not even going there," she muttered.

"What?" Duncan shouted.

"Nothing!" The drums reached a fever pitch, and Carys realized that Harold's river barge had reached the dock in front of Lud's Hill. "I'll tell you later. It looks like the coronation is about to start."

KING HAROLD'S coronation was as raucous and as rowdy as the drums and crowds had promised it would be. There was dancing and singing. There were shouted speeches projected by fae magic and a light show in the sky over the river.

The Great Serpent breached the darkness of the river and showered the surface with a feathery gold illumination, which everyone in the crowd took to mean a blessing and divine approval for the new regent.

It was a sign to celebrate, and the city did.

An hour after Harold had ascended the throne, draped in blood-red garments trimmed in white fur, the ceremony at Lud's Hill had spread through the city while the newly crowned king departed to his castle on a river barge guarded by the Great Serpent of the Tamis while the crowds cheered.

There was dancing in the meadows along the river, and the smell of roasting meat floated through the air by the time Cadell found them in King Dafydd's box.

"We will fly to the castle for King Harold's party," Cadell shouted. "Let's get to the coracle."

Dafydd himself had been plucked from the royal box by Mared in beast form, while Carys's two cousins, Anwyn and Dylan, grasped the giant claws of their dragons and stared down at Carys as they flew away.

"Show-offs," Laura muttered. "You could totally do that." She glanced at Carys. "If you weren't wearing a dress."

"I just wore what Eamer picked out for me." Which was an emerald-green gown sewn with seed pearls and embroidered with gold and silver thread. It was a dress fit for a royal coronation, but it wasn't conducive to flying with a dragon.

Duncan took both hers and Laura's hands before he led them down the stairs and through the swiftly departing crowd. "Still glad we can fly by dragon instead of going by carriage. It would be faster to walk than ride tonight."

They made it to the luxurious coracle moments later, and Carys breathed a sigh of relief when the heavy door thunked closed.

She sat on the bench and whispered, "Cadell, get us out of here."

Her heart was heavy, and every time she closed her eyes, all she saw was Lachlan looking kingly.

It did nothing to diminish the attraction. If anything, seeing her former lover step into the leadership role he'd been born into made him more attractive, not less. He was noble and serious. Warmth still emanated from his expressions, but there was a gravity that had joined it.

He was a chief. A leader.

Carys felt a warm hand slide into her own, and she opened her eyes to see Laura watching her.

"You okay?"

Carys nodded.

"Too much noise?"

"Yeah." It was an easy excuse. "I don't know how Dafydd thinks I'd survive being queen of Cymru" —she let out a harsh laugh— "when I can't even handle watching a coronation without getting a migraine." She pressed her lips together. "The party at the castle will be quieter, right?"

"I have no idea." Laura's sad smile told Carys she knew it wasn't just a headache troubling her friend. "It was a very cool experience. Completely different than the high chief's dedication. Way more beer at this party."

Duncan was sitting across from Carys, his eyes scanning the ground, one hand on the bolt that secured the massive coracle door.

Carys nodded toward him. "He takes his guard duty seriously."

"When you told me Duncan was Lachlan's complete opposite, I was expecting a surly asshole because Lachlan is so sweet and charming," Laura said. "And he can be. But Duncan's also one of the most conscientious men I've ever met." She nodded at Carys. "He takes care of you and everyone you care about. I like that. Even if he is a collection of sharp edges at times."

"Well, he does make swords in his spare time."

Laura smiled. "I saw Lachlan tonight."

"Yeah." Carys kept a smile firmly in place. "He looked great, right?"

"He looked like a CEO and a politician," Laura said. "Like a king."

Carys nodded. "I'm sure he's going to make a good one."

"Even though he says he doesn't want it?"

Carys shrugged. "He goes back and forth."

"And you?" Laura raised an eyebrow.

"I was going back and forth." Carys kept her voice low and glanced at Duncan. "But maybe not anymore."

CHAPTER THIRTEEN

"Remember" —Cadell led Carys across the torch-lit drawbridge and into Harold's castle right next to the river — "this is a party, but this is also a show of strength, a political theater, and an occasion to declare alliances." The dragon kept his voice low. "Be careful who you are seen talking to, and be *very* careful who you dance with."

Dammit, she knew the dancing thing was important. "What does a first dance signal?"

"It depends," Cadell said. "But in a situation like this, it's usually a declaration of alliance."

Alliance, huh? Carys looked over her shoulder to where Duncan was smiling at Laura. Had Carys declared an alliance with Duncan when he claimed the first dance at the welcome banquet?

Laura and Duncan were laughing and joking as they walked into the party. They looked like they were ready for fun, not being lectured by a dragon.

"The participants of a dance can be very significant," Cadell continued. "Harold will likely not dance at all."

"Because he doesn't want to show favoritism?"

"Because of that and because he is the guest of honor." Cadell looked up, scanned the growing crowd, and nodded to someone in the distance. "The dances are to amuse him. He's the audience, not the entertainment."

"Got it." She scanned the courtyard as they made their way through the heavy military presence and into the main hall. "I don't see Lachlan."

"I imagine he's already inside. Harold was raised for many years in the Alban court. The alliance between Alba and Anglia is as close as it has been in centuries. The seating tonight will reflect that."

"And Cymru?"

"We have always been separate." Cadell spoke carefully. "And that is by design. It is not prudent for a small nation as powerful as Cymru to show favoritism. And that extends to social interactions."

"So I shouldn't spend too much time with Lachlan is what you're saying?"

"Seren and Lachlan's marriage was a turbulent time." Cadell's voice was wooden. "I suspect the four royal courts of Briton are looking forward to more tranquility during Harold's reign." He glanced at Carys. "You should know that since it might influence decisions that are in your hands, my lady."

Fine. Message received. Lachlan was a bad romantic bet for lots of reasons, and one of them happened to be world peace.

Cadell navigated them between a row of red-clad sword-bearers, bronze blades raised to form an archway that all guests walked under.

"Two messages," Cadell said. "In Harold's house, we are under the protection of the Anglian throne. We are also under its blade."

"Got it." Carys's head was spinning. There was a reason she'd never much cared for political science. It was one thing to dissect hidden meaning in myth and literature. It was a whole other thing to have to parse every word and action so as not to cause a war that could affect thousands of people.

Tell me the truth, Carys said in Cadell's mind. *Does anyone besides Dafydd want me near the throne of Cymru?*

"Absolutely not," Cadell's voice was low and urgent. *But you should not tell anyone that right now.*

Carys blinked. "Why not?"

"That's for your uncle to decide, not you."

Okay, so maybe she'd been too free speaking to Anwyn. Yet another reason she probably shouldn't be queen.

Cadell spoke to her mind. *Be very conscious of your station tonight, Nêrys. Every movement, every dance or conversation, matters.*

"Right."

So be royal. Or a royal possibility.

But not too royal. Or too interested in being royal.

Fuck, this was complicated.

They entered Harold's grand hall, and the musicians were already playing, pink-red wine passed by them in blown glass goblets, and the hall was lit with red and white illumination supplied by dancing air sprites fluttering silver-tipped wings.

Above their heads, candles floated among the zipping fairies, and the scent of roasted meat and spices wafted through the air.

Carys breathed out a sigh of pleasure. There were a dozen social and royal traps she might fall into that night, but for a moment, just a quick moment, she wanted to enjoy the magic of the evening.

The newly crowned king sat at the head table with his guests of honor joining him. Harold was a plain man in person, but the crown and the robes did a lot to make him more impressive.

Next to Harold, Carys saw Lachlan and the silver-haired woman, both in royal-blue tunics. Dafydd and her cousin Anwyn were seated next to Lachlan in intricately sewn leather armor and verdant-green robes.

On Harold's other side, the fae and Éiren nobles completed the head table, Orla's cool beauty glowing like moonlight while Cian's face appeared lit by an invisible sun.

Immediately in front of the head table, a crowd of gold-clad musicians played before the king and his guests while fae, humans, and unicorns danced in circles under the lights.

Soldiers in bright red with white trim ringed the hall, staring at the revelers with faces frozen in ceremonial rigor.

But despite their solemn presence, bursts of laughter punctuated the feast, and even the solemn-faced wolves in their grey-and-silver uniforms appeared to be having fun.

Floating overhead and through the room were golden ribbons of magic that wound between the candles and zipped around the silver sprites.

"Oh my God," Laura breathed out. "This is so much magic."

Even Duncan was impressed. "In all my years visiting the Shadowlands, I've never seen the like."

No one could mistake Harold's coronation party for anything but a massive show of sovereignty, wealth, and supernatural power.

Oblivious to the revelers, Cadell continued his lecture in Carys's mind. *If you're ever in a tricky situation when it comes to dancing, tell your prospective partner your next dance has been promised to either your cousin Dylan or me.*

Cadell was an obvious if reluctant choice, but her cousin? "Why Dylan?" *I'm pretty sure that Dylan hates me.*

Your cousins may not like your presence here, but they were both raised to think of the Cymric throne above their own self-interest. "Dylan never dances," Cadell said aloud. "So he'll always be available. He's also smart. If you walk up to him and say you're ready for a promised dance, he will not blink."

Sounds like someone who might be suitable as a king.

"Hmm." The dragon made a rumbling sound at the base of his throat.

That's your "I have thoughts but I'm not sharing them" sound.

Now is not the time.

They got caught in the crowd, and Carys looked back at Laura. "I'm getting the rundown of coronation protocol from the tall one."

Laura grimaced. "Does anyone think to—I don't know—have

this talk with you a couple of days *before* the super-important event instead of right as you're walking in?"

"This is what I'm saying," Carys said to Cadell. "No preparation time."

Cadell pursed his lips and said nothing.

"Useless," Duncan said.

Carys raised her eyebrows. "Preparation is useless?"

"You'd forget half of it because your brain wouldn't be focused by panic," Duncan said as his green eyes scanned the crowd. "Then the dragon would have to remind you right before the event anyway."

Carys glared at him. "I don't need you to be correct and insulting at the same time."

Duncan shrugged one massive shoulder. "Am I wrong?"

"Maybe," she muttered. "Where's the food?"

Between being sewn into their dresses, hair braiding with numerous extensions, and last-minute dancing-in-heavy-velvet lessons, Carys and Laura hadn't eaten anything since that afternoon.

"They'll serve it when we sit down. I see our table." Cadell came to a halt so quickly he nearly yanked Carys's shoulder from the socket.

The dragon cursed under his breath in very rapid Cymric.

"What?" Carys's heart leaped, and she reached for the dagger that usually sat at her waist except she was in a velvet gown and no weapons were allowed at the coronation ball.

Cadell, what it is?

We have been seated directly between Godrik's wolves and a contingent of fae from Éire.

Okay, who did we piss off?

"I have no idea, but we will tread softly," he said quietly as he ushered Carys toward their table. "Laura?"

"What's up, dragon butt?"

Cadell blinked and froze before he slowly turned to face Laura.

Carys barely kept from bursting into laughter. Duncan didn't even try.

"Fuck me." The blacksmith snorted. "His face, Laura."

"What?" Laura's cheeks were red as she stared at Cadell. "You need something?"

"We are…" The dragon seemed to struggle to collect his thoughts. "We're sitting between traditionally antagonistic parties. Whether by accident or design, I have no idea, but tonight would be an excellent night for you and Carys to play up your foreignness and be intriguing."

"Keep them too curious about the weird Americans to snipe at each other?" Laura nodded. "Can do."

"What about me?" Duncan said. "What can I do to help?"

Cadell frowned. "Nothing. You're a mundane Brightkin. They might question why you're here, but no one will be interested in you."

Duncan crossed his arms over his chest. "Say it again when I have steel in my hand."

"I will." Cadell started walking again, keeping Carys's wrist gripped in his massive hand as he weaved them through the crowd.

"That dragon is so damn irritating," Duncan muttered.

"If it helps," Carys said. "I don't think you're mundane."

The corner of Duncan's mouth twitched. "I appreciate that."

"Except in the magical sense. Then Cadell is actually correct."

"Mundane?" Duncan pulled Laura's hand from his arm and deftly switched Laura and Carys's positions, leaving Cadell gripping Laura's hand while Duncan pulled them toward the dancers. "Say that again when we're dancing, Carys Morgan."

CARYS TRIED TO STOP IT, but before she could say a word, she was pulled into a stately waltz with Duncan holding her close as they moved in time with the music.

"Duncan." She tried to be stern, but her heart leaped when he wrapped his arm around her and took the lead.

"What?" He winked at her. "The old scaly one giving you that lecture about how dancing makes a statement?"

"Yes, and he's not wrong." She tried not to get distracted by the shadow of his beard where it cut along his sharp jawline. "I'm... I mean, we're not—"

"We're not what?" Duncan pulled her close and slid his hand to the small of her back, slowing his steps as the music's tempo dropped, and the energy around the room went from grand to intimate in a heartbeat.

The dance wasn't limited to male-and-female couples as Carys and Duncan were joined by pairs of men who appeared to be taking the opportunity to chat or even conduct business, women who whispered secrets or flirted as they passed from arm to arm, and various magical creatures of every race.

Unicorns and fae. Humans and even a few stoic wolves in uniform.

The sound of a woman's voice rose in a heartbreaking melody that had violins weeping and Carys melting in Duncan's arms.

"Carys?" Duncan held her close and leaned his head down to whisper in her ear. "We're not what?"

She tilted her head, and the scent of fresh pine and whiskey made her head swim. "I don't remember what I was going to say."

"Then don't say anything." His voice was soft. "Just dance with me, Professor Morgan."

Professor Morgan. How did the man make a title she'd heard a hundred times from a hundred different plaintive undergrads sound sexy?

She felt her body heat, and she didn't know if it was from the heavy velvet dress, the exertion from dancing, or the aching need Duncan was stirring in her belly. She should have been concentrating on the complicated political tapestry weaving itself around her, but all she wanted was for Duncan to secret her away to a hidden corner, feed her, and kiss her senseless.

"You look stunning tonight." Duncan moved effortlessly through the steps, guiding Carys even when she stumbled. "If I didn't say so when I first saw you, it was because I nearly swallowed my tongue at the sight of you."

Carys couldn't stop her smile. "What a truly graphic compliment."

"It's true. If I'd tried telling you just then, I'd have squeaked like a twelve-year-old whose balls just dropped."

A woman in pink who circled next to them gasped at Duncan's words.

The Scotsman only tipped his head. "Madam."

"My word," the woman murmured before her fae partner swung her away.

Carys bit her lip to keep from laughing, but that only made her snort. "You'd better stop or you'll cause a political incident."

His eyes twinkled. "Too blunt for you?"

"With lines like that, it's truly a wonder you're still single."

The music changed and Duncan pulled her close, leaning down to whisper into her ear. "Honey may not drip from my lips when I compliment you, but it'll drip from somewhere else if I can get you alone."

And now she couldn't talk. Heat rushed to her face, and her cheeks felt like a dragon was breathing on them.

"Fuck me, but I cannae wait to find out if your tits flush like your cheeks do when you're excited," Duncan continued. "Give me a chance to find out, and I promise you won't be worried about politics tomorrow."

The orchestra finished the song just as Duncan stretched out his arm and turned her in a circle. The crowd around them clapped politely, and partners bowed to each other, murmuring polite parting words as they drifted to a new partner or away from the dance floor.

Duncan Murray tucked Carys's arm into his own and guided her off the dance floor as if he hadn't just planted a dozen sexual fantasies in her mind. "We should find our seats." He scanned the crowd. "I tried to bring you a lunch tray earlier today, but the ladies' maids ran me off."

"I'm starving." For several things at that moment, but food seemed to be the safest to bring up. "And they do."

Duncan raised his eyebrows. "Do what? Chase off men trying to feed you?"

"No." She looked up at him with an innocent expression. "My tits do get flushed when I'm turned on. If you look down, you'll probably notice even in this light."

Duncan's jaw dropped.

And so did his eyes.

Carys saw him discreetly adjust himself as they walked through the crush of the crowd, and she didn't try to hide her smile.

Good.

At least if Carys was going to be turned on and uncomfortable all through dinner, Duncan would be too.

"That's why it's imperative for various shifter factions to police *themselves*." The fae woman spoke with an Éiren accent and a pointed tongue. She glanced at Cadell, who had positioned himself between her and Godrik, the North Wolf shifter. "Surely you must see the wisdom in that, Lord Dragon."

"And what of the fae?" Godrik spoke through a clenched jaw. "Do you not need *policing* of your own?" Godrik glanced at Carys. "Cadell's lady was not killed by a wolf." He looked at his mug of ale. "*Former* lady, of course. No offense intended, Lady Carys."

"None taken." Carys lifted a wine goblet to her lips and reminded herself to sneak in some better wine next time along with her coffee. "I like to think that my Shadowkin's spirit is still very alive in the world."

The fae woman, whose name was Ruda, examined Carys as if she were a bug under a microscope. "Surely you are not implying that

Princess Seren's death was anything but a tragic accident." She glanced at the head table where King Harold was leaning toward Dafydd. "Accidents happen."

What was she implying? Was King Edgar's death not an accident after all?

Say nothing.

She glanced across the table at Cadell. *I wasn't going to.*

Your eyes are the size of walnuts. Compose yourself.

"Ruda, how did you travel to Anglia?" Laura was quick to jump in and redirect the conversation. "We arrived by fae gate from the Brightlands, but I understand from the Kheta Inwe in my home country that fae often choose other ways of travel even though the gates seem like the quickest way to us."

Throughout the dinner, Ruda had conducted herself with obvious superiority, condescending to everyone but Cadell. She alternated between subtly insulting the wolves and openly insulting mundane humans in ways that she appeared to think the humans were too dull to perceive.

The fae woman's smile was indulgent. "We have magic that speeds our travel in much more elegant ways than the old gates. But your naivety is delightful."

Ruda wore her dark curly hair in a pixie cut that showed off the many richly jeweled rings she wore in each pointed ear. Her clothing reminded Carys of silken armor embroidered in a deep plum that brought out a rose flush in her light brown skin.

She was stunningly beautiful. And so patronizing it made Carys want to puke.

"Oh, that's great to hear." Laura's voice dripped with sarcasm. "I'd hate to think I brought grating sophistication to the party." Laura turned to Carys. "How embarrassing would that be?"

Ruda wore bright crystals in her hair and an air of glamour shared by the half-dozen fae on her end of the table. She and all the fae seemed oblivious to Laura's sarcasm.

Cadell cleared his throat and offered Ruda a stiff smile. "Laura is a trained mage in Pauwau Aki. She's remarkably talented at reading runes and connects with elemental magic."

Ruda smiled. "Then she's unusually talented for a Brightkin."

Carys was starting to see why the wolves hated the fae. The arrogance was on another level. Interacting with Dru and Naida hadn't prepared her for any of the fae party they'd met that night.

Godrik rose to his feet. "Lady Laura, would you honor me with a dance?"

Laura glanced at Cadell briefly before she smiled at Godrik. "I'd love that, but be aware that I'm not very familiar with many of the dances here in Briton, so I may step on your toes."

"Fortunately I'm wearing boots." Godrik held out his arm and Laura joined him.

"And Lady Carys" —Ruda offered Carys a coy smile— "what about you? Would you honor me with a dance?"

Cadell's eyes locked with hers. *Careful, Nêrys.*

Carys did a dozen quick calculations in her head, but she couldn't figure out if she should accept or not. *Should I refuse?*

She's a fae noble of equal station to you. You can refuse, but she will be rightfully insulted.

"I would be honored." Carys smiled brightly. "I'll offer the same warning though. I'm still learning the Anglian dances."

Another condescending smile. "I am an excellent leader."

Ruda held out her hand for Carys's and led her toward the crowded dance floor. As they walked, Carys glanced up and noticed that Queen Orla's eyes were fixed on them.

"My queen would like a word with the human indebted to the Crow Mother." Ruda's voice dropped to a low murmur as the music started and the dancers began to move. "But as she cannot dance this evening, she has sent me."

"I have no idea what you're talking about," Carys said. "I'm not in debt to anyone's mother." She didn't even want to admit she knew who the Crow Mother was to this fae woman whose hand gripped her fingers like cold iron.

"Don't play the fool." Ruda turned Carys to guide her backward through a double column of dancers. "We know what you are."

"I'm nêrys ddraig," Carys said. "Admittedly, it's an unusual situation, but the magic does what it wants, I guess."

"You feign ignorance of your blood? Fine." Ruda turned her and pulled her close, wrapping a long arm around Carys's waist as they waited in the middle of the column for the others to pass through. "Your secret is your business and has no bearing on the fae, but the queen must know if the Crow Mother has gained passage into the Brightlands."

"I honestly have no idea who you're talking about or where she might be." Carys's mind was spinning and she wanted to shout for Cadell, but she didn't want to miss what Ruda was saying. "Are you talking about someone from Pauwau Aki? Many people from my home country revere crow gods. I can ask Laura if you want—"

"Your lack of cooperation is not amusing." Ruda dropped her right arm, turned in a circle, and gripped Carys's hand again, tugging her close so they were face-to-face. "If you won't give Queen Orla a direct answer, she has other ways of finding the truth."

Carys dropped the innocent expression. "Then I suggest you tell your queen to find those other ways. I know about Regan. I know everything. And I have nothing to say to any of you."

There was a gold glow that lit Ruda's eyes for a dark moment, and then the music broke, the dancers clapped politely, and Ruda backed away.

"Lady Carys." She nodded slightly. "It appears that Seren's spirit is very much alive. I will be sure to let my queen know."

Carys smiled and felt a curl of anger unfurl in her belly. "You do that."

CHAPTER FOURTEEN

Cadell and Laura sat across from Carys in her bedroom the next day.

"The fae know what you are?" the dragon asked.

"They *say* they know what I am." Carys sipped her coffee and tried to calm her stomach. "*I* don't even know what I am, so they could say whatever they want and we don't really have any way of disproving it."

"The only one who may know the truth of your history and your magical abilities is your mother, who is dead." Cadell glanced at Laura. "We need to speak to someone in Epona's cult. Followers of the old gods sometimes have oral histories or records that—"

"I know we both want to find out what the hell I am and why we bonded, but that's probably not the main priority right now." Carys's belly rumbled and she groaned. "Why did I eat so much last night?"

Laura said, "Because the banquet lasted until three in the morning and there's only so much you can dance?"

The food the night before had been a parade of roasted meats and crispy fish, creamed roots and vegetables, a dozen different cheeses, and honeyed fruit served across a dozen different courses that had stretched through the evening. Each course had been served with a different wine, ale, or mead.

Forget her assumptions, Anglian food was amazing.

And Carys's stomach was in revolt.

Cadell's appetite clearly hadn't suffered. Earlier in the morning, he'd devoured the heap of venison sausage the maid brought and was currently picking at the bread as he finished his coffee.

Laura was nibbling on apples, but she was eating light.

"Coffee is it for me today." Carys set down her cup and rubbed her temples. "I ate enough to last an entire week. What time is the meeting?"

Cadell stared out the window, a frown fixed on his face. "Captain Wynnflad is arriving midmorning with Godrik, purportedly to consult on the market rebuilding project."

Cadell and Winnie had made their plans to meet the night before, passing messages to Godrik, Lachlan, and the rest of their secret alliance, but that was before Carys had gotten confirmation from Orla's spokes-fae that a plan was very definitely in the works.

"I know you think that my identity and the source of my magic is important—and it is to us—but right now I think Orla's scheming is the priority."

"Orla and Cian, you mean." Cadell nodded slowly.

Laura said, "From an outsider's perspective, the Éiren and the fae do have an opportunity if they want to take the advantage."

Cadell turned to her. "Explain."

"The islands of Briton have suffered a series of unexpected transitions," Laura said. "Seren was murdered, and the truth about her death—"

"Which obviously is still a secret to most people," Carys said, "but the royal houses all know what really happened."

"Exactly," Laura said. "That leaves Cymru without an heir right now."

"Yes." Cadell finished his coffee and set down his mug. "Then

King Edgar dies and there is a new king in Anglia, but his was an untimely death."

"Exactly," Laura said. "Harold is obviously building loyalty and trust with a government that his father put in place. They're not his people, so he has to focus on that."

Cadell added, "And there appears to be some debate about whether Lachlan or Rory should be high chief in Alba."

Carys blinked. "That's news to me."

The dragon nodded. "I heard several Anglian courtiers last night gossiping about Lachlan's *diplomatic* campaign. They seem to think the reason he's down here instead of his brother is to cement his position as heir."

"I didn't know that."

Did it change anything? Not if Lachlan was in Anglia to gain allies. Clearly that meant he wanted to be king.

"The islands of Briton are two small dots in a large ocean, but they hold four different kingdoms and millions of human and magical lives," Cadell said. "Tensions are always high, but the Queens' Pact holds the peace."

Laura said, "But if Orla and Cian are looking to disrupt that peace, now might be the time they would try."

"Agreed." Carys picked at a pear, but the thought of eating anything was too much. "My identity" *—and my love life—* "is not the priority. We should do everything we can to figure out what the Éirens and the fae are planning."

Cadell stood. "I'm going to the library. Your uncle agreed that meeting in the hall might attract too many eyes. Fae spies are everywhere."

MEETING in the hall might not have been the best course of action, but Dafydd's library was not the cavernous chamber Carys had found in the Alban castle. By the time two large Scottish men, a seven-foot dragon, and a wolf shifter the size of a small shed joined Carys and Laura, the library felt more than a little bit crowded.

Godrik glanced at Carys with suspicion. "Anwyn and Dylan are not here? Does that mean the Cymric heir has been—"

"It means that my uncle has other tasks for them and would prefer to keep them out of this for now." Carys spoke quickly. "Please do not assume anything else."

Godrik grunted and lowered himself into an upholstered leather chair that groaned as he sat. "My father and Harold are worried. Did Winnie tell you?"

Cadell said, "She told us a little bit. Why are the old fae gates such a concern?"

"Because that's how they move." Godrik's voice rumbled. "They may use magic now—secretive twats—but the old gates? The old magic? It's still there. They used them in Éire when Cian slaughtered the wolf clans there. What's to say that they won't use them in Anglia for the same thing?"

"Do you think that's what they want?" Carys asked. "You think the fae want to kill off the North Wolves in Anglia like they did in Éire?"

Godrik shrugged. "I hear your skepticism, but the wolves are the backbone and magical defense of Anglia. If we're taken out, Harold and his entire country are weaker."

"Why do the fae hate the North Wolves so much?" Laura asked. "Forgive my ignorance, but I don't know your stories, and I feel like that might be important."

Godrik scooted forward. "There is no apology needed. Our stories are our own. Wolves are not native to Briton. At least, not magical ones. We came with the Anglians when they crossed the sea and invaded over a thousand years ago."

Laura nodded slowly. "So the fae are native to Briton, and they see you as invaders?"

"Fae are everywhere," Duncan said. "They take different forms, but they're everywhere. They spread across the Shadowlands after the old gods went quiet, so they can't judge the wolves for migrating."

The library door opened, and Captain Wynnflad joined them. "Sorry I'm late." She looked at Godrik. "It's not the migration."

"It's the magic," Godrik said. "The wolves are resistant to fae magic."

"As are other magical races," Laura said. "But the fae don't seem to antagonize them as much."

"It's prejudice," Lachlan said bluntly. "Old-fashioned prejudice. Most fae of the Temris Court—the high fae, not the wild—see North Wolves as less than the other magical races."

Cadell looked at Laura. "I've heard fae say that wolf minds are more animalistic—"

Godrik growled.

"An insult and an excuse," Cadell continued. "Obviously. But they see the wolves as less, yet they can resist fae influence more easily than humans."

"They can't control us," Godrik said. "And we tend to settle arguments with tactics they find distasteful."

Laura looked around the room. "Which are?"

"Trial by combat is popular when we have conflicts."

Lachlan said, "Yet historically, most fae kings or queens were chosen via challenge, so I've always found that ironic."

Godrik humphed. "Blood prices are acceptable among our own if someone is injured or killed." He shrugged. "We keep to the old laws. But that's only among ourselves. With other races, we abide by the king's law."

North Wolves love war. A unicorn had told Carys that once, but to her, it sounded more like the wolves of Briton kept to an older code that was definitely brutal but she couldn't classify as warlike. Not exactly.

"So the fae hate the wolves and the wolves hate the fae," Laura said. "And the humans?"

"The Anglian throne has always allied with the North Wolves,"

Godrik said. "We conquered Anglia together and staked out our territories. We have always supported the Anglian throne and always will. But Edgar was…" Godrik's expression looked like he'd smelled something nasty.

Winnie jumped in. "My uncle was less allied to the wolves than his mother was. He was fascinated by Queen Orla and had quietly campaigned to marry one of her daughters." She nodded at Carys. "Your aunt actually. He wanted the connection to Orla and Cian, but Eamer preferred Dafydd."

"Any hard feelings there?" Carys asked.

"Not really," Winnie said. "It wasn't a matter of affection. And it didn't matter to Edgar—he still increased the number of fae courtiers in his council and started handing out favors to Orla and Cian's people."

Lachlan said, "My father and I believe that Orla saw an opportunity with Edgar. And as he grew older, she became more determined to cement fae influence in Anglia. And from the Éiren perspective, there *are* better trade routes to the continent via Anglia, especially now that the Frisians have spells that control the leviathans in the Channel."

"She was building a land bridge," Carys said. "Between Éire and the rest of Briton."

"She was," Winnie said. "But Seren discovered what she was doing."

"So they killed her." Lachlan's voice was rough. He glanced at Carys. "Or Regan did. Maybe Orla and Cian have decided that reviving the old gates is easier than a land bridge."

"But why?" Carys asked. "What does Queen Orla want? Money? Territory? Just pure power?"

"The fae draw their power from the land," Lachlan said. "If they control more land, they have more power."

"I know I'm not an expert here," Laura said. "But as someone who is trained in elemental magic and is new here, I can tell you that this place" —she held her hands out— "Anglia. London. Everything in the magic around here feels very... off."

Godrik frowned. "What do you mean?"

"You're magical creatures, but you live here." Laura looked at Cadell and Godrik. "If this imbalance has been happening for a while, you might not have sensed it. But the magic here is restless. It's..." Her entire body shivered. "It's very hard to explain, but there is a lot of tension. Almost like a fault line before an earthquake if that makes sense."

"I believe you," Godrik said, "but what does that mean for us? For the wolves?" He glanced at Winnie, then at Lachlan. "For all of Briton?"

"Briton doesn't have earthquakes." Duncan, who'd been silent for most of the conversation, finally spoke. "But now Orla and Cian are reaching for more power. The magic is unsettled. The thrones are in play." He looked at Carys, then at Lachlan. "I'm just saying that there is more than one kind of earthquake, and there might be one brewing in Anglia."

"We have to figure out what Orla wants," Carys said. "And what this offering to the Crow Mother might be."

GODRIK AND WINNIE couldn't stay all afternoon, not without tongues wagging, so they departed only an hour after the meeting had started.

Duncan grumbled something about finding Angus before he left the library, and Cadell and Laura went to gather some of the wood and herbs she would need to perform magic, leaving Carys alone with Lachlan in the cozy library where a fire was burning and Carys was surrounded by books.

She crossed her legs in the massive chair and stared at the fire.

"You're in your happy place," Lachlan said.

Carys blinked. "My happy place?"

Lachlan looked around the room. "Fire. Books. Comfortable chair. If I grabbed some tea and a blanket, you'd never leave."

She smiled. "You know me."

"Aye, I do." He stretched out his legs and set them on the low table in front of the fire. "I missed you last night, but you looked like you were having fun."

"I've never danced with that many women before. I was a little worried about stepping on toes that weren't covered in big heavy boots."

Lachlan's eyes twinkled. "I don't know. Godrik's sister had boots on, I'm sure of it."

"I believe she did." She leaned back in the chair and watched him. The room was dim, and most of the light came from the fire and the narrow windows that illuminated the old library. "There are rumors swirling that you came down to Anglia to cement your position as the Alban heir to the throne."

Lachlan's eyes didn't move from the fire. "I came to Anglia to see you."

"And attend Harold's coronation."

"Yes. We grew up together."

"And cement your position?"

He frowned. "It's not... a single thing, Carys. Nothing in my life is ever wholly for one reason or another. There are layers to everything I have to do. The one time that I did exactly what I wanted and only what I wanted was when I left the Shadowlands to find you." He blinked and finally looked at her. "And obviously that didn't turn out the way I expected either."

She took a deep breath and let it out slowly. "So your brother Rory is angling for the throne."

"Yes, he is." Lachlan leaned toward the fire. "I have a feeling he knew what Seren's and my plans were when we married. He's a bright boy, and he grew up in Dafydd's court. It's very possible he knew our plan was to hand the Alban throne to him when my father died, and even after Seren was killed, he decided he wanted it."

"And you don't want to hand it over anymore?"

He looked into her eyes. "Do you love me?"

Carys blinked. "I loved you very much, and you know that."

"But do you love me now? You are nêrys ddraig, but obviously you and Cadell have made things work in California. You have a life there. You're not going to take the Cymric throne; I don't care what Dafydd's dreams are."

"You've got that right."

"So do you love me, Carys? Do you want me?" He leaned forward. "You say the word and I hand it to Rory. When my father dies, I'll give him the throne. I'll move back to California and leave all this."

"And you wouldn't miss it? You wouldn't feel like you were abandoning your responsibilities?"

A muscle under Lachlan's eye twitched, but he said nothing.

Carys leaned toward him. "It's not a simple thing. You said it yourself. Nothing you do is ever only for one reason. And Lachlan, I respect that. I maybe..." She laughed a little bit. "I maybe respect you more than I did before, because I see you stepping into that role. I see you sacrificing your own wishes to do what you think is right and necessary for the people you might rule."

"You respect me," he said quietly. "But do you love me?"

She blinked back tears. "I don't know anymore."

"That's fair," he whispered. "I don't expect things to be the way they were. They can't be." His forehead wrinkled in thought. "And I see the way you look at Duncan. I see the way he looks at you." Lachlan closed his eyes. "He's a good man, Carys. He would... he would do anything for you. He could be anyone for you. Anyone you needed him to be."

She sniffed. "I don't want anyone to be anything other than themselves. I don't want you to change yourself for me. I don't want Duncan to either."

Lachlan leaned back, and his eyes smiled at her with a wisdom that made Carys feel young and foolish. "But that is life, mo chridhe.

We all grow and change. We all have to bend. Only children expect the world to revolve around their wishes.”

“I don't expect the world to revolve around my wishes, but I want to find my own path. I need to find my own path.”

Lachlan's eyes were warm and glowing. “When you find it—because you will—you let me know if you want my company walking with you.”

CARYS STARED at the wood beyond the meadows where black-faced sheep were grazing.

The magic of the Shadowlands was unsettled. There was tension. She was too new to magic to have felt it, but Laura had perceived it immediately.

Like a fault line before a quake.

Night on the river with the Crow Mother lurking in the trees and the river fae putting on a show. Riddles spoken between a fae exile and a triple-faced sorceress with power that even Queen Orla had to appease.

An offering.

Carys tried to piece together what Orla could offer a powerful fae like the Crow Mother that she couldn't simply take for herself.

None of this made sense. The Queens' Pact had kept Briton at peace for centuries. The agreement, forged centuries before, demanded that royal children be fostered in foreign courts to secure the peace of the islands. It wasn't always agreeable to rulers, but it had been successful for generations.

Briton's people were thriving, and their rulers cooperated. Unlike empires in the Brightlands, the magic of this placed kept human ambition in check. It kept human empires in check.

The fae ruled over humans; they were at the top of the food chain. They controlled the gates. They controlled everything in the Shadowlands.

"Are you the reason the river folk are singing a kingsong and the serpent has risen from the deep? Won't Cian be pleased?"

"You let me worry about Cian and don't bother yourself with mortal matters, old one."

"Old one," Carys whispered.

Carys flashed back to her memories of the Crow Mother in the woods. To the moment when Dru arrived and they spoke in riddles before the Crow Mother changed her appearance and disappeared.

She'd shown them three faces. The mature, vital woman Carys had bargained with, but two others flashed quickly in the shadows. A dark-eyed maiden. A bent old woman.

Carys blinked.

No.

Oh no.

Cadell. She called out in her mind, hoping the dragon was near.

Nêrys?

Can you come to my room?

He didn't answer, but a few minutes later, she heard a knock on her door.

Cadell was standing in the doorway, towering over her with a grim expression on his face. "What is it? What is wrong?"

She pulled him inside. "How many faces can fae take?"

Cadell frowned. "What do you mean?"

"Humans have one face. I mean physically, we have one face." She pointed to her own. "Shifters have two, obviously. Your beast and your human face."

"Yes." Cadell nodded as if she was a rambling child. "And the fae have one face. Like humans."

"One face." She let out a breath. "And their glamour?"

Cadell shrugged. "It *changes* their face in subtle ways. It can make them more attractive or more foul, but it's still the same face."

"So who has three faces?" Carys leaned toward him and dropped her voice. "Who has three aspects? Three completely different forms?"

Cadell blinked. "Gods."

"Yes." She nodded. "The gods. Duncan and Lachlan thought Angus was a fae, but he's not. Clearly he's not. He can handle iron."

"But he presents himself as fae," Cadell said cautiously. "And you think—"

"The Crow Mother is not fae," Carys said. "She's some kind of god, some kind of deity with a triple aspect. There are any number of possibilities, but the fact remains that I traded passage to the Brightlands not to a fae who is going to lose her power there but to a god who could be just as powerful in the Brightlands as the Shadowlands."

Cadell's face went blank. "The magic is unsettled."

"Maybe the magic is unsettled because an actual *god* has left the Shadowlands."

He frowned. "What does this have to do with Orla and Cian?"

"I have no idea." She gritted her teeth. "None. But I tell you one thing, we need to get some fae perspective on this. We need to know what kind of offering a god might want from a fae. Because that might be what all this is about."

"Fae perspective?" Cadell crossed his arms. "We're trying to stop a fae war. What kind of fae can we trust?"

"I don't know. Maybe one who doesn't want war."

CHAPTER FIFTEEN

At midday the day after Harold's coronation, Carys waited on the edge of Hyde Forest. She had whispered her request into the roots of an old yew tree with daffodils growing at the base.

Dewch ataf fi, Naida.

In all honesty, Carys had no idea if the ellyllon would hear her. She didn't have Dru's power, but she was hoping a tree that was so clearly fae-touched might carry her message.

Carys.

I'm here. Cadell had wanted to come with her, but she'd refused the offer.

You are asking another favor of a fae, the dragon said. *This is unwise.*

I'm asking a favor of Naida. She's not like other fae.

Ellyllon will still expect something in payment.

Carys knew that. She also knew that of all the fae she could go to for answers, Naida was the one who had helped her when she needed it.

Carys waited, sitting on a large stone a little ways away from the yew. She was starting to get nervous about dusk and the wolves in the forest when she heard a quiet voice singing through the trees.

"Write me a poem of heather and firth, where forest
touches night and night becomes earth..."

Carys stood and walked back toward the clearing where the yew tree lived.

Naida sat at the base of the yew, and the tree's roots reached up and curled around her like a cat searching for attention.

The small fae woman ran her palm along the old roots and looked at Carys. "You called for me, Nêrys Ddraig?"

"I appreciate that you came." She was making a gamble talking to Naida, but there were multiple reasons for that gamble, and her power was only one of them. "How is Dru?"

Naida waved a hand. "He's long healed."

And yet the fae mound in front of Dafydd's house where Dru and Naida had disappeared was still there.

And still blooming flowers.

Carys waited, but Naida didn't elaborate. "So I met some of Orla's people last night at Harold's coronation."

Naida's eyebrows went up. "Is that so?"

"They acted like they knew who I was."

The fae woman smiled. "I think everyone in Briton knows who you are, Carys. Brightkin of a dead princess. A human from the other side who bonded with a dragon. There's only one like you."

"Is there?" Carys walked over and sat in the grass in front of Naida. "Lachlan crossed the gates. Others have too."

Naida leaned forward. "You wonder about your parents?"

"I know my father was Brightkin because Dafydd is here. But what about my mother?"

"What about her?" Naida narrowed her eyes. "Nothing is born here but by magic, Carys Morgan. Shadowkin cannot bear children, not even if they travel to the Brightlands."

"Are you sure of that?"

Naida shrugged. "Are we ever truly sure of anything?"

"I'm sure that Orla is plotting something with Cian," Carys said. "Something about the old fae gates here in Anglia."

Naida reared back, resting her head against the yew. "Is she?"

This was a risk. Cadell wasn't convinced the ellyllon wouldn't align with the high fae in Éire. But Carys thought it was worth taking a chance. And if Naida ended up spilling Carys's secrets to Orla, would it be anything the Éiren queen didn't already know?

"The ellyllon keep their own company," Carys continued. "You are known to be solitary. Nonpolitical."

Naida looked up into the trees. "We don't like politics and we tend to the wild. That puts us at odds with our brethren sometimes. What are you asking of me? I do not speak for anyone but myself."

"I wouldn't ask you to." Carys scooted toward Naida. "You know who came after me in Alba, right?"

Naida's blue eyes were as bright and swift as a jay's. "I know what really happened to your Shadowkin." She lowered her voice. "Who *really* killed her."

"Aisling might have poisoned Seren, but it was Regan pulling the strings. And Orla's plans didn't die with her daughter."

Naida looked at the roots of the yew tree that cradled her. Then she pushed herself to her feet and began to move away. "Walk with me."

Carys stood and caught up with Naida, passed out from the shadows of the trees and into the grazing land on the edge of Dafydd's property.

"The trees listen and gossip like the elders they are." Naida looked at Carys. "What are you asking me?"

"Orla and Cian are planning something, and the Crow Mother is involved somehow. Either way, Dafydd and Harold are convinced that Orla is willing to break the Queens' Pact. They want more power."

"That sounds terrible." Naida was speaking the truth. Her

expression was grim. "Truly, that would be… terrible. Cian is powerful enough."

"So help us try to stop them."

"And what would you give me in return?"

Carys sighed. "I don't know."

Naida stared at the forest. "Tell me, who is *us*?"

"A company of seven—magical and human—who value peace." Carys held out her hand. "I think you value peace too. We have humans, dragons, wolves. But no fae. And I think that's a mistake."

She smiled. "You think I can be trusted?"

"You're ellyllon."

"Ah." Naida smiled, and her dimples popped out. "We're little wild fae, aren't we? Sweet and harmless. Not a threat to anyone. Not *ambitious* like the others."

"I don't think you're harmless in the least," Carys clarified. "But I do think you love peace. Am I right?"

Naida looked into the distance. "All wild fae value peace. We just want to live our lives and take care of the land."

"So help us. And I will owe you a favor."

"That is very vague, Carys Morgan."

"It's the best I can do right now."

"I might consider it, but not by myself."

She frowned. "I told you, there are seven of us who—"

"And if I joined you, it would be eight." Naida shook her head. "Eight is an unlucky number. The old gods wouldn't be happy."

Carys and Cadell. Lachlan and Duncan. Laura and Winnie and Godrik. She couldn't think of anyone who could drop out and not be missed. "Is eight really that bad?"

Naida grimaced. "Oh yes."

Carys hadn't thought about eight being unlucky, but maybe for the fae of Briton it was. If they were in Asia, eight would be the perfect number. Either way, she'd learned to be cautious around unfamiliar magic.

"But nine," Naida continued. "Nine is *very* lucky."

"Absolutely not." Lachlan was adamant. "We're trying to avoid a war, not start one."

"Do you have any idea who he really is?" Duncan's voice was a thunderstorm. "Do you have any idea—"

"Yes!" Carys put a hand on Duncan's shoulder, which was positively vibrating. "I know. Or I know what Naida told me."

Carys and Laura were in the kitchen garden outside Dafydd's house the following morning, and Carys was cutting rosemary because she couldn't stop thinking about the smell. Duncan's soap smelled like rosemary.

Lachlan was as worried as Duncan was even if he wasn't as explosive. "It's not that I don't have an... affection for Dru, but you have to know that bringing him in adds a layer of fae politics to this matter that we were hoping to avoid."

Laura sat back on her heels and squinted up at the two men. "But fae politics is at the heart of all this. I'll bet you some of Carys's coffee that's exactly where the smoke takes me when I do this ceremony."

Laura had agreed to do a reading from her rune stones and was cutting sage for the cleansing ceremony while Cadell was at the international market downriver, searching for tobacco and sweetgrass. Laura had already gathered cedar from Dafydd's woods.

"Cian is the closest thing to a fae king that there is in Briton." Duncan sat on a low brick wall that bordered the kitchen garden beds. "And he's the consort to the Éiren throne. He's been building his power for over a century now, and he *will* go to war to keep Dru from taking his crown."

Lachlan was pacing. "Whatever Orla may be up to, the last thing anyone in Briton wants is to spark a fae civil war. The last one killed half the human population of Briton."

Laura blinked. "Seriously?"

Lachlan nodded. "Seriously."

"But according to Naida, Dru doesn't *want* the crown," Carys said. "And he's not here to take it."

"No, he's here because he's in love with Naida," Duncan said. "But that doesn't mean Cian will see it that way, particularly if Dru's presence becomes known more widely."

"He needs to go back." Duncan looked at his brother. "I'll tell him. It was foolish of me to ask him to come. If I had known—"

"You can do that," Carys said. "But if you do, any help from Naida is out. She says we need him if we want to counter whatever Orla and Cian are planning."

"Of course Naida says that," Lachlan paused in his pacing and glared. "She's in love with him as much as he's in love with her. *And* she feels guilty because she's the reason the fae of Briton have no king but an Éiren consort more concerned with his power than his people."

Laura stood up and stuffed her herbs in the wicker basket she was carrying. "Okay, maybe all of you have this backstory, but I do not. Explain or I'm out."

Lachlan looked at Duncan, and some wordless communication passed between them before Duncan shrugged and started talking.

"Cian and Dru—Diarmuid is his proper name—are brothers, the children of the light fae Queen Aine who ruled over all the fae of Briton for centuries," Duncan said. "She was the one who returned the fae to peace after their last war."

Lachlan continued, "Aine had two sons. Cian was the oldest and the son of the old god Elatha, who came from the Fomorians."

"In Irish mythology, Fomorians are kind of…" Carys squinted. "Not gods but god adjacent if that makes sense."

"The Fomorians were monsters," Lachlan said. "But Aine took a step toward peace when she had a child with Elatha, who was seen as one of the more… peaceful of the Fomorians."

Duncan said, "And Cian was raised as Aine's heir until the queen fell in love with Lir."

"The sea god?" Carys asked. "So Aine married Lir after being Elatha's lover?"

"Aine never married either of them," Lachlan said. "The old gods never stay in one place long enough to rule anything. They keep to their own faithful, and they honestly don't have followers here the way they used to. When was the last time you saw fires lit for Lugh at daybreak or grain offerings to Cernunnos?"

Duncan said, "Most humans in the Shadowlands know that magic exists, but they're also modern people. They honor the Tamis because it's tradition, but they don't think much of the old gods anymore. That's why their power has waned."

"Other than a few cults like Epona or Sulis, they're not really worshipped anymore."

"Followers like Epona's daughters." Carys looked at Laura. "We think my mother's Shadowkin might have belonged to Epona's cult." Or actually her mother. But Carys wasn't saying that out loud yet.

"So Aine falls in love with Lir," Duncan continued, "and from all accounts, Lir loves Aine equally. Dru is Lir's son, and he immediately became his mother's favorite."

"Ah." Laura nodded. "Suddenly it's not so clear who will become the next fae ruler."

Duncan pointed at her. "Exactly."

Carys stood and put her rosemary into Laura's basket. "Where does Naida come into all this?"

Duncan continued with the story. "Aine becomes tired of the throne, and according to fae stories, she goes to the sea to live with Lir, leaving her sons to rule the fae of Éire and Briton. The dark fae will remain the keepers of the fae gates while the light fae remain in power in Temris, ruling the courts, the wild fae and interacting with the other races."

Lachlan took up the narrative. "The two brothers agree that since Cian is the eldest, he will marry Orla, officially uniting the fae and the Éiren royal houses."

Duncan said, "And Cian will pluck the finest soul placed at the gate to be Orla's daughter, and eventually that daughter would become Dru's wife."

"Oh, that is so messed up," Carys muttered. "Can you imagine picking your own sister-in-law and raising her as your daughter before you hand her over to your brother?"

"Who you don't really like much," Duncan added.

Laura asked, "And Dru was okay with this?"

"Dru isn't ambitious," Duncan said.

"It sounds like it was a compromise," Carys said. "One they could both live with."

"Exactly." Duncan looked directly at Lachlan. "Most political marriages are."

Lachlan ignored his brother's pointed look. "And remember, fae don't have morals the way humans do."

"That is very clear," Laura whispered.

"Orla is well over a hundred years old," Lachlan said. "Her Brightkin is long dead, but she still looks like a thirty-year-old woman. But she *is* mortal. Eventually Orla will die, but as long as Dru married her daughter, her line would continue."

"Which daughter?" Carys asked. One of Orla's daughters was married to King Dafydd. "I mean, Eamer looks good for her age, but she's definitely older than thirty."

"Finola is Orla's eldest daughter. She's the heir to the throne, and she's the one Dru was supposed to marry," Duncan said. "Except..."

"Naida." Lachlan shrugged.

"Dru was supposed to marry Finola, but he fell in love with Naida?" Laura shook her head. "So messy. Can you imagine if they made this into a reality show, Carys? *The Unreal Housewives of the Light Fae Court?*"

"Naida is ellyllon." Lachlan got the discussion back on track. "They're elder fae. Not a touch of Fomorian blood. They're respected but seen as weaker. The high fae would never accept a prince marrying an ellyllon and messing up Cian and Orla's carefully built power structure."

"So instead of marrying Finola for political reasons," Duncan said, "Dru left. He told his brother to fuck off and left for the Brightlands."

"And Naida didn't go with him?" Laura asked.

Lachlan shook his head. "Naida will never live in the Brightlands. Her people are doubly sensitive to iron. She'd wither and die there."

Duncan said, "But Dru was determined. If he couldn't have Naida, he didn't want anything to do with any of them."

Lachlan said, "So Finola married another fae consort so she wouldn't age, but rumors say she's still bitter about the whole thing."

"And now Naida is saying that Dru has to be a part of" —Duncan waved his hands— "whatever it is we're doing to keep the peace in Briton and keep the Queens' Pact alive."

"Except Dru being involved is more likely to disrupt the peace." Laura wrinkled her nose. "I have to say I'm seeing their point, Carys."

Lachlan turned sad eyes on Carys. "It's not that we don't sympathize," he said. "I know what it's like to feel like your relationship is doomed, but Carys..."

Carys crossed her arms over her chest. "What?"

"It really *is* doomed." Lachlan kept his voice low.

"If Dru claims the crown," Duncan said, "which Cian knows he *could* do, there would be war among the fae. The reason Dru left for the Brightlands was because he wanted to avoid that."

"Would Dru be a better fae ruler than Cian?" Carys looked between Duncan and Lachlan.

Lachlan nodded. "Probably."

"But is Cian so bad that it's worth starting a war?" Duncan shrugged. "That's the real question."

"Agreed," Lachlan said. "Having Dru helping us will make Cian think that the humans of Briton are siding with Dru against him."

"Whatever he and Orla might be planning, it would jump-start it, not stop it," Duncan said.

Lachlan continued, "We *must* leave Dru out of this if we're trying for peace."

Carys felt her cheeks heating. "But Naida won't help us without Dru."

"So we leave Naida out of it," Lachlan said. "We don't need her."

"What other fae do you trust?" Carys looked at Duncan.

Duncan shook his head. "No one."

She looked at Lachlan. "You?"

He folded his arms over his chest. "I don't trust *Dru*, and I don't know why you would."

"I don't trust him," Carys said. "But I trust Naida, and Naida wants him. That's the point."

Laura frowned. "Are the fae that devious here? I'm suddenly feeling very thankful for the Kheta Inwe."

"You two think we can actually find out what is going on with Orla and Cian without any fae help?" Carys looked between the two men again. "We don't think the way they do. We don't understand their magic and the extent of it. If we want to know what the fae are planning, we need to know what they want, what they can do, and what this offering to the Crow Mother might be."

Lachlan sighed. "Fine. We need fae knowledge. But not Naida and Dru."

Laura nodded. "Okay, so who do you two suggest?"

Neither Duncan nor Lachlan spoke.

"Helpful," Laura said. "So helpful. That's amazing."

Carys grimaced and grabbed the basket from Laura's hands. "Naida is the only fae that either Cadell or I trust." She and Laura started toward the kitchen. "And Naida wants Dru to help. If you two brilliant strategists come up with a better idea, feel free to let us know."

Laura cleared a space in the center of Dafydd's garden after Cadell returned, burning the four sacred herbs in an earthenware bowl placed on the bare ground. She wafted the smoke over stones etched with ancient symbols from various parts of North America.

The song Laura sang was in Yurok, but the symbols on the runes were used across the Pacific Northwest. The scent of tobacco, sage, sweetgrass, and cedar were all familiar; however, the song Laura sang under her breath was not for Carys's ears, so she tried to keep her distance.

Cadell stood at Carys's shoulder in human form. "What is she doing?"

"I suspect she's trying to connect with the magic here."

Laura held the stones in one hand and dug her hands into the earth with the other.

Cadell frowned. "She is Brightkin."

"She is." Carys nodded. "But she has a formal role in Pauwau Aki, which means she has trained in magic. It's not as powerful as her Shadowkin's magic, but she can connect."

"Maybe that's part of your magic as well," Cadell said. "You were raised in a place where the border between the two worlds is more permeable."

Carys nodded. "Maybe. I hadn't thought of that."

Laura's voice rose, and her face lit with a bright smile. She leaned down and spoke to the ground she was sitting on, pressing her forehead to the earth.

"She's a striking woman," Cadell said.

You can say she's beautiful. Carys spoke to his mind. *She's my best friend, but you're my dragon.*

"*Beautiful* is far too common a word to use for her." Cadell kept his eyes on Laura.

Laura gently tossed the stones on the ground, then took the bowl where her herbs were burning and blew gently, coaxing more smoke from them as she murmured over her stones and the earth.

Carys saw the stones begin to move slowly, rolling over the

ground and rearranging themselves in a distinct pattern. Laura watched them and glanced between the stones and the smoke.

After a few moments, she stood and looked at Carys and Cadell. "We need to follow the smoke."

Laura left her stones on the ground and picked up the earthen bowl, carrying it in front of her and singing under her breath.

The smoke rose and lifted into the air, seemingly impervious to the gusts of wind that moved the trees as they walked through the back garden, through the kitchen garden, and around the side of the house.

Carys tried not to wince as she watched Laura's bare feet sink into the cold, sticky mud on the edge of the garden.

"Her feet must be freezing," Cadell said. "I will make sure warming blankets are gathered after her ritual."

They walked toward the courtyard where soldiers were drilling and dragons rested in beast form like a fleet of fighter jets waiting for orders.

Cadell and Carys followed at a short distance, and Carys kept her eyes on Laura, whose eyes were locked on the smoke that traveled through the wind.

As they entered the courtyard, Cadell barked something in Cymric and the soldiers who'd been drilling scattered.

There was a low thrumming sound as the dragons surrounding the house tuned into the energy floating through the air. Carys had heard the sound a few times before, most notably when Cadell was greeted by the dragons from the Chahta nation who had come to help train her in California.

Dragon vocalizations weren't often the roar they emitted when they were angry or belching fire. There was a deep vibrating noise they made when they recognized each other that nearly sounded like a large feline purr.

If your cat was a terrifying aerial raptor with a wingspan nearly as large as a jumbo jet.

Cadell was in human form, but clearly the dragons in the courtyard understood what he was saying because they rose on their back legs and spread their wings, blocking some of the wind as their keen golden eyes detected the magic and the smoke.

The air around Carys grew still and the smoke curled upward, spinning in the familiar glyph of an intricate spiral as it gathered over the fae mound where Naida had taken Dru to heal. The smoke spun and twisted, circling and circling until it broke into the familiar Celtic triple spiral that Carys had seen on megalithic structures as old as any in Briton.

The glyph formed over the mound, glowing in the fading, pearlescent light and circling gently over the fairy hill that grew thick with grass before her eyes.

The thrumming sound from the dragons grew louder, and beyond the courtyard, Carys saw Duncan and Lachlan run out of the stables, jolting to a dead stop when they saw the triple spiral hanging over the fae mound.

Laura lowered the bowl with the burning herbs and walked toward Carys and Cadell. "I asked the magic in this place to show me the key to bringing things back into balance." She lifted an open hand. "And this is where the smoke led."

Cadell nodded. "Then the earth has answered."

Carys watched the slowly turning triple spiral that showed no signs of drifting or dissolving even while the wind picked up. "I'm going to have to agree with the dragon."

Laura turned and faced Duncan and Lachlan on the far side of the fae mound. "I know you two may not like this answer, but I think it's pretty clear that whatever it is we need to do to keep the peace here, Dru and Naida are going to be a part of it."

CHAPTER SIXTEEN

Godrik glared at the small fae woman and the willowy man with the bright blue sigils on his face. "I don't like this."

Dru, for his part, seemed unbothered. "Of course you don't. My brother is the one who slaughtered the wolves of Ireland, and ancestral memory runs deep."

"Dru has done nothing to you or your people," Naida said. "Do you want us to examine the old fort or not?"

Carys, Duncan, Laura and the two fae had flown by coracle to Godrik's home territory north of London. The hills were rolling and green, and large settlements crawled along the many rivers and inlets that led to the ocean.

There were sheep everywhere, along with large mills and modern but primitive factories. Cadell told her much of the wool fabric that was exported to the continent came from Godrik's home territory, and Carys could see why.

It was a prosperous region dotted with forests, and they were standing in the middle of one. In front of them, a large, grass-covered mound rose up among the oaks and the yews, an old fae fort that Godrik claimed had changed the most over the previous year.

"This has to be at least twelve feet higher than it was a year ago," Godrik said, still keeping one eye on Dru. "Before that? Not even the oldest wolf in our clan remembers fae here."

"No." Dru stepped closer, his eyes narrowing on the green mound. "The invaders built with stone and cut down trees." He took off his leather boots and walked toward the mound. "You built great halls and wore shoes on sacred ground. Of course the old fae abandoned it."

"We had people to feed and clothe," Godrik said. "We can't conjure riches by magic. Were we supposed to live in the mud? That's what the fae want, isn't it?"

"Not what I want, wolf." Dru stared at the ground. "Fae are not a monolith any more than humans or wolves."

To Carys's eyes, the landscape around them was verdant and lush, but on closer inspection, she could see traces of humanity everywhere. Stone walls and willow fences. Cobbled highways and mill after mill after mill. If they were run by smoke and steam instead of waterwheels, there would be black smoke staining the air.

"This fort is old." Naida bent down and dug her fingers into the soil. "It's had time to rest. I feel new life here. Along with something very, very old."

Cadell and Duncan stood at a distance speaking quietly while Laura and Carys walked with Naida.

"What has changed?" Dru sank his feet into the ground as he approached the mound, and as he walked, the grass grew up around his feet. It was the coolest and weirdest thing Carys had seen in a long time.

"The height, of course." Godrik walked with him. "And strange plants we don't normally see."

Birds clustered around them, singing in a riot of song as they swooped through the air as if in celebration of the fae prince's visit.

Naida waded into the brush next to the path and bent down.

"This type of foxglove is unusual in Anglia." She looked up. "Dru, did you see the blackthorns?"

"I did, my love." Dru was looking at the ground, frowning at something he saw in the grass, when a small bright creature flew to his shoulder and alighted with a dreamy flash of gold wings.

"Hello there." Dru smiled and angled his head to the side. "What's that you want to tell me?"

"It's a sprite," Carys whispered to Laura. "See its wings? How they glow? Probably a tree sprite. They're related to the water sprites we saw by the river."

The small creature looked like a tiny fairy with a tuft of nut-brown hair, a body that appeared to be covered in leaves, and bright flashing wings that beat as quickly as a hummingbird's.

It leaned up to Dru's ear and whispered something that none of the rest of them could hear before it flew away as quickly as it had come.

Dru's eyes followed the sprite as it disappeared into the trees, then spread his arms and held his hands out flat. "Humans and wolves, back away from the mound slowly."

The fae man started backing away himself, but Godrik didn't move.

"What?" the wolf asked. "What did that wild fae tell you?"

Carys heard Cadell's voice in her mind. *Nêrys, we should not be here.*

"Cadell says we shouldn't be here," Carys whispered to Laura and Naida, who had joined them on the path.

"That tree sprite is a friend and a generous messenger; you should have more respect." The blue sigils on Dru's face glowed, and his voice lost its usual amusement. His voice dropped to a whisper. "Come away from the mound, wolf."

"Or what? It will open up and steal me away?"

Dru's eyes rose to the top of the mound where cracks were starting to appear in the earth. "We were mistaken; this isn't a fairy fort."

Godrik finally realized that Dru was serious and stepped away from the earthen structure. "What is it?"

Dru backed up slowly, his arms outstretched and his eyes locked on the grassy mound, which was starting to move. The grass beneath his feet crawled higher and higher, nearly to his waist.

"I don't know his name," Dru said, "but he's something far older than you or me or any of our companions. Back. Away."

"Laura, I think we need to get back to Cadell and Duncan." Carys gripped her hand and turned, but a burst of movement at the top of the hill made her turn back to the rising earth, and the rumble of the ground beneath her feet stole her breath and froze her in her tracks.

Naida stepped forward and her eyes went wide. "It's a forest god."

A stony head ringed with grass rose from the earth, the god stretching its shoulders and rising as dark soil poured off it like water.

Its eyes were black rock, and what might have been a mouth stretched and opened as a primeval groan that sounded like grinding stone emanated from the creature's gaping jaw.

Flowers sprang up on the crown of its head, and as it rose to its full height, moss and grass crawled over its earthen body like a moving green robe.

Carys couldn't look away. "Oh my God." It was the most fascinating and frightening thing she'd ever seen.

Dru looked over his shoulder and shouted, "Run! All of you, run!"

Nêrys!

She felt a tugging in her chest and turned to see Cadell dissolve into a shower of gold before emerging in his dragon form with a terrifying roar. His green, iridescent body shimmered from the fire already burning at his throat.

He rose up on his back feet, nearly as tall as the forest god, and spread his wings as he let out a bellow.

Godrik let out a terrifying snarl that pulled Carys's eyes back to the forest god. The wolf's human body disappeared, and his beast form burst from a shimmering grey fog and lunged toward the green giant, who lifted a trunk-like leg and kicked the massive wolf into the trees.

The crunch of wood told Carys that the trees had broken as much as the wolf might have.

"Carys, get out of there!" Duncan shouted from the edge of the clearing, running toward them with his hand on the hilt of his steel sword.

The ground lurched beneath her, as if something was emerging from the deep, and she fell. Her ankle twisted when it caught between two rocks in an open crevice.

"Carys!" Laura ran to her and tried to pull her up.

"I can't move. It's stuck." She felt her heart racing. "Oh shit."

The ground was rolling and jumping every time the forest god moved.

Nêrys, come to me.

"I can't, I'm stuck!"

Cadell breathed a stream of fire across the tops of the trees, and the forest god took a massive step forward toward the dragon, bellowing something that sounded like boulders scraping against rocks.

The earth rolled as he walked. He didn't have feet, but his legs were planted into the soil like tree roots that curled and twisted like tentacles as he stepped from the footprint of the old fae fort and into the forest surrounding him.

Cadell stood on his hind legs, bellowing and trying to draw the giant's attention away from the humans and fae at his feet.

And Dru stood in front of the ancient creature, his shoulders back and his face defiant.

Duncan ran and reached down into the crevice, folding his

massive hands around her ankle and pulling gently but firmly. "It's twisted, and it's starting to swell." He looked up, and his eyes were wide and panicked. "I can't break the rocks."

"They're *rocks*." Despite everything, Carys had to smile. "Even you're not strong enough to break rocks, Duncan."

"Damn it!"

"I'll try to move it from here." Laura's eyes darted between the forest god and Carys. "Maybe the earth will listen to me."

She put her hands in the ground and began to whisper as Duncan continued to try to pull her leg from the narrowing crevice.

Nêrys? Cadell was shouting at her mentally. *What is happening?*

My foot fell into one of the crevices, and it's stuck between two rocks. Duncan and Laura are with me.

I'll keep him moving. Perhaps if the earth shifts again, it will loosen.

Cadell took to the sky, soaring over the forest god's head and drawing his attention up and over the trees, before he swooped back and circled the forest.

Trees and bushes cracked as the giant moved. Birds flew out of the treetops in panic, and animals and creatures that had been sheltering in the woods ran and scattered.

Deer bounded from the shadows, furtive lynxes darted away, and rabbits raced into the meadows and country lanes. A pair of unicorns fled from the shadow of the trees, glancing over their shoulders as they ran away. A flurry of glowing sprites followed them.

"Nothing yet!" Duncan continued to keep her ankle in one firm hand while he shoved the tip of his sword into the ground to try to dig around the rocks. He glanced over his shoulder at the roaring giant who was watching the dragon swoop around his head. "I've never seen anything like that. It's a nightmare."

While Cadell was flying, Dru spread his arms and the ground around him answered. Two columns of earth shot from the pathway in front of him and jabbed at the forest god, knocking the giant creature off-balance for a short time before he turned, opened his massive maw, and bellowed at the earthen spears before him.

When the forest god opened his mouth, living earth poured from the gaping cavity like drool from a dog's mouth. It appeared as if his teeth were made of white stones, his beard was dripping moss, and though he had no tongue, the earth itself moved within his mouth, crunching and grinding as the creature roared in anger.

The god brought his great arm across the stone columns Dru shot toward him, bashing and breaking them as if they were made of sand.

Twisting roots made up the architecture of his arms, and curled branches that ended in bunches of verdant-green leaves took the place of hands. When he reached, the branches curled and twisted toward the ground, grabbing a twisted blackthorn tree and pulling it from the forest.

The giant lifted the tree and swung it toward Dru like a slow-moving sword, but the fae prince ducked and let out a roar of laughter.

"Look at you, old man!" Dru shouted. "Ah, for the love of the old gods, you are a gorgeous thing, aren't you? I haven't seen your like in five hundred years."

"Dru!" Naida shouted at him. "Get away from it!"

Cadell was still flying around the giant's head, trying to draw his attention. No bellowing, no fire. He watched the massive creature with wary gold eyes.

I do not want to harm him, Cadell said in her mind. *We are trespassing on his home.*

If you leave, will he calm down?

Perhaps, Cadell said. *But I cannot leave you.*

Carys looked down at her stuck and twisted leg, then at the forest around them. The ground was ripped and bare roots exposed. The forest god might have been the one who had planted this forest and made it grow, but now it was the one destroying it.

Creation was destruction was creation. In the oldest stories, you often couldn't separate one from the other. They were inextricably linked. Like a forest fire, this old god's fury might be the very thing that made this forest renew.

Nêrys, his corporeal form does *appear to be made of branches.*
I understand.

Branches were wood. Branches could be burned by dragon fire.

Carys had a vision of the forest god tromping along the Essex countryside, kicking at sheep, squashing humans and animals like bugs, and tearing up wool mills as it ripped up the roads and fences that scarred the land.

Then she had a vision of the old god twisting with fire, his verdant-green cloak turning black and his massive leg-trunks burning to ash.

Don't burn him. Not yet.

Carys shouted at the ellyllon. "Naida!"

She was standing on the edge of the forest, her back to an ancient oak and her arms spread out, as if she could keep the trees safe from the marauding forest god. "What?"

"Dru said he woke up."

Naida's eyes were wide. "Obviously yes."

"So can we put him back to sleep?"

Duncan looked up and glared. "What the fuck are you talking about? It's not a baby!"

"Maybe." Naida walked to the tumult of the clearing where the ground rippled and rolled and put her hands on the churning earth.

A bloody Godrik in wolf form was limping from the trees, his teeth bared at the forest god, snarling and howling.

In the distance, the faint echo of other howls came back. One, then two, then a dozen.

"The wolves are coming," Duncan said. "This is going to get messy."

"Nothing." Laura gasped and looked at Carys. There were tears in her eyes. "The earth is so confused right now. I can't connect at all."

"It's okay." She could feel her heartbeat in her leg as it swelled. There was pain, but she had so much adrenaline coursing through her system she barely felt it. "If we can't move the rocks, Duncan has his sword."

"What the fuck are you talking about?" Duncan roared.

Dru paced back and forth in front of the massive creature for a few moments as the god shook his grassy head and looked around the landscape that surrounded them.

"He looks confused," Carys said.

"Dru said he hadn't seen his like in five hundred years." Duncan was smashing the hilt of his sword against the rocks holding Carys's leg, and his palm was bloody. "Can you imagine how bloody confused you'd feel after a five-century nap? Fuck!" He tossed his sword to the side and reached his massive hands down into the crevice, trying to move the stones with his bare hands.

"Duncan." She put a hand on his shoulder. "It's going to be okay."

He looked up and his eyes were red. "Not if you're hurt."

Dru shouted something at the forest god in a language Carys didn't recognize, but it caught the creature's attention, and the green face peered down to the ground to look at the fae prince.

"What is he doing?" Laura asked.

The giant leaned over, his head angled as he watched Dru like he would a bug.

Dru shouted again, and it wasn't Cymric, Éiren, or Alban at all. This was some older tongue that had the god paying attention.

"Maybe they have their own language," Carys said. "Maybe the gods have another language and Dru knows it because of his father."

"Dru, tell him to let Carys go!" Duncan shouted.

"Shhhh," Laura said. "Don't distract him."

The god, staring at Dru, opened his mouth, and a slow, deep roll of sound issued forth.

"Oh my God, that thing is speaking," Duncan whispered. "Those are words."

They were words spoken at the pace of a geological event, but sometime later, the forest god finished speaking and Dru said something else.

"What is he doing?" Carys asked.

"I have no idea." Naida walked toward them. "But I can feel the animals coming back. Carys, what's wrong?"

"She's stuck." Duncan began to dig around the rocks again. "It's like her foot is encased in bedrock somehow."

Carys heard the birds first. They flew in giant flocks, settling in trees and singing loudly, as if they had stories to tell. A few moments later, a pair of deer poked their head into the forest, and two fawns followed them.

The forest god saw them, and something about the ancient and stony face softened. He moved toward the footprint of the old mound where he'd been sleeping and sat down, his knees bent up and his long, branchy arms reaching out to welcome the birds that came to fly through his branches. He let out something that seemed like a sigh, and bright white flower petals filled the air, falling over the broken earth like snow.

Dru was still speaking, and the cadence of his words was nearly a song.

The fae is lulling him back to sleep, Cadell said.

Carys smiled. "And it's working."

"What?" Duncan asked.

"Whatever it is Dru is doing." She rested her cheek on Duncan's shoulder. "Look, he's calmed down."

As the forest god sat and rested, Cadell landed at a distance. He didn't shift out of his dragon form, but he settled on the ground and curled his wings back.

Godrik, too, sat on his haunches, watching Dru as he spoke softly to the giant.

"Naida." Dru reached out his hand.

Naida whispered, "Just stay still. I'll help you in a moment." She stepped forward and walked to the fae prince's side. Without a word, she opened her mouth and began singing.

Carys didn't recognize the song, but the forest came alive.

Ground churned up by violence smoothed and settled. The earth beneath her seemed to sigh, and the rocks that gripped her ankle released.

"Yes!" Duncan gently pulled her leg from the ground. "Thank God. Thank you, God." He bent down and kissed Carys's scraped knee. "Oh lass." He wrapped a hand around her ankle and Carys winced. "Sorry," he whispered.

Duncan pulled her into his lap and held her as Naida sang.

The new dips and mounds that the giant had pulled up didn't smooth, but grass grew over them and moss covered the open wounds of trees and bushes marked by the footsteps of the forest god.

Birds and sprites flew over the forest giant as he settled and slumped on the ground, heaving a great sigh that had vines and moss crawling over his rocky shoulders like a green blanket.

Minutes passed, animals crept back into the forest, and Naida's voice grew softer and softer.

The forest god closed his hollow black eyes and laid his body down, melting into the forest as the moss and grass grew over him and the trees stretched up toward the sky.

CHAPTER SEVENTEEN

After Naida had healed Carys's twisted ankle and Godrik had sent his wolves home, Cadell flew them to two other fae gates. The first was on the edge of a wolf town, near a school, and while the abundant flowers growing across the meadow delighted the children, all the adults were worried.

The other was on an island where two rivers met, and the magic there felt dark and seductive. Carys understood immediately why Godrik was concerned about both. While none of them were resting places for ancient forest gods, Dru and Naida both confirmed that magic that should have been sleeping was very much awake.

That night they gathered in the library in Dafydd's house. Carys's ankle was still a little red, but the swelling was gone. She sat near the fire with her leg propped up on a small table as the rest of them shared a drink.

"So you see why we're concerned." Godrik sat near the fire, a bandage wrapped around one arm and a long slash across his jaw. "This is not common magic for our territories. And the one near the school is especially concerning."

"But fae gates are everywhere." Naida was drinking bright red wine. "Some are more active than others, but surely your people expect to feel their magic."

"Not like that." Godrik leaned forward and raised his bandaged arm. "Not like this."

Carys said, "That wasn't from a fae though. That was a forest god."

Dru lifted a glass of whiskey. "True indeed, Carys Morgan."

"Fine, but why did he suddenly decide to wake up?" Godrik asked. "Did I miss something? Did you do something to wake him, fae?"

Naida leaned forward and narrowed her eyes. "I do not care for your form of address, wolf. We risked ourselves trying to help you today."

"My love." Dru reached out his hand toward Naida. "I did nothing but connect with the ground, Godrik. The old one was already waking up. I might have sped up the process when he felt my father's magic, but he would have woken up eventually. Sooner rather than later."

"So is that because of something the fae are doing?" Godrik persisted. "Is this part of Cian and Orla's plan? Or is it something else entirely?"

Dru raised one eyebrow. "An excellent question."

"Yer not fucking giving us many answers though, are you?" Duncan sat across from Godrik, nursing a whiskey and a foul expression. "I've spent a decade working out some kind of defense against the fae in this damn place, but I don't have any defenses against a fucking god."

Dru frowned. "That old one wasn't harming anyone. He's unique. He only cares for that patch of ground."

"Are they comin' after the humans?" Duncan persisted. "The wolves? Why did the earth trap Carys this morning? I swear to you, those rocks were *holding* her. Every time I dug around them, they just gripped tighter. And I was digging with steel."

Naida shuddered, but Dru only shrugged. "The old gods care

nothing about iron. They exist on both sides of the gates. It was the *Brightlands* that birthed them. They just retained more of their magic in the Shadows. Steel and iron are nothing to them."

Laura spoke from the corner. "Where Carys and I come from, the old gods are still alive and moving. The salmon never lost his power. The crow still flies and we honor all of them, human and magical creatures both. Do the gods hide here?"

"Not exactly," Naida said. "But they're not active."

"Something is waking up old magic." Dru looked at Laura. "That is what you're feeling. In Briton, the old gods retreated as humans stopped honoring them. They allowed the fae to take their place."

"But there are still cults that honor the old gods," Carys said. "And most of the magical creatures do as well."

"Yes, but most humans don't," Duncan said. "To most humans here, the fae are the higher power."

"And fae are not gods." Dru shook his head. "Even though they may act it at times."

"So where does that leave us?" Godrik asked. "What am I supposed to tell Harold?"

Dru stared at the fire for a long moment. "Tell Harold that making offerings to Tamis and the other river gods in the city would be wise right now. If the old gods still sleep, it will be seen as a nod to tradition. If they are waking—for some reason—then it will appease them."

Godrik nodded. "Not a bad idea. I wouldn't have thought of that."

I told you we needed fae allies. Carys thought it, but only Cadell, sitting outside in beast form, heard her.

It's not polite to brag, Nêrys.

Naida added, "And it will put the fae in their place. Remind Orla and Cian that they're not deities. They're magical creatures like the rest of us."

"Should I tell the king and Winnie about the forest god?" Godrik asked.

Dru and Naida exchanged a look, and some unspoken conversation happened between them.

"That would probably be wise," Naida finally said. "Harold should have all the information he needs. I don't believe in coincidence. The fae gates, the forest god" —Naida looked at Carys— "the Crow Mother asking for passage to the Brightlands. Some greater plan is in the works, and all of us must be ready."

CARYS STARED at the ceiling in her room, watching the flickering light from the fire as it cast shadows across the painted beams.

Shadow. Light.

Old gods. Fae.

What was magic? What was elemental?

And what was Queen Orla planning?

Was Queen Orla behind any of this? Or was it Prince Cian?

Her bed was massive and cold. Her body ached from so many hours in a coracle and the multiple jolts of surprise. Her leg ached a little bit, but it had accepted Naida's healing.

Laura had gone to bed soon after they finished in the library.

Cadell had gone to visit his children at the horde nesting grounds.

Carys had been an only child. She knew how to be alone.

She didn't *want* to be alone, but she was almost asleep when someone knocked on her door.

She rolled across the massive bed, then threw on the wool wrap that kept her warm in the old stone house and slid into a pair of deerskin slippers.

She walked to the door and somehow wasn't surprised to see Duncan on the other side when she opened it. "Hi."

"Hello." He leaned his massive shoulder against the arched doorway. "How are you? How's the ankle?"

"Sore but better. Tired." She was tired. She was… weary.

"Can I come in? Just for a minute."

She opened the door and let him inside. "I have to tell you, if you're planning any seduction-type activities, I am probably not up for it tonight." She wanted a bath something fierce, but this wasn't the place to hop in the bathroom for a quick "freshen up" shower. Taking a bath meant planning ahead.

Duncan smiled and wrapped his arms around her, lifting her off her feet and wrapping an arm around her bottom, then carried her to the bed. "Are you sure? I might be able to change your mind."

He probably could. She could take a very cold sink-bath, right? She probably didn't smell that gross. And she was only kind of sore. As long as he wasn't expecting gymnastics—

She winced as he set her on the edge of the bed.

"Kidding." He tucked a piece of her hair behind her ear and ran his warm fingers along her jaw. "Jesus, Carys, you scared me to death today. And when you told Laura I had my sword—"

"Listen, if it's between losing a foot and dying, I would rather lose a foot, and I don't think that's a crazy thing to say."

Duncan pulled a stool over the edge of the bed and sat in front of her, settling her sore ankle on his lap and looking up. "Do you know what that would do to me?" His voice was rough, and his eyes were shining. "Even the thought of hurting you—"

"I would have made Laura do it," Carys jumped in. "She could cut off a limb for me if I needed it. She's very practical, and she's kind of mean."

"Fuck me." He let out a harsh laugh, bent forward, and leaned his forehead on her knees. "I can't believe you're joking about it."

"Hey." Carys reached out and ran her fingers along the short crop of his russet-brown hair. "I'm okay. Nothing bad happened. I have a twisted ankle and a giant bruise on my butt. But that's all. Remember when I thought I was leaving you to the terrifying fae bear in the murder forest? This was not nearly as bad as that."

He turned his head to the side, rested his cheek on her legs, and let out a long breath. "Let me take you back to London tomorrow.

The real London. Fuck all of them. This isn't our fight. You and Laura and me—and your fucking dragon, obviously—we can just go. Fly back to California and forget about all of them. I need to fuck off and take a vacation anyway. Fiona's been at me for months because I've been in a foul mood."

"You just used *fuck* in three successive sentences with three different usages. It truly is the best curse word."

Duncan looked up, and his entire face was smiling. Eyes. Mouth. Beard. All of it. "I adore you, Professor Morgan."

Her heart flipped over in her chest. "You know, I was talking with someone the other day. Someone who reminded me of you."

His smile dimmed a little bit. "Is that so?"

"Don't get that look." She pulled on his beard a little bit. "He told me that you..." She let out a long breath. "That you were a good man. But you're not just good, Duncan. You're one of the best men I've ever known."

"Don't make me noble, Carys." He shook his head. "I just told you we should run away from a fight. I'm only noble in small quantities."

"This person who reminded me of you, he also said you'd do anything for me. Be anything."

Duncan's green eyes burned. "Then he does know what he's talking about, because I would."

"And I told him I just wanted you to be yourself," Carys whispered.

Duncan stood slowly, parted her legs, and moved between them, leaning into her. "The man I want to be is the one at your side, Carys Morgan. The one you call when you're hurt or lonely or just need to vent. The man who helps you fight your battles and fucking... washes your socks if that's what you need. I just want to be with you. I just want to be yours."

Enough.

Carys reached up, pulled him down, and kissed him.

Duncan wrapped an arm around her waist and drew her into his body, settling the heat between her thighs against the prominent erection behind his pants. Carys arched into him, needy with desire and ignoring the pain in her body.

"Oh fuck." She closed her eyes and let her head fall back when Duncan's kisses trailed from her mouth to her neck. "I'm warning you, I haven't had a bath in two days."

He tugged the hair at her nape and angled her eyes to his. "One, I don't care. But two, if you really do, there's a hot bath waiting in my chambers."

Her eyes flew open. "Are you serious?"

"I asked for it and then couldn't stop thinking about you and I came up so—"

"Take me to your room right now," she whispered.

His eyes laughed at her. "Just for the hot water?"

"Let's start there and see where it goes."

He glanced down at her ankle. "You can't walk that far."

"I'm not in that much— Oooh!"

With one swoop, Duncan had hoisted her up and over his shoulder.

"Don't worry, I'll carry you."

"You cannot carry me through the castle like this!" she whispered, trying not to laugh.

"Watch me."

He strode to the door, opened it, and then slammed it behind them as he walked down the stone hallway, which was lined with torches.

Carys was a little uncomfortable lying over Duncan's shoulder, but she was mollified by the truly excellent view of Duncan's ass as he walked.

The man might be a laird, but he also enjoyed physical work, and it showed. His thighs were thick as tree trunks, and his ass was rounded with muscle.

"Are you staring at my arse?"

"Yes."

He reached up and slapped hers, and Carys winced. "Bruise!"

"Oh fuck me!" His hand smoothed over her bottom. "I'm sorry, darling, I completely forgot about that."

Okay, but if he kept his hand there, that wasn't bad.

Moments later, Duncan carried her through the doorway of a smaller chamber, and the scent of rosemary filled the room.

He kicked the door closed and slowly lowered her to the ground. "Hello there."

Carys looked around at the cozy room. It was smaller than hers, didn't have as many windows, and thus it was a *lot* warmer. Duncan's room had a four-poster bed with heavy curtains covering the sides, a small table and a set of chairs by the fire, and a large wooden bath in the corner, surrounded by wooden screens.

She spun around, taking it all in.

"Carys." Duncan's voice was soft. "Truly, lass, I've been playing with you. If you'd like a bath, please take it. I can wait in the hallway to give you privacy or—"

"Stay." She pulled him down and planted a kiss on his full mouth.

Duncan hesitated for only a heartbeat before he wrapped his arms around her, angled his mouth over hers, and feasted.

His lips were soft and his beard was rough, but all Carys could think about was the sensation of his mouth moving over hers, his callused hand gripping the small of her back, and the hand that smoothed over the bruise on her left buttock.

Her head was swimming as Duncan lifted her and walked her toward the bath, setting her down on the thick rug next to the wooden tub. He drew back and silently unwrapped her dressing gown before tossing it on the bed behind her. Then he reached down and took her nightgown by the edge and pulled it slowly up and over her head, leaving her completely naked save for her woolen slippers.

Duncan knelt in front of her and lifted one foot, then the other, staring up at her, his eyes scanning her body, taking in every inch.

Carys had never felt more exposed in her life. "Duncan—"

"Beautiful." His voice was rough. "You're so beautiful, Carys." He leaned forward and kissed her hip where a bruise was forming. Then a small scar next to her belly button. "I want to taste every inch of you." His tongue licked out and his teeth scraped along the soft flesh of her belly. "God, I want to ravish you, but I know you're sore."

She pulled at his shirt. "It's a big bath. Why don't we both get in before it gets cold?"

His eyes met hers, and they glinted with amusement. "I do like the way you think."

Duncan stood and quickly disrobed.

It was... surreal.

While he and his twin were identical in looks, their bodies were remarkably different in build. Duncan was thick everywhere. Shoulders, arms, legs.

And yes, the minute he took his pants off, she looked. How could she not?

His cock was thick, erect, and it had an intriguing curve to it. She felt her body heat up, and she couldn't drag her eyes away.

Duncan caught her stare. "If you keep looking at me like that, this bath is going to get cold."

Carys climbed in and she was glad they hadn't waited, because in the chill of the evening air, the water was hot, but it was cooling off. She sat down and reached for his hand. "Come on then. Sit between my legs and give me some of that soap I love. I'll wash your back."

"You're testing my patience, Professor Morgan."

"Indulge me."

The heat of the water was as delicious as the rippling muscles on his arms and back, and Carys didn't hesitate a moment before running the chunk of fragrant soap over his skin.

Duncan let out a sigh and leaned back into her touch as she wrapped her legs around him. He ran his hands along her legs and cradled her foot and ankle in his strong hands.

"How's this?" He touched her ankle. "The swelling is almost gone."

"It's good. That magical healing is the best." She arched her foot and managed to run a toe along the length of his erection.

Duncan hissed. "I wasn't wrong before—you're a menace." He pressed his back against her. "I love the feeling of your tits on my back."

She was washing him, but she was also feeling him up, her fingers slipping over the ridges of his arms, along his side, and across rippled abdominal muscles that made her body clench.

Carys reached under his arm and ran the soap across his chest, marveling at the rock-hard span of muscle under her fingers. "You are... incredibly strong."

"Hmm." He grunted. "And you are..." His hands reached back, trailing along her wet legs and the outside of her thighs. "...soft as silk." He grabbed the soap from her and lathered it between his palms, then thoroughly washed her shoulders, arms, and hands, dipping her fingers in the water so he could take them in his mouth and slowly suck them, running the tip of his tongue along the soft folds where her fingers joined.

It was an obvious demonstration, but Carys didn't want to rush. She ran soapy fingers down Duncan's chest, along his abdomen, and down below the water, wrapping both her hands around his erection as he arched back and turned his head, searching for her mouth.

"Woman, you'll kill me."

She whispered in his ear. "They call it the little death for a reason."

He captured her lips with his own, groaning into her mouth as she stroked him.

Duncan's kiss grew desperate and his body grew harder. Impossibly hard.

There was a low growl in his throat as he ripped her hands away, spun around as quickly as he could turn his massive body in the wooden tub, and reached for her.

"That's enough of that," he growled. "I want my mouth on your sweet tits and my cock in your—"

Carys leaned forward and kissed him again, her hand going back to his erection. She tore her mouth away as Duncan's fingers slid between her thighs, and she was nearly overcome with lust until Duncan froze and sat back.

"What?"

He slapped a hand over his eyes. "Condoms."

"Oh fuck." Carys nearly growled with frustration. "Well—"

"Good."

"Good?"

Duncan stood, dragged Carys out of the cooling water of the tub, and threw a towel around her before he picked her up and tossed her on the bed. "Yes, good."

She crawled up the bed, confused and still turned on when she saw him naked and marching toward her. He didn't look like he was second-guessing anything.

"You're injured—"

"Ish," she protested. "Injured-ish."

"Still, wouldn't want to rush a good thing." He crawled onto the bed, and his grin was wicked. "I'll figure out the condom thing tomorrow, but that doesn't mean I can't taste you tonight."

"Oh." Her entire body flushed, and Duncan's lips grew red.

"Fuck me, you were right. It all turns red, doesn't it?"

"Yes."

He licked his lips and eyed her pussy, but first he crawled up and over her, capturing her mouth in another bone-melting kiss that had her seriously considering throwing all her careful safe-sex lectures out the window.

She dug her hands into the muscles of his shoulders as he trailed his mouth from her lips to her neck, nibbling along her collarbone before he gathered both her breasts in his hands and kissed each nipple delicately.

Carys let out a harsh breath. "You're going to make my head explode if you don't— Fuck!"

As she was speaking, Duncan opened his mouth, drew one pointed tip between his lips, and lapped at her as if she were candy. He sucked and bit lightly; her breasts swelled under his touch, aching from the pleasure.

Carys dug her fingers into the muscles of his shoulders and pushed. She needed him...

She needed more.

"Aye, lass, those are delicious." He scooted back and gently raised her injured ankle before he placed it on his shoulder, baring her sex to his hungry eyes. "But Carys Morgan, I've been thinking about getting my mouth between your thighs for months now, and I don't think I can wait."

Without another word, he bent down, put his mouth directly on her sex, and ran his tongue up the dripping folds of her pussy until he reached the apex.

He circled her swollen clitoris with his tongue, teasing and stimulating her with his mouth as his hands stroked over her body, the fingers of his right hand teasing her breasts while his left kneaded her bottom and his thumb caressed her entrance.

Carys was awash in the most intense arousal she'd ever experienced, and her mind went blank. Duncan's fingers threaded through her own as her body began to seize.

She was sensation and hunger. And Duncan...

Duncan.

He was everything she needed.

When her climax took her, all she could remember was his hand holding hers.

CHAPTER EIGHTEEN

She woke the next morning naked and curled into Duncan's side. She couldn't remember the last time she'd slept so well. And she couldn't remember ever waking up and feeling like she might have fallen into bed with a grizzly bear.

It wasn't that Duncan was hairy. He had a completely average amount of hair.

He was just massive. Big arms. Muscular legs. Broad shoulders. He took up roughly two-thirds of the bed just by existing.

He must have already been awake, because his hand was running along her shoulder, lightly dragging up and down in soothing strokes beneath the linen sheets.

The light in his bedchamber was tinged with blue, and she heard a fire crackling.

"Why is your room so much warmer than mine?" she murmured and snuggled closer to his body.

"Privileges of being a nobody here. Smaller bedroom means it's easier to heat."

She smiled. "Is it nice kind of? Being a nobody here?"

His chest moved in silent laughter. "It is actually. Not a laird here. Not the boss. Not anything magical at all. I'm the *mundane* human here."

Her warm hand spread over his muscled abdomen and drifted lower. "I don't think there's anything mundane about you." Her fingers curled around his erection and squeezed lightly. "Mmmmm."

"No." He moved her hand away.

"Why not?" She pouted and looked up. "You didn't come last night."

"No, I did not."

"If you think taking care of that would be a hardship for me, you are very much mistaken." Her hand slid south again.

"Menace." He laughed and grabbed her hand, weaving their fingers together.

"Why not?"

"Ahh." He grinned. "You'll think I'm a Neanderthal."

"What? Why?" Her eyes went wide. "Do you not like it?"

Both eyebrows went up. "Strike that thought from your mind, Professor Morgan."

"You have naughty teacher fantasies, don't you?" she whispered.

"Wouldn't you like to know."

"Yes, I would. I have a tweed blazer and reading glasses, for your information."

He grabbed her hand and placed it back on his even-harder cock. "You're not helping."

"But I *could* help."

Duncan growled, rolled her to her back, and caged her under his massive body. "Fine. Neanderthal time. The first time I come with you" —he arched up, pressing his cock into the juncture of her thighs — "I want to be *in* you. See? Neanderthal."

Hot. Something about that was so unbearably hot she wanted him even more. "Where do we find condoms here?"

"We don't, because they don't need them." He laughed. "Ah,

imagine that. No need for them. At all. It's free love in the Shadow-lands, darling. No pregnancy here. No diseases that can't be cured by a potion." He tapped a finger along her hip. "But you weren't born here, and neither was I."

Fuck.

"You know… I'm just putting this out there, but I brought coffee."

"If you're saying I came on this trip very unprepared, you do not have to remind me." His eyes softened. "In my defense, I was trying to give you space."

"I know. I appreciate that." She rested her chin on his chest. "I don't think I want space from you."

Duncan's eyes were soft. "I'm not going to ask."

Carys frowned. "What?"

He blinked. "Sorry. Misspoke."

"No." She sat up. "Not going to ask what?"

Duncan sat up next to her, grabbing a wool blanket and throwing it around her shoulders. "Forget it, darling."

"You know I'm not going to." What was he doing? "Why are you being weird?"

"I'm not…" He scowled. "*Weird.* What kind of thing is that to say after last night? *Weird.* The fuck, Carys?"

"You're being weird. Talk to me."

He threw his legs over the side of the bed. "We should get dressed, and you need to eat something. You barely ate any dinner last night. Don't deny it—I noticed."

"Duncan."

"Fine!" He grabbed for his clothes. "I'm not going to ask if you still have feelings for Lachlan, okay? That's what I was *not* going to ask, but then I had a slip of the tongue and now I've asked it and I'm an arse."

Carys's racing heart calmed as she watched him throw on his tunic and pull on his pants from the day before. "You're not an arse."

Duncan froze and looked up. "I'm not?"

"I *can't* say I don't have feelings for Lachlan, but... not like this." Her cheeks went red. "They're not like the feelings I have for you."

The hunger and the craving? She'd never felt that with Lachlan. Not on this level. Not ever. Being with Lachlan was as easy and comfortable as slipping on a familiar pair of shoes.

Being with Duncan was like bashing your head against a brick wall before the brick wall hugged you, fucked you, then fed you a hearty snack.

"Oh." His eyes narrowed. "Ever?"

"What?"

"You *never* felt like this about him?"

This was too messed up to even examine before coffee.

Carys crawled out of bed. "Do you know where my robe went?" Her feet hit the ground, and she immediately got goose bumps. "And where are my slippers?"

"Fine, we don't have to have a conversation about this, but be aware that I am not backing off. *Ever.*" Duncan tossed one slipper across the bed. Then the next. "And if you suddenly get feelings for Lachlan again, I'm not stepping aside." He pointed at a window for some reason. "That's princely bullshit, and I told you, I'm only noble in very small quantities."

"Trust me, I get the picture!" She found her dressing gown tangled in the blankets at the foot of the bed. "Now do you want coffee or not?"

She was storming toward the door when Duncan caught her around the waist, swung her close, and planted a kiss on her scowl. "Och, you're bonny when you're angry, lass, but you do know how to sweet-talk a man in the morning."

LAURA FOUND them moments after they got back to Carys's room and called for boiling water. "Hmm." She narrowed her eyes and looked at Carys. Then at Duncan. Then back to Carys. "You two had sex."

"How?" Carys hissed. "How do you always know these things?"

Duncan frowned. "Christ, she's good."

"One, you're both wearing the same clothes you wore yesterday, which in this place is not a dead giveaway, but two, there's just this…" She waved a hand as she walked to the wardrobe where Carys hid her coffee. "There's a thing."

"Aye, well, let's not talk about it, shall we?" Duncan lowered himself into a chair, and his expression was stormy.

"And I can see the blissful morning-after feelings are blooming like flowers in springtime." Laura sat across from Duncan and placed three coffee packets on the table. "Hey, grouchy pants. Looks like we have to be friends now, so try smiling when I get you a coffee."

Duncan smiled, but it was closer to gritting his teeth.

There was a tap at the door, and a maid wheeled in a cart with a steaming pot of water. Carys nearly leaped on it. She was pouring water into three coffee cups before anyone could say another cross word. "We've just had a complicated morning, that's all."

Laura shook her head. "Mornings after sex are always complicated, right? I mean, especially for you guys."

The maid let out a small gasp, and Carys realized that news of her sex life was going to quickly spread across the castle. She looked at Duncan to find him staring back at her.

Without a word, the maid fled the room, shutting the door behind her.

"I do not care," Duncan said carefully. "She can announce it at dinner if she likes. I would prefer that everyone in Briton knows that I'm fucking you. It might make life easier."

Carys sank into her chair. "This is so… awesome."

"Well," Laura said, "you can't say he's not direct. I like that for you." She stared at Duncan as she sipped her coffee.

"What?" he finally asked.

"I am noticing a certain… ease in my dear friend there." She nodded at Carys. "You, not so much." She pursed her lips, and then her eyes went wide. "Ohhhh."

Carys knew the moment she realized what happened. "Laura—"

"No condoms here." She winced. "*Shit*. And not exactly available at the corner store. Dude, that sucks, but speaking of sucking, there are other ways—"

"I'll take my breakfast in my room." Duncan rose and started to walk away, but then he turned back and planted a hard kiss directly on Carys's mouth. "Professor Morgan, I'll see you later."

"See me now." She pointed at the chair. "I have an idea, and it involves both of you. And maybe Cadell, but maybe not."

Duncan frowned, and Carys lifted the cover on the tray. "Also, hot breakfast is already here, and you need to watch me eat, don't you?"

Duncan grabbed a plate from the tray, filled it with sausages and eggs, then set it in front of Carys before he sat down. "Eat."

Laura smiled at him. "He's such a nurturer. It warms my heart."

"I think" —Carys sliced off half a fried egg— "we should go back to London, as in Brightlands London."

Duncan blinked. "Seriously?"

Laura set her coffee down. "Okay, I can tell the sexual chemistry is very much alive right now, but going through a fae gate just to get condoms—"

"And more coffee," Duncan muttered.

Laura opened her mouth, then closed it. "Okay, you have a point." She reached over and clinked her coffee cup against Duncan's. "*Still*, it seems a little excessive when there are world-changing magical tides turning at the moment."

"We're not going to get condoms and coffee," Carys said. "I mean, we are definitely getting those things, but that's not the *main* reason."

"So what's the main reason?" Laura reached across the table and grabbed for the scones. "If you're out, I'm out." She traded a serious look with Duncan. "For real. You got hurt yesterday, and there may be some kind of war brewing. I am not authorized to fight for any foreign entity, so—"

"If you need to go back to California," Carys said, "I get it. One hundred percent. You signed on to come to a coronation and a few fancy parties. Parties and coronation are done. But I did something a few days ago, and I'm starting to wonder whether it has way more implications than I realized."

"The Crow Mother," Duncan said.

"Aren't you all a little bit curious what she's been up to in London? I mean, other than sunbathing, of course."

"No," Laura said.

"Yes." Duncan reached for a plate. "Yes. I'm worried too. Especially after yesterday."

"First Dru comes back and they're being all cryptic with each other, and then Orla's fae mentions an offering—whatever the hell that means—and then fae gates start waking up and the forest god yesterday and—"

"We get it, it's been busy." Laura's face was grim. "What were you and Cadell talking about?"

"That the Crow Mother isn't fae." Carys kept her voice low. "That she can't be. She showed me three faces when she trapped me in the forest by the river. Three faces. I met the mother when we struck the bargain. Nurturing mature woman in the cottage in the forest, right? Cauldrons bubbling. Happy to receive visitors and gifts."

"And bargain for a year of your life or your firstborn child," Laura said. "I remember the story."

"Your firstborn child?" Duncan's eyes went wide.

"Which obviously I did not trade," Carys said.

"Very interesting that he focused on that one though," Laura whispered. "Just saying."

"She showed me the mother then." Carys tried to ignore both of them. "But when she caught me alone in the forest, when Dru came and found me, right at the end, before she disappeared, I saw two others. A maiden and an old woman."

"A three-faced fae?" Duncan asked. "Was it a glamour?"

"I don't think so, and neither does Cadell." Carys swallowed the lump in her throat. "I think the Crow Mother is a goddess. Maiden, mother, crone. Which means—"

"You invited one of the old gods to Central London," Duncan said. "And unlike the fae, gods do not lose their power in the Brightlands."

CHAPTER NINETEEN

"This is a ridiculous idea." Cadell might have thought it was a ridiculous idea, but he was still going with them.

"Thank you, Cadell; you're the best dragon in the whole entire world." Carys walked next to Cadell as they started to cross the Night Bridge on foot. Laura was on his other side, and Duncan led the way. Night was falling, and the last of the pearl-grey light was fading in the Shadowlands. By the time they crossed the fae gate, dawn should be breaking in London.

"I know there's a lot going on, but I think Carys is right to be worried," Laura continued. "Orla mentioned the Crow Mother, and the Crow Mother mentioned Orla. This could all be part of the same thing."

Cadell did not look convinced. "If she's a goddess—which I believe is correct—that means that the Brightlands is not foreign to her. In fact, she was born there at some point in history. I have no idea why she might have been banished or what was keeping her from passing through the gate, but we have no control or influence over divine powers."

Duncan kept silent as they walked, casting glares anytime someone looked like they might approach.

"I'm curious," Carys said. "If I unleashed something on the Brightlands—"

"It would be out of your control," Cadell said. "Cross Human, can you convince her?"

Duncan glanced over his shoulder. "I can convince her of nothing most of the time."

Cadell frowned. "Not even now that you're sexual partners?"

"Ha!" Laura crowed.

Carys felt like her face was on fire. "Does everyone in Anglia know?"

The cross human shot her a rakish grin. "Hopefully."

"Nêrys, we are mentally and emotionally bonded. Of course I will know when you take on a new sexual partner."

"Does this mean I'll know if *you* get a girlfriend?"

Cadell glanced at Laura. "No."

"Unfair."

Were Cadell's cheeks red? Just a little?

"In truth, I do not know," he admitted. "My prior matings did not have an emotional attachment. If Seren noticed anything, she did not tell me."

Wait, did that mean Cadell had never had sex just for fun?

Carys saw Laura staring carefully ahead and guessed that her friend was wondering the same thing.

Interesting.

And also kind of weird.

A stout troll with a stony face and grey tufts coming out of his large ears stepped in front of Duncan near the end of the bridge, glaring at Cadell.

"That dragon isn't welcome in the market."

"He may not be welcome," Duncan said, "but he'll pass through."

The troll puffed up his chest. "Says who?"

Cadell stepped forward and seemed to grow several inches as his voice dropped and a red glow appeared at his throat. "Do we have a problem?"

Duncan jabbed a finger toward Cadell. "Says himself. We're passing through, warden. We don't want trouble—we're only making for the fae gate."

The troll narrowed his eyes at Cadell, then looked at Duncan, Laura, and finally Carys. "Yer the one," he muttered.

Carys's eyes went wide. "I don't know what you mean."

"The one who started the trouble." He bared two curved fangs at Carys, but then he curled his lip and pointed over his shoulder. "Get on with you. Straight to the gate and don't talk to no one."

Carys jutted her chin out. "If no one talks to me, I won't talk to them."

Duncan put a hand on her shoulder and guided her past the troll and off the bridge. "We're moving."

Carys muttered, "He's acting like I'm the one who burned down the place."

"Did you see the badge on his chest?" Duncan asked. "He's the warden of the market. At least they have one now. It's his job to keep the peace."

"And I'm not the one who broke the peace in the first place." She scanned the cobblestone lane along the river where the fire-scarred skeletons of ramshackle buildings and open stalls remained standing like withered matchsticks. The three humans and the dragon picked their way through the remains of the troll market where soldiers patrolled and a few intrepid vendors still set up stalls.

The fae bookseller was there, reading a scroll that unfurled itself. Her booth was parked next to the troll with the scaled hands. It was too late for fish, so he had switched to hawking fishing equipment like lines and charmed nets.

There was a round-faced troll woman selling crystals and charms, and an elderly human in a turban carefully measuring herbs.

Carys saw no humans being sold; the vendors that remained in view of the patrolling soldiers all appeared to be legitimate businesspeople.

"There." She pointed out the lane that she couldn't forget. "This is the way."

"I remember." Duncan walked forward, disappearing into the narrow lane as he walked to a corner where two lanterns sat on a narrow stoop.

"Follow Duncan," Cadell said quietly. "I'll watch your backs."

"Is this smart?" Laura asked quietly.

"We're heading into the Brightlands," Carys said. "At least the chances of running into malevolent trolls are a lot lower there."

LAURA WATCHED an early-morning drunk peeing against a wall in an alley off Wilton Place. "Lower, but not zero."

"What?"

Laura pointed her chin at the stumbling man, who still had his penis dangling out of his pants as he shuffled away.

"Ah, the charms of London," Laura said. "All the stories are true."

Duncan snorted. "You show up anywhere at this hour and you're bound to get the worst of a city. Joggers and drunks."

As if on cue, two men in black running clothes passed by the end of the alley, heading toward Knightsbridge Road.

"We're here now." Cadell looked around the grey walls and paved streets with a glare. "How do you propose we find one woman in a city of over eight million people?"

Carys had already been thinking about that. "Where are the oldest existing forests in London?"

Duncan blew out a long breath. "Believe it or not, there are quite a few forests in London. Hyde Park you know, but there are parks and woods all over the place. It's hard to say which one might be—"

"Gorne Wood." Laura piped up.

All of them turned to look at her.

She shrugged. "I remember because I looked it up before we left. I figured there might be a fae gate there. It's right in the middle of the city, and it's the last part of the Great North Wood that's still standing. It's been continuously forested for over four hundred years."

Duncan frowned. "I've never heard of it."

"It's not really a park or an actual forest. It used to be an old scouting campground or something. It was just bought and preserved by a local foundation. It had been in private hands before, but it was all run down. After the scouts stopped using it, it kind of became a dumping ground. People sold drugs there. Lots of crime."

Cadell looked at Carys, staring at her for a long moment.

"Cadell," she whispered.

"What?"

"I can't hear you." She pointed at the buildings around them. "Brightlands, remember?"

"Ah." He straightened and threw his shoulders back. "I was telling you that a secluded place that has been wild for four hundred years and has untouched earth would be exactly the kind of place a god might seek out."

Laura said, "The article did mention that it might be dangerous because of the crime. It's been fenced off, but I'm sure we can find a way to sneak in."

"Where is it?" Duncan asked.

"South London?" Laura closed her eyes. "Brockley? Brockney? Something like that. I think they said it's only six miles from Westminster."

"Brockley." Duncan nodded. "We should get a cab before traffic really gets going. This time of day, we might get lucky and get there in under an hour."

"Old forests, seclusion, and crime?" Carys nodded. "Sounds like just the kind of place the Crow Mother might hang out."

A HALF HOUR LATER, the black cab dropped them off at the end of Courtrai Road in Brockley, a tidy neighborhood in South London where neat houses lined up in straight rows, family cars lined the streets, and a children's play area was set up at the apex of a dead-end road.

Gorne Wood wasn't marked by anything remarkable. There was a chain-link fence set up in an attempt to keep trespassers out, but it was clear from the litter and churned-up grass on the other side of the crooked gate that it wasn't as effective as the local activists probably liked.

"Gorne Wood." Cadell took a deep breath in. "I don't smell any fae."

"You're in the Brightlands," Carys said. "You don't have a dragon nose here."

There was a metal padlock on the gate, but Carys was sure she could climb it. It had been a few years since she'd hopped fences, but it wasn't that hard when you were short.

The men, on the other hand, might have a harder time.

Cadell frowned. "My senses are stronger in Baywood. I can usually sense fae even on the Bright side of the gate."

"Thinner walls, remember?" Laura didn't wait for them to gather attention from passersby. She promptly started climbing up and over the fence. "The gates in Baywood are more porous. You guys coming or not?"

"Right after you." Carys started to climb the fence, only to freeze when she felt Duncan wrap his hands around her waist.

"I've got you," he murmured. "Don't want you to rip your clothes." He lifted her up nearly to the top of the gate, and all Carys had to do was throw her foot over and drop to the other side.

Did his blatant display of manly strength leave her a little turned on? Okay, yes. Yes, it did, but that was understandable. Not every man was built like Duncan Murray.

Cadell frowned at both the women, looked up at the top of the fence, then walked over, twisted the padlock in his fist, and broke it off. "There was really no need to climb over the fence when there's a gate."

Laura looked up at him. "You could have done that before I nearly twisted my ankle."

"You could have waited for me to open the gate." He pushed the metal gate open, and he and Duncan walked through. "Don't blame me for your impatience."

She tried to hide her smirk. "You gonna make another joke about delayed gratification right now?"

"No." He walked past her and bent down. "But if you want something from me, you should state your desired expectations clearly."

Laura turned and narrowed her eyes at the dragon.

Carys grabbed Duncan's hand and quickly walked past them, heading toward the large shed that was leaning to the side.

Duncan wove their fingers together and chuckled. "Don't envy that dragon one bit." He squeezed her hand. "Are you a hand-holder then, darling?"

She turned, her cheeks a little red. "I mean, it's holding hands. It's nice."

"I agree." His eyes were dancing. "I like learning these little things about you."

"Really? What else do you want to know?"

They walked under an alleyway of gnarled oaks, their twisting branches bright green with spring leaves. As the sun rose and light filtered through the limbs, a dust of spring pollen drifted through shafts of light, lending the green tunnel an otherworldly air.

"What's your favorite music album?"

"Ever of all time?"

Duncan hummed a little bit. "Favorite of all time and favorite of the past... five years or so."

"Okay." She took a deep breath and kept her hand firmly in his as they walked deeper into the woods. The light grew dimmer, and the trees grew taller. She heard Cadell and Laura walking at a short distance behind them, but the wind rustling the leaves overhead drowned out whatever they were talking about. "Obviously the greatest album of all time is John Denver's *Christmas with the Muppets*, which is both seasonal and timeless."

Duncan snorted. "God, you're fucking adorable, Carys Morgan. But that is a ridiculous pick."

She turned her head and gawped at him. "How dare you?"

"It's not even the best Muppets album," Duncan persisted. "Which is obviously *The Muppet Movie* soundtrack."

"Unbelievable," Carys muttered.

The path in front of them abruptly stopped, and the trail narrowed to a thin, beaten track that twisted through a dark bramble of weeds, bushes, and a few scrappy wildflowers that defiantly bloomed in the filtered light.

Duncan looked back. "You feeling anything now?"

Cadell nodded. "There's something here."

"I feel it too," Laura said. "There's a weight to the air."

Carys wouldn't have said it like that, but she knew exactly what Laura was getting at. The air around her felt pressed in and heavy. The pollen drifting from the oak trees stuck to her skin. As she stepped off the path and around the tall bramble blocking her view, she heard a distant humming and a faint, eerie song.

"Carys, watch out." Duncan grabbed her arm.

Looking down, Carys had nearly tripped over the outstretched leg of a young man lying half in the bramble and half out. He was shirtless and wretchedly thin with blue veins crawling up his pale forearms. He must have been no older than eighteen or nineteen, the same age as the freshmen in her Intro to Mythology class.

"Hey." She gazed at the young man, who appeared to be staring into the canopy overhead. "Hey, you."

"Yank," the boy muttered. "Whadya want? Yer not allowed here."

The caw of a crow sounded in the distance along with the faint voice of a young woman singing.

"Oh, the oak and the ash, and the bonny ivy tree. How
I wish once again in the west, I could be…"

Cadell stepped forward and nudged the young man's leg with
the toe of his boot. "I believe he is enchanted."

"He's high," Duncan growled. "Look, boy, get out of here. You're
playing with things you can't even imagine."

The boy looked up, his pupils dilated and a smirk on his face. "Yer
not the boss around here, are ya? She's the boss."

"Who?" Carys asked.

"Ma… cha." He seemed to drift off, staring back into the trees. "Of
course."

A blurry idea in Carys's mind was taking shape.

A three-faced goddess. The Crow Mother.

Dru's words in the woods: *"You're speaking nonsense, Badb."*

And now the name Macha.

"Carys," Laura whispered. "There's more."

She took another step into the overgrown bushes and saw more
legs sticking out of more brambles. Sneakers and sandals. A pair of
black boots and more than one set of bare feet. There were dazed
youth everywhere—all but one were young men—and half of them
appeared to be smoking something, but there was no lingering smell
of smoke.

"This is her." Carys kept her voice low. "I know it."

And she was starting to understand just whom they might be
dealing with. The possibility was… not great.

"She's gathered acolytes," Cadell said. "Deity is looking more
accurate than fae."

They kept to the path, and Carys ducked under the low-hanging
branch of an oak tree, looking up and to the right where the song
was coming from and a pale leg dangled from the crook of the tree.

The leg swung back and forth in rhythm with the quiet song that
a young woman in the gnarled oak was singing.

"While sadly I roam, I regret my dear home, where
lads and young lasses are making the hay…"

The song stopped, and the woman leaned forward, her dark red hair falling over her shoulders as she looked down on her new visitors. "Look at that," she said. "A dragon, a thief, and two halflings have come to visit us." Her blue eyes twinkled with amusement. "If you think I'm going back to the Shadows, you're very much mistaken."

She was stretched naked along the twisted limb of an ancient oak tree, soaking the morning sun into her pale white skin while a small murder of crows kept watch in the branches above her.

Carys looked up and met the goddess's bright blue eyes. "Hello, Morrigan."

CHAPTER TWENTY

"Do you feel clever?" the goddess asked. "You've finally got it right."

"Morrigan?" Cadell's voice was grim. "You're a long way from home."

"Ah-ah." She shook her finger at the dragon. "Many years ago, I blessed this land by coupling with its king." She lifted a curl of red hair and held it in the sun. "Even their queens carry my mark." She lay back and closed her eyes, her leg starting to kick again. "All land I walk upon is mine, dragon. My crows fly everywhere."

The birds above her laughed in a cackled chorus.

"They even keep ravens in their white tower." She opened one eye and smiled at Carys. "A small offering, but I will graciously receive it."

"Morrigan," Laura said. "Isn't she…" She seemed to remember that the goddess was right in front of her. "You're a war god, right? Washing the bloody clothes of the dead or something?"

"It's more complicated than that," Carys murmured.

The Morrigan was as much a fertility goddess as a war goddess, though popular depictions of her tended to lean toward the dark and macabre. This nubile redhead hanging out in the remnant of an ancient forest and lording over intoxicated teenagers was as much a part of her worship as bloodshed would be.

"War." The Morrigan sighed. "Everyone remembers the blood." She rolled to her side and the crows fluttered, rearranging themselves around her. "I granted these islands their sovereignty. Even those who came to invade them eventually..." She shrugged. "Well, they all just fucked and now it's a... a tapestry, isn't it?" She kicked her leg out again, surveying the young people around her with a tender smile. "Look how beautiful they are. This forest has changed so much since the last time I saw it, but I can find my Fianna anywhere I go."

"Why are you here?" Duncan, as always, cut to the chase. "And why did you call me a thief?"

"Because you stole a branch from my forest! Orick should have killed you." The Morrigan bared her teeth at Duncan before she turned to Carys. "Why him? The other one has much finer manners."

"I am so not getting into this with you," Carys said. "And you're one to talk about manners. Didn't you imply that you like to eat babies?"

"Oi, that's disgusting," a young man leaning against the trunk of the oak muttered. "You don't do that, do you, Macha?"

"Don't be silly." The Morrigan winked at Carys. "I was playing a part."

"Why?" Duncan demanded again.

She turned her face up to the sun. "Because I wanted to see the sun, of course."

"You're a goddess." Cadell stared at her. "The magic of the fae gates shouldn't bind you."

The young woman blinked. "Shouldn't it?"

"No, it shouldn't," Cadell said. "You were born here."

"Was I?"

"The gods can walk between words," Cadell said. "It is known."

The Morrigan parroted him again. "Can we?"

Cadell frowned, but Carys knew exactly what the Morrigan was doing.

"Come on." She grabbed Cadell's arm and turned to leave. "She's not going to answer our questions. Bye, Macha, or Badb. Or maybe Anu. Not sure what you're going by today."

"Oh, you're so boring!" the Morrigan shouted. "Ugh."

Carys spun around. "Why are you here? What offering is Queen Orla going to give you? What's the big plan, Morrigan?"

The goddess stretched her arms out and hung on to a branch, bouncing a little bit.

Even Carys was distracted by her breasts.

"I'm here to visit the trees," the Morrigan said. "I was worried about them."

"Yeah." Carys started to turn again. "She's not gonna tell us. We should go."

There was no way an ancient three-natured goddess of war and fertility was going to tell them her plans, so Carys wasn't going to waste their time. It was entirely possible with an old deity like the Morrigan that she had no plans at all and just wanted to irritate someone to amuse herself.

But the longer they spent in the Brightlands, the more havoc Orla and Cian might be wreaking in the Shadows.

She knew where the Crow Mother was now, and seeing the Morrigan surrounded by drunk teenagers was actually a little bit reassuring. If they needed to find her, all they'd probably have to do was follow the police reports.

"Come back!" the goddess shouted. "I can curse you, you know."

"Okay." The thought sent a chill down her spine, but Carys kept walking.

Duncan leaned down. "You're the mythology professor, but shouldn't we—"

"Nope. The surest way to give a god power is to pay attention to it."

"Ah."

Powerful she might be, but other than the kids hanging out in the forest, there were very few people in modern Britain who were actual acolytes of the Morrigan, and if there was one thing that Carys knew about old deities, the gods obtained power through sacrifice, elemental strength, natural phenomena, but most of all through human adoration.

That meant in modern London, the Morrigan likely had less power than the latest contestants on a reality dating show.

"Are we really just ignoring her?" Laura whispered.

"She's a goddess," Carys said. "And gods love the sound of their own voices. She'd like nothing more than wasting hours of our time, talking us in circles." She looked over her shoulder as they made it back to the wider part of the forest path. "We're not going to get answers from her no matter how long we stay."

In the distance, the song picked up again, drifting faintly through the rustle of the trees.

> "Oh the oak and the ash and the bonny ivy tree. They
> flourish at home in my own country... how I wish
> once again in the west, I could be..."

"So that's it?" Laura asked when they were back in the cab. "We're just going back to the..." She glanced at their driver, who was bopping along to the latest Punjabi pop hit and talking rapidly to someone via an earbud. "You know, the other place."

Cadell stared at the mundane human who began singing along with the car stereo. "Human, we're four travelers from a hidden magical dimension where dragons, fairies, and unicorns exist. Can you get us to a fae portal forthwith?"

"Eh?" The driver cocked his head. "I get you to the... Mandarin Crown on Knightsbridge, right?"

"That's correct." Cadell looked at Laura. "I believe we can speak freely here."

Carys leaned toward Duncan. "There's a pharmacy right on the corner of the—"

"Already thinking ahead," he muttered. "You and Laura grab some instant coffee at the corner market, and I'll—"

"Yep." It was only midday in London, so they'd be returning to the Shadowlands in the middle of the night. "We'll get it done."

The black cab stopped and started through the clogged streets of Central London as Carys leaned into Duncan's arm and closed her eyes, enjoying the warmth of the sun on her face. She was sleepy. It was a little like jet lag, and the feeling of the sun on her skin was another kind of enchantment that was its own magic.

Duncan knit his fingers through hers and leaned over, kissing the crown of her head as she dozed.

"You're so like your mother."

Carys blinked and sat up. She wasn't in the cab anymore but sitting on the edge of the loch near Sgain Castle, staring at a woman with long wavy hair the color of chestnuts and dark brown eyes.

The woman stood on the edge of the water, but she was looking at Carys.

Carys looked around and rubbed her eyes. "Where am I?"

"In a taxi cab driving through London."

"No." Her head swiveled from side to side. "I'm obviously not."

The woman smiled. "Aren't you?"

"I'm dreaming."

"Yes."

Carys blinked. "Are you... are you fae?"

"The fae cannot visit dreams." She turned from examining Carys and stared across the loch and the still grey water that mirrored the cloudy sky.

She might have been in a dream, but that dream was set in Alba. Carys was dreaming of the Shadowlands. "You mentioned my mother."

"I did." The woman walked over and sat in the green verge that flourished along the edge of the loch. "Your waking mind belongs to your darling father, and your dreams belong to your mother."

"I don't know what you're talking about."

"Of course you don't." She leaned back on long arms, and her dress floated around her body like a whisper.

As Carys stared at the beautiful woman who could have been thirty or fifty, she realized she'd seen her before. It was in this very place, standing on the edge of the loch and speaking to the dark apparition of a man who became a vicious water horse.

The woman had been speaking with the kelpie and hadn't shown an ounce of fear. "I saw you talking with the kelpie."

"Did you?" Her face lightened. "So that's why your dream pulled me here."

"I pulled you here? How?"

"That's an excellent question." She wrinkled her nose and leaned forward. "How did you do that?"

"You're not a fae."

She chuckled a little bit. "Oh no."

"Are you a goddess?" Carys asked.

"You're closer to the truth, but you'll never catch the whole of it." She turned from her examination of the water. Her brown eyes were soft with emotion. "Your mother knew me once. I've always hoped I'd meet her daughters."

Carys's mind was spinning. "How?"

"That's an excellent question."

"My mother traveled to the Shadowlands."

The woman smiled. "That's one way of thinking about it."

"Who are you?"

"Do you mean to steal my name?" she asked. "Collect it in your pocket like a greedy fae?"

Carys shook her head. "I don't know how to do that."

"Names have power, you know. Names can conjure power. Names can trap." Her brown eyes glittered. "Call a name often enough, and its owner might even become a god."

Carys suspected she'd offended the... creature. "I'm sorry. If you don't want to tell me—"

"Your mother called me Rhiannon."

Rhiannon was a complicated figure, as much myth as reality. A queen or a goddess or maybe both. She was a central figure in Welsh mythology, a royal consort, a mother, and maybe even a deity. "Is that your name?"

"It's one of my names," she said. "You may call me Rhiannon. Many have."

"*I see you too, blood of Rhiannon.*" The water horse's voice had come to her in a whisper not unlike the way that Cadell spoke to her.

"Someone told me once that the goddess's daughters walk between worlds," Carys said. "Was he calling me your daughter?"

"Are you my daughter?" Rhiannon spoke in a whisper. "If you were, I would tell you to go back."

"Go back where?"

"Go back, Carys."

"Back to California?"

Her eyes went wide. "Go back now!"

Carys sat up so fast she banged her head on the edge of the door.

"Lass, what's the damage?" Duncan winced and leaned over, pressing his palm to the sore spot on her head that was stinging. "You were sound asleep."

"I had a strange dream."

Strange dream might have been an understatement. Her heart was racing.

"You are here." The man reached his hand through the window. "Brompton Road. I only take cash."

"No, you don't." Laura, ever the practical tourist, pulled pound notes out of the purse she carried at her waist. "All licensed taxi drivers in London have to accept cards and contactless payments."

The driver stared at her. "But you have cash."

"Yes." She handed it over. "Because I'm nice. But I want my change."

The cab driver muttered under his breath but handed Laura her change while Carys got out on the sidewalk and Cadell and Duncan unfolded themselves from the back seat.

Carys was still stuck between sleep and the waking world.

Go back now!

Go back where? To California? To Shadow London? What was Rhiannon trying to tell her?

After the driver had sped away, Laura walked over. "Grocery store before we head back?"

Carys wanted to shout no and run for the gate, but she had no logical reason other than a weird dream, and the others were nodding.

"Coffee," Cadell said. "As much as we can carry."

"And I just..." Duncan pointed over his shoulder. "I have a quick errand to run at the pharmacy. Meet in front of the restaurant when we're finished?"

Duncan's voice slapped her back to the present.

The pharmacy. She caught his eye. "Sounds good. We'll get coffee."

She grabbed Cadell's hand and dragged him along the sidewalk before he could make a comment.

"Why are you embarrassed?" the dragon asked. "I approve of the surly human's instinct to protect you from disease or untimely pregnancy."

"Great." Her cheeks were flaming. "I just don't want to talk about it with you."

Discussing her sex life with Cadell was a little like what Carys imagined it would be like talking about it with a judgmental brother.

They walked to a nearby city market that promised fresh food on the go, and Carys and Laura split up to look for the instant coffee while Cadell surveyed the plastic-wrapped packages of deli sandwiches, wraps, and salads.

Carys was debating the larger instant jars of coffee versus the smaller individual packages of espresso when someone bumped into her.

"Pardon me." A woman in a business suit turned and grabbed Carys's shoulder, steadying her as she tried to keep the jars of coffee from falling off the shelves. "Have you got it? Richard, let me call you back—I'm attacking tourists in the Sainsbury with my briefcase."

Her voice was clipped, but her accent was delicately Welsh and had Carys looking slightly up and into familiar blue eyes set in a face that nearly stopped her heart.

"Mom?"

She was still standing frozen in the coffee aisle when Laura and the dragon found her.

"Carys, what's—?"

"I saw my mother."

Laura's face grew pale. "That's impossible. There was a report. There were two bodies—"

"Her Shadowkin," Carys blurted. "No, her... I mean, it was her but it wasn't, and at first I thought there was just a resemblance, but it was too exact. Even her voice was..."

Her heart was racing. Her skin felt clammy. She'd suspected. They both had.

Carys looked at Cadell. "It was her. It was—"

"Her Brightkin." Cadell put his arm around Carys and pulled her close. "Laura, can you take the coffee from Carys?"

"Got it." Laura was already taking the jars Carys clutched to her chest. "Honey, go outside with Cadell. I'll check out."

"We knew." Carys looked up into the dragon's fierce gold eyes. "I don't know why it was such a shock, because we... I mean we knew, Cadell."

"We suspected, Nêrys." He kept his voice calm as the aisle cleared in front of the massive man. "Suspecting your mother's origins is entirely different from seeing your mother's face on another and knowing that she was not what you thought."

Carys was staring at a blackened smear of gum on the sidewalk when she heard Duncan's voice.

"What's going on? Is everything okay? I waited at the restaurant, and it's been—"

"Carys met her mother's Brightkin."

The air was filled with the sounds of imaginative Scottish cursing. Seconds later, the watery vision of the smeared gum was gone, and she was crushed to Duncan's chest.

The crushing felt good. It broke her mind out of the frozen pattern she'd been circling before.

"Oh, lass." He pulled away and tipped her chin up to meet his eyes. "What do ya need? A good cry? Privacy? We can go to my mother's house if you want. We don't have to go back right away if you'd rather—"

"I called her mom." Carys blinked, and tears fell down her cheeks. "She must have thought I was insane. And she was wearing a suit."

Carys couldn't get the image of the tidy woman who reminded her slightly of Helen Mirren out of her head.

Tegan Morgan hadn't worn a business suit a single day in her life. She wore long flowered dresses, linen pants in the summer, and the occasional pair of faded jeans with feathers embroidered on them "to cheer them up" when she was gardening or hiking.

"Come on." Duncan put his arm around her and hustled her down the sidewalk. "You're in shock."

"She's not in shock," Cadell said. "We knew this was a possibility. We already suspected—"

"She saw her dead mother's face on a living woman," Duncan snarled. "Shut your mouth or go back to the gate, but don't tell me she's not in shock."

Carys felt like she was spinning, stuck in a car skidding on ice. Her mind raced from one thought to the next.

Her hair was grey.

Her mother's hair was only silver at the temples.

But this woman was older than Tegan had been when she died. Her mother never cut her hair; it hung nearly to her thighs. It looked nothing like the smart grey bob the woman in the shop had worn.

Of course it wouldn't be the same. That woman was years older than her mother had been when she died. Of course she was different. She was Tegan's opposite, in fact.

Dafydd was boisterous and a bit explosive. Nothing like her father's steady, quiet demeanor, so of course her mother's Shadowkin—

Brightkin.

That had been her mother's *Brightkin*.

Which meant Tegan Morgan—painter, dreamer, mother who left out milk for the brownies at the hearth—had been born in the Shadowlands, her essence brought to life in the shadow of the fae gates and pulled into reality by magic.

Nothing was born in the Shadowlands except by magic.

Her mother was Shadowkin. She'd crossed the gates to the Brightlands just as Lachlan had.

Don't be curious, my Carys. Leave the rabbit to the wolf. Never follow the lights. They want to lead you away from me.

Carys murmured, "They want to lead you away from me."

Her mother had known. Somehow Tegan had known that even

though she'd crossed into the light, a little of the shadow lingered in a place where the gates between myth and reality were thinner.

Rhiannon's daughters walk between worlds.
  Go back now!

"Carys?"

She looked up and realized that Duncan had led them off the main road; they were standing on a residential street where white-tipped dogwood trees arched over the narrow lane, dropping petals on them as the breeze rustled their branches.

"I'm okay." She wiped her cheeks and tried to get her bearings. "I'm... okay. It was a shock. I was just surprised."

"Of course you were." Laura was still clutching the paper bag from the market. "Do you want to go to Duncan's house?"

"No."

Go back now! Rhiannon's words pushed her toward the fae gate.

She frowned. "We should head back. We need to go back."

"You've had a shock," Duncan said. "Are you sure?"

We've been gone too long.

"I'll be fine."

"You're not fine." Duncan bit out the words. "I cannae imagine what you're feeling, and I've met both my parents' Shadowkin."

She looked at Cadell. The dragon's eyes were steady on her, and his face was stoic. "We knew. I knew. I think as soon as I crossed the first gate, I knew."

There was a reason the shadows had always felt familiar. There was a reason the gates tried to grab her and hold on.

"Your mother must have pleased the gods greatly." Cadell's voice was soft.

"Why do you say that? She left the Shadowlands."

"But they gave her a child." Cadell smiled. "Even when she crossed into the Brightlands, she would not have been a mother without the help of the gods. And from what you have told me, being a mother and having a family was Tegan's greatest joy."

"It was her." Rhiannon. Epona. The Celtic goddess of horses, the Welsh mythical queen. *"Your mother knew me once."*

She looked at Duncan. "I dreamed about Epona. I think it was her. Or Rhiannon. Or maybe they're the same. I don't know. But in the car—earlier today—I dreamed about her."

"And then your mother's Brightkin just happened to run into you at the grocery?" Duncan shook his head. "What is happening?"

Carys looked at Cadell. "She said I pulled her into my dream. How is that possible?"

"I don't know, but I agree with you," Cadell said. "We need to get back across the gate."

CHAPTER TWENTY-ONE

Crossing the gate with their smuggled coffee tucked in pockets, all Carys could think about was the woman in the market and her mysterious dream in the cab.

"Names have power, you know. Names can conjure power. Names can trap. Call a name often enough, and its owner might even become a god."

The rowdy night market was abnormally quiet, though business continued in a muted fashion. The black river flowed in the background, glowing, golden trails rising to the surface every now and then from the serpents and water sprites that called it home. The night was clear and moonless, and no stars shone in the sky.

There was a faint golden aura hanging over the city like a fog of gold light from torches, fires, and the oil-burning streetlamps that lined the embankments and roads.

As the group walked down the cobblestone street, which still held muddy ash from the fires less than a week before, the trolls all stared at them from behind their booths and counters.

"They probably smell the coffee," Cadell said.

"Something is wrong," Laura said. "Don't you feel it?"

The Kingsguard, in bright red uniforms and bronze and leather armor, patrolled in groups of four and six, joking among themselves and chatting with some of the vendors that remained.

"It's too quiet," Duncan said. "There are usually fae musicians that play on that corner." He nodded toward the start of the bridge over the Tamis River. "They're not playing tonight."

Fae musicians.

Carys looked around the market, but the fae bookseller was gone. She scanned the tents and booths propped up against the brisk breeze coming off the river. "There are no fae here."

Duncan looked around, and Cadell's eyes narrowed.

"No fae at all," Carys said.

Nêrys! Cadell froze, shouting in her mind. *We must go now.*

"What's going on?" She turned and grabbed his arm. "Cadell?"

"Mared is calling me." His throat burned and he stepped away, leaping toward the bridge and transforming in a shower of gold sparks that had the trolls in the market screaming and running for their lives.

Cadell, what is happening?

The Kingsguard ran toward them, but before the soldiers could reach them, the dragon whirled around, let out a burst of fire, and snatched Carys, Duncan, and Laura in his massive, curled claws, hurtling into the air with a heave of his great wings.

"What the hell is happening?" Duncan was furious. "Carys?"

Mared is shouting for me. She's summoning the horde.

"Mared is summoning the dragon horde," Carys shouted into the wind as Cadell soared over the river and across Hyde Forest, toward Dafydd's estate.

An old fae gate burst open near the nesting grounds. They rushed in, and two children were taken before the minders realized what was happening.

"Oh my God." Carys felt cold rush over her body, and it wasn't only because of the wind. "A fae gate opened near the horde nesting grounds. Two children were taken."

"What?" Laura shouted.

As Cadell soared into the air, a dark cloud appeared over the city.

Not a cloud, but a massive flock of crows that swooped and cawed as they dropped something from their claws.

Feathers?

No, not feathers. Papers. Pamphlets.

What did you do when you wanted to get a message out but there was no television or radio? Crow-pamphlet, Carys was guessing.

Slips of paper flew in the wind, blowing over the twisted streets and wooden roofs of London, tossed in the currents of the river, and landing in shining puddles throughout the muddy lanes.

One stuck to Carys's cheek as Cadell flew through the night. She grabbed it, trying to read in the glow of the dragon's fire.

The words on the paper flickered and moved. "'People of Briton.' It's in Anglian!"

"It's glamoured." Laura had grabbed one too. "Because it's in Yokut for me. They've used some kind of spell so that everyone will see it in their own language."

"But it's the same message?"

"'For too long,'" Laura read, "'you have ignored the old magic. You build your cities of stone and metal. You school your children, but you teach them nothing.'"

They set down in Dafydd's courtyard. Cadell dropped them as gently as he could, but her sore ankle still jolted when she landed in the mud. Then, without a word, her dragon flew into the darkness.

Carys heard the soldiers milling around the courtyard—all of them had fae pamphlets in their hands.

"'You offer no sacrifices to your house spirits,'" one soldier read, his forehead furrowed. "What is this?"

A maid reached down and grabbed a pamphlet from the mud.

"'You cut down trees that are older than the cities that have grown up around them.'" She looked around in confusion. "Who sent this?"

"'It is time...'" Laura continued reading the pamphlet in her hand. "'...for you to forget the lure of the Brightlands and the false worship of human leaders. It is time that you pay homage to your *true* rulers.'"

"True rulers?" The maid tossed the pamphlet in the mud. "I serve King Dafydd. Who wrote this nonsense?"

Laura's face leached of color as she looked at the bottom of the page. "It's signed Cian of Temris, High Lord of Éire, Consort of Queen Orla, and..." Laura looked up. "High fae king of Briton."

Duncan said nothing, but his face was grim, and Carys knew exactly what he was thinking.

The fae had just declared war.

"What's happening?" she shouted at the nearest dragon rider she saw. There was chaos as every nêr and their dragon readied their coracles to fly to Cymru.

"You!" Anwyn was clinging to the side of a war coracle, and her dragon was beating her wings, waiting for the signal to fly. "In the hall now! The king wants to see you."

"The children—"

"The remaining nestlings have been moved to a new nesting ground," Anwyn shouted and slammed the door to her coracle. "Go and speak to the king."

Cadell was stormy and silent in her mind. She could feel his desire to mount the sky and follow the nêr ddraig who were already winging toward the mountains, but he crouched near the stables, waiting for Carys.

Nêrys, do not ask me to take human form right now.

Are they your children?

All dragon children are my children.

"I understand."

"What are we doing?" Duncan said. "Carys?"

"Anwyn said Dafydd wants to see me." Carys was already walking into the hall, and Duncan and Laura followed her. "So I'm going to see the king."

There was a red-coated messenger standing next to Dafydd in the hall.

"Carys, you're here." The king's face was grim. "Harold has just sent a messenger. The news is everywhere. Crows and ravens filling the skies. They struck all over Anglia. They took wolflings, humans. We have not heard of any missing unicorn young as yet, but there are gates opening all over Briton."

Carys asked, "Were Cymric children taken as well? Other than the dragons, were human children taken?"

The king's face was grim. "We are waiting for news."

Duncan asked, "Have Orla and Cian formed an army?"

"We don't know yet." Dafydd's face was dark, and his eyes were fixed on a map spread on the table. "But we know that children all over Anglia have disappeared. Snatched from their beds in the middle of the night, lured into forests. They've disappeared into fae mounds and barrows that we cannot breach."

The red-coated messenger spoke. "Over two hundred children have been reported missing so far. Dozens of barrows are popping up all over Anglia."

"Oh my God," Laura said. "Why children?"

"Children are the most precious thing in the Shadowlands," the messenger said with a bleak face. "I imagine they know we will do anything they want to get them back."

"Hostages," Carys murmured. "They've taken over two hundred hostages."

Duncan crossed his arms over his chest. "What do they want?"

"There have been no demands as yet." Dafydd looked up with a grim stare. "Just the pamphlets the crows dropped from the sky."

He pointed to the map. "Carys, the dragon nestlings have already been moved. Make sure you tell Cadell so he doesn't panic."

Cadell, the king says the rest of the children have already been moved. Mared has told me.

I'm still with the king now. Anything you want me to share? Anything you need to know?

Mared is speaking with me now.

Carys was nothing but a green soldier when it came to any kind of combat. She was a decent shot with an arrow, but her main strength as a new nêrys ddraig was simply being the human voice for a big, bad dragon.

But her people had been attacked.

Her people. Cadell's children.

"What do you want us to do?" Her heart was racing. "I don't know if I can help, but—"

"You can help." Dafydd pointed to Duncan. "And you too."

Duncan frowned. "Has Lachlan called?"

"Not yet. I imagine he's trying to communicate with his father right now. Probably trying to find out what is happening in the north."

"Ravens have been sent from the palace," the messenger said. "But Harold and Lachlan have not heard back from Robb, and there is a fear that any raven or crow could be loyal to Cian."

"I've sent Dylan and his dragon Tamsin to Alba to coordinate with Robb and Rory." Dafydd looked at Carys. "One of the dragon young taken was from Demelza's last clutch. Anwyn and Demelza are flying to Cymru immediately."

Her clutch? What does that mean?

Cadell's voice ached. *All children are our children, but that means one of the missing is Demelza's own blood.*

Dafydd was speaking with Harold's messenger. "Once Dylan and Tamsin are close enough, they will be able to communicate with the dragons in the north. My niece Carys and her dragon Cadell will remain here in Anglia. I need to fly to Caernarfon, but my niece will remain in Anglia to communicate with Harold's people and be my voice here. Please let your master know."

"You have our gratitude, King Dafydd."

It wasn't as good as a mobile phone, but dragon's mental communication was surprisingly far-reaching.

Dafydd continued, "I'm sure Lachlan will stay here in Anglia with the Alban troops already in the south to coordinate with Harold and back up his armies."

"Armies?" Laura's voice was quiet, but everyone turned to listen. "They're not attacking with armies, Your Majesty. They're taking children." Her eyes were wide and tear-filled. "Armies are not going to get those children back."

"You're absolutely right," Dafydd said. "But we can surround the gates. Keep the fae from taking any more. Keep them contained."

"They've brought old gates back to life," Carys said. "Remember? That's what Godrik was worried about. Do we even know where all the fae gates are?"

"No, and that's why I need you." Dafydd pointed to the map spread out in front of him. "Every fae gate, fort, and barrow we know about is marked on this map. I have charged my personal scribe with making you another copy of this map as we speak."

Carys nodded. "Okay."

"You and Cadell will take a surveying trip over the southern part of Anglia. Cadell and Seren were well trained in mapmaking and surveying. He'll know what to do. We must identify any new gates so we can surround them."

"I'll do my best." She couldn't draw to save her life, but with Cadell's help, she was certain she could mark any new fae gates on an existing map.

"And you" —Dafydd pointed at Duncan— "will go with her. I know you have an iron sword, and I expect you to carry it."

"I have no idea what you're talking about," Duncan said. "But I'll send a message to Lachlan, let him know I'll be staying here."

"How can I help?" Laura spoke again. "I'm probably not

supposed to get involved in foreign conflicts, but I feel like I have to help somehow."

"The fae that you called have disappeared," Dafydd said. "You probably didn't even notice in all the commotion, but the mound in the courtyard is gone."

Carys blinked. "Dru and Naida left us?"

"Fae are disappearing all over Briton," Dafydd said. "We don't even know if household spirits have remained."

Duncan said, "Brownies and other household fae should have protected any children of a household they watch over. How could they have been taken?"

"Maybe they did," Carys said. "Not every house has a brownie."

"The disappearance of friendly fae means that human mages are more important than ever." Dafydd nodded at Laura. "If you are willing to stay and ward this house in some way, I would be grateful."

"Of course," Laura said. "And I could never leave Carys."

"The fae cannot all be on Orla and Cian's side," Duncan said. "I know more than one fae, and they would never—"

"They may not stand with Orla and Cian," Dafydd said. "But the wild fae may not feel strong enough to stand against them either." He looked at Laura. "If you can call Naida and Dru, call them. I know who Diarmuid ap Lir *truly* is. If there's anyone who might be able to get these children back, it's him."

CADELL WAS NEARLY CRAWLING out of his skin with his need to go to his children, so Carys released him to fly to the mountains for the rest of the night while Duncan dragged her away to get a few hours of sleep.

"There's no use trying to survey fae gates when it's dark, and Cadell needs to comfort the young dragons." Duncan dragged her up the stairs, her hand firmly wrapped in his. "You need to rest while you can."

Carys still couldn't wrap her mind around what was happening. Days ago they were dancing under torchlight and celebrating King Harold's coronation. Prince Cian and Queen Orla had been there!

And now the most vile crime had happened, children were missing, and the country was in confusion.

"Is this always what happens when a war starts?" Carys asked. "You feel really confused and nothing seems real?"

Duncan put his arm around her shoulders as they walked. "I don't know. We've been lucky, haven't we?"

Peace is not natural to the Shadowlands. We are magic and myth and every dark impulse that exists inside you. We must claw civility from the mud with power and domination. Because when peace breaks, good people become animals to survive.

"Eamer told me once that peace wasn't natural here. That when the world breaks, it's women and children who pay the price."

"Spoken like a woman who has studied history," Duncan said. "She must be heartbroken right now, knowing that her own mother is the one who planned this."

"Did she though?" Did Queen Orla have it in her to provoke a war? What could be the motivation? Did the Queen of Éire really want to rule the whole of Briton? "Was it her or was it Cian?"

Carys was thinking aloud. She didn't really know anything. But Orla's fae consort was the closest thing to a king that the fae in Briton had, and he wasn't well-liked.

"Do you think Cian knows that Dru is back?"

"Yes. I think he does." Duncan opened her bedroom door and walked inside. "Stay here." He left her by the crackling fire and inspected under the bed and in the dressing room before he returned. "I don't see any danger."

"I'm sure we're safe in Dafydd's house."

"For now we take nothing for granted." He frowned. "I'm going to check Laura's room too. I'll be right back." He reached to his waist, grabbed a thin scabbard, and shoved it toward her. "Stab anything you don't recognize."

"She's right next door."

"Like I said, stab anything you don't recognize." He stomped out of the room and came back less than five minutes later. "She nearly stabbed *me*."

Carys smirked. "She grew up with sisters. You can't really take Laura by surprise."

Duncan tossed his pack on a chair by the fire, then walked to her wardrobe. "Warm clothes. Socks. It's cold in this room."

"Are you fussing?" She sat on the edge of the bed.

"Fussing?" He dropped his arms, which were holding up a warm wool tunic. "Did you just accuse me of fussing?"

She collapsed back on the bed, patting the mattress beside her. "I'm taking off my shoes and sleeping."

"You're changing." He walked over and tugged at the ties holding her trousers up. "You're changing because you've been wearing these clothes for hours and you will sleep better out of them."

Had she been in London only hours ago? Her shirt still smelled like sunlight.

Carys watched Duncan, eyes half closed already, as he swiftly undressed her. "This is not how I imagined your first night in my bed would be."

The corner of his mouth ticked up. "It's not our first night in bed, and there will be no fucking. We both need to sleep." He tugged off her trousers and let them fall on the floor.

"Last night wasn't our first night in bed. It was our first night in bath."

Duncan snorted as he pulled her up to sitting. "You're exhausted."

"Are you staying with me?" She didn't want to be alone.

"Yes." He took a deep breath and looked longingly at her nearly naked body before he put the nightgown over her head. "But no fucking."

"Do you know that fuck is one of the oldest profanities in English? First recorded usage was in the... fourteenth century, I think."

"Fascinating, Professor Morgan."

"And it's likely from an earlier Indo-European root because both Germanic and Romance languages have some version of it that has the same or related meaning."

He threw back the heavy coverlet, picked her up, and set her in the bed before he drew the covers up. "That must explain why it's such a useful fucking word."

"It really is, right?" She was already drifting to sleep when she felt him get in the bed, scoot closer to her, and wrap his arms around her body. "So many..." She yawned. "...different parts of speech."

"Sleep, Carys."

She had one moment to feel the comfort of Duncan's arms around her before she completely lost consciousness.

CHAPTER TWENTY-TWO

Nêrys.

She opened her eyes at the sound of his voice. "Cadell?"

Duncan was still sleeping, and the light outside her shuttered window was pearly and pale blue.

She eased out of bed and wrapped herself in a heavy dressing gown that Duncan had placed at the foot of the bed, then walked to the hallway, but when she opened the door, she saw nothing.

Nêrys.

Cadell, where are you?

In the garden. His voice sounded hollow. As empty and grieving as the first time she'd heard him in her mind.

Carys tiptoed down the stairs, nodding at the green-clad soldiers who patrolled the halls, and walked out the back corridor to the kitchen where she borrowed a pair of heavy boots that were sitting near the door.

She found Cadell in human form, sitting on a stone bench and staring at the fountain in the center of the garden.

Carys sat next to him and took his large hand in hers. "I'm sorry."

"I must believe they are not dead. The fae would be fools to hurt them." He didn't break his stare. "But they must be terrified. Dragons that young are never alone. Never away from their clutch."

"You mean their brothers and sisters?"

He nodded. "Dragon children are raised communally, I have told you this."

"Yes."

"They have never been alone. Not for a moment. Not in their entire life. They have never been away from their family group. They are babies."

"How old—"

"Only ten years old."

Okay, Carys wouldn't classify ten-year-olds as babies, but dragons had much longer lives, so it made sense that the adults still saw them as babies after a decade.

"Have the fae ever stolen dragon children before? I mean, there is story after story in human mythology of the fae stealing children and replacing them with changelings or just stealing them for..."

So many horrible reasons.

"Never," Cadell said quietly. "Why would you risk the wrath of the dragons to steal a child you cannot control with glamour or magic?" He frowned. "The human children can be lulled into sleep or glamoured to not know that is happening, but the magical children, the dragons and the wolves—"

"They'll know they've been kidnapped."

Cadell nodded.

Carys squeezed his hand. "They'll also know that their horde will come for them."

"We cannot sense them," he said. "One of the babes was born of Demelza's own body, and she cannot feel her. They have used *powerful* magic to hide them, Nêrys. Very powerful magic."

"Demelza is bonded with Anwyn?"

"Yes." His head hung. "She is frantic. And she feels even more guilt than the rest of us, but I should have known—"

"You should have known that the fae would do something they've never done in history at a gate that you didn't even know was active?" Carys snapped at him. "Don't be ridiculous, Cadell."

He raised his face and looked into her eyes. "Tell me the king has a task for us. I know you have never been to war, but—"

"War isn't going to get those children back," Carys said. "Dafydd wants us to survey the south and find as many gates as we can so Harold's army can surround them and hopefully keep this from spreading further. Since you and Seren had experience surveying, he thought that would be the most immediate use."

He nodded. "We can do that." His eyes glinted. "And if we happen to kill any condescending, superior, marauding fae that might be passing through those gates, that cannot be helped."

"Half the fae—maybe more than half—are in hiding, Cadell. Dru and Naida have disappeared. None of the fae who are normally at the market were there last night. I have a feeling that this was not a plan the majority signed on to. They *know* this is going to paint a target on their back."

"Because it should."

"Why?" Carys blinked. Her steady, levelheaded dragon appeared to have disappeared. "So that the Queens' Pact crumbles to dust? So there's another fae war where half the human population dies?" Carys stood. "We need to get those babies back, but killing every fae on sight is not going to accomplish that."

He looked up, and his eyes flashed. "Do you forbid me from killing the fae as my nêrys?"

As his nêrys? As his commander?

"You're like a knight."

   "Your knight. I answer only to you, Lady Carys."

   "Please just call me Carys."

   "I answer to you, but you do not command me."

Carys had never seen Cadell so cold. "I am asking you to think of the greater good and not just revenge." She poked at his mind, trying to speak to his mind and his heart, but it was like a wall had slammed down between them.

Cadell said nothing, but his eyes locked her in place.

"I will never keep you from rescuing your children or protecting the vulnerable," she said. "I will never forbid you from protecting me, but we will not take part in the death of random fae who had nothing to do with this."

He held her gaze for a long moment, and Carys refused to look away.

"I will take your suggestion under advisement." The dragon stood and walked toward the house. "Be ready to fly in an hour."

CARYS LEANED out of the coracle, speaking mentally to Cadell as she and the dragon flew over the gently rolling landscape of Southern Anglia. *Where is it?*

Four o'clock, Cadell said. *Do you see it?*

She looked and saw a shimmering light over a dark green spot on the hills. *Got it.* "Duncan, fae fort at four o'clock—do you see it?" The high walls of the coracle protected them from wind, but Carys still had to shout.

"I see it," he yelled. "Marking."

Since sunrise, they'd spotted five fae forts that were not on any of Dafydd's maps. They were eerily quiet, but the land around them was rich with magic. Forests had grown up overnight where there had been pastureland before, and the trees seemed wilder, the animals more bold.

Magic was reasserting its dominance over the Anglian landscape, and Carys was desperate to know what else was changing, but this was the Shadowlands and there was no national news.

Ravens and dragons were the fastest form of communication in times like this, but dragons had congregated in the Cymric Mountains to guard their young, and ravens were fae-friendly creatures with minds of their own.

Carys pulled her head inside the war coracle and looked across at Duncan. "We should land somewhere," she said. "I hate to be the human here, but I really need to pee."

Duncan snorted. "Things they don't include in the fantasy movies, right?"

"I'm pretty flexible, but an isolated bush would be appreciated."

Duncan looked up with a raised eyebrow. "You know every single bush or tree here has some kind of nymph of sprite, right?"

"If a sprite wants to stare at my bare butt, that's on the sprite," Carys said. "But we need to land." *Cadell?*

The dragon was still being standoffish and cold, but at least he wasn't shutting her out.

I heard you.

Seconds later, they were wheeling down in slow circles, aiming for a meadow on the edge of a wooded hilltop where sheep were grazing and two white-coated sheepdogs stood guard.

The canines stood at alert and let out a few barks as the dragon landed, but other than that, there was no one in sight as Carys ran for the edge of the forest, Duncan on her tail.

"I do not need an escort to pee!" she hissed.

"That's what people say right before they get kidnapped by fae," the surly blacksmith grumbled. "It's not like I haven't seen your pretty arse before, darling."

"Seeing me in sexy context versus seeing me pee in the woods are two very different things." She ducked into the middle of a thick bramble, keeping Duncan in sight as he stood near the edge of the trees with his sword drawn.

Carys did her business as quickly as possible, then stood to tie the laces on her woolen trousers, her back to Duncan and her eyes adjusting to the heavy shade of the forest.

It took her a moment to realize what she was seeing in the shadows.

Hidden between the trees and crouched in the bushes was a small group of fae, staring at her with wide eyes. A man and a woman stood on either side of an oak tree with bows drawn and arrows pointed right at her.

She opened her mouth to shout for Duncan, and they pulled their bows taut.

Carys sucked in a breath, and her heart raced until she noticed a small pair of eyes duck out from behind a pair of legs.

There was a fae child with silver hair and bright blue eyes peering between the legs of one of the archers. His golden-brown skin blended into the woods, but that silver hair was impossible to miss, as were his sharply pointed ears, still devoid of the gold rings that would mark him as an adult.

If he was human, Carys would say he looked no more than four or five, but he could be decades old as a fae.

A woman lunged forward, grabbing the child and pulling a dark hat over his silver hair. Her eyes weren't on Carys, they were on the dragon just past the tree line, standing in the meadow.

"Do you want to kill us all?" the woman hissed to the two archers. "We should run while we can. The moment that dragon sees us, the entire wood will be up in flames, and we promised the trees—"

"These woods are our home." The fae man stared at Carys, never moving an inch. "We have lived here for centuries."

Carys raised her hands. "I don't want to harm you."

Nêrys, what is wrong?

For the first time ever, she lied to Cadell. *My drawstring has a knot. I'm fine.*

"Carys, that dragon—" Duncan turned and walked into the trees, halting when he saw the fae archers. "Fae." Duncan raised his sword, and the fae turned their arrows on him.

"They're a family!" Carys stumbled out of the bushes and between the fae archers and Duncan. "There's only four of them, and they have a child."

"Aye, they're right to be worried," Duncan growled. "More than one parent is missing a child today."

"We had nothing to do with that," the female archer said. "If the prince would claim his seat—"

"Eldra, be quiet," the male archer said. "We want no trouble. We're making for the fae gate near Lewes."

"We don't know Éire at all," the woman said. "But it's safer than Anglia now."

Three fae and one fae child, and they'd probably be shot on sight by Harold's soldiers. Carys stared at the small child with bright blue eyes. "Don't go to the fae forts," she blurted. "They're not going to be safe. By now all of them are surrounded by the king's soldiers."

Duncan's voice was low. "Carys—"

"He's a child." She pointed at the little one. "They're a family. They're not a threat."

Duncan narrowed his eyes at the archers, who had still not lowered their weapons.

"They're running away, Duncan."

"Eldra." The fae woman on the ground met Carys's eyes and nodded. "Desmond. Lower your arrows."

Slowly they both lowered their bows, and Duncan lowered his sword.

"She's right," Duncan said. "The king's armies and the wolf clans are surrounding the gates and the forts. You won't be able to get through."

"We can go underground," the female archer said. "My sister speaks to the earth."

"Maybe." Duncan nodded. "That's a possibility. But Harold has sorcerers too. The gates might be warded, and they might know when you try to break through."

The man's shoulders slumped. "What are we supposed to do?"

"Stay here." Duncan's voice had softened. "Stay hidden for now. If you have friends among any local unicorns, they might be able to keep you safe."

The fae woman named Eldra nodded. "We know the chief of the local blessing. She might hide us."

There was no one more trusted in Briton than the unicorns. Even royal soldiers would think hard before they violated the sanctity of unicorn territory. If unicorns were willing to hide these fae, they likely had nothing to do with Cian and Orla's plans.

"Go," Carys said. "Find the unicorns. These woods won't be safe for long."

AFTER THEY FINISHED their surveying run, Cadell flew Carys and Duncan back to Dafydd's estate where Laura greeted them in the courtyard.

"I just got an update from the castle," she said. "Dafydd told me to wait here for you, but it wasn't like I had plans to go anywhere anyway."

Cadell shifted into his human form and approached her. "What did the letter say?"

"It was from Dafydd. He flew over to meet with King Harold and Godrik at the castle," Laura said. "Dylan is in Alba, but I didn't get an update on stuff up there. And Anwyn and Demelza are in Caernarfon, overseeing the fae gates and forts in Cymru."

Carys asked, "With Eamer?"

Laura shrugged. "I would assume so? She's the queen, but her mother is also the one who... you know."

Carys nodded. "Right."

Queen Eamer was in a difficult position. Her loyalty was to the Cymric throne where she was queen, but it was her own mother who had initiated this attack on the rest of Briton.

"Has anyone heard from Lachlan?" Carys asked.

Duncan shot her a look, but she ignored him.

"Dafydd said he's at the castle, but that was all."

No sooner had Laura finished her update than Cadell shifted into his beast form again and took to the sky. *I hear Mared.*

"Mared is returning," Carys told Laura. "That means Dafydd is on his way back." She handed the rolled-up map with the new fae positions to Laura. "Can you make sure he gets this? I need to go clean up."

"Of course. Go." Laura's eyes were fixed on Cadell as he circled the estate in his dragon form. "How is he?"

Carys sighed. "Angry."

Just like the burly man towering over her, but Carys was emotionally tapped out.

The missing children.

The furious dragon.

The terrified fae in the woods.

Added to all that, a day of riding in a coracle had made Carys's hair a bird's nest, and her skin felt crusty and dry.

She passed a maid on the way up to her room and asked for a hot bath to be brought up when it was possible. She hadn't had a bath since her night in Duncan's room, and she was aching all over.

Halfway up the stairs, Duncan caught up with her. "Lachlan is doing his duty."

"Okay." She glanced to the side. "And I'm allowed to ask about him."

He was silent until they arrived at her room and the door was shut behind them.

"Perhaps this isn't the best time," Duncan said. "But maybe I'd like to know if you have plans to continue... seeing my Shadowkin while you're fucking me."

Carys's mouth dropped open. "You're right. This is a really bad time."

He crossed his arms over his chest. "I'd still like an answer."

"Wow." She was honestly gobsmacked. "So you think I had plans to just... jump between beds maybe? Enjoy the Murray-brothers buffet for a while?"

He cursed low and under his breath. "Don't act like I'm being unreasonable."

"I was with Lachlan and you knew that." She pointed to the bed. "Before we ever—"

"Doesn't mean I have to like it!" he shouted. "And that doesn't mean I'm willing to share."

"I didn't have any plan to *share*!"

That took the wind out of his sails, and he had the grace to look abashed. "Carys—"

"No, I'd like you to leave." Her face was burning up. "I realize that this is not a situation either of us has ever been in, but..." Carys realized that actually, she had been in this situation. In fact, she knew exactly how Duncan was feeling. "Do you think I was jealous of Seren?"

Duncan had started toward the door, but he stopped in his tracks. "What?"

"Even before I knew anything about this place or this parallel world or who Seren really was, do you think I was jealous of her?"

Duncan frowned. "I have no idea."

"I knew Lachlan had a dead wife. I knew that there was someone he loved deeply, long before he met me. Someone who had been his first love. Someone he *still* loved, in fact."

"It's not the same thing."

"No, it's not, but if you're going to keep bringing up my past with Lachlan when we're together, that is going to be a problem."

Duncan stepped toward her. "Well, it's not exactly a settled issue, is it?"

"And you think this is the way to settle it?" She marched over to him and glared up at his stubborn, handsome face. "I had a life before I met you. In fact, that's the life that led me to you. So if you cannot handle that, if you're going to always doubt me because somewhere in the world there is a man that I loved before I met you—"

"He's still here!" Duncan pointed toward the door. "There's more than half a chance he'll be in this house before nightfall."

"And you think that means I'm going to sleep with him?" There was a hot ball of anger in her chest, and she felt like punching him in the stomach, but that was far more likely to break her hand than him. "If you think I'm the kind of person who will just—"

"I'm fucking in love with you, Carys!"

Dead silence in the room when a timid knock came at the door. "Lady Carys, your bath is ready."

Carys felt frozen as she walked to the door, highly conscious of the effort it took to heat water in the castle. Sending the chambermaid away when she'd asked for a bath would be impossibly rude.

She let the maid in, then stood back as two stewards carried in a wooden bath. The maid walked to the pipe mounted to the wall, whistled out the window, and pulled down the spout, aiming it over the bath before she pulled the bronze chain that controlled the water.

Duncan murmured, "I'm going to—"

"Don't you dare leave," she hissed.

Carys felt like two dragons were battling in her chest.

One was ridiculously happy and spinning circles.

The other one was slightly terrified and breathing fire.

And neither of those dragons was willing to let Duncan Murray leave her room after he'd said that he loved her.

Did she love him?

Yes.

Oh fuck.

Yes. She did.

Did that mean she didn't love Lachlan anymore?

That was more complicated.

Duncan's shouted declaration hung in the silent air as the maid finished with the hot water. She cleared her throat and looked at Carys. "If you'll just give it a few moments to cool, Lady Carys, the temperature should be perfect. Do you need any help washing your hair?"

"No, thank you."

"Very well." The maid gathered her things, closed the window, and folded the pipe back up against the wall.

It was possible to love two people at the same time, but was it possible to love them in the same way? The love she'd felt for Lachlan felt so rooted in her heart that it made her cross a world to find him.

And the love she felt for Duncan was a bright, burning, wild thing that couldn't be tamed.

And definitely could not be denied.

All the servants slipped out of the room, and Carys turned to Duncan, taking his hand and looking up into his eyes. "I love you too."

CHAPTER TWENTY-THREE

Duncan Murray's green eyes went soft and his face relaxed. "Carys—"

"But I can't tell you that I don't love Lachlan at all," she whispered. "I do, and I think a part of me always will."

Duncan pulled his hand away. "No."

"Do you want me to lie?" She blinked back tears. "If I'd only ever met him, I probably could have loved him forever. That's the truth. But then I met you, and…" She choked back a laugh that was almost a cry. "You're like an eclipse. You block everything else out. There's a war going on outside this castle, and somehow all I want is to be with you."

He lifted his hand to her cheek, his fingers hovering inches away. "What are you saying?"

"I don't want to be with Lachlan," Carys whispered. "I have feelings for him, and I always will. But those feelings are nothing compared to what I feel for you."

Duncan's eyes burned in satisfaction. "You choose me. You love *me* most."

"Yes." She swiped at the tears that fell down her cheeks. "It kind of pisses me off right now, but yes."

His hand softened, and his palm cupped her cheek. "I love you, lass. I love how brave you are. I love how loyal you are to your friends. Even to fucking Lachlan, I suppose."

"And I love you. I love you in a way that I've never loved anyone. I love you in a way that scares me to death, because if you ever took it away" —she clutched a fist to her chest— "I don't know what I'd do."

"I'm not going to take it away," he whispered. "I'm not going to leave you."

"Good." She sniffed and wiped angrily at the tears that kept falling down her cheeks. "Because I've crossed two worlds now, and I think you're *it*. You're the one. You're my fate or my destiny or whatever that means, so if that's not enough for you—"

"Shut up." His mouth fell on hers and he drank her in, enfolding her in his arms and lifting her up.

Carys wrapped her legs around his waist and her arms around his shoulders, falling into his kiss and away from the madness that beat outside their door.

If war was coming, she wanted him. She only wanted him.

Duncan walked her to the edge of the bed and set her down. "Fuck me, but I love these tall beds." When he set her on the massive four-poster bed, her body was perfectly aligned for the rock-hard erection behind his woolen trousers.

He stared down at her desperately. "I don't know if I can wait for a bath again."

"Don't want to wait." She was ripping at his shirt, eager for his skin. "Bath later."

The fire in the hearth crackled, and the water in the bath warmed the room. Carys reached down and pulled her shirt up and over her head.

As soon as her breasts were exposed, Duncan was on them, gripping her back and lifting her body to his mouth, feasting on one breast, then the other, his tongue and his teeth arousing the most ferocious hunger.

She was already wet and aching for him. She reached down, her fingers sliding under the waistband of his trousers, searching for the heat and the steel of his erection. Her hand closed around it, and he groaned against her skin.

She wanted to feel him in her. "Please tell me you have—"

"Yes." He lifted his head, his eyes fixed on her bare breasts as he reached for the pocket of his trousers and pulled out a slim packet that he tore open with his teeth.

Carys pushed his trousers down and slid her hands around his cock, stroking the heated skin there before he pushed her hands away and rolled on the condom.

"In me," she panted.

Carys pulled him by the shoulders, covering her body with his as he hooked his fingers around her pants, tearing them down her legs before positioning his cock at the aching center of her heat and slowly pushing himself to the hilt.

His eyes locked with hers. "Say my name."

"Duncan," she choked out. "Oh my God, Duncan." There were tears in her eyes; he felt so painfully good. And right. And everything.

He was everything.

Duncan fell forward, bracing his arms near her shoulders and leaning down, seducing her mouth as he drew back and then pushed forward with aching tenderness.

His mouth left hers, and he pressed his cheek against her own, whispering in her ear as he made love to her. "I love you, Carys Morgan."

He rocked her back and forth, teasing her clitoris with every thrust of his erection. "*This* is the real magic. You." Thrust again. "And me."

Carys threw her arms around his neck and clung to him as her body began to shake. She felt her climax over every inch of her skin. She felt her pleasure hit like a burst of sparks over her body, and when she cried out, he held her closer.

The flutter of her climax seemed to loose something feral in Duncan, and he lifted up with a roar, gripping her hips with his fingers and rocking into her harder and faster.

He reached down, lifting her ankle to his shoulder and changing the angle so that her pleasure seemed to go on and on. He felt even harder. Bigger. He consumed her.

Duncan turned his head to the side and bit the soft flesh of her calf as his fingers dug into her hip. His thrusts grew wild and uncontrolled until he shouted her name and came, his hands shaking and his muscled body shining with a burst of perspiration in the heated room.

Carys felt like she'd been dropped off the side of a cliff. Her lungs were heaving, and every nerve in her body was on fire.

Duncan fell into bed beside her, grabbing her in a wholly proprietary way and wrapping her in his massive arms before he pulled her against his chest. "After we take that bath, I'm sleeping here tonight. If we're sleeping."

He was as bossy as she somehow knew he was going to be.

Carys didn't want to talk at all, but she forced herself to speak, breathing hard as her ear pressed to his chest, enjoying the drumbeat of his racing heart.

"My body says yes," she panted, "but my brain says we probably need to sleep for whatever is coming tomorrow."

He kissed the top of her head. "Practical girl."

Carys didn't want to be practical. She wanted to hide and bring Duncan with her. But she knew that wasn't going to be an option. At least not for a while.

She closed her eyes and listened to his steady and strong heartbeat. She felt safe in his arms. And a little bit like she'd been run over by a truck. Emotionally anyway.

Duncan's arms tightened around her. "Say it again," he whispered.

Carys closed her eyes and smiled. "I love you, Duncan Murray."

His heartbeat picked up again. "I love you too, Professor Morgan."

ACT III

CHAPTER TWENTY-FOUR

Two hours later Carys was freshly bathed, her hair was braided, and she was sitting at Dafydd's table in the main hall with the king on one end, Winnie and Godrik flanking him, and Lachlan sitting right across from her.

"The king is horrified." Winnie was speaking. "Shocked. They're counting on the shock for us to freeze, but we've already pushed past that." She looked to her right. "Godrik's people were the first to surround the fae forts and gates that are known. And Carys and Cadell—along with other surveying pairs—have identified the new fae gates that were reported, those that we didn't have record of."

"What are the king's plans to get the children back?" Duncan was sitting beside Carys and definitely not looking at Lachlan.

"Right now we're waiting." She sighed, and her professional mask slipped. "We're waiting for word. Now that we've contained the fae, all we can do is wait."

"Is there any sign of the children?" Carys asked. "Has anyone been able to—"

"If the dragons can't find their own young" —Lachlan's face was drawn, and it looked like he hadn't shaved in two days—

"it's highly likely that they're in heavily warded locations. Barrows. Forts. Judging from the way the attacks occurred, they were likely dispersed." He glanced at Carys, then looked at Dafydd. "The human children could be glamoured and sleeping under fae mounds we know nothing about and not emerge for a century."

Carys felt powerless.

That is how they want you to feel. Cadell spoke to her mind.

A moment later, he and two other dragons strode into the hall. "Your Majesty." He nodded at Dafydd. "Demelza has sensed her young."

Dafydd rose to his feet. "Where?"

Winnie was still on her feet. "Are there any human children with the dragons? Any wolves?"

"Where?" Dafydd repeated.

Cadell's gaze was steady. "A fae fort that appeared near Maen Llia."

"Go. Mared and I will return to Caernarfon. Let Anwyn and Demelza command the wing."

Cadell's eyes were burning. "Yes, Your Majesty."

"You and Carys will join her." Dafydd locked his eyes on Carys. "Gather your things now."

Lachlan and Duncan both rose to their feet.

"She's not ready," Lachlan said.

Duncan said, "I'm going with her."

"Sit down, both of you," Dafydd roared. "My niece is nêr ddraig, and she has more magic than both of you. Sit your bloody arses in your chairs." He glared at Carys. "Leave this world now or join your dragon."

Carys felt a shivering and terrifying sense of purpose. She'd been training for this. She hadn't imagined she'd ever be called to actually shoot arrows from a dangling wooden boat in the sky, but she could. In theory.

But more, Cadell had lived his entire life to protect his people, and there was no way she was taking him from this battle. Carys stood. "Yes, Your Majesty."

Thank you, Nêrys.

She met Duncan's eyes for a brief moment before she walked to Cadell's side.

Laura was sitting next to Lachlan. She gave Carys a short nod. "Be careful."

"I will."

One last glance at Lachlan, then at Duncan.

Carys looked up at Cadell and nodded. "Let's go."

THE WIND WAS FREEZING, but all communication was mental. Carys was seated in a small coracle with high sides and strategically placed arrowslits as Cadell's massive wings surged west toward the southern Cymric Mountains.

She was dressed in leather armor and carrying the bow she'd trained with back in California, but she had a short Cymric bow in reserve.

Two dragons had flown with them from London, and another joined them ten minutes into their journey.

Then another.

And another.

Now there were thirty dragons with them and at least two dozen nêr ddraig who had joined them en route to Maen Llia, an abandoned stone fortress in the southern valleys of Cymru.

As they approached the mountains, the clouds grew heavier. The sky was pregnant with mist and fog, and Carys's teeth chattered from the cold.

She tilted her leather helmet back and peeked out of an arrowslit at the silent flock of dragons who flew with them.

Who are they?

Dragons from Eryri mostly. But a few who heard the call and joined us. There are solitary dragons in Southern Anglia.

The dragons must have been speaking to each other with their mental voices because Carys could hear nothing but Cadell.

I'm scared.

You are scared because you're not an idiot. His voice was softer. *Nothing will happen to you.*

Carys blinked back frosty tears from the wind. *And I'm scared for the children.*

Dragon children are not without their defenses. Cadell's voice was grim. *Not even babies.*

She felt when the wing began to descend.

Listen for my command and my direction. You remember your arrow positions?

The arrowslits were built into the war coracle at forty-five-degree intervals, and Carys's job was to listen for Cadell's command to fire arrows. He told her which position and what angle from the horizon, and Carys fired. She couldn't see the ground; she had to depend entirely on Cadell's targeting.

Fae archers on the hill at two o'clock.

Her heart began to race. "What do I do?"

Don't speak aloud. They might be able to hear you even from the ground.

Okay fine, what do I do?

Wait.

There was a deep rumbling and a high scream, and then Carys saw the gloaming lit up by a burst of orange-and-red light to her right.

Position six. One fifty degrees. Wait.

Carys's movements were automatic. She moved to the sixth arrowslit, nocked an arrow, and mentally aligned herself with the center post of the coracle, angling her bow down one hundred and fifty degrees toward the ground.

She called back to Cadell, *In position.*

Fae archers. Fire on my word.

Ready.

Now.

Carys nocked another arrow from the quiver at her waist, shooting one, then another, then another in rapid succession.

Hold.

As she was shooting, she felt the response under her feet. Rapid thunks against wood as arrows hit the bottom of the coracle, and one sped past the coracle and pierced Cadell's wing.

Carys felt it in her own body, but she said nothing. Heat filled her chest as she felt Cadell's magic rush to the wound, but there was nothing she could do in that moment.

Going back for another pass.

How many archers?

I am following orders. So should you.

It went against everything in Carys's being to act as an automaton commanded by someone else, but she could see very little, and she had to trust Cadell's eyes and the eyes of every dragon in the air that night.

Turning. Cadell wheeled around, throwing Carys back against the wall of the coracle. *Position three. One hundred and ten degrees.*

Carys fought her way into position and braced her legs as the coracle rocked and rolled with the wind. She kept her back parallel to the center post and leaned her shoulder on the wall of the coracle.

Just then a shower of arrows hit the wall of the coracle where Carys was leaning, and the tip of one pierced just far enough through the wood to jab into her arm.

"Shit!"

Silent!

"Fuck that! They can't hear me down there, and why the hell aren't we just razing this entire field with fire, Cadell?"

There are wild fae in the trees, Nêrys. There are unicorns in the valley. Should we kill all of them to retrieve the small ones? That is what Demelza would like to do.

Carys closed her eyes and leaned against the center post, positioning herself again.

In position.

Fire in three... two... now.

Carys let loose with another volley of rapid-fire arrows from her quiver. She had two more quivers waiting in the coracle, ready to go. The arrows that Anwyn had given to her were massive things—long, thick, and designed to pierce fae armor. She felt clumsy with them, but she hoped that anything she could do would help.

Anything?

The archers have run back to Maen Llia. The dragon began to descend. *Demelza has heard her daughter's voice.* There was a shot of joy through her bond with Cadell. *I can hear her too.*

There was a fierce scream and another rumbling roar before Carys saw the night light up with fire.

She ran to the other side of the coracle, peering out the arrowslit to see a dragon strafing the valley below them with a river of fire.

It was eerily silent as a squad of dragons descended, Carys and Cadell among them.

What's happening?

Demelza knows where the children are. We are landing. Brace and arm yourself.

Carys grabbed her bow, nocked an arrow, then steadied herself against the back wall of the coracle as they descended. Moments later, the round-bottomed coracle scraped along the ground before Cadell let go, rocking the unit forward and back until the door burst open and braced the coracle on the ground.

Carys aimed her arrow at the foggy night, waiting for the signal to come out of the vessel and wary of anything that might come through the narrow door.

"Carys!" She heard Dylan's voice, but she waited. The fae could imitate voices. It was only when the young man marched toward the coracle and Carys could see his face that she lowered her arrow and stood.

"What's happening?"

There were screams in the distance and the crackling sound of burning wood.

"Demelza has found the fort, but she can't break the wards," Dylan said. "We're blocked."

Carys searched the landscape, but the night was fully descended. "Are there woods here? Have you tried calling an ellyllon?"

Dylan's eyes went wide. "They're fae."

"They're Cymric!" Carys shouted. "We don't have sorcerers or mages, do we?"

"The fae are the ones who *took* the children, you idiot."

"And the fae are the only ones who can open those gates." Carys started to run toward the sound of screaming. "Dylan, we need their help."

A rust-skinned wyvern had braced her wings wide and was sweeping fire across the top of the hill. Carys could see blackened bodies scattered on the hillside and others running away.

"This is madness." Carys turned to Dylan. "We're never going to get them out without fae help."

Dylan's eyes turned hard. "What about you? Do you have fae powers?"

Carys blinked. "Oh my God, is that what people think?"

Dylan shrugged.

"You're idiots." Carys ran to the nearest copse of trees she could find and knelt down, pressing her face to the ground. "I'm sorry. I'm so sorry."

She felt the earth move beneath her, as if it were sighing. When she lifted her eyes, she saw the wide, frightened gaze of a tiny tree sprite, her cheek blackened from ashes and her wings drooping. The creature was hiding in the brambles and trying to blend in.

"I'm sorry," Carys whispered. "I know you didn't have anything to do with this."

The sprite clung to the branches of the bush that was shielding her.

"Can you open the gate?" Carys asked. "There are stolen children inside. That is what is making the dragon so angry. She's frightened for her child."

The wood sprite crawled to the base of the bush and whispered something into the ground.

The earth beneath the bramble began to rumble and shake, and Carys had a flashback to the forest god that had risen and trapped her foot.

"What did you do?" Dylan shouted.

Cadell called out to her from his position near Demelza. *Carys, what is happening?*

I asked for help. Whether they got it was going to depend on how much power that little sprite had and how much she could rouse.

Carys had a feeling that the gentle residents of this mountain valley just wanted all these dragons to go away.

A moment later, the ground went quiet and Carys's heart sank. Maybe the earth was too angry with the dragons. Maybe the fae wards were too strong.

Demelza rose on her back legs and spread her wings, her head turning up as a scream of rage and sorrow erupted from her throat in a feral and gutting cry to the sky.

Moments later, a bright green light erupted under the soil. It arrowed through the valley, turning and twisting around rocks and roots, arrowing toward the fae mound where bodies were scattered and the grass was charred and black.

"What is it?" Dylan's voice was in awe.

"I don't know."

The glowing green power disappeared under the mound, then moments later, the earth yawned open and Carys could hear children's screams.

"No!" She ran toward the black, gaping hole, but no sooner had she reached it than a dozen children crawled out of the darkness, two of them running straight toward the hovering dragons while the others stumbled and blinked their eyes with confusion.

"Mam?" A little girl rubbed her eyes. "Tad?"

"They're human!" Carys ran toward them, ignoring the two small human-shaped dragons who were immediately enveloped by a squadron of dragons who hid them from view. A moment later, Demelza took off, a coracle clutched in one foot while Anwyn hung from her other leg.

Dylan let out a sigh. "They're safe."

"Tad?" a little boy called. "Jory?"

Carys took the hand of one child and reached for another. "The other children need help."

Both the little ones who took her hands started speaking in rapid Cymric, far too fast for Carys to understand, but within moments, a dozen dragon riders had run over and picked up the children, explaining where they were.

They spoke hurriedly, cuddling the children against their leather armor and wiping their tears. There were cries and sniffles, but none of the children appeared harmed.

Carys waited for Cadell to reach her in human form before she went to the open, earthen mouth of the fae fort. She took a deep breath before she walked inside, bracing herself to find... whatever it was they might find.

"Are you ready?"

Cadell nodded, and Carys nocked an arrow.

"Let's go."

CHAPTER TWENTY-FIVE

"There was nothing," Carys said. "From what I could see, I'd guess the human children had been glamoured. There were sleeping mats but no food. No signs that the kids had even been awake."

"But the dragon children had been conscious the entire time," Cadell told the group of allies as they sat in the library. "Demelza's daughter was able to call to us when we got close enough. That's how we were able to locate the fort."

They were sitting in the library with Godrik, Winnie, Duncan, Lachlan, and Laura. It was nearly midnight by the time Carys and Cadell were able to return to Dafydd's house.

Dafydd remained in Cymru with his people while Anwyn and Demelza guarded the children. That left Carys and Cadell as the only nêr ddraig in London to coordinate with Harold and his forces.

"How?" Duncan sat next to Carys, rubbing salve on her fingers, which were bloody from shooting. "Harold's sorcerers and mages have been looking for ways to break through the fae wards, but nothing so far has worked."

Cadell shot Carys a dark look and shook his head. "Dragon children have their own magic," he said vaguely. "That's all you need to know."

They had both seen it. Carys and Cadell had seen the blood on the walls and the sharp rocks scattered on the ground that the small dragons had used to cut themselves and bleed into the soil that bound them. It was that dragon blood that had allowed the children to fracture the fae spells keeping them imprisoned and call out for help.

Fae didn't realize how much iron was in dragon blood, and no dragon in the world wanted them to know. It made the creatures' blood oxygen rich and helped their massive bodies to fly.

That iron also meant that dragon blood could break fae wards. At least enough for two small dragons to send out a distress call.

"What other news do you have?" Carys looked at Winnie and Godrik. "Are there any signs of the wolf children or the missing Anglian kids?"

"Nothing so far," Winnie said.

Lachlan was staring at the fire. "At last count, there were forty human children missing in Alba and five wolves. No unicorns. Not a single one."

Laura was sitting next to Lachlan. "You don't think that the unicorns—"

"No!" Lachlan shook his head. "I don't think anyone suspects that they're working with Cian and Orla, but it's... odd."

"Unicorn magic is elemental," Carys offered. "It might be similar enough to fae magic that hiding their children wouldn't be effective."

Duncan added, "Or maybe they just didn't want to piss the unicorns off."

"But they were willing to piss off dragons?" Winnie shook her head. "I don't buy it."

"Maybe the fae *want* to keep the unicorns neutral." Carys thought about the fae family in the forest who said they would try to seek shelter with the local blessing. "Unicorn blessings are powerful; no one wants to threaten them."

Duncan glanced at Carys. "If the unicorns are neutral, they can be a safe haven for fleeing fae who had nothing to do with Cian's plans."

"So even the fae don't want to provoke them?" Lachlan shrugged. "It's as good a theory as any, I suppose." Alba had the greatest concentration of unicorns in Briton. They were loyal to the Alban chiefs, but they were also aloof. Them being neutral wasn't exactly a surprise.

Godrik was staring at Carys. "You did something. I heard the soldiers talking in the courtyard. They said you did something to break open the wards."

Carys shook her head. "I didn't do anything. I was on the ground, and I noticed this little tiny tree sprite that was hiding in a bush." She looked around the room. "She was terrified. I mean, we have to assume that none of the wild fae like the sprites or the pixies or the brownies have anything to do with this."

Godrik muttered, "I will admit that it's highly unlikely that wild fae and minor fae were in on Cian's plans, but they're also not powerful compared to the high fae of Temris. Do these wild fae even matter?"

Duncan frowned. "I wouldn't say that. Wild fae can be *very* powerful. They're just more solitary."

"And they tend to be loyal to their specific forest or river." Lachlan leaned forward, resting his elbows on his knees and staring at the fire. "Or house for that matter. A brownie or an úruisg would never harm a child of their house."

"Annoy it, maybe." Duncan cracked a smile. "God knows Auld Mags used to play her pranks on us when we were children." He glanced at Lachlan. "Particularly if we were annoying her. But harming them? Stealing them away from their beds?" He shook his head. "I can't see it."

Carys nodded slowly. "It would violate their bargain with the home. If the family living there was feeding the brownie or taking care of the forest where a sprite lived, harming that family would break magical rules."

Laura said, "In our home, not even a powerful deity could make one of the Kheta Inwe betray the forest or the village they care for. It would go against their nature on an elemental level."

"Fine," Winnie said. "They might not have taken the children, but they didn't stop Cian's people from taking them either."

Godrik lifted his chin. "Not every home in Anglia has a house fae. Most wolf houses don't have them at all."

Winnie narrowed her eyes. "You're right. Most houses in the city don't hold fae." She stood and started to pace. "Hosting a brownie or a gnome in the garden is kind of seen as a country thing."

Carys blinked. "Is possible Cian and Orla's people only stole children from houses with no house fae?"

Winnie stopped pacing. "It's something to ask. And it might even be a way for families to defend themselves."

"If that's true," Laura said, "that means the brownies, the sprites, and the gnomes might be allies."

Carys turned toward Godrik. "You asked me what I did in Maen Llia, but it wasn't me at all. I told the tree sprite there were children locked in the fort, and she did something. That's what the soldiers saw, but it wasn't me. I'm almost sure it was the sprite."

"There was elemental magic," Cadell said. "It seemed that the earth itself responded. The ground broke open, but it was from inside the fort, not outside."

"So the minor fae" —Lachlan leaned forward— "the brownies and the sprites—"

"Mermin and the water serpents," Winnie added. "There are so many in the Tamis."

Godrik nodded. "And people still offer sacrifices to the river," he said. "Even if they ignore the household fae, everyone recognizes the magic in the river."

"Selkies, the Great Serpent." Winnie's eyes were sharp. "They could all be allies. We have to reach out to them."

"You must have court mages," Laura said. "I'd contact them first."

Duncan pulled Carys's arm into his lap and held her hand. "Cian's court isn't likely to coordinate with the wild fae, are they? In a way, they're as bad as the humans are. They mostly ignore anyone who's not high fae."

"We should return to the castle," Winnie said. "But I'll ask the families with missing children about house fae. If they have them and those fae didn't protect the children, they may be working with Cian and Orla's people."

"But if they didn't," Cadell said, "then Anglia has a powerful and overlooked ally that can help you find the missing."

Godrik stood and held his hand toward Cadell, who took it.

They grasped forearms, and Godrik said, "I'm relieved your young are safe."

"I wish the best for your hunt," Cadell said. "If my nêrys and I can be of any help, please send a messenger."

"There were ten human children being kept in that mound with the young dragons," Carys said to Godrik. "They only remembered falling asleep; then they woke up in the fae mound when the wards broke open."

"We can hope that the Anglian children are glamoured as well," Winnie said. "It might be a comfort to their parents to know that they're probably not terrified."

"Wolf children won't sleep." Godrik's voice was cold. "Fae spells do not work on them."

Laura stood as well. "Has anyone heard anything from Orla or the fae? Have they made any demands?"

"Nothing specific." Winnie held out a pamphlet. "Another one of these was dropped last night, but it's doing nothing but causing trouble with the people."

Carys looked over Laura's shoulder and began to read.

The humans of Briton have forgotten their duties to honor the fae.

They mix with foreign magic and welcome Valachian monsters to their skies. They have forgotten who they are and from where their children come.

"We've got some gross fae nationalism happening with this one, huh?" Carys muttered.

Because the humans of Anglia forget their past, their fields will be cursed and their animals will lose the protection of fae blessing.

Honor the true fae king of Briton.

Bow to Cian, high fae king.

"Carys."

She turned on her way out of the library to see Lachlan waiting in the hall.

Duncan still had her hand in his, and he squeezed it.

Carys turned to him and looked up. "Hey. Give us a minute, okay?"

Duncan glanced at his Shadowkin, then back at Carys. He nodded. "I'll wait for you in your room," he said loudly.

"Thank you," she said, "for informing the entire first floor about that."

Duncan shrugged before he dropped her hand and walked toward the entry hall.

Lachlan watched him walk away, his arms crossed over his chest. "Walk in the garden?"

"Sure." She was exhausted, but she'd rather have this conversation sooner than later.

He followed her toward the kitchen and then out the door to the vegetable garden. Her room overlooked the back garden. If Duncan wanted to watch them talk, she wasn't hiding anything.

"You and Duncan are together now," Lachlan said.

Carys walked past the beds of rosemary and turned to him, her arms crossed over her chest. "We are."

Lachlan nodded, and his eyes were sad. "I can't blame you. He's a good man."

"He is."

"Does that mean..." Lachlan cleared his throat. "I mean, will you be moving to Scotland?"

"I don't know. We haven't really talked about it."

Lachlan stared at the fountain burbling in the distance. "I'm going to step back," he said. "Rory wants to be king; I do not."

Carys blinked. "But at the coronation—"

"I'm man enough to know when I'm not suited for a role," Lachlan said. "I love my people, and I'll be honored to serve in my brother's court. But during all this, the people have rallied around my father and Rory."

"Because you're here."

Lachlan shrugged. "He took advantage of the timing to consolidate his influence there. It's not something I would have thought to do. But it's something a king would do."

"Ah." Carys nodded. "So you think he'll be a better king because of that?"

"I hope so." Lachlan sat on a stone bench and looked up at her, his vivid green eyes glowing in the torchlight. "Either way, I don't *want* the crown. Far better if it goes to him."

"Okay." Carys walked over and sat beside him. "You know that's not why I decided—"

"You don't have to explain yourself to me," Lachlan said. "I see how you look at him."

She laughed a little bit. "With annoyance? Irritation? How do I look at Duncan?"

Lachlan's voice was soft. "The way I wanted you to look at me."

Carys blinked. "Lachlan—"

"Maybe that was the way that I used to look at Seren," he murmured. "She was the beginning and end of my world, but she drove me absolutely crazy at times."

She cocked her head back to look at the starless sky. "I'm going to think about that later. I'm not going to be able to stop myself."

Lachlan frowned. "What were we doing, Carys? Was it all just grief for the ones we lost? Seren? Your parents? I know I love you. I *still* love you. Even while you're choosing him. There's this…" He clenched a fist to his chest. "I feel this ball of anger in my chest that I know you don't deserve. I'm jealous as hell. But I can't hate either of you."

"We loved each other." Carys felt tears creeping up again, and God, she was tired of crying, but she couldn't seem to stop. "We loved each other, Lachlan. We really did. I know that."

"But you love him more."

Yes. She didn't want to say that; it felt cruel. She swallowed the hard lump at the back of her throat. "Maybe it's not more or less. Maybe it's just different."

Lachlan nodded. His shoulders were tense. His muscled arms crossed over his chest. "I can accept that, but I still love you. If my love is not what you need right now, I accept that too." He looked at her. "But know that I'll never stop loving you. Not ever."

Lachlan picked up her hand, lifted her palm to his lips, and pressed a chaste and fervent kiss there. He closed his eyes and whispered, "I will *always* love you, Carys Morgan. Good night."

Blinking back tears, Carys watched him stand and walk back to the house.

Then her eyes rose, and she saw the curtains in her room snap shut.

Carys was wrapped in Duncan's arms when she heard a tap on her door early the next morning.

"Carys?" Duncan's voice was sleepy.

She pulled away from his hold and sat up in bed. "It's Cadell."

You need to wake up.

It was early morning, and she could already hear the house stirring. Horses were neighing in the courtyard, and the heavy beat of dragon wings sounded overhead.

"Go ahead." Duncan rolled out of bed and cleared his throat. "I'll go back to my room and get ready."

"I don't know what he wants." She opened the door to see her dragon in human form, already standing on the other side with his arm braced against the top arch of the doorway. "What's up?"

"We're hunting with Godrik today." Cadell glanced at Duncan. "The human can join us. Bring your sword."

"Done." Duncan threw his overcoat over his shoulders and frowned. "I mean, I would anyway, but is there a specific reason?"

Carys knew before Cadell said it. It hit her like a flash. "The iron. If the iron in the children's blood could break through the wards—"

"What the fuck are you talking about?" Duncan growled. "What children's blood?"

Cadell stepped inside the room and closed the door. "The young dragons who were being held in the fae fort cut themselves to break through the wards and call out for the horde. If the iron in their blood could fracture the fae spells, it's possible that any fae fort that is holding a wolf child might fracture from the iron in your sword."

Only five living people in all of the Shadowlands knew that Duncan's sword was forged with dragon blood, and they'd tried very hard to keep it a secret.

"So we hunt with Godrik." Duncan nodded. "Guess the rumors about my blade are about to become more fact than rumor."

"It's worth it if it finds these kids," Carys said.

Duncan leaned over and kissed her forehead. "Not even a question in my mind, lass. I'll get dressed and meet you at the stables." He glanced at Cadell. "You two flying or riding?"

"I'll fly overhead and spot from the sky," Cadell said. "Carys can ride with you and Godrik's people so we can communicate."

"Good thinking," Carys said.

She watched Duncan open and shut the door before she started to get ready. Cadell turned his back and watched the fire as she moved behind the screen in the corner by the wardrobe.

"You've settled on the surly one then."

Carys had known he was going to bring it up. Cadell acted like he had no interest in her personal life, but he was as nosy as Laura was.

"Yes," she said. "He's..." She didn't know what to say.

The human one? The smart choice? Those weren't the reasons she'd fallen in love with Duncan.

"You love him," Cadell said simply. "You don't have to explain."

Okay. Well, that was a relief. "He understands me."

"He does. So does Lachlan."

Carys was half-naked when she poked her head out from behind the screen. "What's that supposed to mean? *Now* you have an opinion?"

"I've always had an opinion," Cadell muttered. "Are you ready?"

"No." She ducked back behind the screen and pulled on a fresh linen tunic. If she was riding, she'd get sweaty, so she didn't want to wear wool. The days had been far more summery than cool. "I don't need your opinion. It shouldn't matter."

But it does, he said silently.

"I know it does," she hissed. "And I don't understand why."

"Because I am your dragon." His voice was soft and mildly amused. "And I am older and wiser than you."

"Okay, old and wise dragon." She belted the tunic around her waist and walked toward the fire. "Why is Duncan a better choice than Lachlan?"

"He's not." Cadell turned. "But he is the one your heart wants. That's what matters."

Carys let out a slow breath. "It hurts, but I love Duncan more."

"Lachlan's pain is his own responsibility," Cadell stood at attention with his hands behind his back. "Duncan Murray is an honorable man who cares for you and is a fierce protector of the people under his authority and care. I respect him greatly."

Carys nodded. "Okay. You're right."

"And he makes you laugh," Cadell added. "He also makes you angry."

"That's a good thing?"

"Anger isn't the opposite of love, Nêrys. The opposite of love is indifference." He raised an eyebrow. "And you have never been indifferent to Duncan Murray."

SHE RODE the beautiful mare named Leuca from the stables that morning, the dappled grey greeting her with a stomp and a toss of her head.

"I brought you an apple," Carys said, holding out the shining red fruit to the mare. "And I'm sorry it's been so many days since I visited."

The mare laughed a little bit, and Carys remembered who she was. "You're Epona's daughter, aren't you?"

A short whinny in response.

Carys leaned close and whispered, "My mother was born here. She was Shadowkin." It was the first time she'd said it out loud. "She served your mother when she lived here. I think she loved her very much."

Leuca turned and pressed her cheek to Carys's body, letting out a happy huff.

Carys didn't hear the horse's words like she could hear Cadell's, but words popped into her mind, and she somehow knew they were from the horse.

I see you. Welcome home.

"My mom always had a strange reaction to horses when I was young." Carys laid the saddle pad and blanket over Leuca's back, chatting as she readied the horse for the day. "I used to think she didn't like them, but maybe it was too painful for her to have that reminder of Epona in the Brightlands."

Leuca whinnied again.

Duncan walked into the stables. "Who are you talking to?"

"Leuca." Carys nodded at the horse. "She's Epona's daughter."

"Ah." Duncan nodded. "Like your mum."

Carys smiled. He was so quick. So unexpectedly intuitive. "Yes, exactly."

"She's a lovely girl." The big man stroked along Leuca's cheek and reached for the saddle that was waiting near the door. "A good friend to have today. I just spoke to Godrik, and he plans to ride hard. There are two different fae forts where they think there might be children hidden."

Carys wasn't an expert rider. She'd become much more comfortable on horseback since her first trip to the Shadowlands, but she was likely the least experienced rider in the hunting party that day.

"I'll stick with Leuca."

"She's more experienced at being a horse than you are as a rider." Duncan put the saddle on the horse, securing the girth and fixing the stirrups for Carys. "If it comes to it, just give Leuca her head and hang on. She'll know what to do."

When the mare was ready, Duncan helped Carys up and then patted the mare's flank before Carys nudged her forward and walked out to the courtyard.

Godrik and the wolves were already waiting, Godrik on horseback and the rest of the wolves in their fur.

The North Wolves of Anglia were massive beasts who were immediately distinguished from the wild animals they mimicked.

Their heads came nearly to the shoulder of Carys's mount, and their eyes were wise and human, though they moved exactly like wolves.

Like the dragons, North Wolves could speak silently to each other, so Godrik was already moving toward the forest when Duncan joined her.

"We're riding south," he said. "There's a fae fort near Effra Green that's just risen in the past week. The farmers in the village say that the unicorns that lived in the woods south of the green moved farther into the forest three days ago."

"The same day the children were taken?" Duncan asked.

Godrik nodded. "It's been surrounded by Harold's men since the attack, and I want to take a closer look. Four children from the village are missing, and it's near to a small pack that roamed near the woodland where another child went missing."

Carys knew at least five families must have been going insane for days, and the sense of urgency caused any enjoyment of the bright, warm morning to flee. "Are there still fae in the forest even though the unicorns have left?"

"Yes." Godrik raised a black eyebrow. "Might be a good time to test your theory, Lady Carys."

They rode south through Hyde Forest and headed toward the river, crossing the wide stone bridge over the Tamis and escorted by a pack of over twenty North Wolves.

Carys didn't know how long they rode, but Cadell was in the sky overhead, and the light was as bright as it got in the Shadowlands by the time they crossed the narrow Effra River and saw the fae mound rising in the middle of a village green.

Sheep and donkeys were grazing around the base of the mound, and the green was patrolled by a line of red-coated soldiers. Other than the grazing animals and the stoic soldiers, nothing moved.

The town looked as if it were frozen. No shopkeepers called out, and the few pedestrians on the cobbled streets were silent and watchful as they passed.

The fairy fort looked as if it had been there for years, not three days. Thick grass carpeted its high slopes, and flowers sprang from the earth. Daffodils spread across the village green, their bright yellow blooms bobbing between the black-faced sheep.

Two of Godrik's wolves crossed the soldier's perimeter and padded over to sniff around the base of the mound. Whatever it was they were searching for, they turned back with drooping tails and went to sit near Godrik's mount.

The wolf dismounted from his sturdy horse and walked over to Carys and Duncan.

"They don't smell anything. The scent of fae magic is so strong that it drowns everything else out."

Carys looked at Duncan, then down at his sword.

"All right," the Scotsman grumbled. "Let's paint a target on my back." He sighed and swung his leg over his horse as he got to the ground. "Carys, is the dragon near?"

Carys mentally reached for Cadell, who was flying in broad circles around woods that bordered the green. "He's nearby."

Duncan glanced at Harold's soldiers, then back at Godrik. "You're not seeing anything you're about to see, understand?"

Godrik looked confused, but he nodded anyway and looked at Carys. "Is this about the magic you used for the dragon children?"

"Again, that was *not* me," she said. "Does everyone here think I have some kind of fae magic?"

"You're a Brightlander who can talk to dragons," Godrik said. "Yes."

Carys walked next to Duncan as he crossed the line of red-coated troops and strode across the green. Then—like a highlander in a movie—he pulled the steel sword from its scabbard, the silver glinting in the sun, and drove the blade into the earth just at the base of the newly risen ground.

The soldiers around them muttered in low voices, and the wolves barked and yipped as the earth around the mound rolled like there was an earthquake. The sheep bleated and the donkeys brayed, scattering from the green as the soldiers moved closer.

Godrik's shoulders went back and his eyes went wide. "I don't know what that was, but I heard something."

A wolf sat back on its haunches and threw its head up, howling into the air; then another joined it and another.

"They can hear the children!" Godrik shouted. "There are children under the ground."

Half a dozen of the wolves ran to the side of the mound and began to dig, furiously churning the earth and tearing at it with their claws as others in the pack continued to howl.

But no matter how much they dug and how much the earth climbed in piles behind the digging animals, the holes they dug seemed to fill as quickly as they created them.

The wards are still intact, Cadell said into her mind. *I can feel them. There is a crack, but nothing that will let them break through.*

Can you break them?

Not without bleeding myself, and you know how dangerous that is.

Carys knew that if she asked it, Cadell would offer his own blood to free whatever children were trapped under the earth, but it would be a massive risk. There would be no way to hide what had broken the fae wards, and if the whole of Briton discovered what dragon blood could do, Cadell's kind could be hunted.

"Duncan, can you drive your sword deeper?"

"I can try, but I don't know if it will help." He pushed the blade farther into the ground, but Godrik shook his head.

"I can hear them now. I can feel them, but it's like they're behind a wall. And now they can hear us and they're panicking." The burly man's chest was heaving in anger and frustration. He threw his head back and shouted, "Damn you to hell, Cian Elathason!"

Carys heard the soldiers begin to yell, and the villagers were running toward the mound, drawn to the howling wolves and the rumble of the earth as it began to shake and roll.

But no matter the rocking and churning, the smooth surface of the green mound did not break open to reveal any way inside.

Carys was starting to feel desperate when she heard a low, droning hum from the forest south of the village.

She turned and saw a dark figure coming through the trees, singing a song in a low, familiar voice.

The wolves grew quiet. The soldiers froze.

The humans in the village turned toward the voice; then one by one, they fell silent, sat down wherever they were, and listened with rapt attention and adoring faces.

Carys saw Duncan staring at the figure as if he was caught in a trance. "Duncan?"

The big man gripped his sword and shook his head. "Damn fae."

Dru walked from between the trees, a green cloak thrown over his shoulders and twigs and feathers trailing from his hair.

Despite his wild appearance, the dark fae's face was regal, and the dancing lights of sprites and pixies followed behind him like a luminous cloud.

"The fae." Godrik growled. "He dares show his face—"

"Quiet." Dru raised his hand, palm up, and the wolf disappeared in a shower of silver and gold sparks until there was no man and a massive wolf crouched near Godrik's horse.

The gelding reared and Godrik let out a nasty growl, but Dru continued to walk forward, kneeling before the green earthen mound.

"Duncan," Dru said quietly. "Take your sword from the earth. You've upset its magic."

Duncan pulled up the sword, and the soil spit it out with a stretch and a settling rumble.

Then Dru put his hands deep into the earth, lifted his voice in a new song, and the side of the green, flowering mound crumbled away.

CHAPTER TWENTY-SIX

There were ten children hidden in the fae mound—two wolves and eight humans. The wolf pups immediately shifted to their animals forms, running toward the adults, who circled them with wagging tails and excited yips.

Minutes after the shifter children ran away with half the pack, the villagers sitting around the green seemed to wake out of their trance and called for their missing children.

"Alfred?" A woman ran to the mound, hesitating only a second before she ran into the gaping cave. "Alfred!"

"Sara?"

"Is Hilda inside?"

Moments later, the humans of the village had crowded into the open fae mound, lifting children from the cave, most of them rubbing their eyes.

They had dirty faces and blinking eyes, but none of them seemed to be harmed.

Carys watched the commotion from the edge of the green, standing next to Dru, who was sitting on the ground with hollow eyes, watching the humans rescue the children.

Carys crouched down next to him. "Your brother did this."

"I know."

Duncan walked over, his eyes shooting daggers at Dru. "Children, Dru. Hundreds of children are still missing."

He turned dark eyes up to meet Duncan's glare. "Are you asking me for a favor, Duncan Murray?"

"Fuck your favors and your tricks." The angry Scotsman pointed his sword at Dru. "Fuck all your magic and machinations. Do the right thing, Diarmuid."

"The right thing?" Dru dug his fingers into the ground. "It's quite a thing to think you know what that is, Duncan Murray."

"You could free all of them. You could—"

"The children of Briton are sleeping." Dru looked at Carys. "They might be the safest ones on the island right now. War with my brother means human blood spilled. The earth will drink the life of this island, and more children than just these missing ones will be harmed."

Something tickled the back of Carys's mind, but just then Godrik stormed over to them, halting when he came close to the fae prince.

"My people are grateful that the children are safe," he said carefully.

Dru nodded. "I wish that this had never happened."

"But it did," Godrik said. "And you freed them."

Dru shrugged. "They were not in any danger. The magic they used put those within the wards in stasis. They would have come to no harm. No hunger or thirst would have touched them."

"But they were away from their families. Their clans." Godrik nodded. "We are grateful."

"I am pleased that your children are returned to you," Dru said.

He might have said he was pleased, but the dark-eyed fae looked anything but happy.

Dru stared at the fae fort, whispering as it slowly receded into the ground.

"Duncan." Godrik turned to the blacksmith. "Can I speak to you for a moment?"

"Of course." Duncan cast one more angry look at Dru, then walked away.

Dru watched them. "The wolf wants to know where Duncan obtained his weapon."

Carys sat next to him and put her hands into the soil, feeling the pulse and life of the earth beneath them. "I'm sure he does."

Duncan wouldn't tell him. He'd never endanger Cadell or the dragons that way.

"Can you feel it?" Dru asked, his hands still pressed to the earth.

"I feel something. Nothing like what you and Naida feel, I'm sure. Nothing like Laura."

"Your friend is a very skilled mage for a mundane human." Dru's eyebrows went up. "It's no wonder your mother chose a place such as the Bay-wood. A place where the earth meets the sea. A place where light and darkness sit next to each other like friends."

Carys smiled. "I don't remember telling you where I was from."

Dru smiled. "I imagine she felt right at home there."

"You called me Carys Morgan, daughter of two worlds."

"Did I?" Dru watched the children waking and the crying adults who wrapped them in blankets and tried to feed them.

"I met my mother's Brightkin when I was in London."

"Did you go to visit Macha?"

"Is that her name?"

Dru leaned back on the grass. "It's one of her names." He looked at the forest behind them. "I feel her. She's not that far from here, is she? Just on the other side of the shadow." He looked off into the distance, his eyes cast over the dense forest. "I'd say about three miles as one of her crows would fly."

"What is she doing there?"

"Reliving her days of glory perhaps?" Dru sat up and brushed his hands. "Reveling in memories of battles she fed from and blood spilled in her name? I should go before thanks turns to blame."

Carys reached out and grabbed his hand before he walked away.

Dru froze, looking at her hand on his wrist. "Be careful. You may be Epona's daughter, but I'm the blood of Lir."

"Diarmuid mac Lir," Carys said. "That is your name. Your proper name."

Dru's easy brown eyes turned sharp. "What will you do with it now that you have it, Carys Morgan?"

"This world is suffering because you chose a path that took you to the Brightlands."

"I had my reasons."

"You could be king of the fae."

Dru's eyes flashed. "I don't *want* to be king of the fae. I only ever wanted Naida, and they will never accept her as my queen."

"So you just opt out?" Carys shrugged. "See ya? Not my problem anymore?"

He narrowed his eyes. "You say you're not asking me for a favor, but you are."

"I'm not asking you to do anything." She let go of his wrist and rose to her feet. "I'm telling you who you are."

Dru lifted his chin and looked down his nose. He'd never looked more wild. Or more regal. "And who do you think I am?"

"Oberon," she whispered. "Wandering prince. Beloved of Aine. Blood of the sea god. You're the one she wanted to rule, aren't you?"

"My mother returned to the sea with Lir," Dru said. "It doesn't matter what she wanted."

"Doesn't it?" She looked at the fae mound. "I don't think you would have done this, would you?"

"I'd never take a consort who would ask it of me."

"Was this Cian or Orla?"

"Does it matter?"

Carys cocked her head. "I don't know. Does it?"

"Elf!"

They turned as Godrik shouted across the green.

"I'm not an elf," Dru muttered. "Barbarian."

Godrik and Duncan walked toward them.

"We should talk," the wolf said. "The human had a surprisingly good idea."

Duncan frowned. "You don't have to sound surprised."

"Come to Dafydd's house," Godrik persisted. "And bring your small mate."

NAIDA LEANED against a bookcase in Dafydd's study. "To be clear, I am not his mate."

The ellyllon was wearing her usual uniform of a green tunic and leggings but with a human-style overcoat thrown over it and a hood to hide her ears.

Being a fae in Anglia these days was not popular.

"Aren't you?" Godrik frowned. "I assumed—"

"You shouldn't." Naida looked annoyed and nervous. "Why are we here? I should be traveling back to Cymru."

"We appreciate your staying." Dru sat near the fire, his long legs stretched out toward the flames. "I myself am waiting to hear the reason for it."

He reached out his hand toward Naida, but she stared at it pointedly, shook her head, and kept her hands firmly in her pockets.

Carys sat across from Dru. Since Dafydd was gone, she was effectively the lady of the manor.

Which was... so weird.

Duncan was helping her out, considering he knew about the running of a great house and she absolutely did not. Shooting arrows from a coracle? She was getting pretty good at that. Telling the house manager how much meat the game warden needed to hunt for the week? Not so much.

"You're here because I am taking you at your word, elf prince, that our children are safe," Godrik said.

"You shouldn't take me at my word," Dru said. "You should never take a fae at their word."

"I thought fae can't lie." Laura was sitting on the sofa next to Cadell.

"That's a lie we tell humans, and for some reason they believe us." Dru shrugged. "You're very gullible."

"You are," Cadell said.

Laura shot him an annoyed look.

"You *are*," Cadell repeated. "Why are the fae here? Naida, if you want to return to Cymru, I will take you."

Naida nodded at him. "Your honor will never be in question, Lord Dragon."

"Stop!" Godrik said. "I am trying..." He sighed. "I am trying to be... diplomatic."

A knock came at the door, which cracked open. Lachlan and Winnie were on the other side. "Godrik, it worked. Partly."

Carys blinked. "What worked?"

Winnie spoke. "We asked a group of sprites in the Kingswood to open a mound. It took some bribery, but they did it."

"Excellent." Dru rose. "Then you've found a way to thwart my brother and his wife. I'll be going now."

"I said partly," Winnie jumped in. "They were able to open the new mound that had formed in the Kingswood. The old fae fort near Lud's Hill is still locked up tight."

Carys waited for Dru to sit, but she could tell the fae was reluctant to stay.

"Dru." Naida spoke to him. "If you help, I'll stay."

Dru immediately sat and turned to Godrik. "What do you want me to do? Ride around to every warded fae fort in Anglia and open them? There are probably a hundred of them. It will take some time."

"No," Winnie said. "King Harold has instructed me and Godrik to lend you our official support in your assumption of fae leadership in Briton."

The entire library sat in stunned silence until Lachlan spoke. "My father, Robb of Sgain, high chief of the clans of Alba, also lends you the support of the Alban throne."

Dru's face was carefully blank.

He doesn't want it, Cadell said into her mind.

And I didn't want to eat my vegetables as a kid, but I did it.

Vegetables are horrible.

This is really not the time to discuss vegetables.

"I haven't spoken to my uncle," Carys said softly. "But you know that if Harold and Robb are both throwing their support behind you, he probably will too."

Carys looked at Naida, who was staring at the fire. Her expression could only be described as desolate.

She knows that their relationship has no future, Cadell said into her mind.

That doesn't mean it hurts any less.

Dru took a long time to speak. When he did, it wasn't what Carys was expecting.

"Crown Princess Finola has taken a fae consort," Dru said. "I have no desire to usurp him."

Godrik immediately responded with a growl.

"There's no reason the fae leadership should be linked to the Éiren throne," Lachlan said smoothly. "That was something that Queen Orla brought in, and there is no historical precedent for it. By its very nature, the fae having such a close alliance with one throne causes an imbalance in the Queens' Pact."

Naida added, "None of the other thrones are so close to the fae in their lands. The ellyllon hold no particular special status in Cymru."

"The fae in Alba are honored residents with their own leadership," Lachlan added, "but they have the same status of any regional lord."

"But in Éire," Godrik said, "the wolves have been driven from the island. The fae hold sway over the human throne. The court belongs to Cian, not to Orla."

Dru stared at nothing, and Carys couldn't read his expression.

"Your brother and his wife killed my Shadowkin," Carys said softly.

Dru finally looked at her.

"They killed Seren," she said. "Regan may have been the glove, but your brother—Regan's father—was the hand in that glove. And he killed Seren to keep her from revealing that they were creating a land bridge. They killed her with no thought to what it would do to Cadell. To Lachlan. To the entire country of Cymru."

Duncan had been silent up until then. He'd been watching all of it from the far corner of the library. "Your brother's not only a murderous bastard," he finally said, "he's a shit king. Every fae creature in Briton is in danger now because of him."

The blank expression that Dru had been wearing cracked just a little bit.

"You don't have to do this for yourself," Carys said. "It's not about your own ambition, Dru. This is about the safety of every brownie, every sprite, and every wild fae in Briton." She looked at Naida. "Naida is the most peaceful fae I know. She shouldn't have to hide who she is or run from London because your brother wants more power."

"This is not about me," Naida protested. "Do not make this about—"

"Fine." Dru's voice wasn't rough or emotional. It was smooth, seductive, and commanding as hell. "You want me to take the fae throne?"

He stood, and his presence filled the room. The fire leaped in the grate, the shadows grew deeper, and his voice took on an echoing quality that shot fear directly into Carys's heart.

"I will take the fae crown." Dru turned to Naida, then looked at Carys. "But remember that you asked for this blood. Not me."

THE MASSIVE FAE mound was back in Dafydd's courtyard—only this time it was nearly as big as the mansion itself.

It didn't look like a fae mound anymore. It looked like a fortress.

Dragons were dispatched to Alba and Cymru to share the news that Diarmuid mac Lir had returned to the Shadowlands and was claiming his crown.

A pall had settled over Southern Anglia, and the Great Serpent hadn't been seen in days. The river fae were silent, and the sky was unseasonably cloudy.

Apple trees that had been setting fruit had begun to wither as wild fae and tree sprites fled deeper into the old woods. Flowers fell on the ground and were trampled by the hooves of horses as Harold called every able-bodied soldier from his vassal lords.

Carys sat on a stone bench in the muddy courtyard in front of Dafydd's house, staring at the bustling activity of the remaining Cymric soldiers as rain began to fall on the ever-rising green mound.

There was a muddy ring around Dru's fortress where wolves were circling. Every now and then, a cloaked fae or a small group of them would emerge from the woods or the lane, pause at the sight of the wolves before they walked to the fort, reached a hand out, and melted into the earth.

They were tall and short but mostly tall. Slim as willows and furtive as foxes. The fae came at all hours and were often accompanied by animals. Rabbits and dogs were common. Owls were often perched on top of the fort. Ferrets and weasels scampered about, and one small, round fae even came with a bear that trotted behind her, his breath huffing steam in the cool morning air.

"Quite the parade."

Carys turned and saw Naida watching Dru's fort in the dying light of the afternoon. The breeze was filled with flower petals from a bright pink hawthorn that had sprung up overnight on the top of the hill. Every time the wind moved, pink petals drifted in the air.

"I've never seen anything like it."

Naida sat beside her. "You've never spent time in the court of Temris, the halls of the aes sídhe."

Carys had done her homework after her first trip to the Shadowlands. Aes sídhe was the Éiren name for the high fae—the "mound people"—also known as the race descended from the Tuatha Dé Danann and the old gods of Éire.

They were the dominant fae of Briton after they had conquered the legendary Fomorians. They were the most powerful practitioners of magic and the supernatural race that controlled the gates to the Brightlands.

And their capital, not so coincidentally, was in Temris, the same place the Éiren kings and queens ruled.

It was these fae—not the ellyllon like Naida or the wild sprites or the humble but powerful brownies—who decided what human souls lived as Shadowkin and which ones became nothing more than magical wisps that congregated by the gates.

These were the fae who had insinuated themselves into the human power structure.

These were the fae Dru had been born to rule.

Carys glanced at Naida. "Have you seen the city of Temris?"

"Once." Naida blinked. "That was how I met Dru. I had traveled to Éire with my mother. We were meeting with court healers." She frowned. "Something like what you'd see as a conference or convention in the Brightlands. Just a gathering of fae and unicorn healers traveling through the gates to share knowledge." She smiled. "It was nice."

"And it was fancy?"

Naida laughed. "It was more than fancy. I had been brought up in the valleys. My people aren't from the north like yours. My mother was born in the southern valleys of Cymru, maybe the most gentle and beautiful place in the Shadowlands." She smiled. "I could be biased."

Carys couldn't stop her smile. "Just a little bit."

"It's a beautiful place, but it's simple. Very small community of ellyllon and humans. Lots of wild fae. The woods and valleys are thick with sprites and gnomes and all sorts of water spirits. The trees are old, and even the smallest willow tree has a fae spirit attached to it."

"It sounds beautiful."

"It is. And peaceful. Going to Temris was like another world. I thought, 'This is what it must look like to see the sun' because the magic of the city makes everything glow."

"It sounds stunning."

"Yes, it's wondrous." She shook her head. "Underground cities and gardens lit by magic. Libraries that are illuminated by sacred fire. Halls so vast you couldn't see the end of them from the door you walked into. And power." She shuddered. "So much power it was like the scent of lilac in spring. Power infused everything."

"And that's where you met Dru?"

"All this glowing architecture" —Naida smiled— "and right in the middle of all this light, there was this dark, brooding, sulky fae prince who looked like he'd been sucking on a turnip."

Carys had such a clear mental picture she nearly laughed out loud. "Did you tell him that?"

"I don't remember what I told him, but I had no idea who he was, and I simply thought he was spoiling the mood. I said something silly to try to get him to cheer up and then something rude when he scowled at me."

"And he fell in love."

"I fell in love," Naida whispered. "And he fell in lust. Or maybe love. I don't know. But eventually someone told me who he was, and thank the gods, I went home the next day."

"Did he follow you?"

Naida looked at Carys from the side of her eye. "He pursued me all the way home, and when I told him that our lives were too differ-ent, he dug a mound in the middle of the valleys and sulked for nearly ten years."

Carys blinked. "Ten years?"

"I was weak," Naida muttered. "I never should have given in so quickly. As soon as I did, my life was turned upside down. Cian caused trouble for my mother. The farmers in the valley had problems with their crops, and the animals became sick." She shook her head. "It was petty, but I understood. Dru and I are not meant to be together."

"Says who?"

"The nobles of the aes sídhe. The rulers of his people." She nodded at Dru's fort. "The ones who will follow him to claim his throne from Cian would never accept me as queen, and that is why I am here and not in there."

"Does he want you in there?"

"Yes." Naida smiled a little bit. "But I know where I belong, Carys Morgan. And it's not on a throne."

CHAPTER TWENTY-SEVEN

"The first thing you must do is hide the children." Dru was hunched over, and he had never looked more inhuman. The fort where Carys and Cadell had been granted access was riven through with roots and vines that crawled down the muddy walls. Green ivy curled around the twisted roots that formed a kind of primitive throne beneath the earth.

The blue sigils on Dru's face were darker now, and a circlet of shining silver ran around his forehead and through his tangled hair.

It must have been a trick of the eye or glamour, but from certain angles, it appeared that two large antlers grew from Dru's head, not unlike the headdresses of the stag dancers they had seen at Anglian parties.

The round barrow was filled with the fae prince's collection of wild fae courtiers. Tall fae, wary dark-eyed brownies, and various beasts with intelligent eyes. Owls perched along the vine-covered walls, and a blue fire burned in the center of the room.

Cadell spoke into Carys's mind. *You see his true nature now.*

Is he light fae or dark?

Light in name, dark in spirit. Perhaps they are more alike than different.

"Hide the children," the prince repeated, speaking to the brownies. "The houses in Anglia who don't have house spirits *must* be protected, or my brother will take more children and hold greater sway over the humans."

"They are weak," a brownie with a gnarled face said. "They offer no sacrifices to the hearth."

"They are ignorant, not weak," Dru said to the wizened old fae. "The ancient ways must be revived. In this, my brother is correct. The humans have grown too mundane, too fascinated with the Brightlands." Dru's eyes rose to Carys. "Some Shadowkin even desire to leave this place and live under the sun. We must remind them what magic can do."

"If we protect the human children" —a long-haired fae with willow branches strewn through her hair spoke up— "who will protect our young?"

"Take them to the unicorns. If there is a safe haven in this world, the pure folk have created it." Dru's eyes went back to Carys. "Leave me with the dragon and his lady. You know what you must do."

The fae creatures in the round barrow slipped away into the shadows, leaving Carys, Cadell, and Dru alone save for the cadre of watching owls.

"My messengers." Dru glanced at them. "They are loyal to me. Crows and ravens are not to be trusted in these times."

"Owls are swifter and more silent in flight," Cadell muttered.

Carys thought about sitting, and as if the earth had read her mind, a twisted bunch of roots crawled from the earth, forming a makeshift bench behind her.

"Sit," Dru said. "Did my message reach your uncle?"

Carys nodded. "All the human families in Cymru have been told to go to houses guarded by wild fae. Brownies mostly, but a few houses have different familiar spirits or animal spirits that guard them."

"Cian will target the children first," Dru said. "They know that, don't they?"

"More have disappeared," Cadell said. "Not dragons or wolves, but more humans."

"He won't eat them," Dru said. "Not around Orla. He'll use them to threaten the other thrones."

Meaning Cian would eat the children if Orla wasn't around? Carys pictured the handsome, golden-haired fae prince from Harold's coronation and shook her head at the thought.

"You're thinking he's civilized," Dru said. "You are thinking he is a pretty face with more care for his long hair than his wife's throne." Dru shook his head slowly. "You are very wrong. Cian is Elatha's son, and Elatha was of Fomorian blood." His eyes reached out to Carys. "Do you know what that means, daughter of two worlds?"

"It means that his father was old." Fomorians were another magical race that were older even than the Irish fae in myths and stories, but Carys hadn't heard mention of them among the modern people of the Shadowlands.

"They came across the sea, grasping for power," Dru said. "My father *was* the sea. Elemental. Eternal. Erratic but enduring. Lir has no need for power because he is power."

"But the Fomorians were conquerors?"

"Cian is hungry," Dru muttered. "He was always so hungry."

"Your brother has glamoured the queen of Éire," Cadell said. "She wouldn't risk her throne if she was in her right mind."

"Don't be fooled into thinking Orla is a pawn." Dru's eyes glinted in the blue fire. "The Alban prince killed the queen's daughter, a daughter she believes was given to her by the gods. A daughter she valued above her other children."

"Because Regan was Orla's natural daughter with Cian?"

Dru nodded. "If open war breaks out, they could very well go to Alba first to seek revenge for Regan's death."

"How will they fight?" Cadell said.

"With magic," Dru answered. "With the shadows and with whispers. That's why it's so important for humans to seek the protection of their house spirits." Dru leaned forward. "The humans *will* turn on each other. Cian will poison their crops. Their animals will die. Soon they won't be able to help it."

TRUE TO DRU'S PREDICTION, shadows grew deeper all over London even as the wolves and wild fae were retrieving many of the children and returning them to their homes.

Carys, Duncan, and Cadell were walking through the green market near the Tamis with a list from Laura, herbs and roots she needed to reinforce the wards around Dafydd's house.

"You there!" a woman shouted. "Stop this, both of you!"

There was a scuffle and a grunt as a crowd gathered in front of a tall cart painted bright blue and stacked with tin canisters.

Duncan strode into the melee with Cadell behind him. "What are you doing, you idiots?"

Two humans were wrestling over a tin canister that rolled on the ground.

Cadell picked up one man by the collar while Duncan wrangled the other man's arms behind his back.

As they were fighting, a woman jumped on the back of the wagon and lifted her arms. "I told all of you, one per person and that's all we have today!"

People in the crowd shouted, but Cadell walked over, tossed the thrashing man to the ground, and roared at them, his throat growing red and his body getting bigger.

"Calm down," the dragon said. "There will be no violence today."

Moments later, red-coated soldiers ran through the center of the market with their shields up, and the crowd settled down.

"What is going on?" Carys righted the canister and heard sloshing. "Is this... milk? You guys are fighting over milk?"

The man Cadell had thrown on the ground stared at the milk

canister with greedy eyes. "We have five families living in a house with one hob to guard the little ones," he said. "We need the milk more than he does."

"You have *five* families?" The man Duncan was holding tried to lunge forward. "Our village had forty cows yesterday, and this morning they're all dead. Every one of them. If the broonies don't get milk, not a child in our village is safe."

Conditions in the city and surrounding villages were growing dire. It was just as Dru had said. The household fae were protecting human families, but brownies were proud folk. Insult them, and they would leave you for another family that was all too eager to bribe them with whatever they had.

All this was happening at the same time that crops and animals were suffering all over Anglia and Alba. The ellyllon of Cymru were offering humans in that country their protection, and refugees were pouring into the southern valleys and the mountains in the north, searching for a safe place for their people and animals.

But in Anglia, villagers had taken to gathering wild roots and hunting game, which were not affected by whatever spells Cian's magic had spread in the soil. Wheat and barley crops withered in the fields, and only wild oats survived.

Hares and rabbits were plentiful, and fish still jumped in the river, but dairy cows were growing sick and dying, and sheep neither gave wool nor dropped lambs on the hillsides. The only domestic animals that seemed to be too stubborn to die were the goats, and if you had a flock of those, you could ask any price for their milk that you wished.

The dead livestock were piled on the outskirts of London and set on fire by the dragons before sickness could spread, but nothing seemed to stop the plague from spreading across the land.

"Thought we had some magic of our own." The man that Duncan held wrested free from the blacksmith's grasp and shook his shoulders. "What's the king doing to stop these fae bastards?"

"It's not all the fae," Carys said. "Remember, the brownies and the sprites are the ones protecting—"

"It may not be all of them." The man's face fell when he saw the canister of milk disappear into the crowd. "But it's enough." His shoulders slumped. "We won't survive this."

Carys leaned close. "Go to King Dafydd's manor north of Hyde Forest. Tell them Carys sent you, and there should be some milk they can give you. So far our cows have been healthy."

Whatever wards Laura had put up were working, and Dru's magic infused the soil. While most of London was withering, Hyde Forest and the surrounding meadows were thriving. The wolves had to patrol the forests at night to keep Londoners from poaching too many of the deer. The city was hungry, and meat was becoming a luxury when venison and beef had been plentiful only weeks before.

The village man looked at the ground. "Thank you, my lady."

Duncan walked over as the man was calling for his teenage son who was waiting by a small wagon. "You can't feed all of London, Carys."

"I know." She sighed. "But I can help him."

Duncan put his hand on the hilt of his sword as Cadell handed management of the milk wagon over to Harold's soldiers. "This is only going to get worse."

"It's like siege warfare," Carys muttered. "What does Cian think he's doing?"

"Honestly? Probably thinning the population before he invades."

It had been a little over a week since the crows had come with Cian and Orla's message and the children had disappeared. London had a new king who hadn't yet consolidated power, a hungry population, and many of the friendly fae had fled out of fear of human retribution.

It was no wonder dark clouds hung over the city.

Carys and Duncan started to walk toward the edge of the river to wait for Cadell. "Any sign of the Great Serpent today?"

"Not that I've heard."

She looked over the slow-moving stretch of the Tamis where otters still played and frogs croaked in a happy chorus.

A few children were fishing in the long grass, and Carys felt her heart clutch, worrying that they might disappear until she saw a few water sprites dancing in the grass, their wings flashing between the reeds as they watched over the little fishers on the banks.

"There's still so much good here," Carys said. "But it's going to get worse before it gets better, isn't it?"

"Tell me when you want to leave." Duncan kept his voice low. "You say the word, and I'll get you to the gate."

"And leave Cadell here?" Her eyes searched for her dragon. "Or take him away when his world is at risk?"

"This isn't our fight," Duncan said. "And you're my priority, Carys Morgan. Not any throne or dragon."

She slipped her hand into his. "Right now we need to be here. Right now I think this is the right thing to do."

LACHLAN'S FACE was grim when he joined Carys, Duncan, Naida, and Laura in the hall. Godrik and Winnie had just left to return to Harold, and the household staff had served them a simple dinner before they returned to their own quarters.

The house was quiet when the Alban prince walked in, slumping into a seat as Carys jumped up to get him a plate from the sideboard in the dining hall.

"Sit," she barked. "You look exhausted. Have you eaten?"

"Not all day." Lachlan's face was pale. "We've had word from the unicorns in the Kingswood."

Duncan frowned. "Finally. What did they say?"

Lachlan had been in Harold's camp for days, coordinating the security of the city while also organizing troops that were coming in from the countryside.

"They are still maintaining their neutrality" —he raised a hand when he saw Duncan's mouth open— "and I understand why. But their ears are everywhere, and they *are* sharing information."

Duncan sat back and crossed his arms over his chest. "What kind of information?"

Carys set a plate in front of Lachlan. "Eat."

"Whatever Dru's magic is doing to block the fae gates, it's working." Lachlan sat up and took a bite of the stew Carys had served him. "According to the unicorns, the fae were planning to invade Anglia via the gates, but something is stopping them."

Carys looked at Naida, but the ellyllon was staring into the fire and listening intently without saying a word.

The "something" that was stopping Cian from using the gates was probably Dru, who had systematically taken control of the fae gates, forts, and barrows across Southern Anglia with the help of the wild and solitary fae who had gathered to him.

They were a hodgepodge of characters and outcasts, and nothing that looked anything like an army, but Dru's people were connected to the wild earth of Anglia and moved effortlessly through the wards that Cian had wrought.

"What's their next step?" Carys asked. "Unless they're giving up?"

Lachlan grimaced and took a drink of beer. "Not likely, though the unicorns also say that this isn't a popular move in Éire. Crown Princess Finola is very against Prince Cian's plans. Behind the scenes, there is a lot of disagreement about this."

"Will that stop Cian?" Duncan asked. "What if Finola just won't break the Queens' Pact?"

Lachlan shook his head. "In the end, Finola is Orla's daughter and heir. She's in charge of the army, but she'll do what her mother commands." He started eating again, ravenously tearing into the bowl of venison stew.

"Do we know what Cian has planned next?" Carys looked at Duncan. "It's been days, and no more children have been taken since King Harold spread the word about working with household fae."

Lachlan swallowed a gulp of beer. "The rumors are that Cian will come via boats from the south."

"Boats from the south." Cadell pushed away from the wall. "Into Kernow?"

The jut of land that was called Cornwall in the Brightlands was Kernow in the Shadowlands, and it was a wild place that was teeming with dragons.

Lachlan shook his head. "They'll avoid Kernow. They don't want to antagonize the dragons any further, and they think the dragons won't strike at them when Cian has proven his people can take dragon young."

"But the dragons got those children back." Carys stood up and walked to pour herself a mug of beer. "And now we're pissed."

Lachlan raised an eyebrow. "We?"

"You know what I mean."

"If they avoid Kernow," Cadell said, "Cian will take boats up to Hampton."

Lachlan nodded. "And from there the unicorns think Cian's army will march to Saris Plain."

The dragon frowned. "Why Saris?"

Naida said quietly, "Old Saris."

Lachlan nodded. "That's what the unicorns say. Cian wants to take Old Saris and rebuild it as a fae stronghold in Southern Anglia."

Laura leaned toward Carys. "Where is Saris?"

"It's Salisbury in the Brightlands," Duncan said. "That's where Stonehenge is in our world."

"It's where it is in every world," Naida said quietly.

Every eye turned toward her.

"For the fae—particularly the light fae of Temris—Old Saris is kind of this mythical place of power," Naida said, "even though the chalk underneath it is resistant to fae magic."

"So why would Cian want to rebuild Old Saris?" Duncan said. "If the land resists magic—"

"Because anyone strong enough to hold the Saris Plain must be the chosen of the gods," Naida said. "It's a place of power in every world. A place of worship, offering, and sacrifice."

"So if Cian wants to reassert fae power over Briton," Carys said, "making a big show of defeating Harold on Saris Plain would be one way to do it."

"It's theater," Naida said. "But it's theater that would impress every magical creature in Briton."

"She's right," Cadell said. "Even the dragons would be impressed. We'd still do our best to kill every fae in sight after what they did to our young, but it would be impressive."

Carys didn't know what it said about her that Cadell's blood-thirsty proclamation was intensely satisfying.

Lachlan continued, "The plain is huge, which will give Harold the advantage because he has numbers, but Cian's army will be traveling up from the ocean along the Yuten Woods, and that's dark fae territory." He rubbed a hand over his eyes. "The fae-thanes there are not friendly to humans. They'll probably lend Cian more people before he meets Harold."

"Unless Dru gets there first," Duncan said. "Have you and Harold told Dru about any of this?"

"He probably already knows," Lachlan said.

"Maybe." Cadell lounged at the end of the table, his legs stretched out toward the fire. "Or maybe not. He might not have made the connection between his brother and the dark fae of Yuten Woods. He's still gathering his people and breaking all the wards Cian put in place around the fae forts holding the children."

"He's playing catch-up," Laura said. "But if he's going to claim fae leadership in Briton, he's going to have to visit these dark Yuten fae himself, right?"

Lachlan nodded. "They're powerful, and they control the southern gates to the Brightlands. They have extensive magic in the rivers there. It wouldn't be a bad idea for Dru to go first."

They all looked at Naida.

"What?" The ellyllon narrowed her eyes. "I'm not your fae emissary. I'm not one of them."

"But you are," Laura said. "Way more than any of us."

"He'll listen to you," Carys said.

"Are you asking me for a favor?" Naida asked. "What will you give me if I ask this of him?"

Carys wracked her brain, trying to think of what she had that Naida might even be interested in. Ellyllon were notoriously hard to bargain with because they weren't greedy.

"I'll give you dragon scales," Cadell said. "For the rest of our lives, if you need a dragon scale for healing, you may come to me."

It was no small gift, but Naida still seemed reluctant.

"The unicorns think Cian's boats have already left Éire," Lachlan said softly. "He'll be in Anglia in days, not weeks, and he'll have an Éiren army with him. Once he is here—if he has dark fae allies—it will be even harder for Dru to take the crown and keep the Queens' Pact from breaking."

Carys saw warring emotions on Naida's face.

Taking the crown meant that Dru would be in charge, and all of Briton would likely flourish because of it. Taking the crown also meant any hope of a relationship with the man she loved was well and truly dead.

"I'll speak to him," Naida said quietly. "But there's no telling how long he might take to decide what to do. He has minions whispering in his ears now, and his relationship with the dark fae is complicated because of his father."

"I can get Dru to Yuten Woods in hours," Cadell said. "I'll fly him myself, and I will get him there safely."

Cadell flying a fae prince in his current mood?

Risky but worth it.

Naida stood up. "All of you." She waved her finger around the room. "I'm collecting favors from every one of you when this is over." She pointed at Carys specifically. "Especially you."

CHAPTER TWENTY-EIGHT

The wide green expanse of Saris Plain was marked by no human habitation save for the occasional simple stone farmhouse and a few footpaths that crossed between the ancient barrows and chalk outlines of horses visible from the air.

Far more than those that existed in the Brightlands, the horse outlines on the Saris Plain showed herds of equines, some big and some small, dotting the hills and overgrown forts they flew over.

"The people of this plain once worshipped the horse goddess." Dru sat on the opposite side of the coracle, and Duncan sat to his left. The three of them were traveling to Yuten Woods to meet with the dark fae there and convince them not to lend Cian any people or magical creatures.

Carys looked up. "The people here don't worship horses anymore?"

"They never worshipped the horses; they worshipped the goddess."

"Who often took the form of... a horse?" Duncan asked.

"Yes. It is an old faith with few adherents in the modern world." Dru's eyes danced. "But you knew that already."

He's talking about your mother's cult.

I know. Carys responded to the dragon's voice in her mind. *And please don't call it a cult.*

But that's what it is.

"My mother revered Epona," Carys told Dru, "before she left for the Brightlands."

"I would be surprised if she stopped revering the goddess," Dru said. "She is an easy goddess to serve."

Duncan snorted. "As opposed to the gods that are difficult to worship?"

"Agronā used to require a sacrifice of newborn babies thrown into her rivers," Dru said. "Matunos used to take the form of a rabid bear and eat the high druid who led his worship on the summer solstice." Dru shrugged. "It was considered a great honor for the druid who was eaten."

Carys was starting to understand how the old gods lost their popularity.

"And Epona?" Duncan said. "What did Epona want?"

"Offerings of burnt grain and chastity," Dru said.

"Yes, I can see how that might be more popular." Duncan's eyebrows went up. "Then again, if chastity was a requirement, I might take my chances with the bear."

"How much longer to Yuten Woods?" Carys scanned the horizon through the narrow window; she saw nothing around them but distant green hills.

"Another hour maybe." Dru looked up. "Your dragon flies swiftly."

Of course I do. I'm a dragon, not a sprite.

"This looks like good farmland." Duncan looked out the window. "But there are very few villages here."

"The soil is thin," Dru said. "More chalk than living soil. That's why it's so resistant to magic. And the trade routes are not good. Sheep and wild horses are the only creatures that like this place. If my brother had to choose a battleground, at least he picked one that isn't in a populated area."

"Why here?"

Dru opened his mouth, then waited for a long moment to speak. "I do not know. Perhaps the isolation appeals to him."

Lie. That was totally a lie.

Every part of this quiet war—from the timing right after Harold's coronation when there were still foreign visitors in London to the missing children and the army of crows dropping messages—was designed to catch attention. What had Naida said?

It's theater, but it's theater that would impress every magical creature in Briton.

If all this was theater, who was the audience?

And what was the purpose of this play?

"Cian chose this place for a reason." Duncan was looking at Dru, and he clearly thought the fae was hiding something as well. "Maybe the dark fae of Yuten know what it is."

THE GROUND WAS green and damp on the edge of the Yuten Woods. Cool light trickled through the dense canopy of beech trees, and the single path into the forest was heavily overgrown with ferns, spring grasses, and the occasional bell-shaped flower peeking out through the green.

Blue wisps—clear evidence of the fae gate nearby—danced in the shadow of the forest, luring travelers into the woods and whispering secrets like a laughing voice in a far room.

Carys stood at the edge of that narrow pathway, her mind flashing back to another path through another forest and the same man who had led her then: the fae prince who stood on the edge of the forest, beckoning her to follow him into the darkness.

Cadell waited on a hillside overlooking the dark fae stronghold. Dru had all but forbidden the dragon from entering unless he wanted to start a fight.

Nêrys, I do not like this place.

She looked up at Cadell in the distance, the light shimmering off his iridescent green skin. *I know. I don't like it either, but at least I'm with Dru and Duncan.*

And I trust neither of them.

He really could be a judgmental dragon.

You told me the woods are not warded and that I can call you anytime I want.

They are not. If you need me, I will burn the forest down to find you.

Okay. So Cadell was feeling a little overprotective at the moment. She didn't want to judge, especially right after he'd carried a fae prince across half of Anglia safely. *That's a little extreme. Maybe don't make that your* first *course of action, okay?*

There is nothing in this forest but dark fae, trolls, and imps. He was sulking. *No one will miss them.*

Imps? Had she run into imps yet?

If Carys was going by books, imps were a little bit like sprites or pixies, nature spirits with a surprising amount of magic who liked to play pranks and cause mischief.

Hopefully they were an annoyance more than a problem.

If the situation becomes dangerous, Cadell commanded, *you will call.*

So you can burn down the entire forest?

Call.

Carys made a mental note to make calling for the dragon a last resort. *I will call if I am in danger.*

Dru glanced at Carys and Duncan, and the corner of his mouth turned up in the hint of a smile. "This feels familiar."

"I was just thinking the same thing," Duncan said. His hand fell on the hilt of the borrowed bronze sword. Dru had warned him that bringing iron into Yuten Woods would get them nowhere but into trouble with the dark fae that made the forest their home.

Carys was carrying her bow on her back along with a quiver of arrows at her waist. *Dru said I could bring my bow.*

Not as effective as fire, Cadell grumbled.

You can always come with us in your human form.

The low growl she heard in her mind was enough to tell Carys exactly what the dragon thought of that suggestion.

Dru held his hand out to Carys. "Last chance to turn back. I cannot bring any other fae with me when I go into the Yuten Woods, so you have only me to defend you."

Duncan grunted. "I have a sword, Dru."

Dru's eyes didn't leave Carys. "As I said, you have only me to defend you."

"Fuck off." Duncan laughed and started walking. "What's in there? A bunch of willowy goth fairies I could knock over with a stick?" He looked up at the flashing blue lights that started dancing as they entered the woods. "Wisps? This looks like the woods behind my house except the trees are smaller."

"Exactly." The fae did not sound happy about it.

As they walked, Carys felt like the wind that had whipped around them as they flew over Saris Plain was still with them. Cold licked at her neck, and her feet were suddenly chilled despite the fact that they were walking swiftly.

"What's this cold on our feet?" Duncan asked. "It feels like there's wind blowing from underneath the ground."

"The trees here are very old." The dark-haired fae whispered something into the shadows, and the wind at their feet calmed.

"Seems like they like you well enough," Carys said.

"They don't like me—they fear me." His voice was cold. "But if I need to invoke my father's name, I will."

"Your father was a sea god," Carys said, "wasn't he?"

"His power covered this land long ago." Dru reached a long arm out and brushed his fingers over the tops of the ferns that lined the forest path. The fronds bent back as he touched them, cowering from his power. "The trees still remember it."

As Carys walked behind him, she saw the optical illusion again, a pair of horns that seemed to rise from Dru's head, branched like a stag's antlers but twisted and curling at the ends.

When he walked into shadow, she saw a flicker, and the moment he passed into the light, they were gone.

She'd only glimpsed the dark fae in Alba, and she knew they looked quite different than the light fae that were the public face of the fae kingdom in Briton. Cadell said the dark fae were far less human than the light, with sharp teeth and wild features.

Antlers were more of a dark fae trait, which made it even more curious that they had appeared over Dru's head when he claimed his power.

"Do you want to know how I know that your mother worshipped the horse goddess?" Dru kept his voice low as they walked.

"I don't know. Do I smell like horses?"

"Your blood smells of magic in the same way that Regan's did."

"Regan?" The half-fae sorceress had been the one who helped kill Carys's Shadowkin. She was also the natural child of Orla and Cian.

A thought suddenly occurred to Carys. "Regan was your niece."

"Hmm. I suppose she did carry a little of my mother's blood," Dru said. "Not much, but a little."

"My father was human, and so was my mother. Why would my blood have magic?"

"A child smells like magic in that way when their birth was a gift of the gods." Dru glanced over his shoulder. "There is usually a sacrifice involved."

"A sacrifice? What kind of—"

"Hush now, daughter of Rhiannon." He slowed, then came to a stop. "The Yuten fae are here."

Carys tried to look around Dru to see the dark fae he was speaking to, but the path in front of them was enveloped in shadows.

"Hello, Ogmi," Dru said quietly. "It's been... well, not long enough."

She was expecting to see tall, frightening figures from a horror movie when she peered around Dru's back, but the only thing that stepped into the sliver of light that crossed the pathway was a short, pale creature the size of a small child with long black hair that fell nearly to the ground and light green eyes that seemed to glow in the shadows.

The small creature widened his thick-lashed gaze and looked up at Dru.

Then Carys nearly fell over when the creature named Ogmi grinned to show off a row of sharp, serrated white teeth.

"Too many of Aine's sons trespass in our woods." Ogmi was sitting at the base of an oak tree whose roots were covered in moss. The small fae lounged against the gnarled wood and plucked grubs from the ground, slurping them into his mouth like delicacies.

The creature had led them into a round clearing in the middle of the woods where they sat on tree roots that had grown into a natural circle under the oak canopy. Tree litter, mushrooms, and moss carpeted the forest floor, and a red fox perched behind Ogmi's shoulder, watching them with clear and clever eyes.

He seemed particularly suspicious of Duncan.

Dru was tall but willowy, and he stretched his legs out, lounging on the ground.

Carys was taller than Ogmi, but far smaller than Duncan, and her smaller stature seemed to set the dark fae creatures that gathered around them at ease.

But Duncan? The massive blacksmith looked like nothing less than a bear perched on a bicycle.

"I would have preferred not to bother you at all," Dru said, "but you must know what my brother has been doing."

"Stealing the wolf cubs." Ogmi cackled. "Provoking the drakes and their precious humans. What of it? Your brother doesn't bother us."

These fae were nothing like the dark fae she'd glimpsed in Alba. They were closer to the Kheta Inwe from the Shadowlands back in California, but their obvious malevolence set them apart.

Short, sharp-toothed fae, all around Ogmi's size, hung from branches and peered through leafy boughs. They were all dark-haired, and most of them shared Ogmi's milk-white complexion, so pale that blue-purple veins were visible beneath the surface of their skin, which was marked with black and blue sigils that weren't unlike the ones that marked Dru's face.

They surrounded Duncan and Carys, often clicking their fangs in agreement or tapping their long claws against rocks when Ogmi was silent and thinking.

Blue wisps danced in the canopy overhead, and though it was the middle of the day, very little light reached the forest floor, blocked out by heavy spiderwebs that shaded the circular glen where Dru and Ogmi conferenced.

The dark fae have surrounded you. Cadell spoke into her mind.

We're fine for right now.

She glanced at Duncan, whose eyes swept the clearing, back and forth. He angled his body toward Carys, and his hand never left the hilt of his sword.

Duncan is keeping guard while Dru talks to the... head fae.

Carys was distracted when a round-faced creature landed in the tree over her shoulder.

A pert-faced fae with wings that looked like those of a beetle, she tapped her sharpened claws against the carapace that covered her shoulders, staring at Carys and licking her lips.

Nêrys?

Remember how you said that there was nothing in these woods but dark fae and imps?

Have the imps found you? Cadell's voice was elevated.

No, but these fae are... not human. Not even close.

"That one reminds me of Auld Mags a bit," Duncan muttered.

Carys looked to the side, and her eyes went wide. "The one that's staring at me like she's hungry?" she murmured.

"Eh, not the beetle bits." Duncan nodded at the beetle fae, whose eyes were darting between Duncan and Carys with interest. "Ma'am. How're ya gettin' on this morning?"

She hissed something at a shadow in the trees, then unfolded two wings from her back and fluttered away with a clicking sound that sent shivers down Carys's spine.

It was instinctual. Elemental. And Carys suddenly realized why beetles had always freaked her out. There was something feral, predatory, and distinctly insectile about the dark fae in Yuten Woods.

Dru and Ogmi were still talking.

"You said Aine's sons have trespassed." Dru ate another grub. "Has my brother already been here, Ogmi Intibus?"

"You're enough." Ogmi wrinkled his nose. "You're enough, son of Lir. You come to this place and threaten our trees?"

The dark fae punctuated the accusation with a sharp yip, and the glen came alive with the sound of clicking and clacking, chattering, and snapping teeth.

"Elatha's son may not bother you now, but what will happen if he takes over this place?" Dru reached for a grub from the ground and tossed it in his mouth as he and Ogmi chatted. Then he looked around the dark forest glen. "Do you think Cian will be happy to let the Yuten Woods remain independent? You know what he's done to the fae gates in Éire."

More clicking and a few hisses as the dark fae considered what Dru was saying.

"My power is rising." Dru sat up and pulled his legs in, sitting cross-legged in the middle of the glen. He lifted his face and looked into the trees around him. "I have returned to Briton with allies. The dragons." He glanced at Carys. "The human kings and queens." He nodded at Duncan. "Even allies from the Brightlands."

A low humming that reminded Carys of cicadas started echoing through the trees.

"You may ignore me," Dru said. "You may even lend your magic to my brother who comes to rule you."

More hissing and clicking.

"But know that whatever Cian Elathason may say with his mouth, in his heart, his father's Fomorian blood is strong."

The clicking and the humming calmed as the dark fae pressed closer to hear Dru's words.

"I am Diarmuid mac Lir," he said firmly, "son of the sea and prince of the light fae." He looked around the dark woods. "*Aine's* son. I have no desire to rule you or change your ways." He nodded toward Ogmi. "I honor the Yuten folk. I will not dig under your forests or cut down your trees to construct my barrows. This is the Yuten Woods, not the high court of Temris."

Did the clicking and the snapping sound... happier? Was that possible?

Carys kept her lips shut and listened.

"In two days, my brother will pass by these woods, coming from the sea to fight me on the Saris Plain."

A hush fell over the forest.

Ogmi narrowed his eyes. "And you want us to leave our wood to fight with you, fae prince?"

"No."

Dru's simple word made Ogmi blink and the forest come alive again.

"This battle is not yours," Dru continued. "This battle is between Cian and me. All I ask of the Yuten folk is that you do not lend your thanes to my brother."

Ogmi pressed his lips together and began to rock back and forth in the tree roots. The humming and the clicking started again.

"Leave this battle for the light fae," Dru said. "He will make promises to you, permissions that the Yuten folk have long sought."

Cackles in the trees and more chittering as the blue wisps raced over their heads.

"But know that whatever Cian gives with one hand, he will take more with the other." Dru leaned forward. "My friends and I will leave now and let the Yuten folk decide their fate."

Dru stood, and Carys and Duncan stood with him. Then Dru reached up his long arms and raked his fingers through the tree branches above as he walked back toward the path leading out of the forest.

"But the Yuten folk would do well to remember that just like these trees" —Dru turned once Carys and Duncan were back on the path and out of Ogmi's clearing— "the son of the sea carries a very, very long memory."

Thunder crashed overhead, and a sudden rainstorm opened up in the Yuten Woods, drenching the dark fae and their creatures with rain. They scuttled back into the shadows and the tree hollows, hiding from the downpour.

And when the water dripped down Carys's cheeks and touched her lips, the raindrops tasted like the sea.

CHAPTER TWENTY-NINE

"What will they do?" Duncan asked. "Will they back you?"

"I don't need them to back me."

Carys nearly tripped over a root that jumped into the path. The way out of the forest was distinctly more difficult than the way in, and Carys was grateful that Dru was leading them.

"I just need them to not back my brother," Dru continued. "And I don't think they will. The Yuten fae are their own breed of creature, and they don't like authority. They've ruled these woods for centuries, and they like their independence."

"You mentioned something that Cian would offer them," Carys said. "Could you offer them the same thing?"

"They want more babies." Dru glanced over his shoulder. "More human children. More changelings sent through the gates. You think I should offer the same thing?"

Carys felt her stomach churn. "And Cian would offer that?"

"He'd offer, but he wouldn't follow through. Population is how he maintains his influence." Dru's attention turned to the right. "The

Shadowkin at the gates…" He trailed off, narrowing his eyes at something in the distance.

Duncan immediately drew his sword. "What is it?"

Dru took a deep breath and closed his eyes. "Trolls."

Carys blinked. "Trolls in the forest?"

"Yes." Dru remained frozen. "And they have imps with them."

"Oh fuck." Duncan drew his sword. "Not imps."

"Why are imps so bad?" Carys asked. "Aren't they a little like— Ow!" She slapped her hand on her shoulder when she felt the sting, and her palm landed on something that crunched. "What the hell?"

Something poked at her palm, and a stabbing pain shot up her forearm. "What is that?"

When she removed her hand, there were two wide, angry black eyes glaring at her from her shoulder.

"Carys, brush it off!" Duncan shouted. "It's an imp!"

"Brush— Ow!" She nearly bit her tongue when the tiny creature bared its fangs and lifted a needlelike blade that he drove it into Carys's shoulder. "Get off me!" She swiped her hand against the imp, but the tiny fae creature opened its jaw to nearly ninety degrees and sank its teeth into Carys's finger.

A spear of pain shot up her arm, but she managed to slap her hand down, and she felt the imp crunch under her palm. It squeaked and burbled before it slid to the ground and the moss crawled over its body.

That could not be good.

"They're everywhere," Duncan shouted.

A gang of imps raced through the forest, some flying with wings and others clicking and climbing from the ground, swarming Carys and Duncan with their gangly bodies, wicked little blades, and needle-sharp teeth.

She grabbed for an arrow and started brushing them off, taking care not to stab herself with the point.

Carys was able to shake off the next one that tried to land on her arm, but there were more coming. And more. They swarmed in the air like bugs.

Even Dru's face was scrunched and his eyes narrowed as he batted the imps away from his face, but his focus was on two tall figures striding through the trees. "Duncan, get Carys away."

"Are those trolls?"

"I'll be fine." He glared at Duncan and pointed to the edge of the forest where the light broke through the trees. "Get the nêrys ddraig back to her dragon!"

What is happening? She heard Cadell's voice in her mind.

Just a bit of an imp situation.

Did they bite you?

Only once.

"Come on." Duncan grabbed her and tucked her against his chest.

The big man was wearing a heavy cloak that the imps couldn't seem to penetrate, and he'd pulled it up and over her as he bodily carried her through the forest and away from the swarm.

"What kind of place is this?" She hid her face against his chest. "Half-size fae with beetle wings, bloodthirsty sprites, and now trolls?"

Duncan paused, shaking his head and swiping one more imp away from his beard. "Dru is dealing with the trolls."

Carys looked under Duncan's arm and saw the ground buckling and the trees swaying behind them. Whatever Dru was doing looked like he was tearing the forest from the roots, and Carys couldn't help but feel a kind of desperation when she heard trees crashing and branches snapping.

Nêrys, I'm coming to you.

"Let me down." She could see the edge of the forest from the path where Duncan had been running, and between the trees, Cadell was waiting. "I need to get back to him before he burns down this forest."

I'm here! she shouted with her mind. *Cadell, just leave it. I'm almost to you right now. Dru stayed behind to take care of the trolls.*

"Haven't seen trolls in the forest before," Duncan shouted. "They usually keep to the ports and the mountains."

"Why do you think they're here?"

"They're greedy." Duncan grunted. "Well, some of them are. If Cian paid them enough, they'd fight for him. But only if they're convinced he can win."

"Can he?" She stepped from under the shadow of the trees and fought the urge to run to Cadell.

"Can he win?" Duncan shrugged. "Anything's possible, Carys."

They walked away from the forest and into the waist-deep waving grass of the hills.

Cadell was lying on a hillside, his glowing gold eyes watching the thrashing trees in the distance. *The fae prince is powerful.*

"Cadell says Dru is powerful."

"I've never seen him fight," Duncan said. "He always seems to be able to talk his way out of things."

Carys.

"What?" She turned to look for Cadell, but the moment she turned her head, the dragon that had been on the grassy hillside was gone.

Carys.

Carys turned in circles and saw the plain empty of everything and everyone save for the golden, waving grass and a white mare and rider silhouetted on the ridge that overlooked the forest.

Carys Morgan.

"Hello?" Carys walked toward the rider, who turned away and disappeared behind a rise in the hillside where a white chalk outline of a horse marked the beginning of Saris Plain.

She walked up and over the hill, but by the time she reached the top, the horse and the rider were gone and the plain filled her field of vision, empty save for a herd of wild horses that grazed among the grass.

"What do you think?"

Carys turned to the right to see the woman with long wavy hair standing next to her.

"I'm dreaming again."

"This time you are not." Rhiannon smiled a little bit. "I simply wanted to show you the plain as it looked before you were born." She spread out her arms. "The plain as it should be. Isn't it beautiful?"

The long golden grass waved in the breeze, and while there was no sun shining, the air around them was warm and the light bright.

"It's beautiful." Carys turned to her. "Why are you here?"

"You were wondering why the fae prince came to this place," Rhiannon said. "You were wondering why Aine's son chose Saris Plain."

"Yes."

"Because more than just the fae prince waits. More than Elatha's son is hungry for power," the horse goddess said. She bent to Carys's ear and whispered, "You must not let them spill blood on Saris Plain."

CARYS BLINKED and the woman was gone. In the distance, Cadell waited for her, and Duncan was calling her name.

"Carys, where are you wandering off to?" The blacksmith hiked behind her. "Dru's back and we should—"

"We shouldn't spill blood on Saris Plain," Carys said. "She told me not to."

"Who?"

Carys closed her eyes and tried to remember her face. "I don't... I can't remember the details, but I've seen her before. In London."

"Your mother's Brightkin?"

Carys shook her head. "No, not her."

You must not let them spill blood on Saris Plain.

"We shouldn't fight here," Carys murmured. "There's something about this place."

"We shouldn't fight anywhere," Duncan said. "And *you're* not going to. Dru may be determined to go to war with his brother, but that fight is not yours."

You must not let them spill blood on Saris Plain.

"You've got stab marks in your shoulder" —Duncan was still yelling— "and your face is slashed."

He touched her cheek, and Carys was surprised when his hand came away bloody. She hadn't even felt it. "That wound is going to get infected. Imps are nasty creatures, Carys. We're going back to London. This has gone far enough."

You must not let them spill blood on Saris Plain.

CARYS STARED across the swiftly passing landscape of Southern Anglia as Cadell flew them back to London.

Duncan was fuming.

Cadell was silent.

Dru was staring at her.

"What did the horse goddess say?" he finally asked.

"She said that we shouldn't spill blood on Saris Plain," Carys yelled over the wind.

"Ah." He nodded. "It is sacred ground to her."

It wasn't just because of the sacred ground. There was something else. Something about hunger and power. Something she couldn't quite grasp as Cadell began to circle down, down, down to the city.

"You're going home," Duncan said. "Enough is enough."

"I'm staying." She needed to be here. She wasn't exactly sure why, but she needed to stay.

The dragon flew over the heavily wooded park on the eastern edge of London, and Carys saw the snaking river in the distance as it twisted and gleamed in the silver light, its water flowing ever outward toward the sea.

Something is wrong.

There was a horn in the distance and bells ringing over the city.

"What's going on?" Duncan leaned over the edge of the coracle. "Cadell, do you hear that?"

The horn blew again, a steady, ominous blast that sounded over and over again.

Dru stared at the wooden wall of the coracle, and Carys saw the air around him shimmer with magic. He closed his eyes, and she saw the shadowy horns rising again over his head in the red glow of the dragon's body.

Cadell, what is happening?

He is swimming toward the sea. The dragon's voice was solemn when it came to her mind. *There are two dragons following him, but he will not speak to them.*

"Who?" she shouted.

"The Great Serpent." Dru breathed out slowly, and his eyes were black and wide. "He is returning to the sea."

"What the fuck are you talking about?" Duncan growled. "The Great Serpent is the protector of the Tamis. The guardian of the city. If he leaves, what the hell does that mean for London?"

In all my years on the earth —Cadell's voice was solemn— *never has the Great Serpent left the river.*

"Are you sure he's leaving?" Carys strained to see more as Cadell swooped down over the city and followed the river, flying behind two smaller dragons who soared over the water, tracking something below. "Maybe he's just going to check something out."

"There!" Duncan pointed at a great ridged fin that surfaced for a moment before it submerged. A rippling current of gold trailed after it, and as soon as Carys saw the gold waves, she finally saw the massive outline of the largest snake she had ever seen in her life.

It was nothing like she had imagined, more primordial monster than eel or whale. There were golden-brown scales down his back and large, fan-shaped dorsal fins that rose on his spine, rising and falling through the water as it moved.

It twisted through the city like the river that was its home, passing Lud's Hill and the coronation throne, swimming by the king's castle and the white tower next to it, dipping under the bridges where panicked Londoners pointed and yelled.

As it swam, the humans across the city ran toward the Tamis, and Carys could see small creatures—otters, river fae, and seals—slipping from the grassy banks of the river and following.

Mile by mile, the serpent swam as Cadell and the two other dragons trailed after him.

One of the dragons in front offered a curious cry and flew lower down to the surface of the Tamis where the serpent rose, answered with a bellowing call that ripped through the water and the air, then disappeared back into the deep.

Where is it going?

He only says he must return to the sea.

What does that mean?

For the first time since she'd known him, Cadell was speechless.

Duncan spun on Dru. "What did you do?"

"Nothing."

"Your father is a sea god!"

"I have done nothing." And yet despite the panic below, despite the confusion of the dragons, the dark-haired fae did not look surprised. If anything, he looked slightly amused. "He's a sea monster, Duncan. Did you think he was tame?"

"He's supposed to protect the city," Duncan growled. "If the Great Serpent is abandoning London, what does that mean for you and your allies?"

Dru shrugged. "I don't know."

"Is this a game to you?" Duncan was shouting. "Because there are people I love following you into battle. And I'm half tempted to throw you over the side of this coracle right now."

I do not know either. Cadell's voice was soft. *Perhaps the surly human is correct. Perhaps you should return to the Brightlands, Nêrys.*

And leave you here to fight without me?

This is not your home, Cadell said. *He is correct. This is not your battle.*

"I'm staying." Carys looked at Duncan. Then at Dru. "I'm staying." She felt a surge of defiance in her breast. "Because let's be honest, I'm going to battle with a dragon." She leaned toward Dru. "A fucking *dragon.* Your brother may have magic and power and maybe even a serpent longer than four school buses, but he does not have *dragons.*"

CHAPTER THIRTY

Harold, newly crowned king of Anglia, stood on Lud's Hill, wearing his fur-trimmed coronation robes and a simple gold crown. His long face was drawn and pale, and the gold-rimmed spectacles he often hid during public addresses were not hidden that day.

He stood in front of the gathered citizens of London as they waited on the riverbank. Carys, Duncan, and Laura watched from the hill where they'd observed Harold's coronation only two weeks before.

To Carys, it seemed like it was months had passed, not weeks.

Diarmuid mac Lir, dark prince of the fae and a frightening specter in black robes, stood beside Harold. On his head was a strange, twisted crown of blood-red coral, and his face was marked by deep blue sigils.

Beside the fae prince, Prince Lachlan of Alba stood in full, shining armor, his long hair tied back and his blue-and-white flag flying.

Dragons circled overhead, clutching war coracles loaded with Cymric soldiers waiting for battle on Saris Plain.

Along the sides of Lud's Hill and up and down the river, lines of red-coated soldiers stood in formation while massive barges waited in the river to take them upstream, where Dru would open a fae gate that would take them to Saris Plain.

"People of London." Harold's voice was amplified by a mage standing next to him, holding a long staff. "Two weeks ago, I stood before you to claim my title as your king. Today I stand before you—my allies at my side—to claim the title of your protector."

"He's not going to mention the Great Serpent," Duncan muttered.

"What can he say?" Laura asked. "Sorry the giant, terrifying supernatural snake that used to guard our city left? I'm sure it's all cool though?"

"I know you have fear," Harold continued. "I know you doubt that your families will be safe. But we know who we are, and we know who we fight for."

A few in the crowd let out a muffled cheer, but an ominous quiet hung over most of the gathered humans and magical creatures of London.

The residents of London stretched out for miles along the riverbank. Some flags flew, but most of the faces who watched the new king were gaunt and worried.

Food had become scarce as crops rotted in the fields. Animals were dying, and pastures that had been bursting with grazing sheep only weeks before were nearly empty.

The only thing that had been feeding the city was the plentiful catch of fish from the river, and now with the Great Serpent gone, even that bounty seemed to be in danger.

"We live in a city where all are welcome," Harold said in a louder voice. "Humans of Anglia. Fae and trolls. Dragons, unicorns, and wolves alike." His voice grew louder still. "Visitors from distant shores are as welcome in London as the smallest sprite that lives on the river."

Carys felt the mood in the crowd shift. In a city full of suspicion and fear, the king was smart to remind Londoners what their community was made of.

"The high fae of Temris stole our children because they wanted us to fear them and hate each other."

A low murmur began to run through the crowd around Carys.

"They *wanted* to divide us," Harold continued, "but we will not be divided. We will not turn on our neighbors."

More murmuring as the mood lightened a little bit.

"Together" —Harold motioned to Dru, who stood in dark regalia to his right— "Prince Diarmuid, the wolf clans, and the dragons of Cymru found every missing child."

Finally a scattered cheer rippled thought the crowd. And if anyone noticed that the unicorns were absent from the retrieval efforts, they didn't mention it.

Harold kept his voice even and firm. "*Every* missing child that was taken by the fae has been returned to their family."

The crowd clapped louder, and a bit of the dark cloud that hung over the city seemed to lift.

Harold looked to his left where a rocky-faced troll and a bent-over brownie with silver-grey hair had joined him.

"The magical population of London has put their powerful wards over our homes and our schools," he said. "Brownies and hobs have protected our children and our elders. Trolls have kept our markets alive and helped our farmers fight the plagues that the high fae have sent to weaken us."

Cheering died down, and the crowd began to mutter again.

Harold shouted, "But we expected nothing less!"

The crowd went silent.

Carys heard Cadell in her mind. *The king is a better orator than his father.*

"We expected nothing less," Harold continued, "because while I may be king of the *humans* of London" —his voice rose— "every sprite or fae, every troll, gnome, hob, or mermin who lives in this place is part of my city. *Our* city. Our home!"

The crowd let out a hearty cheer, and red-striped flags waved.

"We are London," Harold said simply. "I am your king. Our allies are with us. We will not bow to fear."

The cheering grew louder, and Carys heard some horns blowing in the distance.

"We will *not* be intimidated." Harold—spectacles sitting on the bridge of his nose—seemed to grow taller. His face glowed with purpose. "We did not ask for this fight," he said. "We want only to live in peace, trade with our neighbors, and raise our children."

Carys felt the energy of the crowd gather and coalesce around the field of soldiers who were standing in formation between the king and the river.

"But we will defend our home from any who attack it!"

Horns blasted, and the formations of soldiers clapped their bronze swords against their shields.

"We will defend our farms and our markets," Harold shouted. "We will defend our rivers and valleys."

Carys saw some of the trolls and magical creatures in the crowd nod in approval.

"We will not uproot our trees or dig up our barrows."

Sprites flipped and turned overhead, zipping through the crowd and leaving trails of gold and silver in their wake.

"We are London," Harold said. "We are Anglia. What we have built here is worth defending." Horns blasting. Roaring cheers rising from the crowds. "And I will defend it."

CARYS STOOD at the front of one of the river barges as it moved upriver, the flat-bottomed boats propelled by magic and unseen creatures that had answered to Dru when he called.

Dru glanced at Carys, then overhead. "You're not flying with your dragon?"

She and Lachlan stood on Dru's right with Winnie on his left.

"Despite my complete ignorance of most politics, I am currently the top-ranked Cymric official in Anglia."

"Really?" Winnie leaned forward. "Where is Anwyn?"

"Flying to Saris Plain with Demelza."

"And Dylan?"

Lachlan answered, "He's coordinating with my father in Alba."

Winnie blinked. "Oh, so you really are it."

She didn't have to sound quite that disappointed. Carys still had a dragon.

That dragon was simply flying ahead of her because he would not be going through a suspicious fae gate opened by a wandering fae prince who was reluctantly helping them.

And he wasn't exactly thrilled that Carys was going through it either, but she had orders from Dafydd.

Carys turned to face the front of the barge as it headed up the foggy Tamis. They were accompanied by Winnie's personal guard of sixty soldiers along with horses for Winnie, Dru, Carys, and Lachlan.

The rest of the massive barge was filled with the wild fae that had aligned with Dru over the past week.

There were fae of every size and shape riding on the barge. Tall creatures who looked more like trees than people. Flying sprites that buzzed overhead and squat creatures who looked more like rocks or tree stumps than anything human.

There were fae that reminded Carys of ellyllon and others that were tall and graceful. There were fae with wings and some with hands that looked more like roots.

A few wore their hair in long braids, and some had no hair at all.

And all through the river, beside them and below them, she could feel magic. Mermin and serpents. Otters and selkies. Carys even thought she'd spotted what looked like a kelpie on the edge of the fog.

It was a hodgepodge of an army, but Carys hoped they had more magic than it looked like. She'd seen pictures in Dafydd's library of fae armies, and they looked terrifying.

The drifting scent of rotting carcasses told her they were heading deeper into Anglian farm country where there weren't as many dragons to burn the animals that had died.

Dozens of barges filled with Anglian troops moved silently behind them.

"Where is the fae gate?" Lachlan asked Dru.

"Just up ahead."

"And why is it on the river?" Winnie asked. "I've never been through a river gate before. Does it go from water to water? Is that how it works? Or are we going to end up stuck in the middle of a forest somewhere, standing on a bunch of boats?"

Dru cracked a smile, his gleaming teeth contrasting with the blue sigils that grew darker and darker the farther they moved up the river. "You are amusing, Lady Wynnflad," he said. "My power is greatest on the water. The gate that I have created will take us to the Saris Avon. From there your soldiers will only have a few miles to march."

"Good. Do you have any sense where your brother is?" she asked.

"Not right now." Dru's eyes narrowed on a fogbank that appeared before them. "But soon."

Carys turned and stared into the fog. *Cadell, we're going in.*

I still don't like this.

You could always shift and—

No.

Carys smiled despite the grim atmosphere of the morning. *Is King Harold in the air?*

He is in the war coracle with Lady Anwyn.

Good.

The surly human is with me. He complains constantly. Is he always going to be like this?

Might not be as bad once we're out of mortal danger.

Carys saw the fog grow so dense it was as if they were walking into a wall of clouds. Lights flashed behind the dense mist, and Dru began to sing a low song as the barge silently approached.

Lachlan leaned down to her. "If anything goes wrong, stay close to me."

She glanced up. "You still think he's trying to trick us?"

"No. But Cian is powerful and smart. And no one can anticipate you more than a sibling."

Carys nodded and scooted closer to Lachlan. "Do you think this fog is freaking out your soldiers?"

"I think it's—"

The fog closed around them, and Carys's world went white.

There were whispers in the distance, slithering sounds and childish laughter.

Something rustled in the long grasses on the banks of what might have been a river or a plain. The lapping water that had pushed against the barge was silent, and all sound seemed to soak into the dense cloud around them.

Carys stared ahead. She knew fog, but this was something far more than natural. "You think it's what?" The only thing she could hear over the rustling grass was the sound of Dru's voice singing a low, droning chant. "Lachlan?"

Carys looked over her shoulder and saw that the line of soldiers directly behind her were frozen in a trance, their eyes wide, unblinking, and locked on something in the distance that Carys couldn't perceive.

She turned and saw Lachlan in the same state, and her heart began to race.

"Goddess-touched."

Carys turned her head and saw Dru surrounded by the fog, a smile flirting around his lips as the fae on the barge examined her with curious eyes.

Carys tore her attention from the crowd. "What?"

"If I hadn't known before, I'd know now." Dru walked over and touched Lachlan's forehead with his finger. "Fae-touched. Your prince has magic. He can access the earth and the air. That's what makes him so charming and so musical." He turned to Winnie. "Fae-touched. She never misses with her bow. The trees speak to her, and she's more at home in the forest than the castle."

He turned back to Carys and reached out, running soft fingers along her cheek. "Goddess-touched. No wonder you can speak with dragons. My magic works on you, but only a little. I should have known the first night I met you in the pub. You truly are Epona's daughter."

A moment later, the world around her came alive. It was as if everything had been muted and then it wasn't.

"—hard to know how they're feeling," Lachlan muttered. "The unknown is usually more frightening than the reality."

She blinked, and Lachlan caught her stare.

"What's wrong?"

"Nothing." She didn't want to explain Dru's words. She couldn't explain them yet.

The fog lifted and the slow, wide river they'd been traveling along was gone. Instead, a narrow, grassy waterway with dense reeds and overhanging trees surrounded them.

The fae with them started whispering and fluttering their wings. Branches cracked and boughs flexed as they moved off the barge, some flying and others climbing on the treelike creatures that had planted their feet into the shallow water and were lurching toward the bank.

The selkies and the mermin in the river drifted into the shadows or slipped below the surface as the second barge came through. Then one by one, each of the massive boats came to rest in the narrow Saris Avon.

"We're here." Dru motioned with his hand, and the barge floated to the riverbank where it bumped against the muddy ground and came to a stop. "Come. We still have miles to march."

RIDING over the grassy landscape of Southern Anglia was making Carys rethink her decision to stay. Even when their horses were unloaded and she was able to mount Leuca, the calm presence of the mare did little to soothe the anxiety in her blood.

She felt Cadell overhead—the dragon had quickly found her the moment she crossed the gate and was now flying overhead, communicating with her as he surveyed the landscape.

I see soldiers in the distance, but they're far off. On the far side of the plain, coming up from the south.

"Cadell said there are soldiers coming up from the south." Carys looked at Dru. "Cian is here."

"Does he see fae or human armies?"

Cadell, are the soldiers fae or human?

They appear to be mostly human with fae commanders. Crown Princess Finola is leading the Éiren army with Cian.

"Mostly human," Carys said. "Fae in command, Finola leading the human army."

"She did it," Winnie muttered. "There goes the pact. Cian is with her?"

"Yes, she's with Cian."

Lachlan and Winnie both cursed as they began to climb the road that led from the river to the edge of the plain.

"The soldiers we'll be fighting will be likely be Éiren even if they are few in number," Dru said. "Cian won't want to waste fae lives if he thinks he can win with human soldiers and magic."

Winnie's face was grim. "That means we'll be fighting against humans who are supposed to be our allies."

"People we've trained with," Lachlan said. "Cian and his fae started this war, but he's using Éiren people to fight his battles."

Dru kept his eyes on the horizon. "The quickest way for us to win is by using the dragons, and he knows that." He glanced at Carys. "But if we butcher the Éiren armies, the Queens' Pact will be well and truly dead. There will be no peace with that much blood spilled."

"And the fighting in Briton will return." Lachlan looked at Carys. "Would Anwyn order a dragon attack on Éiren troops?"

Carys shook her head. "I have no idea. She might wait for orders from Dafydd."

"And King Dafydd will want to preserve the Queens' Pact if he can," Lachlan said. "This should be a fae battle, not a human one."

Dru shook his head. "I will try to reason with them, but I can make no guarantees."

"What's your strategy, Dru?"

"I will send a messenger to Cian's people." Dru nodded at a large walking tree at the front of the company. "Alafair will tell Cian's fae that I am asserting my claim to the throne of Temris and that they may choose to back me if they do not want to fight."

Carys said, "So you're going to just ask nicely for them to pick you as their king instead of Cian?"

"I have to try." Dru surveyed the wild fae at the front of their company. "I am hoping that if Cian's people see that the wild fae of Briton support me, they may decide it's time for new leadership."

Winnie was already thinking ahead. "I hope they take your deal, because Anwyn *will* order a dragon attack."

Lachlan frowned. "Why are you so sure?"

"She's pragmatic," Winnie said.

"It's pragmatic to kill humans who are supposed to be our allies?" Lachlan said. "It's pragmatic to decimate an army we drilled with two weeks ago?"

"It's pragmatic because a dragon attack will be decisive and will likely end this quickly," Winnie said. "Think, Lachlan. The worst thing that could happen would be for this battle to turn into an extended war. That's what happened last time, and it led to centuries of fighting and death. The Anglian people are already starving because of Cian's plagues."

"But there will be no peace with Éire." Lachlan's voice rose. "And my kingdom, having the closest ties, will suffer the most. The Éiren people are linked with Alba through blood and history. Alban troops will not want to fight against Éiren soldiers."

Winnie lifted her chin. "The Éirens have allowed the fae to drag them into this. They're not innocent."

"They're following their queen."

"Who has handed over her authority to her fae consort! They took your children too."

Carys knew there was a rift swiftly growing between Alba and Anglia.

"Have you ever seen war?" Eamer's voice of caution whispered in her mind. *"Do you know what happens when society breaks?"*

Carys knew this was exactly the situation her aunt had been speaking about. Alliances were cracking. Loyalties were already being tested.

And innocent people were going to pay the price.

Carys heard Cadell in her head.

Anwyn will think about Cymric lives first, and a dragon attack is the fastest way to end this battle, he said. *A dragon attack will keep Cian away from Cymru even if it leads to greater war with the other kingdoms in Briton.*

Carys's heart was racing when she turned to Dru. "We really need to convince Cian's fae not to fight," she said. "Because Cadell agrees with Winnie. Anwyn will absolutely order the dragons to attack."

The deep blue sigils on Dru's face pulsed with a dark light, and they almost seemed to move. "Alafair, go."

As they crested the top of the hill, a sweeping, treeless plateau stretched before them.

In the center of the plain, there was a massive stone circle, twice as large as Stonehenge, as if giants had erected it. Beyond the plain on the other side of the shallow bowl, Carys saw the shadows of a tree line and a shimmering cloud of magic that hovered over a line of horse-mounted troops.

A wild fae as tall as an ash tree stepped onto the rolling green land. With each footfall, his rootlike legs broke open the ground, creating fissures as he walked. At his shoulders, two owls flew, and the ground closed behind him, leaving chalk-white scars across the landscape.

Carys spotted Cadell flying overhead, circling the plain with wide, arching sweeps of his wings, joined by two dozen dragons, both small and large, all carrying war coracles that were perfectly balanced to drop and release armed Cymric troops.

A shadowy figure rippled in the periphery of her vision, and Carys turned her head.

On a horse the size of a Clydesdale, Rhiannon sat silently, her finger pressed to her lips as a voice whispered in Carys's ear.

You must not let them spill blood on Saris Plain.

She watched Alafair walking into the distance, and halfway across the plain, just to the side of the great stone circle, the fae halted and froze. Moments later, one of his owls circled overhead and turned back to Dru, swooping down to fly low over his head.

The animal must have communicated something to Dru, because Carys saw the tall fae freeze.

"What is it?" Lachlan asked. "What did he say?"

The red, twisted crown over Dru's head glowed, and his voice was cold when he finally spoke. "Fomorians."

The ancient race of giants and monsters was supposed to be a legend. Something out of even Shadowland nightmares. Monsters from beyond the sea.

Dru's eyes were fixed on the army across the plateau. "My brother has brought the Fomorians to lead his army."

CHAPTER THIRTY-ONE

Without waiting another moment, Dru shouted something at the top of his lungs and charged toward the center of the Saris Plain with the wild fae army behind him.

"What do we do?" Carys shouted at Lachlan. At this point, blood on Saris Plain seemed inevitable, but that didn't mean Carys couldn't at least try to stop it.

"Hold!" Lachlan shouted as the soldiers behind them began to stomp their feet. He raised his fist. "Hold!" His face was leached of color, and his eyes were fixed on the center of the field. "The only thing powerful enough to defeat this enemy is the dragons."

"I thought Fomorians were a legend even here," Carys shouted.

"Nothing is a legend here." Winnie's mount was restless, tossing her head and trying to surge forward.

Nêrys, I am coming to get you.

"Cadell is coming to get me." Carys jumped off her horse, grabbed her bow and quiver, and patted Leuca's neck. "Go! Head back to the river and wait for me."

Without a word, the horse turned and slipped away through the columns of soldiers.

"What are you doing?" Winnie asked. "We have to wait for orders."

"I'm not your soldier," Carys said. "My dragon is coming for me, and I'm not going to ignore him." And if there was anything Carys could do to stop this battle—or at least end it quickly—she was going to find it.

Lachlan eyed her quiver and bow. "Don't do anything rash."

"Who, me?" Carys walked forward, spotting Cadell in the distance. "I'm just hitching a ride with a dragon."

A moment later, Cadell landed, dropping a narrow war coracle that rocked for a moment before the door flipped down and it braced.

Duncan popped out from the open door and held his hand out. "Get in here!"

Carys ran.

As soon as she was in the coracle, Duncan cranked the door closed and waved his arms over his head. "Go!" A moment after that, they were in the air again, Cadell plucking them from the ground and swooping up to the sky.

"I never thought I'd be so grateful to be back in the air." Carys pulled out her bow as Cadell flew over the battle below. Maybe if they could take out some Fomorians, then the human battle could be prevented.

A grim dread settled in her belly, but the adrenaline coursing through her system quickly overrode everything other thought. She nocked an arrow and peered out of the arrowslit at the chaos in the middle of the plain.

"Fomorians," Duncan said grimly. "I've only ever seen pictures, and they're so much worse than I thought."

"Your sword isn't going to do much against them."

"Lucky I brought this." Duncan picked up a bow and quiver and walked to the arrowslit across from hers. "I'm not as good a shot as you, but I can try."

When Carys imagined the mythical race of superhumans, she had always imagined giants, but what she saw when she peeked through the arrowslit was so much worse.

There was a massive creature with claws like a badger ripping through the white chalk soil and tearing open the plain, grabbing fae from the battlefield and tossing them into his cavernous maw.

There was a three-headed wolf as big as an elephant, its claws ripping up the ground as it plowed through Dru's lines.

Dru was fighting back, his followers defending their leader as he planted his hands in the soil and pulled water from the ground beneath the surface.

As Fomorian giants ripped up the ground, the water came swiftly behind them, pulling the giants back under the earth and flooding the fissures they left behind.

"Is Dru bigger somehow?" Carys asked. "Is that just a trick of the light or—"

"No," Duncan said. "He's almost as big as they are."

The fae prince is the son of the sea god, Cadell said in her mind. *If anyone can defeat these monsters, he has the power. He has only been reluctant to use it until now.*

"Cadell says Dru can win." Carys nocked an arrow and pointed it at a Fomorian monster with the head of a goat and the body of a giant.

As dragons circled overhead, Carys saw arrows raining down and knew that other nêr ddraig had the same idea she did. They might not be able to strafe the plain with fire without harming Dru's people, but they could rain down arrows from the sky.

Cadell began to send positions to her as he flew over the battle. *Position four, one sixty degrees.*

Her first shot at a giant goat-man bounced off his curled horns, but her second hit him square in the eye. He reeled back, grasping for the arrow in his eye, and while he was distracted, one of the tree-fae rose up, shooting a branch from his arm through the belly of the Fomorian, then wrapping that same branch around the goat's body and squeezing until the monster was pulled to bloody pieces.

Alafair picked up a massive leg and kicked the head of the goat-monster away from the battle.

"Cadell, go burn that head!" Carys shouted.

Yes, Nêrys.

"Why?" Duncan yelled.

"I don't know for sure, but if he has elemental magic, he might be able to regenerate."

But there was no regenerating from ash. The dragon bellowed a stream of fire at the rolling goat head, scarring the plain with blackened grass and turning the Fomorian's remains to nothing more than a pile of ashes.

Carys heard Dru shouting.

"Turn back!" she said.

Cadell wheeled around, and it was obvious Dru had seen what Cadell had done. He was shouting at his people, who seemed to catch on quickly because one by one, they all targeted a Fomorian and tried to draw it away from the center of the battle, ripping off pieces where they could and tossing them as far as they could manage.

Like Cadell, other dragons swooped down, shooting fire at the pieces of Fomorians and turning their bodies to ash.

"It's working!" Carys had no sooner said it than she felt something massive knock the side of the coracle, and she flew across the wooden carriage, her head smashing against the wall.

Everything went black.

CARYS WOKE to see Duncan driving his sword through an arrowslit while blood poured into the coracle. There was a great beating wind driving down on her face, and she could feel something dripping down her neck.

She touched her throbbing head, and her fingers came away wet with blood.

"Carys!" Duncan roared.

She was confused, blinking at the giant black-brown feathers floating into the coracle. Massive wings nearly as wide as Cadell's body beat against the side, and she saw Cadell's belly red with fire.

An odd, disembodied voice whispered in her mind. *...cannot believe you are doing this instead of me.*

Duncan pulled his sword from the arrowslit and ran to her. "I don't know what it is, but it's stuck to the side." He put his hand on her head. "Can you move?"

Get your bow, idiot.

Carys blinked, still confused by what she was seeing when a long, black face with bloody, tangled hair peeked over the high wall of the coracle and opened its mouth.

It screamed, and Carys saw blood dripping from its fangs.

Shoot it.

Cadell was shouting in her mind: *Nêrys, there is a harpy attacking the coracle!*

The Fomorians brought harpies?

Duncan was bending over her, blood all over his clothes. "Carys, can you talk?"

"Help me up." She struggled to sitting and reached for her bow. The air around her grew strangely still, and her peripheral vision grew dark.

Aim for the eyes.

Maybe it was the head wound that was making her hear voices, but Carys nocked an arrow, drew it, and all she could see was the eyes of the monster trying to climb into her coracle as she drew back her string.

Thwoosh. The arrow hit one eye and the harpy screamed.

Again.

Carys quickly drew another, aimed, and fired faster than she ever had in her training.

Its center of gravity is thrown back, stab it now.

The harpy was still clinging to the side of the coracle with two clawed wings, but its head was flailing and one claw was slipping off.

"Get your sword!" Carys yelled. "Stab it!"

Duncan picked up his sword, ran to the arrowslit, stabbed the harpy through the opening, then pulled back and swung the blade up and over his head.

Thunk! The sword cut clean through one claw and sank into the wood.

The harpy screamed again.

Duncan yanked the sword from the solid oak and swung it at the other claw.

Thunk!

The harpy shrieked and fell back, and as soon as it released, Cadell wheeled to the side, surged into the air, and Duncan was thrown against the side of the coracle where Carys lay as the dragon let loose a stream of fire that lit up his belly.

The searing heat cut across the coracle, and Duncan threw himself over Carys to shield her from the blast.

The scent of burning feathers filled the air.

There are harpies attacking the dragons, Cadell said. *There are dozens of them.*

Carys struggled to her feet as the coracle evened out. "There are dozens of harpies," she told Duncan. "As many as there are dragons."

He ran to an arrowslit and looked out. "I see them. They look like a flock. They're grouping and clinging to the coracles."

Release the coracles. Carys was still hearing the strange voice in her mind.

"Some of the dragons are landing," Duncan shouted. "No, they're just dropping the war coracles and flying again."

We cannot kill the harpies with the coracles in our grip, Cadell said in her mind.

"Drop us if you need to," Carys shouted.

She ran to an arrowslit and saw Demelza, Anwyn's great red-skinned dragon swooping down over the harpy-covered coracles and plucking a feathered beast from where it clung. Then she lifted the harpy into the sky and tore it to pieces with her claws.

"I've never seen anything like this," Duncan said.

"Cadell, are there any around us?" Carys felt a rush in her blood.

The harpies appear to be congregating around the Fomorians and fae in the field below. At this altitude, we do not have their attention. Shall I continue circling?

"We're fine, go lower!" Carys knew that Cadell was trying to protect her, but she wanted to return to the fight. "Have Lachlan and Winnie charged yet?"

Carys heard horns in the distance and knew the Alban and Anglian troops wouldn't be long from the fight.

The wolves are on the plain, Cadell said.

"There's something dark— Wolves!" Duncan yelled. "The North Wolves are here."

Carys ran to another arrowslit and spotted them.

Like a dark cavalry, the wolves charged ahead of the human soldiers, Anglian foot soldiers running with them as the Alban cavalry fell back.

"What's Lachlan doing?" Duncan cried. "He's off to the side now, the idiot!"

Flank the enemy, the voice in her head whispered. *Divide their attention.*

"The fae have the front lines with the Fomorians and the wolves have their back now." Carys ran to another arrowslit as Cadell began to circle lower. "Lachlan is flanking them."

"I suppose he's not as big an idiot as I thought then." Duncan stepped back and used a piece of his coat to clean his sword.

The harpy blood was sizzling on the blade. It looked like harpies didn't like iron much either.

"We're going down again." Carys picked up her bow and nocked an arrow, ready to start shooting again. "Keep your sword handy in case the harpies try again. Eyes and claws."

"Eyes and claws." Duncan braced himself along the wall of the coracle and kept his eyes up as Carys aimed and started to fire at more Fomorians on the field.

Carys's arrow found a bloody monster's eye a moment before the badger-headed giant swung down, slashing a wolf with its massive claws.

Around them, the Saris Plain was wet with Fomorian and fae blood. Wolves and humans charged forward, and dragons ripped harpies apart in the sky as Cymric longbowmen fired toward the back of the Fomorian line.

Chaos reigned, and the Éiren soldiers had not even joined the fight.

CHAPTER THIRTY-TWO

She felt like her bones were going to fall from her joints as Cadell swooped over the battle for another pass.

"Lining up," Carys said.

The bald Fomorian with the long arms, Cadell said. *Position eight, one forty degrees.*

"Got it." Carys's arrow struck the monster in the back of his bald head, and his great webbed hand covered the wound as blood spurted through its fingers.

As the monster reeled back, a black-coated wolf leaped on the creature, tearing it to pieces and dragging its body away from the battle.

Moments later, a dragon swooped down and blew a stream of fire at the monster's remains, leaving it charred and smoking.

Duncan had hacked off two other harpies that had managed to attach themselves to the coracle, and the smoldering bodies of the aerial monsters lay scattered across the Saris Plain, their feathers falling across the ground like angled drops of blood spatter on waving green grass.

Every time a Fomorian fell, another seemed to rise from the

broken earth, grasping and gripping the white chalk before Dru's fae and the Anglian wolves and humans attacked it.

There was progress, but it was slow and creeping. But monsters fell and harpies bled in the sky, and the Anglian line moved ever closer to Orla and Cian's armies.

Yet through all the bloodshed and tumult, the Éiren soldiers remained along the ridge that backed against the trees, watching frozen as the forces of Briton battled against the invaders.

The queen's flag flew over the mounted crown princess and her guard while Cian watched from the front as Fomorians wreaked havoc on his brother's fae allies.

Look at them. The strange voice that had been with Carys through the battle whispered again. *Look closer.*

Carys looked over the distant army and realized that while Cian and a few fae commanders in front of the armies were riding back and forth, the armies hadn't moved. Not even a little bit. There was no sound coming from the ridge, not the stomping of horses or the trill of pipes or horns.

Look closer.

"Cadell," she shouted, "can you fly over the Éiren army?"

The battle is on the plain, Nêrys.

"I know, but they can spare me for a minute."

Duncan looked up from the arrowslit. "What is it?"

"I need to look at them."

Cadell wheeled to the north, then turned so they flew over the Éiren troops.

"Lower," she called out.

That will put us in archery range.

"I know." She watched the air around the frozen army. "I have a theory."

If your theory gets me a bolt in the wing, I'm going to ignore you next time.

"Yeah, that's fair."

They flew lower, but still nothing moved. Not a soldier. Not a fidget and not a foot out of place.

Cian's face turned up to the dragon, but all he did was squint before he turned back to watching his brother fight the Fomorian monsters.

Green-and-gold flags flapped in the wind, and Carys saw horses' manes blowing, but there was no rustle of restless feet, no horns blasting, and no drums, though their drummers lined up at the front of each stack of troops.

"They're just standing there," Duncan growled. "What the fuck do they think they're doing?"

"Just a little lower, Cadell!"

The dragon grumbled, but on the final pass over the Éiren troops, a pass so low that she could see the gusts from Cadell's wings stirring the banners, Carys saw it.

The enchantment was so strong she felt it from the sky.

Duncan braced himself against the wall of the coracle. "What is that?"

"Do you see it?" she shouted. "Duncan, Cadell, do you see it?"

There is a fae ward over the entire army, Cadell said.

"What is that?" Duncan shouted.

"They're enchanted." She craned her neck to see out of the arrowslit and spotted the fae commanders in front of the troops watching them. "Do you see it? Dru did the same thing on the boats as we brought the army through the river gate, but this is even bigger."

"They're bloody frozen in place." Duncan narrowed his eyes. "I bet if you started shooting at them, they wouldn't move an inch."

"The Éiren people did not march on Briton." Carys pointed to the troops on the ground. "Those soldiers probably don't even know where they are."

Duncan nodded. "Look at the crown princess. She's not moving either. Cian has enchanted his own daughter."

Princess Finola, her long brown hair blowing in the wind of

Cadell's wings, was as frozen as the troops behind her. She wore gold-and-silver armor that didn't appear to be just for show.

She was a formidable-looking woman who appeared to be in her mid-thirties; she had a strong jaw and a steady brow.

The crown princess was the kind of woman who looked like she could lead soldiers into a battle, but she was frozen in place as Cian and the other fae looked at the dragon flying over them, seemingly unconcerned by anything overhead.

Break the enchantment, the voice whispered in Carys's mind, *and you end the battle.*

"There." Carys spotted hunched figures in green robes crouched at the front of the columns of troops. "Do you see them?"

I see them, Cadell said. *But my fire will not penetrate fae wards.*

That's why Cian and the fae commanders seemed so unconcerned.

Break the enchantment, the voice came again. *End it before more blood spills.*

Duncan looked at her, his hand resting on the hilt of his sword. "What do you want to do? Should we head back and tell Dru? He could break his brother's ward to get to Cian."

"Dru is in the middle of the battle."

There was one other option, but Carys knew that neither Duncan nor Cadell was going to like it. *Cadell?*

Yes, Nêrys.

Duncan's blade can break that ward.

Yes. The dragon's voice was cautious. *It could.*

Carys walked to Duncan and put her hand on his shoulder. "Cadell is going to drop the coracle in front of the line!" She pointed to the ground. "We can use your blade to break the ward, and then Cadell can kill the fae who are enchanting the troops without killing the entire Éiren army."

King Harold was in Saris. Crown Princess Finola was in Saris. Maybe with the fae out of the way, a ceasefire could happen before more blood spilled.

"Let me get this straight," Duncan yelled over the roaring wind. "You want us to run in front of thousands of heavily armed Éiren soldiers and *break* the spell that's keeping them from joining this fight?"

Don't be ridiculous, Nêrys. Let the surly human out, and you stay in the coracle. I will lay down fire along the front of the Éiren army and kill the fae sorcerers who have enchanted the Éiren troops. He'll be fine. Probably.

"I'll be with you!" Carys yelled. "Cadell will lay down fire and kill the fae sorcerers after you break the ward." *I'm not leaving him on his own in front of a giant army.*

Yes, because your expert archery skills are enough to take on three thousand Éiren troops.

Duncan's eyes were wide and his chest was heaving. "Carys, that puts both of us in danger. You can't—"

"I don't think they're going to attack us," Carys said. "I don't think the soldiers down there even know where they are."

"You're guessing!" Duncan shouted.

"Yes." Carys had no idea why she was so sure this was going to work except for that persistent voice that might have been a goddess telling her to break the enchantment and end the battle. "But I'm pretty sure I'm right."

We're going back to the line. Cadell started to rise and turn back to the plain.

"Stop!" Carys shouted at the dragon. "I think if I can tell Finola what is going on and how Cian is using the Éiren army, all this will stop. The Queens' Pact won't be broken. Harold will negotiate. This battle can stay between Cian and Dru!"

Duncan kept his eyes on hers, but Cadell was already turning.

"I must be fucking in love with you, Carys Morgan, because I think you're right too." Duncan grabbed her around the waist and pulled her in for a ferocious kiss. Then he released her and yelled, "Dragon, put me down!"

I'll put him down, but you're staying in the coracle.

I'm going with him.

Then we're not setting down.

Cadell, put us down. Carys stared into Duncan's eyes, willing her confidence into him as her dragon roared his frustration overhead.

Nêrys, you have no backup! This is foolish and I will not drop you. We'll find a way to get a message to Dru.

No. She kept her eyes on Duncan's, nodding as she saw the resolve settle in his eyes. *This is the right thing to do. This is going to work.*

Duncan gripped her hand in his. "All right. I'm with you."

How do you know?

The whispering voice came again to Carys's mind. *Ogwen Valley. Just say Ogwen Valley.*

"Ogwen Valley!" Carys shouted.

Complete silence in her mind; then Cadell wheeled around, descending rapidly, parallel to the line of the Éiren army.

A moment later, she felt the bottom of the coracle rock along the ground.

CHAPTER THIRTY-THREE

The coracle rocked forward.

The door slammed open.

Before Carys could even draw her bow, two fae warriors were at the door and Duncan slashed across their chests.

Silver blood burst from their skin as their armor dissolved to nothing and they stood, naked and shaking with wounds in their chest and eyes wide and terrified.

Carys didn't even wait a moment before she let loose with her bow.

Without armor to block it, the arrow flew through the fae's chest and stuck out the other side, knocking the man back as the other ran.

"Iarann!" he shouted as he ran down the angled door of the coracle.

"Get that blade in the ground!"

Cadell was already swooping down, laying a narrow line of fire in front of the fae commanders. It did nothing to break the shimmering magical ward, but it kept more fae warriors from running toward them as they stayed safe behind their bubble of magic.

Duncan ran out onto the field and plunged his sword into the earth, the force of his arms driving it so deep that the green grass split open, the ground rocked, and the shining bubble of magic wavered.

Prince Cian of Temris, Elatha's son and Prince Consort of Éire, turned his head to look on the human who'd struck his ward with a dragon-steel blade, and the fae prince's eyes went wide.

He urged his mount forward and roared, "Who brings iron to my lands?"

Duncan yanked the steel blade from the earth and drove it in again. "Just a mundane human, ya bastard."

Carys stayed behind Duncan, firing arrows at the fae commanders, but it didn't do much. They bounced off the magical shield, but she saw the ward begin to shimmer and the bubble of protection started wavering.

"Keep going," she said. "It's working."

Cian rode his mount back and forth behind the ward, his eyes moving from Duncan to the dragon overhead. "Human, stop."

"I know your brother, you know," Duncan said. "Don't like either of you fae much, but I like him a bit more."

Cian's eyes turned conniving. "I have riches, human. Would you like gold and jewels?"

"Ah, fuck off." Duncan's brogue got thicker as he drew the sword from the ground, walked a few yards forward, then plunged it in the earth again. "I'm already rich, ya blond numpty."

Cian cocked his head. "Your wealth is nothing to what I can give you. Gold and cattle. Fertile lands and—"

"And fuck you" —Duncan pulled the blade from the ground before he ran it in again— "for ruinin' ma blade. I'm goin' to catch hell from Angus. I've probably bent it, and it took ages to make."

"It's working," Carys said softly. "Keep going."

Nêrys, the ward is weaker but still intact.

She could see the pearlescent surface of the magic wavering, a faint rainbow shimmering like a bubble floating in sunlight. She looked at Princess Finola on her horse.

The princess blinked.

Carys's heart leaped and she nocked an arrow, aiming it at Cian. "Duncan, one more time!"

The prince's horse reared, and the fae's face turned from cajoling to furious. "Stop that this instant, you craven—"

"Oh fuuuuuuck oooooff." Duncan yanked his sword from the ground one more time, then walked over and—keeping his eyes on Cian's—plunged the sword down once again.

The enchantment broke with an audible crack.

Carys let her arrow fly at Cian's chest, but the fae prince batted it away.

Cadell roared in the distance.

Nêrys... RUN.

"Come on!" Carys pulled Duncan's arm, grabbed his hand, and fled from the line of fae troops and frozen, white-eyed Éiren soldiers, running toward a copse of trees just over a fold in the hills as arrows whizzed by them and she felt Cadell approaching.

Stay low, the dragon warned.

Duncan and Carys took cover behind a thick stand of bushes moments before the dragon flew along the front line of the Éiren army, laying down a line of fire that caught the fae commanders, the green-cloaked sorcerers, and the front lines of the Éiren cavalry, stopping short of incinerating the Éiren crown princess before he swooped up to the sky again.

Finola's horse reared, and the Éiren troops woke from their enchantment, screaming and scrambling for cover.

"Dragan!"

The cries erupted from the columns of troops, and Carys saw the princess, mounted on a great brown stallion, put her head down and ride forward, aiming straight for Cian.

Finola had her sword already drawn, but before she reached the fae prince, the ground beneath her opened up and her horse went tumbling.

A voice boomed over Saris Plain. "Cian Elathason!"

Coming up from the plain, his wild fae army arrayed behind him, walked Diarmuid mac Lir. His height stretching to over eight feet tall, his hair flowing down his back like dark water, the fae prince's arms were spread wide as the sea and doom was on his face.

His eyes were fixed on his brother.

CHAPTER THIRTY-FOUR

Diarmuid mac Lir, the son of the sea god, strode across the land, and beneath his feet the water rose up, splashing against his legs as he marched toward his half brother.

"So the wandering bastard returns." Cian sneered at his younger brother, dismounted from his horse, and walked toward Dru, with each step growing in stature until his height was even greater than the dark prince's.

His arms grew long, and from his right hand, a gold-tipped spear emerged.

"We will end this." Cian's voice filled the air everywhere. "You and me."

"Gladly." Dru reached into his black cloak and drew out a silver sword. "This fight was always and only between you and me."

The wild fae hung back as the two sons of Queen Aine wrestled for power in the stone circle where the oldest humans had prayed.

The wolves came to ring around the fight, but the remaining fae hung back, watching the two princes meet to decide their fate.

Dru lifted his sword and swung, but Cian struck first, his gold spear stabbing Dru just underneath his ribs.

Duncan hissed, but Carys's attention wasn't fixed on the battling fae princes. She kept one eye on them and grabbed Duncan's hand, keeping low as they scuttled behind the hills below the Éiren army.

"What are we doing?" Duncan asked.

"Looking for Finola." She was searching for Finola's guards as the fae and the human armies' attention was fixed on the battle between Dru and Cian. She hadn't missed the look of rage that the crown princess had sent her mother's consort.

"I have a feeling there's no love lost between Finola and Cian." She spotted the crown princess watching the battle with two tall knights on either side of her.

Cadell. She could feel the dragon circling overhead and knew he was dying to fly down and pluck her off the field where she was surrounded by soldiers.

Nêrys, there are too many people. Run toward the Anglian line and—

Did Seren know Princess Finola?

The dragon was silent.

Cadell!

You need to leave the battle. The situation is volatile, and I cannot protect you on the ground.

Did Seren know Finola?

Yes, they met on many occasions, and Seren had great respect for her.

"Okay." Carys breathed out slowly. "Seren knew Finola."

"What does that mean?" Duncan muttered as they crouched behind a rock. "I don't need to remind you that you are not your Shadowkin."

Carys, I am coming down to meet you. Tell Duncan to stay with you until I am there!

"No!" She turned her head up to the sky. *Stay overhead. Watch us. Cover us from above.*

Nêrys—

Please trust me. She grabbed Duncan's hand and looked at him. "Trust me."

"What are you going to do?" Duncan whispered. "Don't be a fool, Carys."

"Seren knew Finola. She respected her. Me looking like a dead woman might just shock her into giving me a moment before her guards start shooting."

Before Duncan could grab her or Cadell could yell more in her brain, Carys rushed toward the Éiren lines, waving her hands over her head.

"Hey!" she shouted. "He-ey! I need to talk to Finola!"

She only got about twenty yards before soldiers grabbed her and wrestled her arms behind her back.

"I'm not fighting!" Carys shouted. "I just want to talk."

Duncan came roaring up behind her with his sword drawn. "Carys!"

"Put it away!" Carys spoke as quickly as she could. "I'm Lady Carys Morgan, nêrys ddraig of Cymru, niece of King Dafydd!" She nearly fell over as the duel between Cian and Dru raged in the distance and the ground rocked with the force of their blows.

A soldier grabbed her and put a knife to her throat.

"Lady Carys Morgan!" Her heart was pounding out of her chest. "Nêrys ddraig!"

The soldier holding her was confused. His knife eased off her neck. "Cymrais?"

"Lady Carys," she said again. "Nêr ddraig." The soldiers only spoke Éiren of course. She pointed to the sky. "Dragon! Ddraig." She pounded a fist against the leather armor she wore. "Nêr ddraig."

A few moments later, a knight in worn chain mail and a green-and-gold surcoat walked toward her and Duncan, speaking English. "You are a Cymric dragon lord and wish to speak with the crown princess?" His eyes were lined, and silver sprinkled his dark hair. His jaw was rough with stubble, and he wore a signet ring on his left hand.

An older knight, a man of some standing, and one with experience. It was exactly the kind of advisor Carys had been hoping to meet.

The ground rumbled again, and a tree shot up between Dru and Cian, its leaf-covered branches reaching out to try to wrap around Dru.

The knight's eyes went wide, but he forced them back to Carys. "What does a dragon rider of Cymru want with our princess?"

Dru spun around, slashing at the tree and gripping the trunk as he ripped the living tree from the soil.

Carys looked the knight dead in the eye and kept her voice low. "I have a feeling that you and your princess and all your soldiers are really confused right now, and I would like to tell you what is going on."

The giant birch tree that was attacking Dru groaned and twisted before it crumbled and dissolved into dust.

The wild fae cheered, but Carys saw the remnants of the Fomorians crawling in the distance, heading toward Cian and Dru as the two fae princes battled.

"Please," Carys said. "For the sake of the Queens' Pact, take me to Princess Finola."

The knight didn't say anything, but she could tell by the flicker of uncertainty in his eyes that he was more than a little confused by everything that was going on.

"Sir." Carys spoke as calmly as she could manage. "I am trying to stop a war."

The tall man looked at Duncan. "And Prince Lachlan?"

"Oh, I'm not him." Duncan shook his head, and the men holding him loosened their grasp. "I'm his Brightkin."

"I see." The man might have said that, but he clearly didn't know what was happening. "Come with me." He lifted his chin at the men holding them and said, "I will take them." He held his hand out to Duncan. "Your sword, sir."

Duncan looked at Carys, who nodded.

He handed over his steel blade, and the older knight took it.

"This is steel," he said in a low voice.

"Yes, it is."

The knight looked at Duncan with no little curiosity, but as the clash of fae swords continued in the background and cheers rose from the hills overlooking the battle, he urged them forward. "Come with me."

On the ridge overlooking two giant, dueling fae, Princess Finola of Laigin, crown princess of the kingdom of Éire and high commander of their army, was bending over a twelve-foot line of scorched earth at the front of her troops, walking among the charred bodies of dead horses, cavalry riders, and cloaked fae sorcerers who were nothing but ash.

Burned and injured soldiers were sitting on the ground, tended by healers and watchful brothers and sisters in arms.

Carys felt a knot of dread when she saw the dead and injured.

Cadell?

Fire burns, Nêrys. War kills.

I know.

Whether they were enchanted or not, Carys's heart ached from the loss of life.

"Princess Finola?" the knight called.

Finola looked up, and her eyes went wide. "Seren?"

"No." Carys raised her hands. "I'm not—"

"They said you were dead." Finola stalked toward her. "What is going on?" Her eyes went to Duncan. "Lachlan, what the hell—"

"Not Seren," Carys said, holding her hands higher. "Not Lachlan either. But I am Seren's Brightkin, and Cadell—"

"Cadell *did* this." Finola's face twisted in anger. "Cadell of Eryri did this to *my* people!"

"I know and I am—"

Finola shouted, "*A dragon attack is an act of war.*"

"So is invading Anglia!" Carys shouted, trying to get the woman's attention. "So is stealing children."

Finola halted. Her mouth dropped open, and then she snapped her jaw shut and stepped so close that Carys felt the woman's breath on her face.

"Back!" Finola shouted at her men.

"Princess Finola—"

"Get back!"

The men stepped away, leaving Finola and Carys nose to nose.

"What the fuck is going on?" the princess whispered. "If you're not Seren, who are you? Why do you wear Seren's face and the armor of a dragon lord? Are you fae?"

"I am not fae; I am Seren's Brightkin and I am bonded to her dragon."

Finola was a tall woman. She stared down her nose at Carys. "Not possible."

"Cadell laid down fire to kill the fae mages who were enchanting your army," Carys whispered. "There was no way that he could avoid the others. Look around you, Princess Finola. You are on the Saris Plain in Southern Anglia. Cian brought your army by boat and marched you here while the fae sorcerers kept you enchanted—"

"That's not possible."

"It was the strongest magic I've ever seen," Carys continued swiftly. "Look at the land in front of you," Carys hissed. "Look at the wolves, the wild fae, the human soldiers, and all the dead."

Finola was silent.

"Your father—"

"Cian is not my father," Finola snapped.

"Your mother's *consort* was about to march you and your army into battle against Anglian troops, and you wouldn't have even known it was happening," Carys whispered. "We *had* to break the enchantment."

"Why are the Anglian forces arrayed against us? We are allies of Anglia."

Carys's heart sank. "Do you even know about the children?"

Finola stepped back. "*What* children?"

"You and King Harold have been drawn into a fight that belongs to those two fae princes." Carys pointed over her shoulder. "Cian tried to use you to break the Queens' Pact, but this battle is not yours. It's not Harold's. This battle is between Cian and Dru to see who will control the fae of Briton." She let out a breath. "And that is *all* this is about."

Finola looked around, and Carys knew she'd been right. The woman had no idea what was happening, but now she had an army behind her, and she needed to regain control.

The fae commanders were dead. The sorcerers were ashes.

The princess was back in charge of her army.

Princess Finola mounted her horse and spoke quietly to her commanders, who fanned out across the ridge.

The princess shouted something over the line of troops, and those within earshot cheered. Then she spoke again at longer length. After she finished, her soldiers fell silent, murmuring among themselves, but Finola turned to face the battle between Dru and Cian, her face a stoic mask.

Duncan walked over to her, and Carys ran to his arms, holding on as Dru and Cian fought and the earth itself seemed to weep from the blood spilled between them.

Dru bled silver from his head, his pierced side, and a long slash across his neck.

Cian's blood was a shimmering gold, and he was in worse shape than Dru. His right leg was weeping blood, and he leaned to the left, hardly able to stand.

The older knight who'd been holding Duncan walked over to translate. "The princess told the army that Prince Cian of Temris has been challenged for the rule of the fae throne," he said. "But that since this was a rightful challenge on the sacred ground of Saris Plain, where the offerings to the old gods were given, we must watch in witness with our Anglian brothers and sisters. That we must respect the judgment of the gods, who will declare the winner."

"Dru *will* win," Duncan said. "Is your princess prepared to recognize the reign of Diarmuid mac Lir?"

The man's eyes flashed with derision. "That's fae business, human. No business of mine."

Carys turned her eyes back to the stone circle and realized Duncan was right.

Dru *was* going to win.

Cian looked faded and broken, and with every strike of Dru's silver sword, every roar from the wild fae around him, the dark prince grew taller, greater, more and more powerful.

The red crown on his head dripped with silver blood, and every place his blood dropped to the grass, a pool of water formed until the plain itself appeared like a shallow sea reflecting the stormy sky.

Clouds gathered over the plain, and a swift darkness covered the land. The watery shroud opened and rain began to fall, but when it touched Carys's lips, it was seawater that touched her tongue.

Cian of Temris stumbled back, then fell forward, dropping to his knees as darkness covered the land.

"Cian, son of Elatha, old god of light." Dru's voice was an echo like thunder over the sea. "Don't you know you are in the Shadowlands?" Dru's smile was wicked as he drew his sword back. "You have no power here."

With one stroke, the black-haired fae swung his sword, and Cian's head fell to the ground.

Gold blood poured from his body, and his blood watered the land.

IN THE DISTANCE, the last of the Fomorians howled in anger, leaping over their dead and driving their monstrous and mangled bodies toward Dru and the wild fae army.

The wolves turned and lined up, the Anglian and Alban armies turned toward the awakened foe, and the Éiren armies—newly awake to the Fomorian threat—began to beat their shields as low, droning horns sounded from behind them.

The king of the fae held up a hand, then bent down, touched the watery surface of Saris Plain, and Carys saw his mouth move as he spoke to the water.

Lightning flashed and thunder ripped the sky. With the fae king bent down, the ground burst open and the Great Serpent, its golden-brown scales shimmering in the flashes of lightning, burst from the watery ground and aimed itself toward the last of the Fomorian army.

His body was the length of a city block, as giant as a great whale, and as his mouth gaped open, Carys saw the jaws lined with two rows of vicious, serrated teeth.

The serpent slithered over the grassy plain as water poured from the sky, and then it opened its great jaws and swallowed the last of the monsters in a single, violent gulp.

"Fuck me," Duncan muttered. "That's something you don't see every day."

Every human on Saris Plain was frozen as the massive serpent turned, its body gliding smoothly over the grassy hills and the watery rills, passing by the Anglian armies, the various fae, and all the staring wolves.

After a pause, the wolves threw their heads back and howled in triumph.

A moment later, the Great Serpent of London twisted his great scaled body, slid into a massive pool of water near the fae king's feet, and disappeared from sight.

In the middle of the howling and ferocious cheers of the wild fae army, Dru spoke words that whispered across Carys's ears, then slipped away without leaving footprints.

CHAPTER THIRTY-FIVE

Three days later, King Harold of London and Crown Princess Finola of Éire reaffirmed the Queens' Pact on the top of Lud's Hill with cheering crowds from across London celebrating the return of good weather, healthy animals, and the Great Serpent, who had reappeared in the Tamis two days before.

The river was filled with flower wreaths, offerings of food, and floating lanterns to celebrate the great snake's return.

Milk was set out on every hearth, and flowers and ribbons hung from the branches of every tree in the forests that dotted the city.

King Harold had declared a week of celebration and unity to commemorate the lost and give thanks to the gods and the Great Serpent for securing peace.

Carys, Laura, and Duncan walked along the river on Oswulf's Way, the large green embankment that bordered the Tamis where wild river sprites danced in the reeds, the occasional mermin peeked out to watch the brightly dressed humans, and otters were back to play in the verge.

The people of London had filled the green space, and Carys in her leather dragon armor was thanked by nearly every Londoner she passed.

Even the trolls.

"You're a hero here," Duncan said. He still had a long dagger at his waist, but he'd left his sword at Dafydd's castle. "You sure you want to go back to the Brightlands?"

"Ha!" Carys looked at the grey sky overhead. Even with the raucous celebrations happening across the city, the brightest the Shadowlands got was a milky-white sky. "I need some sunshine."

"So not London then," Duncan said. "Or Scone."

"Or Baywood for that matter," Laura added. "It's June Gloom time back home."

"June Gloom?" Duncan asked. "What, the sky you mean?"

"Yeah, it's a thing by the coast from the ocean fog," Laura said. "May Grey. June Gloom."

"No-Sky July," Carys added. "*Fog*ust."

Duncan frowned. "Wait, is the weather in Baywood *worse* than Scotland? I didn't think that was possible. You're in California, for goodness' sake."

"It's a big state," Laura said, "with a lot of cold ocean."

A pair of brightly clad children ran past them, nearly causing Carys to trip. They giggled and raced through the crowds on the river walk as their father shouted at them to "apologize to the dragon lady, for Tamis's sake."

Carys squinted at them as they disappeared into the trees. "Were those kids wearing Spider-Man shirts?"

"One was Deadpool, I think."

"Ah, the troll markets are back in business," Duncan said. "The Shadowlands are healing."

Carys felt a bubble of happiness in her chest.

The Shadowlands—at least in Anglia—*were* healing.

She and Cadell had flown over the southern counties yesterday. Saris Plain was green again, the water had drained away, and grass grew over the hills where the earth had covered the remains of monsters and enfolded the bodies of the humans and fae who had died.

Flowers had burst from the ground, waving in the breeze as wild horses and unicorns returned to the stone circles and barrow lands.

The fae mounds that had sprouted up across Southern Anglia had not receded, but the sheep grazed over the grass, and sprites and birds rested in the branches of the shrubs and hedges that grew around them.

Though Anglian lives had been lost, with the affirmation of the pact, greater war had been averted, and the new fae king, the first true fae leader in centuries, had retreated to the subterranean halls of Temris to bring the fae of Briton under his command.

Queen Orla of Éire, after over one hundred years of life and decades married to a fae consort, was quickly fading with the death of Prince Cian.

Whispers and rumors said that within months, Princess Finola would be queen.

Laura must have been thinking along the same lines as Carys. "I think Finola will be a good ruler," she said quietly. "I was impressed by her speech with Harold."

The young ruler and the crown princess had both addressed the crowds on Lud's Hill, surrounded by Éiren knights, wild fae ambassadors, and Anglian wolves.

"I agree," Duncan said. "She's learned from her mother. Her fae consort is much weaker than Cian. According to Lachlan, he's a follower and has no desire to lead."

Carys hadn't seen or spoken to Lachlan since the ceremony on Lud's Hill, though she knew he was still deep in talks with Harold, Finola, and Dafydd about the future of Briton.

"Have you heard from Dru?" Laura asked Duncan.

"No." Duncan shook his head. "I don't know what'll happen to his pub now that he has to go and be king and all, but that's not my problem to solve."

Carys's mind went to Naida, but no one had seen the ellyllon for days.

Whatever happened between Naida and Dru, Carys had to take Duncan's attitude as her own.

It was not her problem to solve.

Nêrys. Cadell was soaring overhead, circling down slowly as humans shouted and ran from the center of the meadow. The dragon gently landed and transformed, walking toward Carys, Laura, and Duncan in human form as scattered humans around him pointed and more than a few clapped.

"Oh, he hates that," Laura muttered.

Cadell's cheeks were ruddy by the time he reached them, and Carys didn't think it was from the wind.

"Hello, Hero Dragon," Carys said loudly.

"Stop." He linked his hands behind his back and joined them as they walked, trying to seem inconspicuous, which was nearly impossible for a seven-foot dragon in human form wearing dark green leather armor.

Despite the beautiful day, Cadell's face was grim.

Carys knew immediately where he'd been that morning. "So you had the meeting with Finola?"

"Yes."

Carys walked next to her dragon, and she didn't say a word. If Cadell wanted to tell her more, he would. But she wasn't going to ask.

"I share her grief over the loss of Éiren life," Cadell said quietly. "It was... necessary but regrettable."

Laura slipped her arm under his. "Their deaths prevented greater bloodshed. If you hadn't broken the enchantment, there might have been war."

You have to believe her, Carys spoke to his mind. *She's right.*

Cadell glanced at her, nodded, but said nothing.

The dragon would be forced to live with the death of twelve Éiren cavalry commanders and their mounts. As would Carys. It had been her plan to begin with. It had stopped the war, but it had come at a price.

Cadell had wanted to face Princess Finola and offer his apologies in person.

He said, "I have offered blood price to their families from the horde, but Finola would not accept."

Duncan's voice was solemn. "She knows the deaths were unavoidable, Cadell."

He nodded but said nothing else.

They continued along Oswulf's Embankment, but though the humans and magical folk of London celebrated, Carys, Cadell, Duncan, and Laura walked in silence.

Peace had come, but peace always came with a price.

DAFYDD FOUND Carys in the library that night, reading by the fire. He sat across from her, and she set down the book she was reading by fae lantern.

"Hey." She smiled. "How's Harold?"

"The young man is rising to the occasion," her uncle said. "Your aunt would approve."

Carys could tell that Dafydd was missing his wife. "How's Eamer feeling about her mother?"

"She has flown to Áth Cliath—that's Dublin in your world—to be with her. Queen Orla was removed from Temris to Áth Cliath when King Diarmuid appeared."

"How is that going?" The new king of the fae would have to create a new relationship with the humans of Éire now that his brother was no longer the prince consort.

"It appears that King Diarmuid has his hands full bringing the light fae court under his rule," Dafydd said. "I don't think he has much time for human queens. Even those once married to his brother."

"So that's... a good thing?"

Dafydd smiled sadly. "Orla will be dead within months without Cian keeping her alive."

"So the children were all—"

"You said once that the Crow Mother mentioned a sacrifice," Dafydd said. "It is possible that Orla thought a very ancient fae might want children as that sacrifice."

And the Crow Mother wasn't even fae. Carys wondered if Orla had known.

"So twisted." Carys flashed back to her last meeting with the Crow Mother in the Shadowlands. She was a very different woman than the nubile goddess who had become Macha in the Brightlands.

"The queen will bring me her offering, and then everything will fall into place."

"What offering?"

"I take offerings of all kinds. Magic. Blood. Babies."

"You might be right," Carys said. "Thank God all the children were recovered." She leaned forward. "Right? All of them were recovered from the fae?"

"Every one," Dafydd said. "I promise. The only blood spilled was the blood on Saris Plain. All the children are fine."

Carys sat back and breathed a sigh of relief. The only blood spilled was the blood on Saris Plain. And despite Rhiannon's warning, they had averted a greater war.

The only blood spilled was on Saris Plain.

Carys blinked. Threads of memory began to weave together.

"The queen will bring me her offering... Magic, blood, babies."

She sat up straight in her chair. Magic. Blood.

Forget the babies.

Magic and blood.

Magic. And blood.

Dafydd looked at her. "Carys?"

"You don't get your average Londoner offering sacrifices to the river anymore."

"Fae are not gods. Even though they may act it at times."

Carys set her book on the table in front of her. "The fae are not gods."

Dafydd shook his head. "Of course they're not."

"But the *gods* are gods." Carys returned to a black circle in the woods as blue and green lights danced over the Great Serpent of London and a fae prince talked to an old, old goddess.

"Depart from this place and cease your meddling, Old One. Your time has passed."

"My time is reborn as I am."

A beggar prince hiding in a darkened alley, grabbing Carys before the Crow Mother could steal away.

"I do wonder what you're about."

"You'll find out in time, and it's no trouble for you or your kind. In fact, it might just be to your benefit."

A bright fae prince, allied to a queen, searching for power that he thought he'd lost.

"...anyone strong enough to hold the Saris Plain must be the chosen of the gods... A place of worship, offering, and sacrifice."

Offering and sacrifice.

Carys looked at Dafydd, and a knot began to form in her stomach. "Cian wanted to rebuild Old Saris because it's a place of power in every world. Naida said so. That's where Stonehenge is in our world, and there are stone circles there in the Shadowlands."

"Yes," Dafydd said. "Humans have never built there because it was a place to offer…"

Carys saw the moment the realization struck Dafydd too.

"It was a place of offering," Carys said. "The children were never the sacrifice, Dafydd. The children were just a distraction."

As Carys rushed from the library, searching for Duncan and Laura, she flashed back to her last memory of a goddess, but it wasn't the Crow Mother or Macha or any of the forms that the Morrigan, the goddess of war and bloodshed, had taken with her.

She remembered a goddess on horseback.

A goddess whispering in her mind.

A goddess her mother had worshipped and who had tried to warn her.

"You were wondering why the fae prince came to this place. You were wondering just why Aine's son chose Saris Plain."

"Duncan!" She shouted for him. "Laura?" She ran through the halls of Dafydd's mansion, searching for her friends. "Cadell!"

Duncan found her first. He walked up the stairs and ran to her. "What's wrong?"

"We have to get back to the Brightlands." Her heart was racing. "I think something is really wrong."

Laura and Cadell found them next.

"Nêrys?"

"What's up?" Laura's face was red as she walked toward Carys. "You sound panicked."

"We have to get back to the Brightlands. Now."

Duncan and Cadell exchanged a look.

Nêrys—

"Carys, what is going on?" Duncan asked. "You want to go back to London tonight?"

"We can always come back if we need to, but I think something is happening. I don't think all this was because of Cian— I mean, some of it was because of Cian and Dru, but the Crow Mother—"

"The Morrigan." Cadell spat out her name.

"Rhiannon tried to warn me." She grabbed Cadell's arm. "She told me not to spill blood on Saris Plain."

"We stopped the battle," Duncan said. "You and Cadell—"

"We stopped the battle." Carys turned to Duncan. "But blood was still spilled. A lot of blood. A lot of powerful, *magical* blood."

Laura's eyes went wide. "So much blood that a giant snake managed to swim all the way to Stonehenge to eat an army of monsters."

"*That* was the sacrifice," Duncan said. "The fae and Fomorian blood spilled in battle."

"That was the offering the Crow Mother wanted from Queen Orla." Cadell put his hand on her shoulder. "Nêrys, pack your bags. Pack whatever you want to take back to the Brightlands. You're right —we need to go now."

"Give me ten minutes," Laura said. "I'll be ready."

"I'll send a message to Lachlan," Duncan said. "Tell him what we think is going on."

Carys ran to her room and started to pack. Her heart was pounding out of her chest as she heard Rhiannon's words over and over again in her head.

"More than just the fae prince waits. More than Elatha's son is hungry for power. You must not let them spill blood on Saris Plain."

CHAPTER THIRTY-SIX

Carys, Laura, Duncan, and Cadell were heading out the door, packed and ready to walk through the fae gate, when Godrik and Naida found them.

"I ran into this one in the courtyard." Naida's face was blank and her nose wrinkled when she said *this one*. "He wouldn't let me pass. As if he has any authority in the Cymric king's territory."

"I didn't say she couldn't pass," Godrik growled. "I simply asked her where she had been. No one has seen her for days."

"That's none of your business." Naida looked up at the giant wolf. "Where have you been? Not in London. I smell the sea on you."

"Because I was in Eskari territory checking on the— You know what?" He crossed muscled arms over his chest. "I don't have to explain myself to you."

"I don't have to explain myself to you either!"

Cadell narrowed his eyes at both of them. "This is a tiresome conversation, and we have things to do."

Both Naida and Godrik spoke at the same time. "The children were not the sacrifice."

Carys blinked. "What?"

The small fae woman and the wolf stared at each other with shock.

"How did you know?" Godrik asked.

"It never made any sense," Naida said. "The children were taken, but honestly, they were not that hard to find. Your average tree sprite could break the wards around them. And taking children like that?"

"And wolves," Godrik said. "We may not keep company with brownies, but we have good relations with the wild fae in our forests, and we're better land stewards than the humans. If Orla and Cian had tried to offer them up to a powerful old fae, they wouldn't have allowed it. Not children."

"The children were not the sacrifice," Carys said. "The blood spilled at Saris was the sacrifice. We were all played."

Naida's face drained of color. "Dru and Cian—"

"She played all of us," Carys said again. "Their rivalry might have inspired it, and Cian's thirst for power might have made it easier, but the Crow Mother was looking for blood on Saris Plain." Carys looked at Naida. "The place of offering to the old gods."

Godrik growled. "She has been starved of the blood of Briton for centuries because of the Queens' Pact. A war would have fed her power."

"We stopped the war, but that might not have been enough." Carys hiked her backpack over her shoulder. "We're going to the Brightlands right now."

Naida's eyes went wide. "Is the Morrigan in the Brightlands?"

"Yes."

"How did she get there? Epona's daughters have bound her here in the Shadowlands for centuries," Naida said.

Carys's heart sank. "Okay, that's kind of my fault, but I'm going to try to fix it." She grabbed Duncan's hand. "But we have to go now."

"I'll go with you." Godrik glanced at Duncan and Cadell. "Unlike your companions, I am adept at combat with and without magic. The wolves train for times like this."

Cadell and Duncan both started to speak, but Carys broke in. "Fine. That's fine. This is not an argument we're going to have right now, so I'm just going to say that's fine."

Duncan grumbled, and Cadell was speaking under his breath in muttered Cymric.

Carys turned to Naida. "I know you can't go to the Brightlands, but if you could—"

"I'll go." The ellyllon's face was pale, but her full mouth was set in a line. "The fae started this, and I'll do what I can to help."

Cadell spoke softly to her. "It's possible that nothing has happened," the dragon said. "It's possible that we are being overly cautious. We did stop the war. You do not have to do this. I know what going to the Brightlands will do to you."

"It's fine." Naida started marching toward the road. "I'll be fine."

She is being fatalistic, Cadell said in her mind. *The ellyllon can be reckless.*

Her true love is now king of a people who will never accept her. Carys started following Naida. *She probably feels like her future is pretty bleak.*

The rest of them fell in line behind Carys and Naida.

"You know the gate near the troll market," Naida said quietly. "But there are other gates all over London. Smaller ones that we should be able to use if you'll lead the way."

"Of course." Carys looked down. "I appreciate it, Naida."

"I won't have power there," she said quietly. "But I'll still have knowledge that might help."

"Okay."

"I might get sick from the iron." She glanced at Duncan. "If he brought his sword—"

"Not much use for a sword in Central London," Carys quickly reassured her. "He left it with my uncle."

Naida nodded, then glanced over her shoulder at Cadell. "I'm reminded of a joke."

The dragon laughed under his breath.

"What is it?" Laura asked. "What's the joke? Or is this magical humor that humans won't get?"

"A dragon, a wolf, and a fae walk into the Brightlands," Godrik said.

Carys was waiting for the rest, but the wolf didn't say anything else.

Duncan finally asked, "So what?"

"Nothing. That's the joke. We cross into the Brightlands and we all become nothing but humans."

Laura said, "That's... not a very good joke."

Naida nodded. "And every magical creature would agree with you."

"Huh." Laura pursed her lips. "Well, I still think being human is pretty great."

"Thank you, Laura." Duncan threw his arm around her shoulders. "I would agree with you as well."

"I think that officially makes you my favorite Scotsman."

"Good, 'cause I'm the one she's keeping."

Carys looked over her shoulder at Duncan, who winked at her.

They walked into Hyde Forest, off the main path and deeper into the dark and twisted old oaks. The ground was soft with new grass, and in the darkness, the nodding white heads of snowdrops sprang up between the trees.

A few moments after leaving the path, Naida led them through a dense patch of brush where a few scattered blue wisps floated in the trees overhead.

"We're going through." She turned to Carys. "You have to lead the way."

Carys looked into a wall of greenery. "Lead where?"

"Just keep walking forward," Naida said. "Follow the wisps."

Follow the wisps. Ah yes, exactly what her mother had spent Carys's childhood warning her *not* to do.

"Following the wisps," she muttered.

She felt Duncan take her hand, and she looked over her shoulder.

"I'm right there with you." He leaned down and pressed a quick kiss to her lips. "Whatever happens, I'll be with you."

Carys squeezed his hand, turned back to the pathway, and walked into the darkness.

THE DARKNESS PRESSED AROUND HER, and laughter echoed in the darkness.

It was Macha's laughter. The laughter of the war goddess, the destroyer and the mother of crows.

There came a rustling of feathers all around her, as if a flock of crows were flying toward her and around her. For a moment she froze.

Nêrys.

She could still hear her dragon's voice in her mind.

Yes?

Why did you say Ogwen Valley?

What?

Carys started walking again, focusing on Cadell's voice in her mind as she pressed through the darkness.

Before the battle, when we were arguing, you said Ogwen Valley. Why?

I don't know. Wait. She did know. The memory of that still, persistent voice was in her mind. *There was a voice in my mind. I think it was Rhiannon maybe? It told me to tell you Ogwen Valley when you wanted to ignore me.*

This voice sounded like the goddess?

No, it sounded like my own voice, but isn't that how the gods speak to you?

Perhaps.

The dragon was quiet after that. Or maybe the magic of the Shadowlands was fading as they pressed through the heavy brush.

The laughter and whispers were dying down, as was the sound of feathers.

"Fae?" Godrik's voice boomed behind her. "You are limping."

Carys stopped and turned. "Naida?"

"Keep walking," the ellyllon replied. "I'll be fine."

"You are limping," Godrik said again.

Carys halted, but Duncan urged her on.

"I can see the light in the distance," he said. "It's going to be dawn in London. Come on, we need to keep going."

"Walk." Naida's voice was stronger. "Keep walking. I'll be fine."

There was a thready quality to her voice, and Carys knew that she was in pain.

"I will carry you." Godrik's voice came through the darkness. "Don't argue."

There was no arguing from behind her, so Carys kept moving forward.

CHAPTER THIRTY-SEVEN

The blue wisps flew away, and the cool grey dawn appeared before her, the brush around her cloaked with fog.

Carys stumbled out from between two tangled yew trees, her ankles catching on some overgrowth in the grass. She walked forward, pulling Duncan behind her, and saw a narrow asphalt track just ahead.

As Carys walked forward from the bushes, she saw Laura emerge from the trees, then Cadell, and finally Godrik walked through, carrying Naida cradled in his arms.

Footsteps sounded in the distance, and emerging from the fog, a jogger slowed, taking out a white earbud as he squinted at the motley crew of people who probably looked like they'd just come from a Renaissance fair.

"Hey." Carys waved at him. "Good morning."

The jogger paused, running in place, then shook his head, put his earbud back in, and muttered, "Fuckin' tourists."

A moment after that, they were alone.

DUNCAN CLOSED the door in his mother's large town house in Belgravia and looked at them. "She's sleeping. I gave her filtered water and tried to take everything metal out of the room that I could find. If she's not better by tonight, I say we take her back through the gate."

"She'll be fine." Godrik was dressed in some of Duncan's Brightlands clothes, and the pale grey sweater highlighted the silver in his hair and his cool grey eyes. "The small fae has a surprisingly strong constitution."

Even in human clothes, he looked like a wolf.

"I have been reaching for my power ever since we passed through the gate, but I feel nothing," Godrik said. "I cannot sense any larger power here. Dragon, what do you feel?"

"Nothing, but if the Morrigan is stretching her power, we might not feel it until we get closer to her," Cadell said. "As soon as Naida is well, we should go to Gorne Wood."

"Assuming the Morrigan is still there," Carys said. "She may already have moved on."

"Remember, she was trying to start a war and we stopped her," Laura said. "We did defeat that old crow, so whatever magical sacrifice she was looking for, it did *not* go according to plan."

"It might not be enough to do anything other than cause some ripples at the gates," Duncan said. "Maybe make the gates here in London more fluid." He pointed at Laura. "Kind of like the way the fae gates are back in Baywood."

Carys let out a slow breath. "That wouldn't be so bad. A little confusing maybe, but not bad."

"Very true," Cadell said. "It might cause a few minor problems, Brightkin stumbling into the Shadowlands and such, but in theory those gates can be secured over time."

"The last thing we need is mundane humans stumbling into a magical world," Godrik said. "Or Shadowkin crossing into the Brightlands without any guides."

Carys had a feeling that in London—especially if there were as many small gates as Naida had indicated—that might cause more than a little chaos.

"Still," Carys said. "That's good news. I can't hear Cadell either, and I've been talking to him, so we were probably overreacting."

Duncan nodded. "I think we were. Better safe than sorry, but once Naida has rested, we can head back through the gates."

"Goodness."

Carys turned when she heard a quiet voice at the end of the hall.

Duncan's mother—Brightkin of Queen Elinor in Alba—was standing at the top of the stairs.

"Mother!" Duncan said. "I've... invited some friends to stay for a few days. I hope that's okay."

Godrik stood up straight, Laura gave a little wave, and Cadell just stared.

"Oh, that's lovely dear." The older woman waved a hand and brushed at something imaginary in the air. "Make yourself at home. Just talk to Randall about meals and such."

"Thank you, Mrs. Murray," Laura said.

"Mother." Duncan took Carys's hand and walked toward his mother. "You should meet Carys. She's a mythology professor and she's my girlfriend, so you'll be seeing her again. Carys, this is my mother, Alexandra Morrison Murray."

Okay, that was... direct. But not incorrect.

Carys held out her hand, seeing Elinor's kind eyes in a new face. "It's very nice to meet you, Mrs. Murray."

"Oh dear." Duncan's mother's expression fell. "You're American."

Duncan growled, "I won't stand rudeness, Mam."

"Then please don't call me *Mam*." She sighed. "It's so... Scottish. I'm sorry." She looked at Carys. "I'm suppose I'm just disoriented because of the news this morning. What can you even make of such things?" She looked back to Duncan. "They think it might be a *volcano*. In Wiltshire, for heaven's sake. It's only a few miles from the Seymours' country place. Can you imagine? Your father used to go on shooting parties there, do you remember?"

Duncan jerked his head. "What are you talking about?"

She frowned, and two deep lines etched her forehead. "Duncan, haven't you heard?"

Carys heard a television somewhere downstairs.

She followed the sound of the very proper English news presenter's voice down the stairs, through a long hallway, and into a cozy study where a breakfast table was set with tea and two maids were holding hands, staring at a small television on a bookcase.

"—more news from Salisbury where the geological event now appears to be spreading into neighboring farmland."

"Carys?" Duncan called her name. "Where are you—"

"Shhh." Both the maids hushed him.

Carys reached for his hand when she saw the picture on the screen. "Duncan."

"I see it."

The footage on the television looked like drone footage over a very familiar monument, but while the shadows of Stonehenge in the morning light looked familiar...

The giant growing barrow next to it was not.

The news presenter said, "We do have a statement now from the Corps of Royal Engineers, who say that this geological event does not match any known faults or seismic activities and they are still investigating but that currently there is no danger to either life or property in the area."

"What about the bloody henge though?" one of the maids asked. "It's goin' to topple the old thing if it keeps growing."

There was a circle of crows flying in formation around the top of the barrow. The grass around it was dead, the vibrant green leached to dull yellow and brown.

"...meanwhile, local law enforcement has been challenged by a group of neo-pagan activists who are trying to enter the site, claiming any attempt to obstruct them is a violation of their religious freedom. Let's hear from Pippa Kulkarni, who's in the nearby village of Amesbury. Pippa?"

"Thank you, Grant."

Laura and Cadell entered the room, and the dragon stepped closer to the television, bending down to inspect the picture of the mound that had grown next to Stonehenge, seemingly overnight.

The dragon straightened, looked at Carys and Duncan, and said, "I don't think the Morrigan is in Gorne Wood anymore."

END OF BOOK TWO

BROKEN VEIL

SHADOWLANDS BOOK III

COMING WINTER 2025

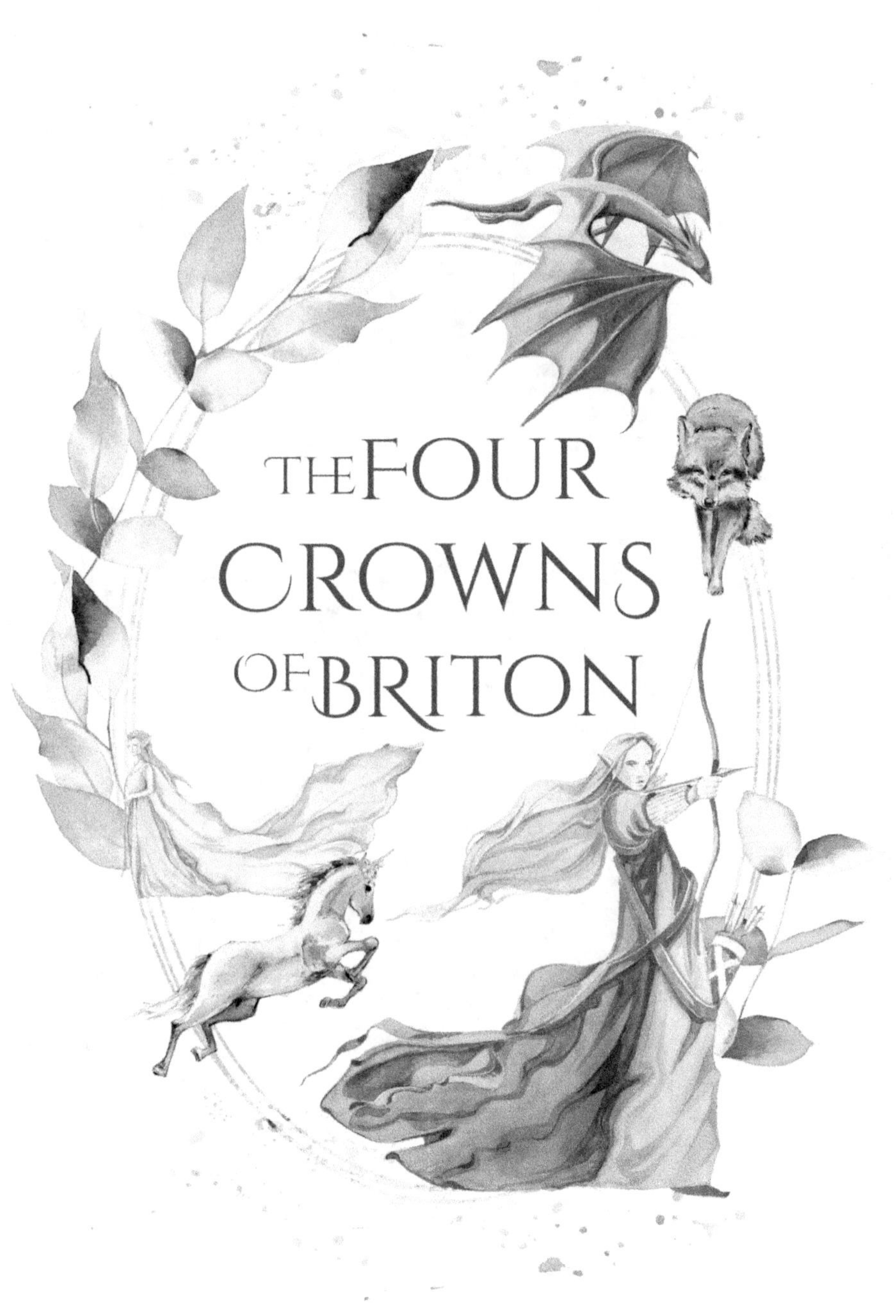

THE FOUR CROWNS OF BRITON

CYMRU

ALBA

ÉIRE

ANGLIA

ACKNOWLEDGMENTS

It's hard to know who else to thank when you've written over fifty books, and you feel like people are probably getting tired of you thanking them over and over, but the same people keep being awesome, so I am forced to acknowledge them.

So if it's you, you'll just have to put up with my endless gratitude.

To my sister and assistant, Genevieve, thank you for keeping me sane and (somewhat) organized. I trust that if I were being attacked by a forest god, you WOULD cut my leg off if it was necessary. But ONLY if it was necessary. *stares at you hard*

To my husband, David, I honestly would be a less happy, less productive, and less sane person without you. So thank you for putting up with my weirdness. Every single romantic hero I write pales in comparison to the reality of you.

To my bestie, K. Thank you for keeping me regularly supplied with baked goods that are definitely good for me. Don't listen to David. The processed sugar and flour is FINE.

There are a bunch of authors who I am privileged to call friends, and there is no way that I could thank all of them, but for this book in particular, Tricia O'Malley was super helpful partly because she's married to a Scotsman, so I'm sending her extra love. (If you ever write a book with an Ethiopian hero, I got you, friend.)

To my extraordinary beta reader, Bee Stevens, you're delightful and special and hilarious. I owe you so many pints of whatever beverage your heart desires.

To my editors, Amy Cissell and Anne Victory, please know that your work makes me so much better, and I am forever grateful to you. And to Linda, who polishes all of it so that my typos are minimal, all of you are magic! (And any typos you find in this book, I probably added back in because I'm contrary.

To my agent, Kimberly Brower, who loves dragons and vampires and all the weird characters I come up with, thank you for all you do.

To Valentine PR for all of their promotional work and advocacy, thank you so much.

To my amazing cover artist, M, thank you so much for one of my favorite covers of all times.

And finally, to my parents for teaching me very young that all books are wonderful, but books with dragons are just a little bit more wonderful than the rest... thank you.

ABOUT THE AUTHOR

ELIZABETH HUNTER is an eleven-time *USA Today* and international best-selling author of romance, contemporary fantasy, and paranormal mystery. Based in Central California and Addis Ababa, she travels extensively to write fantasy fiction exploring world mythologies, history, and the universal bonds of love, friendship, and family. She has published over fifty works of fiction and sold over two million books worldwide. She is the author of the Elemental Mysteries series, the Irin Chronicles, and other works of fiction.

ELIZABETHHUNTER.COM
ELIZABETHHUNTERSHOP.COM

ALSO BY ELIZABETH HUNTER

www.ingramcontent.com/pod-product-compliance
Lightning Source LLC
Chambersburg PA
CBHW070307310726
48976CB00005B/1614